Valley
of the
Queen

A Treacherous Pursuit of a Mythical Queen's Treasure

William Diebold

Cover photographs and graphics by William Diebold © 2021

ISBN: 0692860487
ISBN: 9780692860489

Valley

of the

Queen

A Treacherous Pursuit of a Mythical Queen's Treasure

William Diebold

Valley of the Queen is a work of fiction.

If you like this book and want to follow the interesting characters further, be sure to read the sequel, *Palace Secret*, available at Amazon and Barnes & Noble.

The journey is the prize…

To Mary Lynn who inspired me to read
And begin that journey at a young age.

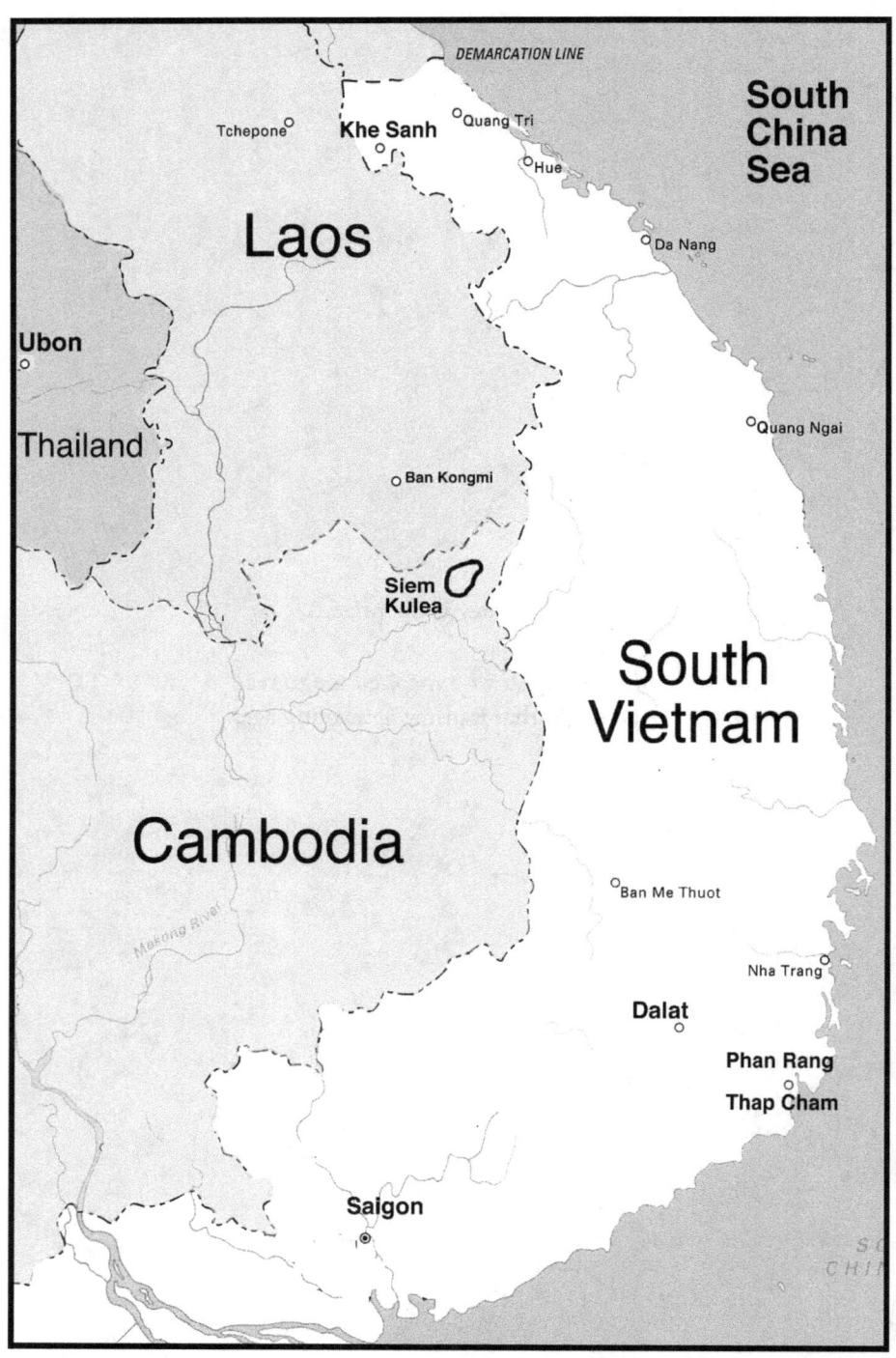

Chapter 1

Panduranga, Southeast Asia, AD 1053
Champa (*Sh-am-pa*)

The four royal guards struggled to free the large wheel of the wooden cart from the muddy hole that stubbornly held it captive. The cart held a chest that was very heavy and made their effort all the more difficult.

They were fleeing the conquering Dai Viet forces, which had recently swept down from the north leaving death and destruction in their wake. Their party included a dozen of the most capable guards in the Champa kingdom along with two Hindu pandits. They brought with them four large, two-wheeled carts that carried the remaining wealth of the Champa Empire that once ruled this land for a thousand miles in every direction. What remained of ornate palaces and temples was now reduced to these four large and heavy chests. Their desperate flight south from the advancing Dai Viet forces was now in its fourteenth day.

Princess Po tapped her foot impatiently as she stood nearby and watched the guards trying to free the cart. The wheel by itself was much larger than Po who was only eleven years old. But even so, she felt a part of the team and wanted to help. She joined the men, found purchase on the wheel and pushed with all her strength. The men made loud grunting sounds as they strained in their effort. She followed their example, but her exertions were heard as a series of mouse-like squeaks that caused the others to spontaneously break into laughter. But with that, the wheel magically worked itself out of the hole, and their laughter became cries of triumph!

Big Sem picked up Princess Po and swung her about joyously. "Little flower, what would we do without you?" he declared.

He weighed more than three hundred pounds and was assigned as her personal bodyguard. Observing how tired she looked, he put her safely up on the front bench of the second cart; the one he managed himself. She settled in and looked at the dense jungle ahead. From her perch peering over the two mules pulling the cart, it didn't appear there was any way forward. But it had been like that since the coast, and they had gone on just the same.

Princess Po was herself one of the treasures of the old kingdom. She was the only remaining heir to the throne of the once great Champa Empire. Though still very young, in a few terrible years she had already lived a lifetime. A scout had brought word the previous week that her parents and two younger brothers were slain at the hands of the ruthless Dai Viet forces.

Princess Po cried desperate protests when her mother insisted that she escape with this specially chosen group of men. They got away secretly in the night before their capitol was surrounded. Her royal presence inspired this small but determined company of dedicated Champa faithful.

Her mother's choices for her to wear on this journey were mundane and presented her appearance commonly as any other child of her age. She wore a colorful weaved skirt and a loose teal top along with boots that protected her feet but that were not as comfortable as the gold sandals she normally wore. Her jet-black hair framed her triangular face and presented her captivating glasz eyes perfectly.

When it became too dark to continue any farther that day, Tap, her teacher who she called Uncle Tap because he was like family to her, ordered that they stop and set up camp. He was the nominal head of the group appointed by the king because he was the king's trusted advisor and Po's mentor. He readily accepted the assignment from the king to save the heritage of the great Champa kingdom, which he considered a sacred responsibility.

Tap saw Princess Po helping to unload one of the carts. He smiled because that was her way and she had endeared herself to everyone in her party by insisting on helping with the work. Tap did not approve but he always acquiesced to her wishes. He took Po's hand and led her to a log in a small clearing by a new campfire. "Sit down, little flower, and talk with me while the men sort out our camp," he said softly while warming his hands. "I need you to lighten my spirits. I confess I am weary after our long walk today."

Tap was not an old man, but not a young one anymore either, and his endurance was little of what it once was. Their escape was successful thus far, but he knew it was only a matter of days before the trailing Viet forces would overtake them if they did not persist in their forced march. He had a desperate plan to preserve their heritage and get them safely away, but only if they arrived soon at their first destination. Tap hoped this night's rest would give them all the energy they needed to continue on their journey at the hurried pace he had set.

As a group they wanted nothing more than to fall onto their mats and sleep. But in deference to Po, they instead took the time to make an orderly camp, set down sleeping areas, and cook rice over a warm fire. The pandits seemed tireless and were very helpful, but afterward, they went off by themselves and went through their nightly prayer ritual. The others talked of many things, and as their bellies filled, they grew more positive in their banter. Po listened quietly with heavy eyes, and finally fell asleep, snuggled in the lap of her teacher.

They were awakened in the middle of the night by a young scout who had been sent behind by Tap to keep watch on the advance of the conquering army. He informed Tap much to his surprise that the invaders were only a day behind but added that they did not appear aware of Tap and his party fleeing before them.

Though still dark, the group quickly repacked their belongings and again made their way through the dense jungle. The path they made seemed ominous in the darkness compounded by a myriad of creature sounds that hid and threatened nearby.

Po was greatly relieved when several hours later the jungle opened to a flat plain of wild grass, cactus, and low brush visible through a mist in the early light just before dawn. She could see foothills leading to high mountains far beyond.

"Is that our destination, Uncle Tap?" she asked.

Tap put his hand on her shoulder and only smiled an answer. He thought to himself *where is it?* He did not remember the temple being this far, but it had been years since he last traveled to this plain.

He was about to seek the advice of the two pandits who were with them when the morning mist cleared somewhat, and in the distance on a hill that overlooked the plain they saw a small temple with three towers lit like a beacon in the rays of the morning sun.

"It is karma, my brothers," said Tap joyously. "The gods are still with us. Come, we must hurry."

Two hours later, they arrived at the mouth of a nearly invisible cave on the far side of a very rocky hill near the temple. Tap went inside to inspect the cave and to see if it was as he remembered. When he determined that nothing had changed, he came out and signaled the carts to be brought close to the entrance.

With six men lifting each one, they brought the heavy chests down from the carts. It took another strenuous effort to deposit them within the cave. The chests barely fit through the opening and were carefully placed back into the confines of the small cave.

On the top of the first chest, Tap placed a scroll on which he had carefully recorded the story of their queen, their history, the royal lineage, and their mission. Before he finally exited the cave, he placed two golden statues of their gods in front of the chests to protect them.

They worked quickly and closed the cave entrance with many large rocks. They gathered brush, and detritus from the adjacent area and covered the entrance to look like the rest of the hill. When they were through they left no sign they had been there, or buried anything within.

It was midday by then, and the two Hindu pandits came to speak with Tap. They were very concerned and after they revealed their secret, they requested that he help them.

They led him to an adjacent hill that was between the cave and the temple. They worked back several large rocks to reveal a partial opening. They explained to Tap that there was a chamber within that was once thought only accessible from the temple. That temple access was bricked over and hidden many years ago as the Hindu pandits began to abandon the area and move back to their homeland. Within this chamber were the collected offerings of devoted Hindu followers over many centuries and from many lands.

The gold within meant nothing to them. There was no reason to keep it because it brought only conflict and suffering when they sought to bring peace and enlightenment to those they nourished with their teachings. Thus the gold was secretly collected and deposited there for as long as any of the priests could remember.

Recently, they had received a message from the last caretaker of that temple explaining that during one of his daily walks, he had discovered this outer cave access. It had become visible after a particularly heavy storm. One of the pandits, Havta, had traveled here at that time to help to cover up this outer access. But it was not as well hidden as the one they just concealed and if anyone heard a rumor of the Champa treasure being in the area, no doubt someone would find the entrance to the buried temple treasure.

Among his many talents Tap in his day had been a skilled builder and he readily consented to their request for help. Moreover, he wanted to make a few additions inside the chamber to ensure that in the remote chance it was discovered, no one would ever be able to take the gold. After he explained his plan to the pandits, they heartily approved.

He chose a golden brick he found within that cave and deviously made the entrance dependent on it. He then looked around the area and found the poisonous plant he needed. He told the pandits to grind it down into a powder and bring the remains to him. He warned them to be very careful because the poisonous powder when airborne was lethal.

By late afternoon his new construction within and the careful undermining of the chamber's entrance were finished with near perfection. In the end, the two hills blended in with those around them leaving their secrets well hidden.

Satisfied with their effort, they gathered their remaining belongings and bundled them onto four mules. They dismantled the carts and as part of Tap's original plan, constructed a comfortable litter for their new queen. The litter looked appropriate and fitting for a queen of any age.

Earlier Tap had given Po royal silks to change into while they worked and even showed her a stream nearby where she might bathe in private.

When she joined them once more, she was surprised and jumped with delight when she saw what they had made for her. Tap sat her down on a rock and fixed her hair in a more formal style that together with a few gold accents and jewelry added to her royal appearance.

Then he put his hand gently on her shoulder and led her toward where her family heritage was now buried in the hidden cave. They stood in silence together for a moment looking at the new rock formation that covered the cave where the Champa treasure was buried within.

Tap bent down on his knees directly before her so she would mark what he was about to tell her. He had done this many times when he was teaching her over the years and she focused on his words as she knew they would be important to her.

"Remember this place, my lady. Someday you must return here. You are our queen now. Our heritage is your responsibility, and the lives and memories of our people will be left for you to preserve for all time."

His voice was broken, and she saw his eyes mist in the reflection of the sun.

She acknowledged his charge to her with firm lips and a solemn nod.

They turned and looked at the area of the former cave once more, but this time she studied it and recorded to memory every detail of the rock formation that guarded her family heritage.

When she was finished, he hugged her warmly and advised, "Your life is going to change now, my lady. Rest assured I will always be here for you and ready to help in any way you wish. Come now, we must be on our way."

When she turned around, she was surprised to find that every man in the group was kneeling before her, indeed with their heads pressed to the ground. She took a deep breath as she realized she was leaving the 'little flower' behind forever. With an almost ritual respect the guards helped Queen Po to a comfortable seat on her new litter.

They walked proudly then, escorting her back down to the plain where they had first entered the area. They stopped and took one last look, as the sun was about to set behind the temple. Po gave a tearful smile, for it was a beautiful sight. The three temple towers looked as if they were ascending gloriously to the heavens.

With no further time to waste, Tap directed the royal party of twelve guards, two pandits and one young queen on their way following the sunset to the distant mountains and their final destination beyond. It was a hidden valley paradise called Siem Kulea. For many years, in that valley a close and devoted following of Champa faithful would prosper and live happily under the wise rule of the young Queen Dau Te Po.

In that far land, time would pass and become memories. Memories would become legends, and legends would be judged in kind.

Chapter 2

Chicago, 1985

People always remember their first impression of Chicago's Magnificent Mile. Especially in the summer the view in every direction can be breathtaking. It is a spectacular stretch of downtown from the river and the terra cotta Wrigley building, to the historic Water Tower and the one hundred story John Hancock building. There are literally hundreds of inviting upscale shops and fashion outlets to explore along the way. It is a feel-good kind of walk.

Feeling good was just what Maisong Sambaht was about. If you were fortunate to pass by her walking along Michigan Avenue that bright sunny day you might turn as many did for another glance in her direction. Her friendly and confidant demeanor reflected her surroundings, and both were inspiring.

Ten years earlier, at the age of eleven she fled as a refugee from Vietnam on a boat with her aunt. When their boat overturned in a fierce storm, her aunt was lost. For a year, she went from one refugee camp to another until a kind elderly couple in San Francisco took her in and gave her a home.

Academics were easy for Mai but making friends was not. There are times when children have been known to be cruel and cold-hearted. From the very start, her fellow students branded 'the new foreign kid' as an outsider. She was judged harshly because of her background at first, and then because of her superior intelligence, which she demonstrated daily in her classes. She grasped new ideas and concepts easily. She was gifted with an understanding far beyond what was proffered by the teacher or written in the books. She skipped a grade twice, first in middle school and then in high school, which only exacerbated her problem of making friends.

Perhaps it was just as well, as she came to regard her fellow students as children preoccupied with adolescent agendas for which she had little interest or time. The girls always talked about boys and boys always talked about sports. Added to this equation was the fact that she was very beautiful and very attractive to boys while girls resented her for the same reason.

It was in her second year of high school that two Vietnamese boys befriended her soon after they arrived at the school. They were brothers one year apart in age and one or the other ended up in most of her classes. The brothers became protective of Mai and from the first meeting they could be seen together whenever possible. They told her they were of Champa heritage, an ancient indigenous people who through time had migrated all over Southeast Asia.

Learning was engaging for Mai and she eagerly devoted most of her time to her schoolwork and studies. She graduated high school at the top of her class but declined to be the Valedictorian. The irony was not lost on Mai. She had been a loner for one reason or another during most of her schooling, yet she was asked to represent her class at its culminating ceremony.

She attended Stanford University on a full scholarship. During her last year, her foster parents died in a tragic car accident on the Bay Bridge in San Francisco. She was alone again, and after graduation she decided it was time for a new start.

She applied and was accepted at Northwestern Law School in Chicago. Again she was at the top of her class, when after two years the money for her tuition and living expenses was depleted. She could have applied for a loan but that was not her way. In the summer between her second and third year, she decided to take a break and find some sort of employment as a source for the funds she would need to finish law school.

As she walked down Michigan Avenue, she looked forward to her first interview and was confident she was well prepared. She visually took possession of every shop along the way because this was to be her city now and she embraced every part of it.

She had done her research and was dressed responsibly in a light teal business suit that mirrored her eyes and would fit well within the corporate world she hoped soon to join.

Her delicate features, triangular face and shoulder length black hair gave her a charming and attractive look. Her smile was engaging with crimson lips and dimpled cheeks. But it was her eyes that held everyone's attention upon meeting her. They were glasz in color, friendly and wise at the same time.

She was smart enough to be aware that the one area where she might be lacking was in social skills. She still had no close friends but had many acquaintances she encountered as an adult who respected her talent and abilities. She hoped her resume would give her a bridge to a new life and perhaps along the way allow her to gain some real friends. She wanted that more than anything. She felt as a flower, blossomed and ready for everyone to notice.

Incredibly, she still had not made up her mind about what particular profession she wanted to pursue as a career. Her interests were varied and pointed in several directions. Her many talents included exceptional skills in programming in six different computer languages. She also had a unique understanding of numbers and data. She could ascertain relationships in data that gave her an advantage over almost everyone, especially when programming and working with figures. She would have been welcomed in California's legendary silicon valley but she did not want to spend the rest of her life immersed in computer programming. She was more interested in the communications industry and in areas such as advertising or television. Whatever she chose, she wanted to be challenged and a part of something grand.

In graduating at the top of her class at Stanford she had accumulated many awards and accolades along the way, all of which were highlighted in her resume and accented by her successful two years of law school. She was positive everyone who interviewed her would be properly impressed and ready to hire her on the spot. She planned to have many job offers from which to choose.

Chapter 3

Chicago, 1985

Two weeks later Mai was still searching for a position that would challenge her skills, engage her interests and provide an adequate income. She had been offered several secretarial positions, but thus far she had not been considered for any position of more substance.

At the end of another unsuccessful day of job hunting, she found herself again frustrated and weary from her lack of success. On the way to the station to board the el for a ride back to her apartment she whimsically dropped into a downtown bar to temper her disappointment with a cold drink. She had never in her life had alcohol of any kind, but that day she decided she needed a drink.

The bar was mostly empty at that time and she sat alone. She candidly informed the bartender it was to be her first drink ever and asked what he recommended. After telling her it was on the house he suggested she try a daiquiri and she discovered she liked her first taste of alcohol.

The bartender's name was Dan and in the next thirty minutes they exchanged life stories and became acquainted. Her sense of him was that he was a good person who was genuinely interested in knowing her story. She found it refreshing after two weeks when she had experienced so much rejection.

At one point Dan offered his learned advice to her. "Life is like that, my friend. It can back you into a miserable corner if you let it and it will affect everything you do. You might get the idea there's a dark cloud hanging over you. But life is just testing you to see if you got what it takes. My sense of you is that you have that and a lot more. Stop worrying. Your future is out there waiting for you. You'll find it and then everything will come easy for you. The future for you starts tomorrow and it's going to be grand!"

Dan's positive attitude made her smile and brightened her spirits. It was while sitting there that her eyes wandered toward the television mounted at the back of the bar. She observed an engaging female features reporter on the afternoon news that inspired her to think there might be a place for her somewhere in the television news industry.

Dan saw her looking at the television and commented, "That's Catherine Marsh. She works at WGNR just down the street from here. I like her features a lot. She does her research and always makes them interesting to watch. She really has her act together. If you ask me, she should have her own show. I would sure like to meet her someday."

The next day, Mai made it through the application process at WGNR, and even gained an interview with the personnel director Milton Briggs. She was surprised with her unexpected progress and hoped it was not another exercise in futility. While waiting she silently tapped her finger on her leg as her foot danced in unison on the floor beneath her chair.

Briggs perused her resume with little comment other than a mumbled 'uh-huh' here and there peppered within a chorus of heavy breathing. His suit coat was thrown over a chair to the side of his desk. By the look of it she suspected he wore the same shirt the day before.

When he was done, he looked up and said, "Your resume is very impressive, Ms. Sambaht. But I am sorry to inform you that we do not have any openings for someone with your talent and particular skills at this time."

She gave a sigh to herself and decided this was further proof that she was going to have to find a different path on her journey to personal success. It appeared that while her attractive appearance could get her in the door, her resume placed her at a level on the corporate ladder where she was not welcome.

She offered him a smile and replied, "That is most unfortunate. I was sincerely hoping to begin my career working at WGNR. I actually thought my resume would be strong enough to merit a position as a part of your team."

"Yes, well, we have very few openings at the moment," he said. "You seem attractive enough, perhaps you would consider a position as a secretary or receptionist. I'm sure my assistant can find you something in that area."

"Mr. Briggs, I came to the United States as a refugee when I was eleven years old. I was an orphan who after some time was fostered by a family in San Francisco that were kind enough to take me in. Even with that start, I graduated college at Stanford University with one degree in Computer Science and another in Communications."

"And you note on your application that you graduated Summa Cum Laude as well," he added. "I see you list a number of awards and accolades among your amazing academic achievements. As I said…most impressive."

"Yes, that's correct, and now I am ready to make a path for myself in the world of television news. I think my resume should warrant more attention than that of a secretary," she protested realizing this interview was ending like all the rest.

Mai's cognitive strength gifted her with a sixth sense, which aided her in judging the people she met. She could not read their minds exactly, but she could gain a feel for a person's sincerity and honesty toward her. Everything she sensed about Milton Briggs was that he did not believe her resume or rather did not want to believe it. He had entirely no interest in hiring her.

Mai bristled inwardly, but she did not let it show. She found a smile instead to hide her true feelings. "I'm sorry this did not work out. I will not take up any more of your time."

Not for the first time Briggs observed that she was strikingly beautiful and a few thoughts made him blush. He quickly recovered as he realized she was now the one judging him and drawing her own conclusions. He became uncomfortable before her gaze and took refuge as he collected her resume along with her application, and pushed them across his desk toward her.

He shrugged his shoulder and folded his hands over his belly in response. "I'm sorry. Even if your resume were valid, we have no use for a computer programmer at this time. We are more personal in our approach to the world around us. It is a necessary part of our daily routine. It was nice meeting you, Ms. Sambaht. I wish you well in your search for a suitable position. Please leave your resume and application with my secretary in the outer office. You never know, something may turn up in the future. Thank you, for coming," he said politely.

Suddenly, the door to his office burst open and the same attractive features reporter who Mai had witnessed on television the night before at the bar marched in. She walked right up to Brigg's oversize desk as if on a mission and declared, "Milton, you promised me you would hire a new producer to work with me on my projects. That was two weeks ago."

She wore a white silk blouse with beige slacks, and appeared ready to do battle if she did not receive an adequate response.

She absentmindedly picked up Mai's resume while she presented her demand. "I can't go on like this. I'm overwhelmed and it's affecting my work on camera. I need...wait...who is this?" she asked reading over the resume.

Milton Briggs perked up at the sight of the gorgeous blond features reporter who was now well known throughout the industry. "Hello, Catherine. I was just finishing this interview," he responded. "Ms. Sambaht was applying for a position here and I told her to leave her resume and application with my secretary.

"Now, Catherine, I assure you we're doing all we can to find the right person for you. But you have to be patient. These things take time."

Catherine did not respond as she continued reading over the resume and then reached for the application form. She looked that over quickly and then looked directly at Mai. "This is your application and resume?" she asked.

Mai stopped gathering her things, and looked up at her. "Yes, ma'am, that's mine. I've just been told it's very impressive but it seems Mr. Briggs is not interested in hiring me anyway," she commented with a glance toward Briggs. "I was just leaving."

Catherine smiled at her candor. She made a decision and said, "Milton I will continue this interview upstairs."

"Well now, wait just a minute, Catherine. I'm the personnel director and I make these kinds of decisions. You have to trust my long experience in these matters and I have already concluded this candidate would not be a good fit for us," he protested.

"Mai…your name is Mai, right?" Catherine asked turning to her.

"Yes…yes it is," Mai replied with a bright face.

"Mai, come with me. I want to talk to you and see if you are indeed as impressive as your resume. Milton appears not to know a good thing when he sees it and you may very well be just what I'm looking for in a producer."

Mai couldn't believe her good fortune. The very woman who had inspired her to look for a job at WGNR was going to interview her! She grabbed up her things and hurried to follow Catherine who was already out the door. She looked back at Briggs as she left and noted he was half out of his chair with his mouth hung open in an unspoken protest.

Mai studied Ms. Marsh from the side as they rode up to the thirtieth floor in the elevator. She thought she was even more attractive in person than on television. She wore her blond hair up and out of the way, the same style Mai had chosen that morning. Her jewelry was functional with a small gold broche added to accent her silk blouse. Mai was genuinely excited and took an instant liking to her.

Catherine led her to a small office with a spectacular window view of downtown Chicago. "This is my office, you may sit here," she told Mai pointing to the empty chair in front of the computer at her desk.

Mai settled in front of the computer and Catherine began. "Mai, as a bit of background, things are changing fast in our industry and those who want to get ahead need to be at the forefront of those changes that are going to affect all that we do in the near future. This computer sitting in front of you is the tool that will drive those changes. I confess I don't know enough about how it works to make the best use of it or even anticipate the changes I have no doubt are about to happen. I see on your resume that you like to write computer programs. That's a plus for anyone wanting to work as a producer for me. I need a program that I can use to collect my interviews and organize the corresponding data. The one that some ding-a-ling in our company bought and placed on all of our computers is cumbersome and not at all intuitive. It's made for an accountant and not for a writer. I hate it and I know we can do better. Can you fix that? Can you help me?"

"Oh, I may have something already, let me show you!" Mai replied eagerly reaching for her briefcase. She pulled out a disk and put it into the front disk drive of the PC. Catherine was surprised to see a formal Menu appear on the screen in front of Mai.

"Wait! What's this? Where did you find that?" she asked.

"It is a desktop presentation software that I developed that makes it easier to use the program. You can see the selections offered for what you might want to do right on the menu," Mai explained.

Catherine quickly looked over a friendly menu of options for a writer. "Mai, this seems much more practical and easier to use than what we have," she told her. "Oh my god! It even has a spell check? May I assume you wrote this?" she asked.

"Yes, of course," Mai replied. "I should have explained that better. I do like to write programs and I think I'm very good at it. If I need something on computer that I don't have a program for, I write one. It is not difficult for me.

"The spell check that you see is still a work in progress. What you see there took some time since a very large class of students took on the project and attacked an entire dictionary by hand. That was when I was at Stanford. But it has become very useful and it's almost complete.

"There is a new commercial program that just came out not too long ago called Microword that is a very good writing program and it has spell check too. But what I don't like about it is that it doesn't connect to a database as my program does."

Catherine sat down beside her. "The program I envision needs to be able to search my interviews and notes for connections and key words, etc. I need my interviews to be able to interact with one another. There is currently no program for anything such as that," she commented. "One thing I would really treasure is if I had a database of my contacts with relevant data on each."

"I have something like that feature in this program. I used it to write all of my research papers for school. It worked very well. Here, I'll show you."

For the next thirty minutes Mai went over the program and features. At one point Catherine replaced her in front of the computer and began using the program. "I really like the main menu. It makes it simple to use and get at the information you need. Mai...this is amazing. But OK ...now I want to send my work to the news editor to review. How do I do that?"

"Look at the top menu. Do you see where it says 'send'? Open that and you will see a list of those you may want to send it to. Do you see where it says 'add'?

That is where you can add the names. Of course, that will remain empty until you set up a network here within the company. I know how to do that if you decide it is something you wish to do.

Catherine was fascinated. She turned to Mai and said, "Tell me about yourself. I want to know everything."

They spent the next half hour talking as Mai told Catherine about her adventurous past. As she talked, Catherine liked her story and even took notes. With a nod she picked up the phone and called Milton Briggs in personnel.

When he answered, she told him, "Milton, I'm hiring Mai as my producer. What are we paying her?" She listened to his answer and replied, "No, no, double that. Hell, I'll bet before the year's out you'll be ready to pay her much more. Trust me, Milton; you do not want to let her get away. She is the real deal and knows her stuff." She listened for a moment and replied, "Milton, I'm telling you, we are hiring her as of now. If I have to get Howard involved in this I will, but you won't like it. You know what happened the last time. My next report very well may be about the discrimination I have witnessed toward hiring women at WGNR, and you can bet I already have a list. Get the paperwork up to me right away. She will be working out of the empty office next to mine from now on."

Catherine put down the phone with a satisfied look on her face. She glanced at Mai and said, "You're hired, that is, if you want the position as my producer. Your paperwork is coming up for you to sign. I hope that's OK."

Mai smiled and observed, "You're something of a real deal yourself, aren't you? Wow! Yes. I want the job!

"Ms. Marsh, This is what I dreamed would happen two weeks ago when I started interviewing. Thank you for taking the time to let me show you what I can do. I believe this was meant to happen. I have a lot to offer in the way of skills that I think can truly help you with your projects. I promise I will work hard and I won't let you down."

Catherine smiled. "Call me Catherine, please. Come on. It's lunchtime and I know a little place nearby where we can talk and get to know each other better. From now on we're going to be working closely together and it's important that you know me, and all my quirks. I should warn you. I decide things on the-spur-of-the-moment and act just as fast. I think I've finally found someone who can keep up with me."

They talked for an hour while they ate, which continued afterward over coffee. People in the small restaurant came and went in that time and they barely noticed. The more Mai learned as they talked, the more she wanted to know. On the other hand, Catherine, the professional and very skillful interviewer kept Mai talking about herself, her past and her amazing array of skills. They became real friends in that short time.

Because Catherine gave her this opportunity and believed in her when so many had brushed her off, she made a personal commitment then and there to dedicate herself to Catherine's success. That was going to be easy because Mai genuinely liked her.

At one point Catherine told her, "I have a very close friend who's in town from St. Louis today. He's a creative director from an advertising agency. I have known him since high school and many regard us a couple. I don't know. I really like Mark. That's his name, Mark Doyle. But I don't see us getting married or anything like that. He's attending a photo shoot with a local photographer named Jack Largent today."

She paused a moment holding her thought. Mai sensed she really liked Mark but there was something else Catherine wasn't telling her.

"Will you see your friend Mark while he's in town?"

"He's taking me to dinner tonight with some of those from the photo shoot. Hey! I want you to come and meet him if you're willing. I guarantee you'll like it…it should be great fun," she said.

Mai was surprised at the invitation and she was eager to accept. She looked forward to meeting Catherine's friends and making some new friends of her own. She was beyond ready. She was tired of being on her own, alone, and in this huge city. Yes, she wanted friends and lots of them!

Catherine did not realize Mai was already convinced. "You have to come, Mai. I insist. You will also get to meet the photographer, Jack Largent. Mark tells me he is one of the best advertising photographers in town.

But then Mai remembered her circumstances. "Well honestly I would love to go. But I confess my reluctance is based on the fact that I don't have anything to wear. I'm afraid you're talking to a pauper. I spent all of my meager funds just to be presentable for these interviews."

Catherine nodded and made a decision, "Okay. We can go back to the office, you can sign all of your paperwork and we can see about getting you an advance. With my approval it shouldn't be a problem. I want you dressed properly if you're going to work for me. You'll be making a lot of contacts for me and recommending those I need to interview as part of your assignment. Heck, you may be able to write it off on your taxes. I know I do. First impressions are very important in our business.

"Since you're starting work tomorrow and I'm between stories, we can take this afternoon off and go shopping. I know just the place. While we're back at the office, I will update my secretary. This should be great fun."

Mai let Catherine's enthusiasm envelope her and then she had a thought. "Sure," she replied. "But I wonder if afterward we might stop at a bar I know and have a daiquiri? I want you to meet one of my new friends. He's not going to believe what has happened. I can't wait to see his face when he meets you!"

Chapter 4

Chicago, 1985

In another part of town, the photographer Jack Largent was preparing a set as part of a two-day photography shoot for Ballantine beer. He watched as his first assistant Kelly placed an empty and specially coated glass back onto the table next to a brown Ballantine beer bottle in the exact spot marked in front of the camera. This would be followed by an artistic spritz with water on the bottle and the outside of the glass in preparation for the pour. That gave it a fresh cold look.

"OK, let's do it again." Jack said, as he closed the lens, cocked the shutter, and gave the big studio view camera over to his other assistant Nick to load the film. In the next few minutes, he and the assistants working as a team photographed two variations of a frosty cold freshly poured glass of beer and bottle on the same pour.

Beer is a particularly challenging subject to photograph well because of the many variables in the physicality of the beer itself. The desired one-inch head reached its peak and stayed there for only a second while the under pour settled up from beneath. The desired look of head and beer was gone a few seconds later. Everything needed to be perfect on the set because the large eight-by-ten-inch transparency film that resulted from this well-rehearsed routine was so clear and vivid, the image would look real, and as if you could reach into the film and actually touch it. Every flaw would be visible, so there simply couldn't be any. Few advertising photographers around the country were able to photograph beer well. Jack was one of them, and only after years of practice and hard work.

"OK, let's clean it up and do it again," he said following that variation.

Kelly pulled the glass off the set ready to replace it with another.

But before they could continue with their routine Nick interrupted, while holding a stack of large eight-by-ten-inch film holders. "Can we take a break to load some more film?" He was young, tall, and good for running the camera because in the studio the large view camera was almost always positioned higher in relation to the set.

Jack nodded. "OK, let's take a break to reload film."

Jack walked across that area of the studio to where the art director Mark Doyle sat on a stool watching them from the opposite side of a peninsula counter. There were eight-by-ten-inch Polaroids of beer shots lying in front of him. Beside them was a layout for the ad they were currently photographing. There was also a full ashtray, a fresh cup of coffee, a half-eaten cheese Danish, and a liar's dice box.

Mark smiled. "It looks good, Jack. Are you going to shoot the other photograph we need, the bottle-pouring ad, today too?"

Kelly joined them and as she sat down she offered a suggestion before Jack could answer. "We could set up the pour this afternoon on another set, boss, and leave this one intact until we see the film in the morning. We can shoot some tests and then do the finals on the other shot in the morning."

Kelly was a buxom, attractive, twenty-something young lady with reddish-brown hair, brown eyes, and a face that lit up when she smiled. She was the most efficient and organized assistant Jack ever employed, and he paid her well because of it. On this day she wore Levi's and a white blouse.

Jack smiled at Mark and commented, "See why I have her around? That's a good plan, and it will ensure you make your afternoon flight back to St. Louis tomorrow. We'll shoot about a dozen more variations this afternoon on this version and then get the film in for processing."

"That sounds good to me," Mark replied. He was thirty-something with dark hair and a dark complexion. He had more lines on his face than necessary for a man of his age. The ad business did that. It could be grueling at times, and the successful people got to where they were by many long, stressful hours and hard work. Doyle wore a dark-brown blazer over a cotton shirt and jeans. He seemed relaxed and comfortable, and that was just what Jack wanted all of his clients to feel when they came to his studio.

The studio front door buzzed. Kelly reached under the counter and pushed a button allowing the woman who was waiting there to enter.

"That's my account person, Susan Aimsley," explained Mark. Kelly got to the door and greeted her. Susan was dressed in a business suit and carried both a purse and briefcase. She said something to Kelly, sat right down on the couch in the client area, and immediately picked up the phone.

Mark called out to her, "For gods sake, Susan, come over and meet Jack first before you go into phone mode." He looked at Jack, smiling. "It's hard to picture her without a phone to her ear. She's the best, and keeps us in good graces with the client." Susan put down the phone and walked over with a smile.

"Susan, meet Jack Largent," Mark said.

"Nice to meet you, Susan," said Jack with a nod, and a light handshake. "Welcome to Chicago. Is this your first time here?"

"Actually, it is. We usually go to New York. The client likes to shoot in New York and I have family there, so it works out great for me," she explained honestly. "Jack just shot our ad at one-third the cost of New York, and it looks better than what we got there the last time!"

"You pay nine thousand dollars a day in New York?" asked Jack.

"Actually ten, and then add on the overtime and extras. It's expensive and overrated. I have to say I have not felt this relaxed on a shoot in a long time. Less travel time, less hassle and professional all the way. Good show, Jack."

"Why, thank you, sir," replied Jack, smiling.

He gave a slight wink to Kelly, who was beaming from ear to ear with pride. She was the one who along with Jack had prepared the set the day before, shot Polaroids and test shots, made adjustments, and reshot tests. She also was responsible for preparing the bottles and glasses for the shoot, which required spraying each of them with a clear surface that would hold the drop-shape of the water spritz.

In the morning, she brought in pastries, fruit, and munchies. She made sure the other assistants knew what they were supposed to be doing on set to support the shoot and the client. She arranged lunch too but cancelled when the client had other plans. She even called St. Louis and talked to Mark's secretary to find out what kind of food and drinks he liked and whether he wanted to see a performance while he was in town. She was the queen of the dog-and-pony show, none better. And the best part about it was that if it went right, no one ever noticed except Jack.

"It looks like you have things well in hand here, and I would like to get out and catch up with some old business friends, said Mark. "We're meeting for lunch, and I want to freshen up a bit first. Oh…that reminds me. Excuse me while I make a phone call."

"Of course," answered Jack. "But don't forget where we're meeting tonight."

"Oh yes, I have it here," said Mark, looking at his notes. "Mr. A's on the park, North Side. Eight p.m. got it." Mark picked up the phone and punched in a number.

Jack had a few more questions for Susan about New York while they waited for Mark to get off of the phone. After a moment he hung up the phone and returned to the conversation.

"Will any of your friends be coming tonight also?" asked Jack.

He nodded. "If it's OK, I just asked a special friend of mine to join us and she's bringing a friend. I hope you don't mind. It's a new producer she just hired…a lady. She says she's young, very attractive and she really likes her. And I insist that charming and efficient Miss Kelly join us too."

Kelly started to put her hand up to make an excuse, but Jack said, "I'm sure she wouldn't want to miss it. So reservations for six at eight o'clock."

Kelly made a note and headed to the office.

Stella Edmund, the office bookkeeper, replaced her almost immediately. She peered over her glasses and nodded a greeting to Mark and Susan with a pleasant smile, as she placed a few papers down in front of Jack. "Here are those figures you asked about," she said, smiling.

He picked up the reports as Stella headed back to the office without waiting.

"Are those our expenses?" asked Doyle

"Yes, and they just went up by seven thousand dollars," Jack quipped, smiling.

Susan broke off a sip of coffee and gave a concerned look.

"He's joking, Sue. Relax!" said Mark. "You know, you don't know how to relax anymore. Don't even think of not going tonight. I'm sure Jack knows a good restaurant and a good time."

Jack compared the paperwork in front of him. "We're about five hundred dollars under our estimate thus far, Susan," assured Jack, smiling.

She beamed a smile. "I'm sorry. The last shoot was a bit of a disaster, and I took a lot of the heat with the client. Thanks for that information, Jack. I feel a lot better."

Nick walked in with a new load of film, and Jack said, "OK, back to the salt mines. Let's get this wrapped up."

"I'll see you all later," said Mark as he put his papers in his briefcase. "Susan, go back and watch them shoot. This is how Chicago does it. In my opinion their routine here is way better than New York." He gave her a nod and a wave before turning to leave.

Susan said, "I have to make a few phone calls first, and then if I don't get called away, I may join you. Please don't let me hold you up."

The two assistants, and Jack returned to the back studio, where the beer shot was still set up. Kelly inspected and replaced the glass with another. After she spritzed the glass and the bottle, she said, "Ready, boss."

And they did it again twelve more times.

That night after dinner, at ten-thirty, they all got out of a limo on upper Clark Street in front of a seamy looking bar ironically named the New York Lounge. Susan laughed when she saw the name, and Jack said, "Just for you, Susan. Actually, we were coming here anyway before we knew you were so fond of New York. I think you'll like it."

Kelly held open the front door of the bar with a flourish, and they entered. But then she held Jack back a bit and said, "Oh my God, I feel like I'm escorting royalty. Are you sure about bringing them here?"

Jack watched Catherine Marsh, the Channel Five features reporter, head for the bar with Mark's hand resting gently on her back. She was dressed elegantly and expensively, in contrast to the bar they were entering. He knew Ms. Marsh was a hot topic in all the trendy local magazines and gossip columns. She was blond and tall, with movie-star good looks.

But what had captured his attention all evening as they dined at the restaurant was the young Asian woman named Mai who came with her. Since her arrival for dinner, Jack took every opportunity to glance her way as he was absolutely taken with her. He could not remember ever seeing a woman so attractive to him. When she smiled he felt it all the way to his heart.

"It's OK, you'll like it too. Just go with it. You won't believe it. Great fun!" he assured Kelly at the door.

An old friend of Jack's named Lenny owned the bar and he was a card trick magician. He performed as part of the entertainment while his patrons sat at the bar and enjoyed the show. He was one of the very best magicians in Chicago, but lately, his establishment and many like it in Chicago had fallen on hard times.

They all sat at the bar as Lenny greeted them eagerly and made places for them. Jack made sure he was sitting next to Mai. They made up one end of the group of six that skirted a corner of the bar. Catherine was seated with Mark on one side, and Kelly on the other.

That night Lenny was in his best form, and Jack's guests were given the full run of his superlative and very entertaining counter-top, card trick routines. As was his manner, he chose Kelly and Catherine who sat beside each other in the middle as the focus of his hour-long show.

Catherine claimed to be hard to fool when it came to card tricks. The highlight of the night was when Lenny produced a card that somehow had landed under Catherine's glass on the bar without her knowing. "Oh no, your card could not have been the queen of clubs because that's been right here under your glass on the bar the whole time!" he exclaimed much to everyone's surprise.

Catherine was delighted. She and Kelly were having a good time and were in a conversation that carried on throughout the evening.

No one noticed but Jack had his own conversation with Mai that began soon after they took their seats and continued throughout the show. To his pleasant surprise Mai seemed as eager to talk with him as he was with her.

Mai was indeed pleased to be sitting next to Jack. She had spent most of the evening at the restaurant sneaking glances at him from across the table. She found herself very drawn toward him in a way she had not felt before about any man. Her feelings confounded her because she couldn't resolve them pragmatically as was her way. She wanted him. She wanted to be close to him. She imagined herself in his arms sharing an embrace. That was a feeling so foreign to her she did not know how to explain it. She liked him and what he made her feel inside. Whatever it was, she was eager to explore her feelings further.

As the evening at the bar progressed she realized that the conversation between her and Jack was centered on her interests. For the third time in two days she found herself sharing her thoughts with someone who seemed to genuinely care about what she had to say. She laughed to herself because this time she was just as eager to know how Jack thought and felt about things.

At one point, when everyone was surprised at the outcome of a trick, Mai put her hand on his. She squeezed it in delight and then held it there. He felt it all the way up and down his body and she did too because she stopped and looked at him seriously eye to eye for a moment. But then she had a question that needed an answer.

"Oh don't tell me you felt that?" he said with his own question.

She surprised him and herself when she impulsively leaned over and kissed him quickly on the lips. That answered her question and was all she expected it would be and more. Mai had never experienced anything like what she was feeling in her entire life. She had never even considered stealing a kiss with a man. She knew he liked her. Indeed she had known it from the first moment their eyes met. *Did he know what he was doing to her* she wondered.

"Oh…I like how you answer questions!" he commented as he took her hand with both of his and held it. They looked into each other's eyes meaningfully for a moment, and briefly kissed again.

For one of the very few times in her life Mai was bewildered and did not understand what was happening with her or why she was acting the way she was. It was her very first time having such wonderful feelings. She never allowed her emotions to get the better of her. Unlike all the rest of the things in her life, this was something that she could not put in a database and analyze. What was worse, she had no close friend with which to share a discussion of her feelings. She was on an island alone trying to sort out her emotions and experiencing something wonderful for the very first time.

They reluctantly gave their attention back to watching Lenny's magic tricks, but took the shared moment and stored it away. They sat closer together after that and became a couple. Hopefully it was the first step in a long and wonderful journey for the two of them.

Lenny was a good showman and he knew from previous nights with Jack not to neglect anyone in the group as the focus of his act. Jack was very pleased when he went to Susan and Mark and spent some time totally amazing them. Susan in particular seemed to be having a wonderful time.

At one point, Jack gave a few clandestine signals to Lenny to bring some of his personal act to Mai.

But Mai was not a good subject for his tricks because her sixth sense always told her where the card was or what he proposed to do. She did not let on and acted surprised and delighted every time. For his part, Jack watched Lenny closely and as usual could not see Lenny work his magic even though he knew what he was going to do.

At the end, Jack worked his own magic in the form of a very large tip for his old friend.

Chapter 5

Chicago, 1985

Jack lived above his studio in an elegant townhouse. The five thousand square foot studio and the townhouse above were near Lincoln Park and provided for a comfortable, urban lifestyle. The building was a welfare clinic before Jack bought it, restructured it, and converted it, all in two months while he lived in a high-rise nearby. Since then he gradually refurbished and redecorated until it was one of the nicer studios in town. There were two kitchens downstairs because Jack photographed a lot of food for advertising, including a lot of the well-known national brands. The smaller studio in the front was next to the main kitchen and was used for most assignments. The larger studio in the back could be used to photograph a car but on most occasions it was broken up into smaller sets for different purposes.

The next morning, after descending the stairs from his townhouse, Jack entered the side door of the studio and picked up the film from the previous day's shoot. It was processed and delivered overnight. After unlocking the main door, he went to the lightbox-portfolio area to look at the film. He laid out the eight-by-ten-inch transparencies on the lightbox for comparison and mounted three that he liked best on eleven-by-fourteen-inch black presentation boards embossed with his name at the bottom.

Kelly arrived with more pastries, cookies, and fruit for the clients. As she began making coffee, she said, "That was amazing last night, Jack. That magician was really good and entertaining. How'd you ever find him? I think Mark and Catherine had a really good time."

"I met him while I was a photographer in Vietnam, Kelly. He was working as some sort of production facilitator for AP at Quang Tri during the Lam Som 719 operation. All the press got tear-gassed one night by the army guys as a practical joke, and as a photographer, I was staying with the reporters and got it bad. I couldn't see and was pretty messed up. He guided me to the showers and helped me get my eyes back. He looks pretty much the same now as he did then. He happened to somehow see my name on one of my flyers and called me up a year ago. He went partners in that bar with a guy when magic bars were booming in Chicago. Since then his partner died and left him all the bills. I think he's going to have to close the bar, but I have hopes that word gets out about him and he can survive. He has stories that go on forever about everything. He's had a very interesting life, Kel. If you ask me, he's one of our national treasures."

"I saw Catherine give him her card," Kelly said. "I think she smells a story there. That would be really cool. And speaking of cool, can you believe how gorgeous she is in person? I'm a girl, and *I* wanted her!"

"Well, you're no slouch yourself. I've seen plenty of guys looking at you."

"Oh yeah? Well, tell me next time, will ya? I seem to have missed them. I think I intimidate guys. But the guy who gets Catherine, now that's a catch! Hey, can you see those two together? I mean Mark is cute and all, but she's on a whole 'nother level. I almost asked for her autograph!"

"Actually, I think they make a great couple. They were sweethearts while she was still in high school, and neither of them has ever married. Did you notice they seemed joined at the hip last night? They're very comfortable with each other."

"Oh yeah, no, I got that. She was running her hand up and down his back all night. But I mean she's headed for the big time. She is definitely media royalty in this town."

Jack pondered that a moment because he hadn't noticed and the thought hadn't occurred to him. But honestly, all he could think about since last night was her friend Mai. His feelings surprised him, but she got away before he remembered to ask for her phone number. He was determined to meet up with her again and he sincerely hoped she wasn't interested in somebody else.

Nick arrived and went immediately to the film-loading room.

"Are the tests back for today's bottle-pour shot?" asked Kelly. "I'm glad we set that one up early and did some tests on it yesterday, boss. That was a doozy to figure out."

"They're on the lightbox, and they look good," said Jack. After they both looked at them a moment he commented, "I want to add a couple more fiber optics inside the bottle itself to get more light inside there. I think it needs that to draw you back into the bottle and add some depth."

"OK...I'll set that up now and shoot a Polaroid," said Kelly, walking away toward the back studio.

Jack turned as the front-door buzzer went off, and he went to greet the client. Stella beat him there and was already saying good morning to Mark, Catherine and her friend Mai. Jack was surprised and particularly happy to see Mai again and gave them a welcome smile.

Catherine explained, "I made Mark bring us this morning because I heard so much about what you do, and last night was...well...unusual and a real kick! With all that, I feel like we're old friends already anyway. I hope you don't mind.

Mai wanted to come and I brought her along to expose her to a real photo shoot. As you know, she just started working as my production person yesterday."

"We're happy to have you and Mai, Catherine," Jack replied honestly. I know Kelly will want to pick your brain. She has always been interested in the news business. She was a communications major in college."

Catherine nodded at that and unconsciously looked toward the back for Kelly. She wore skintight beige pants with a white silk blouse accented with a gold necklace. Mark took her hand and led her over to the breakfast spread and a cup of coffee.

Mai surprised Jack as she put a hand on his arm and commented, "I want you to know I had a great time last night and I really enjoyed spending some time with you. It was the best time I've had in a very long time. Since I came all the way here to see what you do, do you think I can get a private tour when you're not busy today?"

Jack nodded with a smile, "Of course! I think we can arrange that."

She let go of his arm and walked over to the breakfast spread to join Catherine and Mark. It took a moment before Jack realized he was staring at Mai dressed in tight leather pants and a blouse similar to Catherine. She had a figure to go with the face. The buzzer at the door saved him. He let Susan in, took her coat and bags, and greeted her warmly.

"OK, I'm a Chicago fan now!" she said. "Thanks. Last night was great!"

Mark called out from the client lounge, as he poured himself a cup of coffee, "Jack, do we have film back from yesterday yet?"

Jack looked at Susan, smiled, and said, "Come on. You'll enjoy this too." He called back to Mark, "Yes, Mark they're on the lightbox." He led them all into the viewing area where the film was displayed on the wall-mounted, four-foot long light box.

Mark studied them seriously for a moment giving no clue to what he thought. But then he nodded a big smile and said, "Wow. These all look really good, Jack! I honestly don't know which one I like best."

Jack nodded in agreement. "There are twenty more variations in the box, and it *is* hard to choose. I picked those three because I like the drips on two and the over pour on the other. The inside is pretty consistent on all three, and I think the color is just as you like it."

"Yes, I agree, these are excellent. Good work, Jack. The client will be very pleased whichever we choose for the ad."

Susan agreed, but then she checked her watch and asked, "How about the straight-at-you bottle pour ad we still need to shoot? When does that happen?"

Jack turned to her and gave her a serious expression. "The logistics of that shot are much more difficult, Susan, because it's straight on and looking directly into the bottle. To get beer inside for the pour we will have to cut off the back of the bottle. Another difficulty is the actual size of the lip of the bottle being one inch, and then enlarging that to the full eight by ten inches in the final transparency. Oh, and we can't forget we need to get all the drama that draws you inside the bottle worked out. It requires very intense lighting that necessitates a lot of planning and setup beforehand. It really is one of the more difficult shots we've ever done here at my studio. Everyone will have to put in a lot of time and effort to get the kind of results you want. It's going to be a very difficult photograph indeed, no doubt about it."

"So will it happen soon?" asked Susan, not hiding her concern.

Mark smiled because he knew Jack by now and got the joke.

"We're shooting a new Polaroid on the lighting setup right now. Here are the tests we shot on it yesterday afternoon," he said, as he put three large transparencies up on the lightbox unmounted.

"These are beautiful!" Susan exclaimed instantly. Right away she caught herself and seemed embarrassed by her honest enthusiasm. Jack was flattered and amused at the same time.

The transparency showed the front of a beer bottle and the circle of the well- lit lip. The beer poured like a waterfall coming right at you in the eight-by-ten-inch transparency. The circled top of the bottle with beer pouring out over the lip made up half of the image. The lighting was dramatic and so clear it looked almost real.

Jack addressed her directly as he explained, "Susan, these are pretty good. But I thought we could add some more light to the inside of the bottle to add a more depth and draw the viewer inside. Ah, here's the latest Polaroid now."

Kelly handed him an eight-by-ten-inch color Polaroid. "Take a look. The Polaroid will not have the luminosity that the transparency has, but it does give a good idea of the lighting."

Susan held the Polaroid and examined it as Mark looked over her shoulder. Kelly greeted Catherine who leaned against the door and stood next to Mai as they watched.

Jack continued, "See how the extra lighting within the bottle draws you in and even adds some pretty cool highlights to the beer inside the bottle?" He drew back while she and Mark looked at it. He glanced over at Catherine and Mai, and said, "Care to look?"

"Yes," Catherine replied eagerly, "if you don't mind. I don't want to get in the way." She joined the two and said, "Oh, I see what you mean, Susan. These really are very good, aren't they?"

She turned to Mai and said, "Come on, take a look. Jack won't mind."

Jack watched as Mai studied the images on the light box. He noticed how the light played on her face and reflected in her beautiful eyes. His heart began pounding again.

Mai commented, "These are extraordinary. I've never seen a transparency so large. It must be very difficult to photograph anything that ends up as a transparency of this size. It looks so real. You must have to work very hard to make everything look so perfect."

Jack was surprised she already understood the issues so well. She was exactly right. But before he could comment Catherine told her, "All the advertising agencies require large film like this for reproduction. They make separations from these and they often have to retouch the large transparencies before going to final. That is why Jack gets paid the big bucks, right Jack?" she teased smiling.

But it was at that moment that Catherine realized that Jack's attention and gaze was focused on Mai as she studied the images on the light box. She thought, *Oh my! Our photographer is smitten!* She smiled to herself. She had wanted to hook Mai up with Mark but instead she saw that Mai had captivated Jack. She noticed at the dinner the previous night that Mai couldn't keep her eyes off of Jack either. It was obvious to her that something was going to develop from this.

"Well," said Jack, "I think we're ready to shoot finals. He touched Mai's hand and said, "Come on back and watch. You'll love this."

Jack said, "Come on, Kelly, let's go! Nick, is film loaded?"

Kelly who stood beside Catherine at the light box nodded, "OK, boss, coming." and from the back Nick affirmed, "All set."

As the rest departed, Kelly turned to Catherine, who was now standing alone. Catherine started to say something but Kelly spoke first, "Come on back and watch us. You might find it interesting and I bet you've never seen a dance like ours before." As Catherine smiled an OK, Kelly took her arm and led her toward the back studio.

Just then Stella announced over the studio loudspeaker, "Miss Marsh, you have a phone call on line one."

Kelly stopped, and pointed to one of the studio phones. "You can use this one, or the one in the front lounge might give you more privacy if you need it," she said before heading on back to the set.

Catherine went to the first phone and looked toward the back at the beer shot that was just starting. She talked for a bit, then put her hand to her mouth in stunned surprise. She hung up the phone, walked over to Mark and said something. Together they approached the set where the routine had paused while they changed the film in the camera.

"I have to go," said Catherine. "It was nice meeting all of you." She went to the front of the studio and explained to Mai what had happened and gathered her things hurriedly.

"Do you need a cab?" asked Kelly, following her.

"No, I'll take her. I have a rental," said Mark, now also gathering his things. "Mai, are you coming with us?"

Mai nodded with a serious expression. She had already gathered her things and was standing by the door. She sensed Catherine was shaken and needed her.

Catherine paused a moment, wrote something on one of her cards, and gave it to Kelly, who looked surprised. Catherine whispered something in her ear and headed for the door.

Mark directed a few final words toward Susan, and then he pushed out the door with Catherine and Mai, and they were gone.

Jack looked after Mai and paused a moment in a bit of frustration amid the silence that followed their exit. He took a breath and said, "OK, let's get back to it. We have variations to shoot, and that set is not getting any fresher. Are you all right, Susan?" he asked.

"Well, yeah, I guess. We're all set here, right? I mean everything's done, right?"

"All we have to do is shoot the film. The difficult part is all done. Why don't you grab a cup of coffee and join us while we shoot? There's a phone back there on another peninsula by where we are photographing. It makes a nice little office if you need to make some calls while we work."

He nodded to Nick, who said to her, "Come on, I'll get you comfortable back there."

Jack looked at Kelly, who was putting away Catherine's card in her pocket. "What was that all about?" he asked, communicating his bewilderment over the last few, rushed minutes.

"I think somebody died," whispered Kelly.

"Oh man!"

Chapter 6

Chicago, 1985

Catherine was overcome with grief upon the death of her mother. But before she could ask, Mai took charge and quickly planned a funeral, burial, and wake for Catherine's mother. Catherine was devastated and not at all herself the entire time. Mai's intervention gave her a chance to recover and was a great comfort to her.

The ceremony was held at St. Joseph's Catholic Church in Kenilworth, a wealthy old-money community north of Chicago. The cardinal, an old friend of the family, called to announce he would be attending the funeral.

The church was packed to overflowing, and Catherine held her emotions in check while she greeted friends and family at the door and well into the mass. But as Fauré's "Requiem" was sung, she fell finally into that pit of deep and unfettered grief and cried freely. She welcomed a clean handkerchief from Mark, who sat beside her in the first pew. Her mother had been the light that guided her all her life. She was a friend Catherine could always talk to about anything. She was there to listen when Catherine needed that, and they made a point to call each other once a day, if only just to say hello.

Catherine was expected to say a few words during the ceremony and collected herself once again so that she could put the best face on her grief. After Father Feagan waved her up, she took a deep breath and stood at the ambo. She looked out at the sea of faces before her, not seeing any one of them, but nevertheless feeling their presence. She paused while everyone waited in anticipation. They did not know that at that moment she heard her mother's voice in her mind giving her loving advice once more to "Buckle up and shake out the butterflies."

"Thank you for coming," she began. "I believe we all share the honest joy that my mother brought to our lives. If I had the opportunity to choose a woman, any woman in life and time, whom I would want for my mother, I would have picked her. If I had to choose a friend from anyone in life, I would have picked her. When I was with her alone in a room, the room was full and complete. She gave me the gift of unconditional love, and I did my best to return it in kind.

"You would expect me to say that, and I have honestly. But even as those memories of her are among the ones I will cherish, there is one memory of her I will carry with me always.

"Many of you know my mother loved to play cards. She liked to play Bridge and spent many afternoons with her friends at the club enjoying the game and banter. Almost every time I visited with her at home, we would go into the parlor and sit at the old oak card table and play a game of Hands and Feet or Russian Bank. It was over cards that we shared our lives and our daily adventures. It was over cards that we spoke honestly concerning our feelings about everything.

"We just heard Fauré's 'Requiem' sung as wonderfully as any choir ever could. Thank you," she said as she nodded up to the choir.

"But many of you will not be surprised when I tell you that the most enjoyable music to my mother's ears was the sound of a deck of cards shuffling. You may laugh, but you will remember that she was wonderfully happy when sitting at the card table. That, my dear friends, is one of my most treasured memories of her. "My mother is the most wonderful person I have ever known and most likely will ever know. But she would not want you to dwell on her death, and instead celebrate her life. In fact, if she were here today, she would probably lecture you as she did all of us so many times, 'You gonna talk or play cards?'"

The large crowd laughed and broke out in applause as Catherine stepped down from the ambo and took her place once again in the front pew. Mark squeezed her hand, and she squeezed back. She took another deep breath, and settled in her seat. *I'm glad that's over*, she thought. *Thank you, Mom.*

Catherine knew, of course, that her mother was wealthy and that their fortune came from old money that had been handed down for generations. Her father died when she was very young. When her mother died, she still lived in the huge mansion she had shared with her father and where Catherine grew up in Kenilworth. Catherine, an only child, moved out when she went away to college and, like Mark, who was also from Kenilworth, never moved back home. Her mother wanted her to monitor the family wealth and get involved in their investments. But Catherine very much wanted a life independent of that, a life of her own making and merit.

When she started working, she bought a condo along Lake Shore Drive near downtown, not wanting to commute too far each day to work. She lived off a considerable trust from her grandfather that left her not having to worry about money and she was very conservative in her choices otherwise. She hid her wealth well and blended in with the middle-class workers she shared time with in the daily production of a newscast. She felt, rightly so in many cases, that there were already too many barriers in place for a woman in the television news business. She was determined that her work, not her beauty or her family wealth, would break down those barriers.

The reading of her mother's will took place the following Friday at Doyle, Bergen, and Reevis, the law firm that handled the family business for as long as Catherine could remember. Mark Doyle's father was one of the firm's partners, and Mark and Catherine met when they were in high school and continued that close relationship later in college.

It was a week after the funeral, and Catherine was wearing work clothes because she was going to the TV station immediately after the reading of the will. Her outfit consisted of a tan skirt and white blouse, dressed with appropriate accents for work. Her fashion choices were expensive but not ostentatiously so. She looked like a businesswoman who was moderately successful with a good flair for fashion.

Gerald Doyle read the will behind his old mahogany desk while Catherine sat politely in a comfortable leather chair across from him. The genteel and well-appointed legal office matched the conservative suit worn by Gerald Doyle. The office was lined with books and memorabilia that served to validate its purpose and were in part a record of historical Chicago.

Catherine suspected her mother left her money to charity, because giving to worthy causes was always her way. She did not expect a substantial inheritance because her grandfather had left her a comfortable bequest when he passed. Also, Catherine continuously declined and avoided getting involved in the family financial matters. This was the only point of contention between her mother and her. She had declined to get involved so often that her mother never brought it up when they played cards and discussed everything else in friendly conversation.

She hoped to keep some of the furniture and paintings that were personal to her or that had meant so much to her mother. Thus she sat quietly while the will was read and the very long list of donations was itemized. Millions were donated as the minutes passed, and Catherine's thoughts wandered to an investigative report her team was putting together, her first since her mother passed away. She planned to go right to a production meeting with Mai from there and was considering some revisions she would make in the script.

"The rest," Gerald Doyle read as he reached the end of the will, "including the house, estate, grounds, and attached holdings therein, will go to my daughter, Catherine, whom I have loved more than anyone can imagine and with all of my heart."

"Oh, good. Thank you, Mom," said Catherine, smiling. "I was hoping to keep a few things, and now I can be sure to keep the ones most important to me. I will have to decide what to do with the rest. I will probably sell the house. Do you have anyone who can handle that for me?"

"Well, yes," said Doyle. "The grounds, including the house, are valued at eighteen million dollars, and the contents will add considerably to that. But Catherine, there are funds here you will want to invest, and you will need an experienced, reputable financial analyst to manage that.

He handed her a small white sealed envelope. "This is a personal message your mother left for you," he explained.

Catherine opened the envelope and read the short missive within.

Catherine, my dearest,

I know you do not wish this money and have other goals in your life. But it is my last wish that you control these funds and that you responsibly decide what will be done with them, as is your right and your duty to our family and me.
I am very proud of you,
Buckle up and shake out the butterflies.
Be wise, my darling.

Mom

"I'm not getting something here. How much money is left, Mr. Doyle?" asked Catherine, confused. Gerald Doyle was a close friend of her mother's for as long as Catherine could remember. But Catherine, who met him the first time when she was a child, always addressed him as Mr. Doyle.

Doyle looked over a few papers and remarked, "Well, as best as our accountants can determine, approximately one-point-two billion dollars after taxes."

"What? *What?* Oh my God!" exclaimed Catherine, with both hands on her cheeks.

"Well, we don't have an exact figure. It may be a bit more than that, but I thought it was safer to give a conservative estimate.

"I never imagined we were that wealthy...Mr. Doyle!" she said, feeling suddenly very light-headed. "I'm not sure what to think about this. How could I not know?"

As Catherine paled and appeared about to faint, Doyle got up quickly and brought her a glass of water. She accepted it while waving a shaking hand over her face.

She sat there speechless for a moment while she considered this unexpected news. She was not sure where all this would lead, but she knew that her mother trusted the man sitting across from her professionally, and he was an old family friend as well. That was important because she could not have needed him more than at that moment.

"Catherine, are you OK?" he asked with genuine concern. "You look about to faint. Do you need to lie down?"

She shook her head and braced herself in her chair as her heart raced. After an extended moment, she began to collect herself and breathe more normal. She took a deep breath and then looked up at him, this time with an embarrassed smile. "Mr. Doyle, this is all unexpected and new to me. I cannot imagine how I did not know we were so wealthy. But I am certain of one thing and that is that I need someone I can trust to manage all of this for me while I consider my options. I trust you like family, and I am sure you know someone you can trust who is good with finances. I want you to be the overall manager on my account. I want only you, Mr. Doyle, and no one else."

"Of course, Catherine, I'm flattered. Thank you for that. Please, call me Gerald. I think we know each other well enough by now," he said.

She nodded. "Don't be flattered, Gerald. Protect me. Protect my family wealth. Please, that's all I ask. I'm depending on you. I honestly have no idea how to proceed with this. I really need your help. Oh, my God. Mom! What was she thinking? Why didn't she warn me about this?" She shook her head and took another sip of water.

"Catherine, your mother and I talked about this almost every time we got together, but she just never got around to telling you. Her death was, as you know, sudden and unexpected, and she never had a chance to brief you on all of this. I know that was one of her priorities."

"I guess that was my fault, Gerald. I kept putting her off making silly excuses, and saying I was busy with this or that. I kept telling her I wanted to concentrate on my career. Oh, I feel so awful now. I just don't know what to do."

"I understand, Catherine. These kinds of things can be a bit overwhelming, even for those of us with more experience. Take a deep breath, and let's talk about it. But first I want to introduce you to someone who you need right now more than anyone, although you may not be aware of it just yet." He settled back in his chair, pushed a button on his desk, and said, "Brad, could you join us now, please?"

A young man about Catherine's age, tanned and well groomed, came in and stood before the desk. He was handsome and impeccably dressed like a fashion model. Catherine noted his style and observed that if his talent was as good as his taste in clothes, he must be very good at whatever he did.

"Catherine, this is Brad Martin. He looks young but has a master's degree in business and a law degree specializing in business law, both from good schools. And more importantly, he has proven his expertise in the last two years he has worked here at DB&R. When it comes to managing finances he's the best we've ever seen, and he is our choice to manage your accounts...with your approval, of course. I assure you he is quite competent. He has already set up a plan to retain the vast majority of your inheritance after taxes, over and above what I quoted you before. I know you will want to consult with him about that very soon."

Brad held out his hand and said, "Glad to meet you, Miss Marsh. I know of your work, and I must say you are even more impressive in person than on television. I don't want to seem forward, but I would like to get to know you better so I can make the kind of decisions on the accounts that you would approve."

"Have a seat, Brad. We're just about to discuss some options for Catherine," Doyle told him.

After Brad sat down and got out a pad and pencil, Doyle continued, "Catherine, you are in a situation where you can do just about anything you want. You're young, with your whole life ahead of you. Very few people have had such an opportunity. If I may ask, do you have a dream or something in mind, maybe a goal you might like to pursue?"

Catherine noted the two men sat straight in their seats focused on her response. "Well, yes, actually, I have several. But I always hoped I would be able to accomplish them after years of hard work. My biggest dream was to have my own production company and do features for the news...you know, like *60 Minutes* or *Dateline*. I like being a television investigative reporter, Gerald. I want to continue doing that. I admit it drives me. It is my passion, and I think I'm good at it."

"OK, that's a start. Let's assume for a moment that you want to pursue this dream in earnest starting today. What do you need?"

"Well, I would need an overall Manager, someone to actually run the company. Someone who knows the business and has lots of experience."

"Do you know someone like that?" Doyle asked.

Catherine looked directly at him and then nodded slowly and thoughtfully. "Actually, yes. Yes, I do."

"OK, what else?" he persisted.

"You mean like a dream team."

"Yes. If you can afford the best, you might as well get the best," Doyle answered. "I suspect a start-up will need all the advantages you can afford to get it off the ground."

"Well, OK. I have an excellent production person already but I will need a good road crew, director, DP, cameraman, drivers, some reporters besides myself, editors, equipment…"

She paused in the midst of her answer and ran her fingers through her hair, pushing a lock behind her ear while she stared out the window.

The two men remained silent and waited patiently while they let Catherine collect her thoughts.

She turned back, facing them, and asked seriously, "Gerald, do you really think this can happen?"

"Yes, if you want it to, that's the position you're in, Catherine. This may take some getting used to, but I have no doubt you're just the woman who is intelligent and organized enough to get it done. What is your next project? Something you came up with and can say that you own?"

"We're doing a feature on some major corruption involved with the demolition of Cabrini-Green, that low income housing development just to the north of downtown Chicago. They are turning a slum-like set of buildings into modern and very nice condos because it's a prime location close to downtown," she said excitedly as the wheels in her head began to spin. "That's my baby completely. I found, investigated, and wrote the story. I have my production girl Mai working on that day and night, and with her unique skills, she has turned up connections I never imagined."

"That could be the first feature of your new production company," Doyle said. "There may be some work-for-hire issues since you're still working for WGNR, but we can deal with that. You'll need a name for this company. Any ideas?"

"Oh, yes! I have always liked the name NearNorth Productions. I put that name on all of my papers in school. It was kind of a joke between Mom and me. She was originally from Canada, and when I said we lived in the northern hemisphere, she always said no, the near-northern hemisphere."

"OK, you have a name for your new company, and you have a project. What do you think, Brad?"

Brad looked up from his notes as if he was already pondering the situation, and then replied, "Well, if you're really doing this, then we have to be concerned about work-for-hire and work-product issues. To start with, we need to get Catherine and whomever she wishes to have on her dream team separated from their present employment ASAP. Frankly, you, the person you mentioned you want for your Manager if they work at WGNR, and that new production person, Mai, was it? You all should give notice and leave today. Legally, that is imperative."

"I agree. Catherine, if you want to do this, you need to start right away, or work product could become a sticky issue, and we need to ensure you make a clean break from your present employment. We can handle the legal problems. OK, what else, Brad?"

"The company name was my first question," he said, crossing it off a list he had already written on the pad on his lap. "We'll be setting up bank accounts. Besides your personal accounts, I suggest three separate corporate accounts. One for your charities, one for your financial division, and now one for your production company."

"What financial division?" asked Catherine.

"Huh? Oh yes, OK," began Brad. "Your investments will be handled by a separate division from your other companies. Those alone will provide the vast majority of your income every year over and above whatever companies you're starting up yourself. In fact, your production company will use a very small amount of your funds initially, in my opinion, and that's with going first class all the way."

"What's a very small amount of funds, in your opinion?" she asked.

"I suggest opening an account this afternoon with twenty million dollars. I can take care of that, all the contracts and forms, signature cards, et cetera. We can disburse funds for your production company from that. That should cover all you need for this venture for a time. However, if you're planning to do this right away, then I'll need names of the principles signing on those accounts. I can handle all of your financial concerns to get started. Mr. Doyle will get the corporation papers done, and he'll be handling all of your legal issues."

There followed another long pause as Catherine considered. Finally, she nodded and exclaimed with an eagerness that even surprised her, "You two have really got me thinking. Yes. I do want to move on this right away! Today. Right now. Oh my God! I am honestly excited about this." She looked at her watch. "One last thing, Gerald, and Mr. Martin. And this is very important. It is a deal breaker for me. I want my wealth kept a secret. Start up NearNorth Productions, and run the funds from there. No one, and I mean no one, is to know I'm involved in the funding. Do you understand? In fact, I want nothing to do with running this company. I want to be a reporter and pursue my dream."

"I understand your wishes, but I'm not sure I understand your reasons, Catherine," Doyle replied.

"I want a career, Gerald," she pleaded, sitting forward in her chair. "I'm twenty-nine, and I want what everyone else has that they take for granted. I don't want to buy my success. I want to earn my success on my own merits and hard work. I will not be fulfilled as a person until I have that. You and my mother instilled that in me, and you should understand why I want that more than anything else."

"Of course. I understand. We can do all of that, Catherine," he said. "NearNorth Productions. OK, I'll get started on the paperwork right away. Can you meet me here tomorrow morning with your new company manager and that production person you mentioned to discuss this further, sign a few contracts and other necessary papers?"

"Yes. Well, I think so. I mean, I haven't asked them yet, have I? Wow! This is really going to happen, isn't it? Thank you, Mr. Doyle...Gerald. I'm going to get my start-up team lined up next thing. I'll probably call you later with a million questions."

"Anytime, Catherine. I mean that. You are now our foundation client. My door is always open to you anytime of day or night," Doyle said.

Catherine stood up. "Well, Mr. Martin, it was nice meeting you. People will be showing up for my production meeting in twenty minutes, and I'll have to cancel it, so I have to run. This timing couldn't be more perfect."

"Would you mind if I tag along right now, Miss Marsh?" Brad said. "I would like to see exactly what's involved with what you do. I assure you I'll remain in the background and out of the way. I'll be just an observer. In fact, you may think of some questions while I am with you as all of this has happened so suddenly."

Chapter 7

Chicago, 1985

They said their good-byes to Gerald Doyle and went downstairs where Brad hailed a taxi to go to the television station. A moment later, they settled in the back seat of a yellow cab, and Brad said to her, "Ms. Marsh, I hope you'll forgive me. I feel it's important and especially in our situation since we will most likely be spending a lot of time together, that you know something about me in order that we start things out right. I want to inform you that I'm gay, so you needn't worry about me hitting on you. This is all business for me and I hope we can be friends around that."

There followed a pause, so he continued. "Uh, this suddenly seems very awkward. I just want to be up-front with you. I'm truly excited about working with you and I admit this is a bit of an adventure for me. If I've overstepped by telling you that, please forgive me."

His candor was disarming, and she found herself amused. "OK, Mr. Martin. Call me Catherine, and thank you for being candid. And I have a secret, our first of many I'm sure, and I want to be assured it will go no further."

"Call me Brad, please, Catherine. I'm really fumbling this conversation. I apologize for that. I'm not usually so befuddled and at a loss for words. You can rest most assured that anything you share with me goes no further."

"You're forgiven. I'm gay too," she confessed.

His eyes became big, bright ovals. Then he laughed, and she laughed with him as the cab pulled up to the towering building that housed the television studio where she worked in downtown Chicago.

Catherine realized she liked Brad Martin, and she was already thinking how to make the best use of his financial talents. Gerald would not have assigned him to her unless he was the best and could be trusted. She suddenly realized how this changed everything. If she was playing cards, she would be holding a terrific hand, and Brad would be the trump card. She couldn't believe her luck. She guided him to the elevator and smiled, as she looked him over from behind.

"Come on, Brad," she said. "Let's go blow some minds!"

She took Brad to her office and asked him to wait a moment while she talked in private with Mai next door in her office.

Mai was talking on her phone when Catherine walked in. "Oh, that sounds great! I can't believe no one has talked with you. I will let Catherine know and we can meet on Monday. Please find out as much as you can and we can discuss it then. Please don't tell anyone about our conversation until we know exactly what we have here. Yes. OK. Thank you. I will call Monday to set up a time."

Mai put down the phone.

Catherine said, "Mai I have something…"

Mai put up her hand to stop her while she wrote frantically on a notepad. "Just hold that thought. I need to write down everything I remember from that conversation while I still have it all in my head."

Then she got up abruptly and went to the filing cabinet and sorted through a few files until she found the one she wanted. She pulled it out and exclaimed, "Yes! I thought I saw that name somewhere. Oh my god…who knew?"

"Mai…Mai stop!" demanded Catherine.

Mai froze and turned around when she realized Catherine was seriously trying to get her attention about something important.

"Oh, sorry, Cat. What's up? Wow! You really are excited about something, aren't you?"

"Mai, I've made a decision that affects us all but honestly I cannot do it without you. I need you on board. Please say you will go along with me."

Mai sat down and started to arrange a number of papers on her desk. She stopped and gave Catherine her full attention.

"I hope you are going to tell me we're leaving WGNR," she said taking Catherine by surprise.

"How could you know? I only just decided this an hour ago myself," asked Catherine.

"I have been here a week, and three days ago I decided you needed to get out of here. As we threw our story ideas back and forth I realized you could not do them here. Time to go. Simple. This place was holding you back," explained Mai. "You are a computer driven microchip and this place is a piston engine. You are very special Catherine Marsh and this place does not deserve your talent and skills."

"Ok. Well, as usual you're right. We are going. This is all top-secret and no one else can know what I'm about to tell you. I have just inherited a huge amount of money. That's the top-secret part. But beyond that I've made a decision. We are leaving this company as of today. Right now we're leaving. I'm forming my own company and you'll be head of production in it. You'll work I hope closely with Howard Lindell, and our financial advisor, Brad Martin. We're going to see Howard next. I am hoping he will approve and come with us as our overall manager. Any questions?"

Mai smiled at her and shook her head. "I'm not at all surprised, Cat." She got up and began sorting things in her office and putting them in a chair together.

Catherine watched her for a moment and then asked, "What are you doing?"

"I am getting my things together so we can leave," said Mai smiling back at her. "What do you think I'm doing? I'll get some boxes for us. How many do you think you'll need?"

"Then you will go with me?" Catherine asked absolutely relieved and beaming now.

"Of course! You saved me! We're a team. I'll get my things together and start making a list. We have a lot to get organized in a very short time and you know that's right down my alley," assured Mai. "You go talk to whoever you have to talk to and I'll make a list of details to attend to as you make your break. Boxes?"

"Huh…Oh five ought to do it. You know me too well already, Mai," Catherine replied. "Brad and I are going to see Howard now and we can talk afterward. Wish me luck!"

"Good luck. I will get things going on this end. To start with I will make a copy of your hard disk before I expunge data and clean both of our computers. I will get that going first and make a list before I sort my office. Congratulations, Catherine! This is very good news and a very wise decision in my view."

She watched Catherine rush out the door like a whirlwind.

Mai had already concluded the station commonly used routines that existed in the past and time was passing them by. Whatever happened at the lawyer's office to get Catherine to make this decision was meant to be. Watching her work, Mai observed that Catherine was a superior journalist and this was not the right venue for her talents. This was going to be a hell of a ride and she was very much looking forward to it. An independent Catherine Marsh was going to be crazy wonderful for both of their careers.

Catherine and Brad walked in on Howard Lindell, the senior production manager at WGNR, who was having a previously planned meeting with her usual cameraman and driver in a crowded office on the twentieth floor. She introduced Brad to the others but immediately asked Howard if she could interrupt and cancel the production meeting and instead meet with him in private.

After the others left, she briefly introduced Brad Martin and then began her explanation, "Howard, what I'm about to tell you must stay between us. It's very important to me that you keep this a secret. Can you do that?"

"Oh, hell, Catherine, I was keeping secrets before you were born," he protested with a curious expression.

"No, Howard, I mean it. This is serious," she persisted.

"OK, I promise. My lips are sealed. What is it?"

Catherine took a deep breath, collected herself and continued, "As you are aware, my mother passed away this past week. As a result I have just inherited a tremendous amount of money. I have more than enough to start my own production company and outfit it with the best facilities, staff, and equipment available. I'm putting Brad, who my lawyer considers a financial wunderkind, up front as the moneyman. If you're willing, I want you to be an equal partner with me in this venture to see that everything goes smoothly and we make the right decisions. That is your area of expertise. I'll be putting up all the money we need, and you will be putting up the industry experience and know-how.

"But there's a catch," she cautioned. "I want to see if I can make my name on my own merits. Therefore, as far as anyone is concerned, I am just a hired hand, one of the featured on-camera reporters. You will be running everything as the overall president with Brad to handle all the financial issues as the chief financial officer."

She paused, and Howard said nothing. He sat up in his seat but otherwise just looked at her with a blank expression as if trying to determine if this was real, and if so, how he felt about it.

She continued, "Howard, you will have carte blanche to get the facilities you want and hire the best people to make this happen. I strongly suggest you get with my girl, Mai, to do a lot of the planning. I know you've met her but you haven't had the chance to work with her yet. I assure you she is the real deal. You will love her and grow to depend on her as I have. Brad can set up all the necessary bank accounts and financing. Work with him on that. As a matter of fact, we'll have bank accounts set up by the end of the day for you and anyone else you may have in mind to acquire what may be needed. But when you need anything further, go to Brad, not me. If there is a decision you think I need to know about, then talk to me in private and away from the crowd. I will always be available to you at anytime day or night. Otherwise, you go with your instincts. I happen to think you're the best. As far as pay goes, we're going to be equal partners and split the profits evenly, but that said, you can name your price as to your pay. What do you think? Are you OK with this?"

"My God! You're serious about this, aren't you." he replied as the realization of what she was proposing came to him.

"Yes, Howard, this is real. I'm very serious."

He thought for a moment in silence, as he considered his options. After a moment in thought he said, "Damn, this is something, isn't it? One of those opportunities that comes only once in a lifetime...if ever. Sure, Catherine." He seemed somewhat surprised by his enthusiasm. "I'm more than OK with it. I've wanted to break away from here for a long time. So if I heard correctly, Brad is the moneyman, and I'm to be the head of this new company you want to form. Correct?"

"Yep. That's the way I want it. I will treat you as the boss, Howard, and I expect you to put me in my place when I need putting, regardless of who is in the room. You have the final say on everything. We're going to hit the ground running from day one."

"Well, we'd better sever our ties here first, Catherine. That should be our very first move. It's bad form to discuss starting a new company while sitting around in your present place of employment. There will be some penalties for me because I will be breaking my contract. Those will have to be paid. That said, we're all giving notice as of when? What's your plan? Fill me in on the details."

"Our new legal representation already advised severing ties right away. Doyle, Bergen, and Reevis will represent us. I'll introduce you to Gerald Doyle in the morning when we'll be signing all the papers. So you, Mai and I, today... we're gone. Everyone else we recruit will give two weeks' notice. We will pay all the penalties whatever they are. You don't have to be concerned about that. We will deal with all loose ends fairly and with great consideration for our present employer. I know we want to keep that connection and make everyone happy. I'm hoping they'll think of us as kind of an extended family."

"OK," he said, standing up. "We have lots to discuss. But first, let's talk with Harry and get his take on this. If his reaction is positive, it will greatly facilitate our getting out of here without much difficulty. I think he has suspected for a long time I was leaving anyway. I don't think he thought of you, though."

At the door, he turned back to her and said, "Catherine, forgive me, I have to ask. You're sure you have enough money to pull this off, right? We're not just spitting in the wind?"

"We have a start-up fund of twenty million dollars and plenty more if we need it to get this production company off the ground. I want to go first class with everyone, and I want the best people working for us. I don't know all the details, but that's where I'm depending on you and Brad. Money won't be a problem, I assure you."

"You're positive about that?" he asked once again.

"Howard, I'm a billionaire. And if anyone finds out, you're fired," she said, smiling.

"That's my girl," he said as they walked down the hallway to Harry Holman's office.

Five days later, after whirlwind meetings with almost everyone on their proposed dream team and getting them on board, Brad and Catherine rode alone together in Brad's Jaguar XJ6, following a rented video van north to Cabrini-Green. The landscape turned bleak and foreboding when they entered the low-income housing project. It was in stark contrast to the beautiful modern downtown area they'd just departed.

"With all the contracts we've written in the last few days, Catherine, there's still one we haven't settled. As it stands, I'm still on contract to DB&R, but I feel like I am working for you now. We need to do something more formal about that."

She turned to face him. "Of course you're working for me. You've been working for me since you walked into Gerald's office three weeks ago. You should make up a contract between us if you want to formalize your work in my company and get properly compensated. I'll pay you what you think is fair to manage my accounts to start, and that will include managing the financing for NearNorth Productions. You can call Gerald to tell him, or I will. But I suspect we're only following his plan anyway. One thing I have learned about Gerald Doyle over the years is that he always seems to be one step ahead of all of us.

"Are you OK with this, Brad? I want you one hundred percent supporting me. I really need you. Are you in?"

He nodded. "Sure, of course I'm in. Like you, I'm excited about all of this. But you are some kind of roller-coaster ride, Catherine."

"OK, right up front you need to know this about me. I make decisions quickly and act on them just as fast. Like what transpired last Friday. The whole world changed for me, and consequently, it also changed for those who work with me. I went with it because it fell into place so seamlessly. Do you know why, Brad?"

"I'm not sure. Things were unanticipated, at least for me," he confessed.

"You, Brad! You were the catalyst that made this happen. I understood I had a fortune to put to good use and, even better, a financial wiz to help me realize my dream. You have the background and preparation that is perfect for this situation. The icing on the cake is that I can hide my wealth through you and the corporations you're setting up for me. I can have my career and live my dream. It was perfect. Meant to be.

"I suspect you're one of the very few financial talents around who can think on his feet creatively and can keep up with me. You sort of proved that this past weekend. You, Gerald, and Howard were like crazy men throwing contracts and financial ideas around. I was lost watching you three, but I wasn't worried, because the entire time you were calm and collected, crossing things off that never-ending list of yours like it was something you do all the time. We're going to be a great team.

"I'm really serious when I say I want to be in the background as just one of the feature reporters in this new company," she continued. "Everyone will be looking to you when the money decisions come up, so make sure your office and Howard's are considerably bigger than mine. I expect Howard to hire many other reporters besides me and to do lots of features for NearNorth Productions.

"Speaking of which, here's something I need you to do for me right away." She handed him a slip of paper. "Here are three people I want to hire to work with us. The top one, Kelly Ryan, is a must. Offer her a good salary, but pay her whatever she wants anyway. She will be a production assistant working mostly with Mai and me. She works for a photographer by the name of Jack Largent. He's a friend. I like him. So keep this quiet until it happens."

Brad put the list and telephone numbers in his pocket.

"Oh, and another thing, Brad," she said, looking at the desolate and intimidating landscape as they got closer to Cabrini-Green. "My mother was a personal friend of Police Chief Wilcot. He used to bounce me on his knee when I was a little girl. This is not a great area, and we don't have any security with us. If we get into trouble doing this spot, this is his direct number." She handed him a slip of paper. "He told me once if I ever needed anything to call him. Hopefully, we won't need to make that call."

Brad reached over and opened the console between them. "Why don't you dial that number on the car phone, so I don't have to look it up, Catherine? Let's have it ready."

Catherine punched in the number, not pressing the connect button, and sat back.

Their two-car caravan stopped before the entrance to eight fifteen-story, low-income brick housing units. They rose out of the broken cement as if they were pushing their bleak existence up to the sky for the entire world to see while demanding a response. This was Cabrini-Green. When they were built, the buildings were a shining example of modern low-income housing. But over the years they had deteriorated into a gang-and-rat infested poverty housing development that was nationally infamous. No one wanted to live there who had a choice. The irony was that these units, which housed more than fifteen thousand people, were on prime real estate near downtown Chicago. City hall had proposed many bills to tear them down and replace them with modern high-rise apartments. It was planned as a modern, mixed community, with a few guaranteed units allocated for low-income housing.

Whoever got the contract was going to make a bundle. So it was no surprise to suspect a pay off might be involved in any decision favoring one of the many individuals competing for the contract. For that very reason, all of the transactions involved appeared to be overt and correct. As it turned out they were not. The person who got the payoff was Chief Councilman Michael Samuels. Catherine had obtained inside information regarding the councilman receiving a kickback from a man working for one of the largest construction companies in Chicago. She was able to confirm her information through Mai's investigative hacking, which revealed enough evidence to possibly bring an indictment for two of the individuals involved.

The plan for the spot they were to film that day was to set up at the entrance of Cabrini-Green with Catherine in front of the main housing complex sign with its eight towers in the background. But when they got there, they found Mai standing with two Chicago policemen who were waiting for them, no doubt sent by the councilman who was about to be exposed with Catherine's reporting.

Mai had arrived earlier with two staff members to prepare for filming the feature. She informed Catherine when she arrived that the police would not let the video crew set up there or park the video van on the street by the entrance. Catherine walked up and bantered with the big beefy cop who stood his ground and insisted they leave. Brad stayed in the car and made a phone call.

Frustrated, Catherine was ready to give up when Brad stepped up to join them. He had his usual pad and pencil and copied down their badge numbers. One cop confronted him and threatened to arrest him. He went so far as to push Brad forcefully with a hand on his chest.

Mai exclaimed, "Hey, you can't do that! We have a right to be here."

Brad, although a head shorter than the cop, calmly stood his ground, and gave no sign of being intimidated. Instead Brad showed him his credentials, and said calmly, "I am an officer of the court and Ms. Marsh's attorney. She has a valid legal permit to conduct her business as a news reporter on public grounds, and that's where we are now standing. I have just notified the chief of police's office. He is a personal friend of Miss Marsh's. They are sending out two cars to assist us in this matter. Should you wish to continue with this abuse of your authority as a police officer, you will most likely be severely reprimanded and probably suspended, with a great loss of pay. You might even be fired and lose your pension. Most likely you will at least suffer a demotion. I suggest that you have done all you can for the councilman, and it is time to move on."

The beefy cop held a staring match with Brad for a moment and then pulled up his belt in surrender. He shrugged, turned to his partner, and said, "OK, I guess this is over. Let's go."

Catherine, Mai and Brad watched them get into their police car and pull away just as two other police cars arrived. Four policemen walked over to them. One of them introduced himself, and asked if there was a problem.

Brad replied, "No, officer, not anymore, thank you. But we would welcome your presence if you can stay while Ms. Marsh records her spot. It shouldn't take more than thirty minutes. We really would appreciate having you here with us, but we understand if you need to go on another call or have other matters requiring your immediate attention."

Catherine smiled at them and said, "I am very grateful, you showed up for us. You can't imagine how much it means to me to have you here while we film this."

Brad continued on a different note. "Oh! Hey, listen, guys. I have some tickets for the Bulls game tomorrow night, but it turns out I can't make it. You can have them if you know of anyone who would like to go. They're pretty good seats, the tenth row up, and just behind the team bench." Brad handed the closest officer four tickets. They all nodded a smiling thank you, set themselves down on a short brick wall nearby, and watched Catherine set up for the feature spot.

She smiled at Brad and said confidentially, "Bulls tickets? How did you pull that one out of your hat?"

"I have four seats about once a month or so. I brought them along in case we needed them. We just got lucky. But Catherine, word will get out quickly that we take care of Chicago's finest, and they will have your back someday when you need it most."

She rehearsed a couple of times and then nodded to Dave, her cameraman. "OK, let's go."

Mai looked on proudly with the script as Catherine prepared to start her report. She was very impressed with their new team and proud to be part of something grand.

Catherine took a breath and began, "I am here in front of the infamous Cabrini-Green housing project on Chicago's north side..."

Chapter 8

Chicago, 1985

Two months later Mai had moved downtown and discovered that city living fit her style perfectly. She resided in a condominium owned and formerly occupied by Catherine. It was well above what Mai would ever choose for herself both in price and comfort but Catherine owned it and insisted she move there and call it home.

Catherine kept Mai very busy especially after she saw what her talent could bring to her stories and investigations.

Mai was a very skilled hacker at a time when such a phrase was relatively unknown. In fact, few barriers or meaningful computer security existed anywhere and Mai trolled a hidden network of public and private computers connected to telephone lines. She was careful and always protected her 'trail' so as not to be discovered. While there were already thirty million personal computers in the United States by that time her back-door access to them was not protected. She was careful to do no harm to anyone and only looked for the deeper story behind some of Catherine's investigations.

Catherine soon came to use Mai's skills in ways she had never imagined when they first met. Since the Cabrini-Green story, Catherine had developed two other big stories that gained national interest and gave her new company, NearNorth Productions, a stronger presence in the News industry. What's more, they now had an ever-expanding database that was itself a resource for many of their stories.

As it grew NearNorth Productions took up the tenth floor in a forty story building in downtown Chicago on Oak Street. Catherine had moved upstairs to a condo on the twenty-sixth floor.

Howard Lindell had a large corner office commanding a superior view of the lake and Chicago's north side. He spent much of his time recruiting and hiring the best young journalists he could find to add to their ever-growing stable of talent.

But Howard soon discovered Mai's talent too and after he got her involved, she found several prospects for him that became the anchor for their young and ambitious investigative reporting team.

Mai was usually too tired to be concerned about her lack of any social life. She always meant to get back to Jack and he had called several times. But the new start up company had too many loose ends for someone like Mai to ignore. She felt an obligation to Catherine for the opportunity she had given her. She pushed any thought of Jack to the side as she diligently took care of business for Catherine. The most important thing on her agenda was seeing that NearNorth Productions had a solid start and she dedicated every minute of her time to that goal.

———————————✦———————————

Then one Saturday Catherine was exposed to a story that would change all of their lives.

Earlier that day, she had attended a special exhibit of Ancient Asian art at the museum. Within the exhibit were two matching golden Buddha statues that fascinated her. She noted that a company called Asian World Investments donated them to the exhibit.

Catherine got her news-nose in gear when a man approached her and struck up a conversation. He informed her that the golden Buddhas might be stolen and part of an ancient treasure. It was a friendly comment from a stranger she did not know and she initially gave the remark the credence it deserved. What's more, after further conversation she judged it came from a man who had designs on getting her under the sheets.

But he continued talking and finally said something that sparked Catherine's interest. He told her there were a lot of rumors about ancient treasures still to be found in Vietnam and many were centered around the base where he had been stationed. She wondered about that and even accepted a dinner invitation from the man to find out what he might know.

He explained to her that he had been a U.S. Air Force rescue pilot flying out of an airbase called Phan Rang during the Vietnam War. He told her there was a temple located just off base. He mentioned there was an incident near the temple where eleven military police were killed in a rocket attack. He also told her of a local legend that there was a treasure buried nearby. It was in an area called Panduranga. That information turned out to be a mistake for him and his designs on Catherine, because after he told her that, all she could think about was the story of a massacre and a lost treasure. She wanted to know more. She cast his romantic agenda aside, and left him disappointed without even a phone number. She hurried home and called Mai.

For her part, Mai became intrigued as Catherine told her about the story. They talked of the possibilities for twenty minutes before Catherine hung up and went to bed.

Mai, on the other hand, had no thought of going to sleep. That story in the land where she was born was something she wanted to pursue and she went looking for something to authenticate the story, if it were possible.

She started with the company Asian World Investments. That was who Catherine said donated the gold Buddhas to the exhibit. She discovered it's founder and president was a former Colonel in the Vietnamese army named Minh Ti Boa, Colonel Minh. She began to investigate him through Stanford's archives where she still had access. Stanford had a huge section dedicated to Asian history and in particular Vietnam and Southeast Asia. It was easy for her to access their extensive database since Mai had created it while she was attending college there as a student. But even she was surprised when she looked for any record of Colonel Minh. He turned out to be the Ninh Tuan Province Chief during the Vietnam War. That also turned out to be the very Province where Phan Rang Air base was located and also a Cham temple just off of that base. It was an area that was formerly called Panduranga.

Mai was so excited she immediately called Catherine back even though it was 4 a.m. Catherine seemed to be mumbling in her sleep until Mai told her about Colonel Minh. She sat straight up in bed suddenly very awake. Catherine told her Colonel Minh was mentioned in the blurb about the two gold Buddhist statues at the museum. Mai told her she was going to find out all she could about the history of the area.

Mai did not tell Catherine she was particularly interested because about the only thing she thought she knew about her family background was that they had lived in Ninh Tuan Province.

Chapter 9

Chicago, spring 1986

Chicago in the spring is an inspiring testimony to nature's annual rebirth and glory. After hibernating all winter, Chicagoans come out of their towering caves with a fresh enthusiasm for the outdoors. Jack decided to dust off his mountain bike and take a ride through Lincoln Park along the lakefront.

Jack kept in good shape by playing power-team volleyball at the local gym. He was between relationships and somehow never discovered the one woman who matched his varied interests and artistic mind-set. He found many who came on to him within the business arena, like prop and food stylists, models, and even other women in the photography community. Because he was talented and successful, women found him attractive in that regard, and for a lot of women, that was a prequalification for a serious relationship. But his dream was a woman with whom he could share an interesting and informed conversation without being bored. He wanted a woman who would challenge him intellectually more than anything. Thus it was not outward appearances he was mainly attracted to but what the ladies had between their ears. That said, Jack would not deny he possessed a secret affinity for Asian women, and perhaps that frustrated his attraction for others.

That was why he could not forget about Mai, the beautiful Asian friend of Catherine's. He had tried to call her several times but she was always out or busy. He came to the conclusion that she was avoiding him for reasons of her own and he had reluctantly decided not to push it. But it was a fact that she was still on his mind.

Jack liked people watching, and that was a great reason to go to Lincoln Park on a sunny day. It was usually crowded, and Chicago featured every ethnic type imaginable all mingled together in a cultural stew.

He entered Lincoln Park on his mountain bike above the zoo and headed for the walkway adjacent to Lake Michigan. As the wide cement path along the lake got closer to downtown, it dropped off six feet directly into the lake on the left side opposite the park. People liked to walk on the side away from the water, so that left a mostly clear path about twenty feet wide for riding bikes on the side nearer the lake. The crowd made it somewhat of an obstacle course. Jack made it even more challenging because he liked to do his people watching while he rode his bike.

As he road toward downtown with the lake on his left, straight ahead he could see the tall buildings of the city directly in front of him. The John Hancock building dominated the others like a giant robot. He was enjoying this view when a female rider passed him on his right and suddenly cut him off. He was able to stop barely short of crashing into her or worse, going into the lake. He was flushed with anger and prepared to share his frustration with the young lady who had stopped a few feet in front of him. She was dressed in a skin-tight gym leotard of deep purple and orange. She wore dark glasses and a Chicago Cubs baseball cap pulled down over her hair.

She spoke first. "Oops. I'm sorry, Jack. I guess I almost sent you into the lake, didn't I? That was very clumsy of me." She removed her dark glasses, and Jack was surprised to see the lovely face of Catherine Marsh smiling back at him. "Catherine!" he said in surprise and then caught himself. "I don't know if I should be talking to you."

"Why? I would have dived in and saved you!" she joked, smiling and enjoying the moment.

"That was the second strike, actually," he protested. You tried to hire Kelly away from me."

"Oh, that. Well, she didn't take the offer, so no harm was done. I know a good thing when I see it, Jack. I was going to make her my production assistant working with Mai. I was impressed with her work ethic and organization when I visited your studio."

"It was necessary to give her a big raise to make her stay, but she deserved it anyway," he replied.

"Yeah. We would have been a good team, though."

"You sure you were only interested in her as an assistant? Kelly told me you came on to her. Are you bisexual or lesbian? I mean, does Mark Doyle know?"

She laughed, and for Jack that only made her more attractive. "Mark has known since high school. That never stopped him from trying, though. I love him, only not romantically. We have been close friends for a long time. He even offered to marry me on one occasion to protect me from those less freethinking individuals who might get in my way up the ladder. But that was never going to happen. He deserves a real love. I think I may have gotten in the way of that. Know anyone?"

Jack thought of Laurel, the creative director he liked in St. Louis, but lately, she was talking about getting serious with someone else. "No, I can't think of anyone. I'm going to tell you up front, Catherine. I don't like you. You take what you want without any regard for the consequences. You use and manipulate people according to your own agenda. People get hurt that way. Please stay away from my studio and my people."

Catherine was surprised and gave him an honest and concerned expression. "Aw, Jack, please understand. It was just business. We're starting up a new production company, and she would have been a great fit. You said yourself that she was a communications major in college. I meant no harm, really. In fact, my biggest concern about the whole matter was what you would think of me for doing it. I like you. You're a talented professional, and I admire and respect that. I'm hoping we can be friends. I really mean that. Why don't you let me buy you a drink? There's a little place up here off the park on Oak Street that I like to frequent. What do you say?"

She looked up and breathed in the sun. Then she took her cap off and shook her hair out. It looked like a shampoo ad. Jack couldn't tell if she was winding him up or just being herself. He didn't know her well enough. She put on her glasses again, and seeing him hesitate at her offer, she said, "It's called the Stroll Inn. I have something I've been meaning to ask you about anyway. Come on!"

Her ten-speed was faster than his mountain bike, and she apparently rode a lot because she went faster than Jack wanted to through the dangerous curves, but he kept up just the same. After the path turned away from the lake toward Oak Street, it was straighter as it went into the park. Jack would have gone back to people watching except he couldn't take his eyes off Catherine. He was of the opinion that one of life's more pleasing compositions was a woman on a bicycle. But watching her from behind wearing that skintight purple-and-orange outfit, almost made him feel guilty about what he was thinking.

After parking and locking their bikes, they entered the restaurant-bar and Catherine chose a high-backed booth in a remote and near-hidden rear area. It was almost like a private room.

After the waiter took their drink orders, Catherine leaned in across the table and said, "You were in Vietnam, right, Jack? You were a photographer there?"

How did she know that he wondered?

He answered, "Yes, two years and three months." *Where was this going?*

"Did you ever go to Panduranga province?"

He took a moment to think because that wasn't right. "We didn't call it that. I was stationed for about eight months at an Air Force Base called Phan Rang. That was near a temple and a little town called Thap Cham. This was all in Ninh

Thuan province…central coast South Vietnam. That area was at one time called Panduranga, I think. It was what was left of the ancient Champa kingdom before the Viets annexed most of it a thousand years ago. Why do you ask, Catherine? What's this all about?"

She didn't answer his question but instead asked him another. "Do you have photographs of the area?"

"Well, yeah. I'm not sure how much is of the area and how much is of the base, but I have some photos."

"Do you have any of the temple or the massacre?"

She watched his demeanor change and she knew immediately he had something. His expression grew serious, as he inquired, "What's this about, Catherine? Where are you going with this?"

Their drinks arrived, and they took opening sips. She waited till the waiter left, and then she leaned in and pressed on with her inquiry. "Do you?"

"What?"

"Have photos of the massacre. Come on, tell me. Oh my god, Jack! You do, don't you!" she said, reaching out and putting her hand on his arm.

"Good approach for a predator," he thought, and he bet it worked with every man she came in contact with.

"First of all, tell me what you think you know, Catherine. I was there," he revealed candidly.

"There…where?"

"The massacre—uh…incident. I was there."

Her eyes got huge, like golf balls. Her jaw dropped in honest surprise. She froze while she processed this totally unexpected information.

She nodded and said, "OK, I heard that a military unit was trapped outside the perimeter of a US air base near an ancient Cham temple and got wiped out. The incident was completely covered up because the province commander and others had something going, like maybe looting a temple treasure. They didn't want any attention to be drawn to the temple during that time."

He shook his head. "Where did you hear that? That's not right."

"What's not right?"

"Most of it…all of it, I think. Where did you hear such a tale?"

"I was at the opening of the new Asian art exhibit at the Natural History Museum. Art history was my minor in college, and I am particularly interested in Asian art. My mother had a few pieces that are priceless, and they are my most valued possessions. Anyway, I was admiring two matching gold Buddhas in the exhibition when this man came up beside me and started up a conversation. He said he was stationed at Phan Rang as a rescue helicopter pilot. I thought he was just telling me a story to get me interested in him, but he was persistent and talked me into going to get a drink with him. Later, after a few drinks, he told me there was a massacre near a temple just off base, and the scuttlebutt, as he called it, was that there was a treasure there. The rest I told you."

"Well," said Jack, "I mean, you have it all mixed up. Some of that stuff I've never heard before, and it sounds like a complete fantasy."

"So tell me what you know. Oh, my God…I never dreamed! Jack, you were there?" She was excited and eager now. She hadn't imagined that she knew someone who might be able to answer all her questions.

But when people asked Jack about his experiences in Vietnam, he hit a wall that he had protectively built for himself. He had spent eight months stationed at Phan Rang airbase before being transferred down to Tan Son Nhut airbase in Saigon. Out of Saigon, he worked with five reporters assigned to go all over Southeast Asia reporting the story of the U.S. Air force involvement in the Vietnam War. For any young man it would have been a dream assignment, but for Jack Largent it turned into a path to the career he would choose for the rest of his life. A lot happened to him after he left Phan Rang and before he left Vietnam over a year later. Some of his friends died in that time, and he never talked about that part. He even put his hundreds of saved photos and negatives away for such a time as he could deal with them emotionally. He couldn't even go to the memorial wall in Washington when he visited because he knew his friends' names were there somewhere. And there were things he had not told anyone and would never reveal. He did not want to talk about that now. He wasn't ready. He looked at her but said nothing.

"Jack, *tell* me," she prompted. She again reached out and held his arm for a moment, and then she called the waiter over and ordered two more margaritas. "I can't, Catherine, or I don't want to. For me, there are some bad memories. I'm sorry. It just doesn't matter anymore. I've moved on. All of that is a lot of bad energy I don't want or need to deal with anymore, and it's not important in my life. Can we just drop it?"

She sat back and didn't say anything unconsciously scrunching her lips. She liked Jack, but she was also dedicated to her work, and she was onto something big. She knew it. She couldn't let it go. She made a decision, got up, and excused herself saying she needed to use the facilities.

Chapter 10

Chicago, spring 1986

Jack considered his feelings. A lot of time had passed since he last thought about all that happened to him in Vietnam. His second year and three months there were exciting but messed up in a lot of ways, and the incident by the temple at Thap Cham had been the start of the bad part. Eleven security policemen were killed in a rocket attack that landed right in the center of where they were bivouacked by the temple for the night. In the next year and one-half Jack discovered the reality of war, and a person only gets that when war takes from you personally.

It had taken from him, and he had successfully used the last fifteen years to forget about it and move on. Now it was going to work its way back in, if he let it. He didn't want that. He was happy and couldn't think of any good reason to bring it all up again.

Catherine returned and sat down as the waiter put down three drinks. Jack started to say something, but Catherine motioned the waiter away with a polite wave of her hand, "Thank you."

Then she paused, raised her glass, and surprised Jack by saying, "To Kelly Ryan!"

Jack liked that. He laughed and raised his glass. "To Kelly Ryan, the best damn assistant anyone ever had."

Catherine had tied her hair back while she was in the restroom. She reached into her backpack and pulled out eyeglasses, put them on, and took out a pad of paper and a pen. She began writing and talked while she wrote. "I get you don't want to talk about Vietnam, but please bear with me just a moment longer. I really think something is wrong about that incident, Jack. I'm not going to lie to you. I want a story. I need a good story to get the production company I work for more national recognition."

"Like the one you did on Cabrini-Green?" Jack said.

"Yes, exactly. I've got a hunch this one about the massacre is big. Let me tell you how I got onto this story, and then you can decide. OK?"

He nodded but asked, "How is Mai doing?"

"Are you trying to change the subject?" she asked smiling.

"Well, maybe partly, but I am curious. So, how is she?" he asked again.

"She is doing very well. As a matter of fact without her I wouldn't have been able to put the whole Cabrini-Green story together. She's a terrific asset and a hard worker. I've been keeping her very busy, too busy. I'm about to tell her to slow down and get out more. She's amazing Jack. When she gets into a project, she is driven much like me. We work very well together."

"Does she ever mention me?" he asked.

There followed a pause before Catherine put down her pencil and looked squarely at him. "I think she's in love with you, Jack," she answered with a smile. "But she never talks about you. She has never said a word to me, or…anyone else that I know of."

"Huh? Well then why do you think that? Why do you think she's in love with me?" he asked surprised and baffled at the same time.

"She has a picture of the two of you framed on her desk,' Catherine told him.

"What picture…we don't have a picture!"

"Sure you do…the one taken that night at the bar. We all got pictures…hey, you paid for 'em," she reminded him.

"Then why doesn't she say something? She doesn't even answer or return my calls," he replied.

"Jack, you obviously don't know her as well as you think you do. I know people, so I picked up on it very early. When it comes to things like this, she's very shy. She's afraid of you, Jack. She feels vulnerable. That's how I know she's in love with you. She's never known anyone who loved her like you do. Yes…I know that too. I told you. I know people. I know she feels the same about you. She has been maltreated most of her life by others her own age and she doesn't know how to accept that someone can truly love her for who she is. She's very smart but as intelligent as she is, she doesn't know how to deal with her feelings or even have such a relationship. That's the honest truth. I think the door is open, Jack."

Jack became visibly elated. "Wow, really? You have no idea what I feel about her. She is all I think about. Seriously. OK then…I'll just have to go and see her in person."

"Still trying to change the subject?" she joked.

"Huh, no I was just curious. Oh my god, Catherine! You just turned my world upside down. You can't imagine! This changes everything!"

She gazed at him and waited with an amused smile on her face.

She said, "Ok, but now you owe me, Jack. Can we get back to the subject at hand?"

He collected himself, took a deep breath and said, "Ok so tell me how you got onto the story about the incident by the temple." He suddenly felt good about everything. He noted how Catherine had changed from living-goddess-to-die-for to an intelligent, informed, alpha woman reporter determined to get her story.

Catherine was eager to share her story. "The golden Buddhas in the Asian art show were what originally piqued my interest. I know you've seen them on the posters around town promoting the show, but I bet you never knew who donated them or where they came from. When I was there, I read the blurb next to the pieces. It turns out they were donated by Asian World Investments, AWI. That got my news nose sniffing away, and I told Mai about it."

She looked at Jack, but he made no sign of recognition, so she went on. "Mai did some research, and on the board of AWI are many prominent and wealthy men from all over Southeast Asia, including Minh Ti Bao…Colonel Minh. His background shows he was a province chief in Vietnam!"

"Damn."

"So you recognize the name?"

"Yeah, Colonel Minh was the province chief for Ninh Thuan province when I was there. That includes Phan Rang, Thap Cham, and the temple."

Just at that moment, Kelly Ryan arrived and sat down beside Catherine. The two smiled and kissed each other, holding it for a moment in front of Jack. When they were done, Kelly turned around as if nothing had happened and reached for her drink.

"This mine?" she asked, smiling. She pulled the ready margarita to her lips and took a sip, while looking at Jack over the rim of her glass.

Jack's mouth hung open in surprise and stayed there. He looked at the two lovely women studying his reaction with amused smiles. He was so dumbfounded, he didn't know how to react or even what he thought. He was stunned.

"Aren't you going to say anything?" Catherine asked finally.

But Kelly, suddenly feeling awkward, spoke first. "Jack, I'm sorry I didn't tell you. I tried several times and got only partway there, like when I told you Catherine came on to me. This is not the way I wanted to tell you, but Catherine convinced me you would be OK with it, and that we should just break it to you and be done with it. I wasn't sure. So…are you OK with it…with us, boss?"

"If you're talking about being lovers, yeah, sure, I guess I'm OK with that. Surprised as hell. But OK. I am suddenly OK with everything in the world," he told her honestly. "But I suspect I am being manipulated again by the world's greatest expert on that particular routine."

Catherine felt she had to explain. "I just told Jack about the picture on Mai's desk. That's why he's suddenly so happy," she told Kelly.

Then she turned to Jack, "Jack, I'm sorry. I mean that. I'm sorry for trying to hire Kelly and how I've handled my approach with you today. You have to believe I didn't know there was a story when I asked you to have a drink with me. I just couldn't believe it when you told me you were there at that massacre. I've been consumed with this story since I first heard about it. I just started with that to get you here because Kelly and I have something else entirely we want to talk to you about. Can we start over? This is really important to me...to us."

Kelly leaned forward. "Listen, Jack. I have known Catherine intimately for four months now. We're living together. I know how she talks, lives, and even thinks. She genuinely likes you and considers you a man worth knowing better and having as a friend in our lives. I love her, and I know she's being straight with you right now. I'm going to ask you to trust her, and be her friend. If for no other reason, then do it for me. I want you two in my life as friends."

They were silent for a moment as he considered Kelly's comment. If he trusted anyone's judgment of people it was Kelly. He took a sip of his margarita and set his glass down.

"OK, Kelly," he said. Then he looked at Catherine. "I admit after what Catherine just told me, I'm happy with everyone on the planet and on top of the world. But, Catherine, if we're going to be friends, you have to promise to never lie to me and never to play me. If you want something, say it straight out. Be real with me, and I'll be real with you, OK?"

"OK," Catherine said, smiling with relief. She put out her hand and they shook on it.

"But I need some guidelines," he said. "Is this relationship public or just between us friends?"

"We're keeping it private for now until Catherine sorts out her career moves," explained Kelly.

Jack nodded and raised his glass. "To friends."

Catherine and Kelly clicked glasses with him, smiling.

"Jack was just deciding if he was going to talk about the massacre at the temple in Vietnam, Kel, but perhaps we should table that for some other time," Catherine explained. "I told him how I found out about it and why I think the whole thing smells rotten. He was there. He was actually there when it happened, Kel! Can you believe that?"

"Really, boss? You were there?" Kelly asked, surprised.

"Yes...No...Well, a few hours later. I was actually above there in an airplane when it happened. We were doing a story on the Shadow gunships that fly each night covering the perimeter of the base. I saw it happen from the sky. When we landed, my security police friend, Daniel Vega, drove me to the site in a jeep and I took photographs."

"That's amazing! I mean that you were there," said Kelly. "Catherine and Mai have been working on this since the day she got back from the museum. We talk about it a lot."

Catherine got serious and leaned forward on the table toward Jack. "That said, the temple incident is not what we really wanted to discuss with you. I never dreamed you had a connection, Jack. If you say you don't want to talk about it, I will respect that and back off. But please, if you ever decide to talk about it to anyone, talk to me first, or I will go nuts!"

Jack tilted his glass to her, and nodded. "Whom are we shooting with next week?" he asked Kelly.

"We have nothing until Thursday and then there are the Puritan Oats box fronts. We're waiting for Jackie Frye to get the milk-splash acrylic model done."

"Good," explained Jack. "Because I think I'll need a lot of rest after today. So what's the real reason you two are double-teaming me?"

"Double-tea—no," said Catherine before she paused her denial. "OK, yes, I guess we are, but we sort of got a crazy idea, and it includes both of us. We need your help, and Kelly thinks you'll go along. I want to say I feel awkward, but I'm desperate at this point…No, not desperate…Oh, hell. I'm doing this badly too, Kelly. Jack has knocked me off my confidence rail. I feel like a little kid talking to her parents. It's just that this is so important to us."

Kelly took her arm and continued the conversation as she snuggled close beside her in the booth. "Jack, I like you a lot and I think of you as a real friend besides being my boss. I've convinced Catherine you would be perfect. We want you to stand in as her boyfriend so we can go out in public. This is just temporary, so people don't start talking about us as a couple."

"You want me to play her boyfriend? Oh, I don't know. I kind of had it in my head to get serious with Mai, especially after what Catherine told me." Jack commented.

"Oh, well, that will be no problem. Trust us…we have a plan all worked out," said Catherine.

And oh…well, yes, but no, not just that. There's more," said Kelly. "We want to have a baby of our own, and we want you to help us do it. There, I said it. It's out."

There was a moment of shocked silence as Jack sat straight up in his seat, and took a moment to wrap his mind around what Kelly just said.

Kelly continued. "Look, Jack. We want to have a baby and while we considered going the traditional sexual intercourse way, we felt it was better for all of us to do artificial insemination. In fact, the more we thought about the idea, the more we liked it.

"Well? What do you think? Will you do it?" asked Kelly.

Jack didn't know what to think. It was beyond anything he ever imagined. He sat back in the booth and just looked at them without saying a word. These were two bright, intelligent, and very lovely women who were gazing at him with fervent looks of anticipation on their faces. Finally, he took a deep breath, thought for a minute, and scratched his head. "Ok, but why me? Of all the guys you could pick, I hardly think I would be your first choice or any choice for that matter."

"We know you, Jack. In fact, we know you very well. You're almost like family. We don't want some stranger's sperm making our child. You are a good intelligent, strong man. In short, you have good genes. We put our heads together and really couldn't think of anyone else we wanted to do this with," explained Catherine.

"Well, I don't know about all that," said Jack accepting the compliment.

"Let's order dinner," said Kelly. "I like it here, and we have lots to consider." To the waiter, she said, "Can we have menus, please?"

Catherine continued, "But I also want you to put on a façade with me for a while too. I'm moving fast now with the new production company, and I need men to stop looking at me as the bimbo feature girl."

"Catherine, I don't think anyone thinks of you as a bimbo of any variety. In fact, I've only heard very positive comments regarding you," said Jack.

"They all want to fuck me," she asserted pointedly.

Jack did not say anything for a few seconds, and then all three of them burst out laughing.

"Well, yes, you are very attractive," said Jack through a smile. *I might have even considered that at some time myself,* he thought.

Catherine looked at him as if reading his mind and raised one eyebrow. "I want them to think of my talent as an investigative news reporter," she explained. "That is very important to me. To do that, they have to get past my looks and desire what I have to say instead. Right now with starting up this company, my image is very important. I don't want to risk any distractions but I also want Kelly close to me always. Jack, I love her dearly.

"We think you would be perfect to fill that role, at least for a few months. One, we make a great couple, and two, guys will believe I could go for you. Our relationship would be readily accepted, and no one will ever think of Kelly and me as partners," said Catherine.

He asked, "I'm curious. Tell me why it's so important for you to have a baby."

Catherine replied seriously, "For me, having a baby is part of being fulfilled as a woman. I gave up hope of that ever happening since I'm not attracted to guys. I feel an honest desire to parent and nurture a child of my own, and that's right there with being successful as a feature journalist and businesswoman. When Kelly first came up with this idea, I felt hope for the first time for this one thing I was missing in my life." She took Kelly's hand.

Kelly continued, "She wasn't the first to mention having a child. I was, selfishly, because I also wanted to have a child, but not my own. I always thought I would adopt. Catherine has saved me in so many ways, and the irony is that she thinks just the opposite. I get it all from Catherine, and the one thing that will complete our life together perfectly is the child we want you to give us. You, our dear friend, Jack."

It was getting noisier in the other part of the restaurant bar, and they thought for a moment in silence as the Miami Sound Machine did their version of "Conga" from the speakers up front.

Catherine said, "Jack, I found a wonderful girlfriend who gave me support and strength, and my outlook changed and evolved. Maybe I just got more in synch with whom I really am. Kelly talks about you like you're some kind of perfect boss and man. You prefer female assistants to male assistants. You pay your women better wages than most men in their positions. You treat them like partners, not employees, and you show them respect. That is a rare thing, Jack, even in the '80s. I feel like the more I know about you, the more I want to know. You must believe I'm not leading you on. I'm being as open and sincere as I can be, but I also understand this is all quite sudden, and you don't know me yet." She took out a Kleenex, wiped her eyes, and laughed.

"Oh, crap," she continued. "Where did that come from? Now I do look like I'm trying to manipulate you. I can't say anything right."

"OK. I'm still thinking about this," he said while considering. "But what is the game plan? I know you've thought out how this will work. So...let's hear it while I'm still sober. I feel somewhat like a sailor who's being shanghaied. Wait a minute! You didn't just meet me bicycling by accident, did you, Catherine?"

"Guilty," she affirmed smiling. "Although almost knocking you into the lake was not part of the plan. Kelly told me you were going to go bicycling in the park this afternoon, so when she called, and there was no answer, I got my bike and hung out in the lower park, waiting and hoping to see if you would come by. It was a beautiful day, and I was all set to go riding anyway."

Their food arrived. Jack didn't remember ordering, but things were moving fast and dizzily in his head. So, like everything else, he went with it. Kelly was making small talk about the schedule in the studio, but Jack was not listening. He kept looking at Kelly as the two women talked and laughed. She was visibly very happy. It was obvious they were very much in love with each other.

"So?" asked Kelly. "So what?" said Jack.

"Will you *do* it...um, literally?" she said, amused with her pun.

"I'm coming around... maybe. But it *is* bizarre, though, isn't it?" protested Jack. "You two have thought this all out I hope, and considered any unexpected repercussions." There was a pause while Jack had further thoughts about the situation. He shook his head. "It's crazy, but I guess we might just pull it off. As to the pretended relationship between Catherine and me, I will only give it three months. If things are not bound up tight so we can move on at that time, then too bad."

There faces brightened into big smiles. "Agreed," said Kelly. Delighted, she squeezed Catherine's hand. "I told you," she said to Catherine.

"But there is one more thing, Jack," Catherine said. "It's pretty important but necessary for it to work. We want you to sign an agreement beforehand, waiving your parental rights. You will be Uncle Jack to our child."

The two women got pensive and looked worried again as Jack sat back, took a deep breath, and considered this. It really didn't matter to him now, but there was no telling how he would feel in the future. On the other hand, it would remove all legal obligations on his part to the child, and he would still be able to visit now and then.

"OK," he said after a bit. "When do we take this show on the road?" The ladies laughed and looked gloriously beautiful to Jack as they did.

"Um, that's the thing," said Kelly. "That's why we pulled this caper on you today. You may not know this, but my brilliant friend here gets ideas and acts on them instantly. While this has been in the works for a month or so, this morning she woke up, kissed me softly and said, "It's time. Let's do it. Let's talk to Jack." Tuesday is a good time to start for Catherine. She has an appointment with her doctor already and we want you to go also. The doctor has already affirmed that Catherine is a good and healthy candidate for this.

Jack looked at the two beautiful, intelligent, and sincere faces, and both holding his hands now in theirs. It was a very close and intimate moment for each of them.

He nodded slowly, and said seriously, "OK."

"Thank you, Jack," said Kelly as her eyes began to water. "I'm so happy. I love you guys!" She leaned over and whispered something in Catherine's ear that made her smile conspiratorially and look at Jack.

Catherine suggested, "Why don't we go up to our place to continue the discussion? I think we'll feel more comfortable than in here."

"Uh…I have my bike outside…so do you, Catherine," Jack commented.

"We're only a block away, Jack, at 37 East Oak Street."

"That new exclusive high-rise? How do you afford that?" he asked, surprised.

"My darling has deep pockets," said Kelly, "of the money-will-never-be-a-problem variety. Our baby will have the best of everything."

Chapter 11

Chicago, spring 1986

They walked into the twenty-sixth-floor condo, which looked north displaying a beautiful view of Lincoln Park. Everything was new, stylish, and impeccably decorated as if featured in an architectural magazine.

Catherine dropped her backpack and said, "Home sweet home."

Kelly walked into the open-concept kitchen with white cabinets and granite counters. She called back, "Coffee, anyone?"

"Me!" answered Catherine.

"Me too," said Jack.

"Me three," said Mai entering from the hallway.

Jack turned around in surprise upon hearing her voice. Mai walked right up to him and said, "Hello, Jack. I've missed you a lot." She kissed him on the cheek. She drew back at arms length still holding him and explained, "I have been staring at your picture on my desk for two months. I feel like we're old and very close friends by now. Catherine called and said you were coming. She told me about your feelings for me and I want you to know mine."

She kissed him full and meaningfully on the lips before pulling back at arms length again.

She continued. "I must apologize for my bad behavior. I have thought a lot about you since we last met. We were so busy I didn't have the time to even think about calling you at the beginning. Then as too much time passed, I was embarrassed that I hadn't called. But I always knew, or hoped we would get together again someday and in many ways you helped me get through all the frenzy and chaos of the last few months! You may laugh when I tell you that I talk to you every day at my desk. But I really do."

She held him tight as if afraid he might run away while she waited for his reply. Mai was dressed in a white blouse tied up at her midriff, revealing a perfect figure, and she wore light-blue shorts and sandals.

Jack was absolutely surprised and elated. He hugged her to him warm and close and didn't want to ever let go of her. She felt comfortable in his arms as he stared into those glorious eyes of hers. He kissed her again on the lips and held it a long time before pulling back displaying a huge smile.

He confessed honestly for want of nothing profound to say, "At this moment I think I'm the happiest man alive."

She laid her head against him on his shoulder expressing her own happiness.

Catherine walked over and said, "Ok you two. Come sit down on the couch." Catherine was amused and enjoyed playing cupid with her two friends.

After a moment, Mai pulled away, gave him one last peck on the lips and then joined Catherine on the couch.

Jack sat beside her and continued to gaze at Mai as she talked with Catherine. Her face was lit by the soft, north light from the wall size windows opposite them. Her smile was captivating, and when she laughed, he was a prisoner.

Ever the good host and referring to her beautiful condo with the exceptional view Catherine asked him, "So, what do you think, Jack?"

"I think she's the most beautiful woman I've ever seen," Jack replied honestly.

"Well, I meant the condo and view, but I see you have your priorities," said Catherine, enjoying the moment. "But I think perhaps we're embarrassing Mai."

"Oh no," insisted Mai. "I think he's pretty too!" and they all laughed.

"The view is nice in all regards," commented Jack. "That's all I'm going to say until I get my foot out of my mouth.

"You have a great interior-decorating talent too, I see," he said lamely trying to gain some control again.

"In reality I have very little talent for that," said Catherine. "I was going to hire a professional, but then Mai jumped in and helped me, and this is what we got. It was really a group project, even Kelly was involved."

Jack nodded and said to Mai, "Do you live here too?"

"No, I live nearby, but we have our offices downstairs on the tenth floor for NearNorth Productions, and I work there every day. Do you want to go over the contract now?"

"Let's hold off on that a bit, Mai," suggested Catherine. "We hit Jack pretty hard with all our crazy ideas before at the restaurant, and we're not in any hurry just now."

"Are you a lawyer too?" Jack asked of Mai with growing admiration.

"Third-year law school, Northwestern, I graduate next June. So, almost, I hope," she said proudly. "I think I'll do corporate law. I like it the most. Do you want me to suggest a lawyer to go over the contract with you?"

"If there's nothing in there other than helping to get Catherine pregnant and giving up rights to the baby, then I'm OK with it. There aren't any other obligations in the small print, are there?"

Mai looked at Catherine, who nodded, and Mai continued. "If both ladies die, you would be responsible for raising the child, Jack. Also, on the birth certificate, the baby will have Catherine's last name, Marsh. Those are the only things, I think. These ladies genuinely like you and don't wish to harm you in any way. You can trust them...and me. This is all as it should be."

Kelly set down the coffee, and they all fixed their cups and sat back.

Mai looked at Catherine, and took a deep breath. She turned to Jack, smiled and said, "There's a movie opening tonight at the Oak Street Theater I want to see, but I don't want to go alone. Will you take me tonight?"

Jack was surprised but pleased by this unexpected invitation. He welcomed any chance to get to know Mai better and was very pleased that she took the initiative however awkward it seemed for her. He looked at Kelly and Catherine, and then back at Mai. "Yes, sure. I have nothing planned. Sounds like fun. What's the movie?"

Kelly whispered a bit too loudly to Catherine, who was sitting next to her, "I told you."

Jack gave her a curious look, so Kelly explained awkwardly, "Catherine and I made a side bet. I bet you would be so taken with Mai you would say yes before asking what the movie was. Catherine and I have been talking about getting you two together for several weeks. I knew you liked each other. So far I'm right...I think. And OK...there's one more thing."

Jack did not remember telling Kelly about his feelings for Mai, but then she had been his stellar assistant for a long time and knew him well.

He let that go in the face of the conspiracy he suspected was playing out before him. He put up his hand and said, "Wait, I bet I know what it is." He paused for effect and looked at each of them in turn. Then he said, " I'm not going to the movie with Mai. As far as the public is concerned, I'm going with Catherine, and Mai will come along."

Kelly spilled some of her coffee as she laughed out loud and quickly dabbed her blouse with a napkin. It was too much. "Oops! Now I think he knows us better than we know him," she said. "That's right, boss. It's the Chicago premiere of *Top Gun*, and everyone will be there. When you watch the movie, you'll be sitting with Catherine on one side and Mai on the other. We have it all worked out. It's a perfect time and event to introduce you two as a couple, and we already have four tickets. It will be Jack and the three musketeers," she quipped.

Jack looked at Mai. "You're OK with this?"

"Yep," she said not realizing she was matching the response common to Kelly. Jack smiled at that in spite of himself. He was in love. He even enjoyed the fact that the three of them had conspired to plan the whole thing. He was outnumbered and loving it.

"It's black tie, so you'll need your tux," said Kelly.

"My tux needs cleaning, so that's a problem," said Jack, concerned.

"I took care of that last week. It's clean and in your closet," said Kelly. "Done."

"I'll need a corsage for Catherine."

"Already taken care of. In our fridge. Done."

"Dinner reservations."

"Claire de Lune at ten, after the movie. Done."

"OK," he said, warming up to the fun they were having with him. "I surrender. Tell me everything, and let's move this production along!"

Mai pulled him back to sit beside her on the couch. Taking his hand, she got very close and said sincerely, "One thing, Jack. I'm not pretending. While we pretend with them, let's see if we are real, OK? I want to get to know you better. So you and me, let's not pretend, OK?"

Jack thought *Top Gun—How appropriate!*

Chapter 12

Chicago, summer 1986

Catherine could not have imagined the amount and range of the publicity that resulted from her and Jack attending the Chicago premiere of *Top Gun*.

Her choice of an elegant Ariadne Mayhew evening gown that showed off her figure was the icing on the cake. Everyone wanted a photograph of her and Jack together, and they were in all the gossip columns and entertainment magazines after that. Jack, who was never much of a socialite, quickly made a lot of new friends in varied social circles, and the extra publicity even helped his business. He could not make the connection, but with the notoriety he was soon booked for the next three months at the studio.

Jack got a lot of kudos from guys he ran into, and he didn't mind that part. It was actually fun. Catherine played it up, showing her pretended love freely with her body language in public. She always focused on him with loving eyes. The more Jack knew it was just a charade, the more she made it seem real. No one seemed to notice or care that Kelly was always around somewhere.

But it was all in the plan, and Jack never got any ideas, even though he did tell her one night he thought she was coming on too strong. She replied by licking his ear and saying playfully, with a big smile, "Jack, guys everywhere would give their right arm to be where you are. I know you like it, and because it's you, it's safe. I can practically fuck you in public, and you won't have the slightest thought of taking it to the next level. You should be an actor. You play your part with amazing perfection. If I didn't know you take your passion to Miss Mai every night, I would almost think you're gay. As it is, she's already thanked me many times for warming you up."

He did wonder if the two grand manipulators, Catherine and Kelly, were smart enough to figure out that diversion for him ahead of time as a necessary precaution for unintended consequences. He already knew Kelly was smart enough to plan ahead for something like that. But in a short while he grew to appreciate Catherine's superior intellect as well.

Catherine was right about her professional model-like beauty working against her career in journalism. At first even Jack did not consider her intelligence. But after spending more time with her, he was learning to respect her mind far beyond her beauty. She was informed on many more topics than he would ever be, and he enjoyed listening to her expound on any of them. He was fascinated by how she could enter a room, size it up in thirty seconds, and then know exactly the best way to work the crowd to her advantage. He learned a lot from her about people, and she was a good judge of character.

She, in turn, liked talking to Jack because he did listen well and was not afraid to tell her she was wrong, or right, and why. They became very good friends over their many appearances in public as a couple, and the fact that they valued each other's opinions was a result of that.

At the same time, Mai quickly locked up his heart. She was everything he ever wanted in a woman. She fit him perfectly in bed, was not at all shy when it came to sex, and taught him some moves he never dreamed. Her body was as smooth as velvet, and Jack just loved running his face against it. She was all curves; one leading to the next like some sort of erotic pathway. But even in the dark, he could see those beautiful glasz eyes with the silky black hair, and he was totally given to it.

Her exotic beauty captured him to be sure, but it was her intellect that amazed him. He had already been exposed to Kelly and then Catherine, both smart in their own ways. But Mai was off the charts. The more time Jack spent with her, the more he was convinced she must have a very high IQ. She devoured information, could speed-read books and remembered with remarkable accuracy what she read. She had a photographic memory and proved it to Jack when she recited a list of three hundred names they invited to a reception for Catherine's production company. She was a wiz on computers and wrote her own programs to do most anything. She was a data freak and got visibly excited over comparing information in ways foreign to most.

Jack considered himself lucky to be friends with these three women and was not in the least intimidated by their superior intellects. He didn't bother trying to keep up with them in that regard. He loved them all the more because of it and had long ago decided he would just enjoy the ride.

It was obvious to the very few who knew of their relationship that Mai mirrored his feelings toward her. She became possessive of him, and Jack did not mind that at all. She considered Catherine's charade a necessary exercise because she had plans for the resources Catherine's company made available to her. Its success would greatly benefit her too. But she made sure Catherine understood that in spite of their game, Jack was her man.

The biggest problem Jack had was getting sleep in between Catherine, Mai, and his heavy work schedule. After the first month, they agreed to live together in his town house above the studio to make things a bit easier. That turned out to be a very comfortable situation for the both of them.

He was surprised when he bounced upstairs one night after a day photographing a cereal box front to find Mai sitting at his glass dining room table pondering a bunch of black-and-white photographic images. Moving beside her, he saw they appeared to be from the Vietnam War era.

She looked up and gave a cheerful "Hi, honey!" before she jumped up and hugged and kissed him warmly. He liked that about her. When they met in private, she kissed him in a way that left no doubt about her feelings for him.

"I was going to ask you how school was today, but instead of law books, I see Vietnam images. What's going on?"

"Oh, it's something for Catherine. She's exploring every angle she can think of about Colonel Minh and that stolen treasure. She wants me to help identify these people in the photos if I can. I actually know most of them, but these guys are not familiar to me," she said pointing to one of the photographs. "She keeps coming up with things like this that might develop leads for her story. She's looking for connections. We thought these guys were the board of directors, but they don't match other photos we have of the AWI board."

"They remind me of some of my photographs from Vietnam," Jack said. "When I first glanced over your shoulder, I thought you had gotten them out. I haven't looked at them in many years."

"Wait. What? Honey, do you mean you have photos here from your days in Vietnam? You never mentioned that before. "I would love to see them. Will it be OK for you to share them with me?"

Jack felt silly for not thinking of it sooner. "Of course you can see them. I don't know why I didn't think of it before. I will go get them. Sit tight."

The boxes were still sealed, as he had done years before when he'd left Los Angeles and Art Center. It was finally time to open them up, and Jack found himself surprised to be eagerly looking forward to sharing them with Mai. Maybe it was because he would be looking at them with a friend who shared many of his same feelings about Vietnam and its people.

He brought the three boxes up one by one and placed them next to the table. Mai collected the photos that she had been examining, and put them back in a folder with Post-its on some of them. She got a knife from the kitchen and gave it to Jack, who carefully cut through the packing tape along the seams at the top of the first box. When he opened the box, he found newspapers stuffed in the top from 1974, when he had packed up and moved to Chicago.

"This is the one with just photographs," he said. "One of the others has all the negatives."

Mai reached in, took out some of the photographs, and began placing them about on the large glass table. She was sorting them, and Jack stopped to watch her. She seemed almost to know what they were and where they were from.

He asked, "What are you doing?"

She explained, "You have so many, I thought it might help to categorize them according to area and whether the subject is military or civilian. Sorry, it's the Kelly Ryan in me."

"No, it's the Maisong Sambaht in you, and it's pretty amazing, my love." he replied. He brought out a handful of photographs, and they went through them, sorting as they went.

Then they opened the box containing negatives and proof sheets. Jack put that aside and told Mai she could look at them at her leisure. He explained that only a few of the negatives had been printed.

Mai walked down to the end of the large table where the Saigon photos were. "I purposely didn't look at these yet. I wanted to really see them, each and every one. I'm really excited, Jack," she said with a giggle. "This is better than Christmas!"

The Saigon images were in three stacks. She picked up the first photo and looked at it for a long time. By the second stack, she was shedding tears. Suddenly she picked up one and exclaimed, "Jack, I lived on this street. This is my street! I know those buildings. My friend used to live right there!"

To Jack, it looked more like an alley than a street, but it was common to Saigon, with lots of kids, dogs, and people selling things; an old French- made taxicab was parked in the distance. The photo was of three smiling young girls mugging the camera, with the entire street environment as a backdrop behind them.

"I can't see my house; it would be in the other direction. Now I have to see the negatives. This is awesome. We have no pictures from Vietnam. They were all lost on the boat when we came over. We came with just what we had on our backs. Oh, Jack." She fell into his arms and began to cry.

That night they ate Chinese takeout from the new restaurant that just opened up across the street on Halsted. Mai used chopsticks, and Jack used a fork. Mai talked incessantly and hadn't stopped since looking at the photographs from Vietnam.

Later, they sat on the back deck, sharing a lounger and drinking glasses of their favorite wine. Mai was still talking, more gently now. As she put her memories into words, Jack took them in and mixed them with his. For Mai it was remembering the very short childhood she had known as a little girl in Saigon.

"I've always wanted to go back to Vietnam. Lately, that feeling comes to me more often," she said. "I have a feeling there's something very important for me to do there. Do you ever get that, Jack? Do you ever feel in your heart that there's a real and dedicated purpose for your life? I seem to have that calling in my mind more and more often over the last year."

"My calling, as you put it, Mai, was photography. Once I decided that, everything fell into place for me, and my life was easy and fulfilling. Maybe you should go back to Vietnam and visit."

"Oh, they would probably throw me in one of their re-education camps, and before you know it, I would be walking around in a tan uniform and carrying an AK-47," she joked.

"Fortunately, those routines are a thing of the past, Mai. But I suspect that with your mind, you would be the one educating them."

"Yeah, GI, you know Vietnam girl smart, huh? Hey, you want boom-boom me?" she said, kissing him.

Jack kept meaning to ask where she'd learned to talk like a Vietnamese bar girl. He rarely went to a bar in Vietnam but when Mai talked like that it awoke the ready passion in him for her. He laughed, grabbed her up, and carried her giggling into the bedroom.

Chapter 13

Chicago, summer 1986

The next day Jack had a client in from Des Moines, Iowa. The business was primarily a mall-outlet hot dog company, but they sold every kind of food depending on the opportunity. Their philosophy was to go into a mall and sell whatever food was not yet taken. Most of the time it was hot dogs, but there were other things too, even pizza. The creative director was a large man named Art Williams. On the set, he was all business and very serious. But when they went out at night, he was his own stand-up comedy act. He was genuinely funny, but sometimes his jokes got too colorful, even for Jack. So Jack needed to be mindful of that when he took him to some of the nicer restaurants in Chicago.

As it happened, one of the more popular restaurants in Chicago at the time was Francisco's Mexican food, located right across the street from the studio. That day Kelly made lunch reservations for eight, and they were seated quickly at a round, corner table by a window overlooking the studio across the street.

After they were seated and gave their drink orders, Art began his usual routine of telling jokes, and everyone was laughing genuinely at his humor. At the time smoking was still common in restaurants and everyplace else in Chicago. As Art was telling a very funny story, smoke began wafting over him from a table nearby. Without missing a beat, Art went on with his story, seeming to ignore the smoke. But while telling the joke, he casually reached into his suit-coat pocket and took out a small red-and-yellow plastic propeller device. He turned it on, held it up, and pointed it over his shoulder behind him. It began blowing soap bubbles toward a table of smokers.

Within a minute a patron at the next table, where sat the four smokers, got up and told Art in very angry words that he was getting soap bubbles all over their food.

Art did not apologize but in a very loud voice declared, "And you're getting cigarette smoke all over mine!" Several patrons nearby who had followed the incident from the onset with amused curiosity broke into loud applause. One table of patrons even stood to clap in support of Art's clever protest. Kelly was laughing and covered her face with her hand as the owner who was a friend of

Jack's walked up and gave him a friendly look of consternation. Jack shrugged, and even the owner broke into a smile because it really was funny, unique, and a good indication of the changing social mores in Chicago. Jack overheard the owner buy lunch for the table of smokers, and as he left, he handed the owner a hundred-dollar bill on the side and thanked him for his patience.

After that day, Francisco's Mexican restaurant had a new smoking section off to one side of the restaurant.

Art always insisted on going to the New York Lounge, and after dinner that night, Jack was happy to oblige. Mai suggested asking Catherine and Kelly, but only Catherine could go, and she seemed unusually eager to join them. They pulled up at the front of the building on upper Clark Street at about ten, but it was all dark outside.

"Looks like they're closed," said Jack. "Sorry, Art, I know you were looking forward to going there."

Catherine said, "Wait, Jack, I think there's someone inside. Let's go knock on the door."

"Oh, I don't know, Catherine," Jack protested. "Can't hurt," said Art.

They parked the car, and the four of them walked up to the door. Art pounded on it and said, "Open up in there. You have important customers out here!"

Suddenly the door opened, and Kelly greeted them with a broad smile. "Come on in, boss!" she said.

The lights suddenly went on, revealing a hundred people in silly party hats, yelling "Surprise!" all at once.

With a big smile Jack asked, "What's the occasion?"

Kelly explained, "I know how important Lenny and this place are to you, Jack, so Catherine and I went temporary partners with Lenny, using it as a loss for now. I paid all the bills and updated and redecorated, but we kept the original bar…oh, and the original bartender. Since your birthday was next Monday we decided to celebrate it here along with Lenny's new opening. Lenny, your turn," she said, gesturing to the old magician.

Lenny stepped forward, and remarked proudly, "Jack, I will never be able to thank you for this. These two young ladies, Miss Mai and Kelly, have been selling me in publications all over town. Now I have so much business I hired three new people this week. You saved me." He pulled out a deck of cards and said, "Pick a card, Jack."

He did, and it was the jack of hearts.

"Lenny, I…" Jack said as his eyes watered over.

"You got some more of that tear gas in your eyes, Jack?" Lenny quipped.

"Lenny, I'm not responsible for all of this," he said. "I would have done it if I could, but it was Kelly and Mai. You should be thanking them."

"Aw, I already thanked them, Jack. They won't let me kiss 'em anymore," he answered warmly. He hugged Jack long and hard, and Jack was honestly moved.

Jack was happy to see that the people there were friends from the ad and photography business; his friends, and not the society crowd. But still, it was necessary for he and Catherine to play as a couple for the night.

After a while, Lenny gathered Kelly, Catherine, Mai, and Jack together and went into the back room with them. He closed the door and said, "You are four of the most frustrated people I think I've ever seen. Why don't you just kiss and get it over with?"

Catherine went to Jack and started to kiss him, but Lenny said, "Hey, Blondie, your girl is over here." He nodded toward Kelly. "And Jack, if you don't kiss Mai, I'm going to take her for myself!"

The four of them looked at each other, then at Lenny, and gave surprised laughs. "How the hell did you know?" asked Jack. "Are we that obvious?"

"Jack, I am the great illusionist. I have been fooling people all my life. I knew your deception the moment you walked in the door with Miss Asian Beauty here. I knew she was with you without a doubt, but don't blame her. She never once let on when we met to arrange for promoting the place. After I figured that out, it was easy to figure out whom Blondie liked. She was looking at Kelly all night while she was running around talking to everybody. Now I want to see a kiss. Now! Before you guys explode!"

The four of them laughed and accommodated Lenny in a passionate display of overdue affection. Then Kelly said, "Your turn, Lenny," and the three ladies surrounded him and buried him in hugs and kisses.

When they broke away, Catherine said, "I have an announcement, and, like our secret love lives, it cannot go beyond this room." She took Kelly's hand and announced, "I am…pregnant!"

Kelly let out a loud squeal of delight before she hugged, and held Catherine in a kiss without an end.

Mai took Jack's hand, and said smiling, "Hey, GI, we go home, you boom-boom me!"

Lenny shook his head and smiled. "Oh, I recognize that language, Jack. Do you need me to translate for ya?"

"No, Lenny," said Jack. "I got this."

Chapter 14

Chicago, 1986

True to her word, after three months Catherine made it known in the local press that she and Jack, in spite of what everyone thought, were just good friends. It was soon thereafter that Catherine took Kelly to the Chicago premiere of Pippin. Everyone saw them holding hands and eventually the questions became more personal. Catherine welcomed them and fielded them adroitly in a way that made everyone comfortable with their relationship. Catherine was relieved to get their relationship out in the open and noted she had been worrying about nothing. Kelly turned out to be very comfortable with the press and pundits alike, and won many allies in a short time. Chicago had a very large gay community and many prominent and famous people had already declared their sexual preferences.

One thing that intrigued Mai, which she quickly learned, and then pursued with a passion, was black-and-white-photo printing. There was a nice darkroom at the studio, and after a few lessons, she could be found in there often during the week, humming happily and printing some of Jack's Vietnam negatives. She explained that it relaxed her after working most of the time at a frenzied pace with Catherine's projects. Jack liked working with her under the orange darkroom lights and snuggling over the tray while the picture appeared like magic in the developer.

Then one day Mai interrupted Jack on the set with a photograph she had printed the night before and left on the dryer. "Jack, what is this?" she asked.

Jack looked closely at the photograph. It took him a moment to recognize the situation captured in the photo. He did not know he had it and was surprised to see a photo of Captain Straker, the military police commander, and Colonel Minh at the site of the rocket attack incident by the temple at Thap Cham where so many had been killed. They were standing near a large crater made by a rocket. He noticed that Vega was in the background, staring at another hole in the ground. On further examination, he realized it wasn't just a hole but appeared to be the entrance of a cave.

"Where did you get this?" he asked Mai.

"It was in with those Vietnam negatives. The sheet is labeled 'Ubon, Thailand,' but two of them at the beginning of the negative sheet were different like this one."

"You say there's another one?"

"Yep, but from a slightly different angle."

"Can you print that one for me too?" he asked.

"Give me a few minutes," she answered.

"Let me see it wet, Mai. Don't wait for it to dry."

She bounced off more like a little girl on a mission than the wonderfully complex, intelligent, and beautiful woman she was. If she had skipped out of the room, he would not have been surprised.

Jack was back on the set arranging food around a Samson microwave with a food stylist when Mai returned a few minutes later. She carried a red darkroom tray with an eleven-by-fourteen-inch wet black-and-white photographic print lying in it. He stopped what he was doing and took Mai back to the finishing room before looking at both prints side by side.

"Holy crap!" he muttered softly. The cratered rocket hole was in the foreground, but in the background, Vega was now covering over what looked like a smaller hole or cave entrance with a poncho or canvas.

"Call Catherine, and tell her to get her beautiful pregnant ass over here as soon as she can. Tell her I have something she will be very interested to see."

"What? What's going on, Jack?" Mai asked.

"You'll know everything soon enough." He put his hands on her shoulders gently. "Please make one more copy of each of these. Then do an enlargement, baby. Try to get in closer to the guy in the background in each of these images and what he's doing if you can. Dry them well, and have them ready for when Catherine gets here."

Mai looked at him with a question on her face. "Is this about Colonel Minh and the stolen treasure?"

"Yes, it is. Honey, please, I can't explain right now. I have to finish this shot, or the food will die. I'll be done in thirty minutes. Better yet, have Stella call Catherine, and you finish the prints, and maybe we'll jump over to Blue Bayou for dinner afterward."

"But tell her to come here first, right?" asked Mai.

"Yes, honey. I can't wait to show her these photographs you found."

Catherine showed up in an hour, looking beautiful and hurried as usual. "Hi, Jack. Stella called me. She said you told her to tell me to get my beautiful pregnant ass over here, so here I am." She turned sideways and showed her bulging tummy. "What's up?"

Kelly came in and joined them. "I thought I heard your voice," she said. "Did you get off early?"

Jack was examining an eight-by-ten color Polaroid. He yelled, "OK, Nick, shoot it!" Then he pointed at the two ladies. "You two come with me." He headed back to the finishing room.

Mai was standing by the big drum dryer as the prints came off and dropped into the bin below. "Good timing, honey," she said. "Oh, hi, Catherine! Maybe you will tell me what's going on. I made some photos with Colonel Minh in them but I don't know what it means."

"I don't have a clue, Mai. Terrific promotion on that article I wrote, though. Thank you. And I heard you contacted *Mix* magazine about me writing for them. One of their people called me today and wanted to know if I was serious. I told him what I wanted to write about, and he said to send it to him as soon as I have a draft. He liked the idea and was sure they would publish. Good job." Mai beamed proudly.

Jack picked up two copies of the prints and put them side-by-side on the finishing table. "Catherine, do you know who this is?" he asked.

"Let's see, that's Colonel Minh and…holy-moley, Jack. Is that what I think it is?"

"Yep," said Jack.

Jack explained how Mai was printing some of his old Vietnam negatives when she came upon these. She thought they were friends of his in Vietnam until she printed them and then she wasn't sure who or what it was.

Jack left the ladies to talk because he still had a shoot to finish.

Thirty minutes later, Nick had the final shot done, the film boxed, and ready to be picked up by the processors at the front door. Maura Delaney, the food stylist of choice for the day, was wiping down the big prep table in the front kitchen. She was all packed up, with everything in bags and ready to leave. Jack was busy thanking her and commenting on the success of the photography that day.

"What was all the yelling about?" she asked.

Jack knew that Maura was not called Western Union behind her back for fun. Gossip notoriously traveled from studio to studio and around town through the food and prop stylists. As the food and sets were being prepared, clients, art directors, and anyone on the photo shoot sat around prep tables and told their stories. It was a real and active grapevine that Jack was wise to guard against in his studio.

"Stella found a dead mouse. No big deal," he lied.

"Oh," she said. "I'll be sure not to leave any food out."

Jack tidied up, and ten minutes later Maura finally left. Nick too made his exit, and the film was already picked up, so Jack put down the big metal industrial grating that covered the glass front door of the studio and made his studio-townhouse into somewhat of a fortress.

Kelly brought a bottle of wine out and was filling glasses on the coffee table. She left one filled with soda water and lime for Catherine, as they all made themselves comfortable in the client lounge area. For a moment no one said anything. Kelly and Catherine sat close together as they sipped their drinks. Mai walked in and sat down beside Jack.

Stella joined them from the office and asked, "What's the occasion? Am I invited?"

Kelly handed her the bottle of wine, and she poured herself a glass before she sat down.

Catherine continued to work along with the mood swings and physical changes, to develop the story about the rocket incident at Thap Cham. The one thing she had not done was get back to Jack with more questions. The main reason was that she now honestly loved the man and would be eternally grateful for what he did for her and Kelly. She knew he did not want to talk about Vietnam, so she decided to honor that and seek answers through other venues.

But Mai kept Jack up to date about what Catherine was discovering about the incident at Thap Cham, and Jack was growing wary of the investigation and his close friends' continuing involvement.

Catherine took a deep breath and smiled at Jack. "This seems a good opportunity to talk about the incident at the temple in Thap Cham during the war in Vietnam. Let's regroup and agree on what we know. Jack, I'm aware this may be difficult for you, but if you know anything and wish to share, we would welcome it. If you would rather not, that's OK too. We can just start with what we've found today and what, if anything, it means."

"What did we find?" said Stella, suddenly intrigued.

"That's what I have been trying to find out for the last hour," said Mai. "And I'm the one who found it!" She handed the two photographic prints over to Stella.

Since sharing his photos with Mai, Jack was comfortable with talking about his experience in Vietnam. He decided to start. "OK, let me tell you what I know, and you'll see why this is getting interesting," said Jack, as he collected his thoughts. He noted that Catherine already had a notepad and pen in her hand and was focused on what he had to say.

"There was a rocket attack at Phan Rang Air Base, Vietnam, in 1970, just off base and close to a Cham temple, where eleven security police airmen were killed, maybe thirteen. I never heard about what happened with the wounded. It happened all at once at about four a.m. It was a close and focused area that was usually a bivouac for Republic of Korea troops on guard duty. I have always thought that the rocket attack was meant to be in retaliation on the ROK troops for their extreme methods in dealing with Viet Cong. In any case, it was covered up and reported that the airmen died as the result of a rocket attack on the airbase.

"Wait, Jack," interrupted Catherine. "We don't have that. You think they were attacking Republic of Korea troops? Why were Americans there instead that night?"

Jack nodded. "OK. We had been attacked on the other side of the base the previous week. The VC even broke through the perimeter wire before security police turned them back. The ROKs switched their routine that week to patrol on the other side of the base and out from the point of the attack. Our security police were not allowed to extend further than one mile beyond the perimeter. So the two protective forces decided to switch places for a week or so to keep the base secure and allow the ROK forces the flexibility to investigate the VC incursion on that side of the base.

"My friend Daniel Vega, a sergeant in the security police at Phan Rang, was an amateur archeologist, more of a treasure hunter, I think. That's him in the background of those photos. Anyway, he believed firmly in the rumor that there was a treasure buried somewhere around the temple at Thap Cham. He even took me and Bill McCann, a reporter friend who worked on news stories with me, out there one day looking out around the temple for anything unusual. He had heard as part of the rumor that it could be seen from the temple. We didn't see anything, so we gave up. We thought it was ridiculous, frankly, and even laughed at him for dragging us out there. We thought it was just another one of those tall tales that make up most rumors, myths and legends.

"He was sold on it though because he claimed that all the indigenous people around the area, the Champas, believed it. The Champas are like our American Indians. They ruled a large area of what is now Vietnam and Cambodia before the Viets came down in about 1000 A.D. and took over. Vega studied and knew all about that stuff. He was fun to listen to as he told his stories but the fact we were usually drinking beer when he told them might have helped.

"An hour after the rocket attack, I went out there with Vega, who was on duty and was one of those assigned later to clean up the area after the bodies were removed. I took a lot of color photos because that was what Vega's commander, Captain Straker, told me to do. That's Straker standing next to Colonel Minh. I shot eight rolls of color film detailing everything just in case there was a military inquiry later. I ran out of color film and loaded black and white, but as I recall, I got off only two shots before Straker told me to stop. I gave him the color film I shot, and I left with some of the security police guys back to the base. Vega remained out there and started the cleanup with the next shift of security police guys who were sent out.

"In the two photos, Vega appears to be looking at a cave entrance that was probably unearthed during the rocket attack. It's not clear enough to be sure, but put two and two together, and I think he found his treasure. In the other photo, he's covering it up with a tarp or poncho. It's not conclusive, but it's a good lead."

Catherine spoke up eagerly. "So we find Vega, and we find the treasure!"

"Uh, no, one problem with that," said Jack. "Vega was killed a few months later on a special operations helicopter mission into Cambodia. I heard about that from the Major who commanded our news group. He had heard about the secret mission through channels and asked me if I knew Vega. So that lead goes nowhere."

Mai was studying the photos carefully. She jumped up suddenly and said, "I'll be right back."

They watched her leave, as Catherine continued. "So, I first heard about it from that traveling show at the Museum of Natural History that had the two golden Buddhas donated by AWI, Asian World Investments, of which Colonel Minh, seen in those photos, is on the board of directors. We have that connection also."

"I think I have something," said Mai as she returned and sat down again with the group. She picked up the close-up of the crater photo. "Does anyone think this looks like the same guy in both photos? I think it might be." She pointed out a man in a black-and-white photo she retrieved from her briefcase of the group Catherine thought was the board of directors for Asian World Investments. She had been studying it when Jack found her the previous week. She compared it to the side view of Vega putting a tarp over the cave entrance in one of the newly printed photos.

"Look at his hair. It's receding in both...like a parrot's beak," said Mai.

Catherine looked at both photos. After a moment she said, "Yes, I think it is. Jack, I think it's the same man...your friend Vega!"

Jack looked at the photo of the AWI board of directors Mai had been working on a week ago over his glass table upstairs. There were twelve men, ten Asian and two Latinos, all dressed well and looking very serious as they posed for the camera. They were standing before a bronze tiger in front of their world headquarters in Bangkok. He had to admit, one of the men did indeed look like Daniel Vega. The mustache was gone, and he looked a little heavier, but it looked to Jack that it was Vega. He didn't know what to say. He looked blankly at Catherine, not able to consider what it meant. Colonel Minh was in the same photograph, but when Jack scanned the other faces, he did not see anyone else he recognized.

The group was silent as they considered this new development. But then they all seemed to talk at once.

Catherine was jotting down notes as she commented, "Mai, you continue to amaze me. Who else would have put this together? We all discovered things that alone mean nothing, but together they point at something big and you found it. So let's look at our leads. One, we have Daniel Vega."

"Uh…no," said Kelly. "According to the caption under the photo, this man is named Emilio Vaillagaros."

"OK," Catherine continued. "Daniel Vega, a.k.a. Emilio Vaillagaros, looks to have found the Champa treasure and is living large. We need to follow up that lead and find out whatever we can about the man.

"Then we have Colonel Minh, who I have been investigating for several months. He fled Vietnam about the same time as the downfall of the South Vietnamese government in 1975, but I cannot seem to find the exact date. I bet it wasn't long after Vega supposedly died."

"Jack, do you know anything about the special ops mission Vega was on when he was rumored to have died?" asked Kelly.

"Not a lot, actually. I was aware that the Air Force had special units that were using specially modified Huey gunships and flying secret missions into Cambodia in the area west of Saigon. That was before Nixon officially invaded that area in 1970. I assume they carried on afterward. Vega and a few security police from Phan Rang were recruited to join these special ops forces. I heard from a reporter I used to work with that a man named Hernandez earned a Medal of Honor on one of those missions. He might be a good lead to follow up on."

Catherine nodded and pointed to Mai, who affirmed, "OK, I will look into that. I've been in contact with the National Personnel Records Center in St. Louis. They keep the archives there. They might have a lead on him."

"So we need to follow up on Hernandez? Do you have a first name, Jack?"

Jack thought for a moment and finally said, "No…I don't recall. But the article they did on him should be in those boxes; in the collection of old *Seventh Air Force News* papers from back then. You saw them, Mai."

"Oh, yes, they're still upstairs. I will look for the name," she said.

Kelly said, "So what do we think happened? What do we think the story is here?"

"We think Vega and Minh found an opening to a cave, revealed by the rocket attack, that held the treasure. They removed the treasure, hid it, and transformed it into personal wealth worth millions for themselves."

"But if they did steal the treasure, what difference does it make, really?" asked Jack. "I mean, who owns the treasure, anyway? I'm not sure it isn't finders keepers."

"That treasure represents the wealth and heritage of an ancient people indigenous to the area," said Catherine. "It cannot be there just for the taking. At the very least, it should belong to the Vietnamese people. And if there was nothing wrong, why didn't Minh and Vega just announce that they found it? Something is hinky here, Jack. Besides, they became rich and powerful from what happened at that horrible incident where all those men died. But I'm not sure how to prove it, or really, even where to take my research next."

"I might have a way," said Mai. "I can check my sources again at Stanford. They have a great research department but I never tried to find out anything about missions into Cambodia. With their network called the Arpanet I can research other sources. We might find something there. It was actually developed by the military to connect with their missile silos during the Cold War, but now it's being expanded into something more. It's pretty revolutionary and really cool."

"The Arpanet. I never heard of it," said Jack.

"Not many people have, Jack," continued Mai. "The idea is taking off commercially, and it's expanding exponentially. You play those text word games on your computer. That's part of it. The whole idea is that groups of computers can join together with other groups of computers, and they all can access each other and each other's knowledge and databases for research. It's going to change everything; how we communicate with each other, buy things, even how we think. It is growing exponentially and Catherine has already added it to her list of stories to pursue."

"Can I access it on my computer in the office?" asked Jack.

"Not yet, but maybe within the year. Several private companies are starting up with ways to access it…but it's a bit controversial. Some of the universities want to keep the network more private and not open to the public and people like you and me.

"Let's make a list of what we want to know, and then let's set about trying to find out that information."

Kelly got a pad and was writing as they all suggested information that might help them build their idea of a conspiracy.

When the suggestions stopped, Kelly asked, "What if we get caught?"

"We're not doing anything illegal," said Catherine.

"I think what Kelly means is what happens if *they* find out we're investigating *them*?" Jack explained. "It would be good if we have a cover story, so they don't get suspicious or even feel threatened and come after us in some way."

"What way? You think they would try to harm us?" asked Mai.

"I'm not saying that, but these are former military types who are comfortable with getting their way through any means possible, and they're probably breaking the law as a matter of routine. I would bet they have their own lawyers and plenty of muscle and mercenaries ready to protect them."

"We will move confidentially and carefully each step of the way," Catherine assured them.

"I'm good with that," said Kelly seeing Catherine grimace. "Kicking again?"

"Yep…ugh! What a tough little guy," said Catherine.

"You know the baby's going to be a boy?" asked Stella.

"Oh no! And I don't think we care either way…Just an expression."

"I say it will be a boy all the way," said Jack, "and just like the two of you. God help us!"

The all laughed except for Mai. She was perusing the information they wanted to follow up on and devising a possible plan. "I have an idea," she said. "Catherine, I think it's time we redecorate your condo. I'm thinking we should go Asian with it and maybe collect lots of really cool Asian art pieces. Do you know of anyone who might have some of those?"

"Excellent idea, Mai!" said Catherine.

"That gives us an excuse to explore the illicit Asian art market without looking suspicious," commented Kelly. "And with Cat's family world reputation for wealth and art collecting, we should be able to get all the info we need in that area."

"You guys handle it for now. I'm with Jack. One crisis at a time," said Catherine.

Chapter 15

Chicago, spring 1987

As it happened, by the spring of 1987, the first part of their drama was resolved. Catherine had a boy. She named him Charles Jonathan Marsh.

She made sure the hospital records were legally sealed. All at once she and Kelly began organizing for nightly bottle routines. He was not going to want for loving parents. But it was a grind nevertheless for the two very active alpha-professional women.

Catherine was back in earnest doing what she liked best not long after Charlie was born. Her no-expense-spared approach applied to skilled employees as well. When she or Howard saw real talent, they went after them and offered a salary that was irresistible to most. She had a young team of investigative journalists working with her who were developing features with national interest in both video and print. With those sort of investigative and timely stories gaining positive attention for NearNorth Productions, they became more in demand and recognized for their biting stories and professionalism. The end result was that in a few short years, she and Howard had a whole package that could compete well with any of the well-known and established news services.

Most regarded the new production company as a phenomenon in the industry, and many young journalists lobbied to work with them. Their star was rising quickly, and they were taking with them many talented young journalists who might have never had a chance in an industry that was losing its traditional focus and building foundations in the new digital media and cable venues.

Brad Martin ensured that Catherine's creative ambitions were unhampered by financial concerns. Working closely with Gerald Doyle, he guided the success of the two other divisions of Catherine's new corporation. One was a charitable foundation and the other an investment giant that was expanding rapidly through their vision of how the world would evolve in media, technology, medicine, and energy. In almost every case, their idea of the future would seem prescient but it was really a result of an appreciation for new ideas, an informed regard for statistics, and a careful analysis of the growing trends in each industry. This was almost entirely due to Mai.

Brad and Mai became acquainted when she tagged along one day with Catherine for a corporate financial briefing from Brad. As a courtesy to Mai, he gave both of the ladies identical folders, which Brad planned to review with Catherine over lunch.

Not long into the briefing Mai began freely expressing her opinion on a number of issues. At first, Catherine was annoyed with her because she thought Mai was interfering with Brad's presentation. But Brad politely waved Catherine off as he became intrigued, and then transfixed while listening to Mai expound on the investment strategies within the folders. He sat back and listened to Mai carefully because he understood that her perspective changed everything and if she were correct, her strategy and estimates could provide a very profitable future for the corporation.

The originally planned short financial briefing turned into a daylong exercise ending with an expensive dinner at an exclusive restaurant where their involved analysis continued late into the evening. Catherine bailed out early because she was lost in the discourse that Mai and Brad found mutually engaging.

After that day, Brad made it a routine to seek Mai's consultation whenever data analysis was involved. She saw things in those sheets of numbers nobody else did, and her opinions about a company or where to invest proved to be correct almost every time. He once told her she needed to get a raise, but Mai fired back that money was boring. "It is not the end that is important. It's the journey that makes life worth living," she told him.

Catherine met with Brad and Gerald Doyle at his office one day to discuss the Mai situation. Brad and Gerald both agreed Mai should join Brad in working with his corporate investments division. Incredibly, as insightful and intelligent as Brad was, he found he was most of the time schooled by Mai and her unique and original perspective as to the financial markets. The problem was that Mai had already turned them down and wanted instead to continue to work with Catherine doing her production work. She enjoyed working with Catherine on her projects and found that work much more interesting, enjoyable and fulfilling.

Brad made a good case to Catherine for Mai coming to work with them. "Among other things, she has developed a formula for analyzing a company and its potential for success with a number of self-designed algorithms that even I have a tough time understanding. We know only that she is right almost every time. Long story short, our Mai is one very smart young lady."

Gerald Doyle continued. "So, since she won't go across town and work in the corporation with Brad, we recommend that you expand to the thirtieth floor so we can move some of our people over there to work directly with her. We want her to have her own office group supporting our financial division, so we have a steady conduit to her. What do you say?"

Catherine nodded. "Let's do it, and soon. I echo your opinion of Mai and her value to this company. But let's be careful. You and I need to work together, Brad, to ensure we do not overwork her. Let's get her involved only in projects where her very unique skills can be of most value to us. In the end, I want her to be happy. That is of paramount importance to me."

Jack was surprised when Mai said she was not ready to formally marry him but wanted to continue living together as they were. She explained that she loved living with him. She did not want any other man in her life but him, and she wanted him with her forever. But that affirmation of her love served only to confound Jack even more. Perhaps in the future, she would have different feelings toward getting married. But for now, she felt it was, in fact, their coming together as two well-grounded individuals that gave them their strength and solid attraction for each other.

The truth was that Mai didn't really know why she didn't want to get married. It was more of a feeling than a reason she could put into words. She felt she wasn't ready to commit to a formal marriage because she had something very important yet to do in her life.

Jack genuinely admired and deeply loved his young Asian wife-partner. He thought of her as his wife, and she always introduced Jack as her husband at parties. She seemed to always have some new thing she was into, and this was beyond keeping up with all of Catherine's whims and Brad's enterprises. Jack noted she seemed to be increasingly unsettled and restless, as if she were anticipating something about to happen.

Chapter 16

Chicago, summer 1988

Mai found herself spending more and more time searching for some sort of self-realization. Her work with data and creating new computer programs was engaging, but it never seemed to satisfy her thirst for fulfillment. If anything, the more she challenged her mental abilities, the more she felt she was being called to a greater purpose. This drive for fulfillment came from within. She came to firmly believe that, but she couldn't imagine what it was that was pushing her so relentlessly.

As promised, Mai quickly spread the word of Catherine's interest in acquiring authentic Asian antiques for her condominium. This eventually led Mai to a meeting by correspondence with a young lady living in the city of Ubon, Thailand. Her name was Su Ling. She was an assistant to Colonel Minh and in charge of marketing his vast collection of Asian antiquities. She sent Mai an exclusive catalog of various items.

It was soon after receiving the catalogue that Mai and Su Ling began to correspond regularly using a new not-yet public program that allowed them to send text messages back and forth between specified computers easily using telephone lines. Mai's sources that were developing the program called it 'email' because it was online. Mai previewed it through her contacts in the industry and suggested some changes that made the program more efficient. She found the program very timely and useful in her correspondence with Su Ling, who she set up with the necessary software as an advantageous experiment.

Their relationship became more complicated one day when Mai asked Su Ling about a design on one of the pieces she saw in the antiquities catalog. It was a photo of a vase encircled with flowers, and Mai asked for more information about the flowers.

Su Ling explained they resembled a wildflower commonly found in Vietnam. It was called the hoa cuc, and it was also the symbol for the royal family of the ancient Champa kingdom that once ruled the area. When Mai told her she had a birthmark on her hip that looked like that symbol, Su Ling became very interested and began asking her a lot of questions. She pleaded for Mai to photograph the birthmark and send it to her, so that she could see it. She also wanted Mai to send a photograph of herself.

After a few days of her persistent entreaties, Mai acquiesced and accommodated her wishes. She FedExed two polaroids to Su Ling the following day, one a close-up of the birthmark and one a little further back in a bikini that showed where the birthmark was located on her lower right hip.

Mai received a telephone call from Su Ling soon after she reviewed the images. She was very excited and Mai had to tell her to slow down and start again because she was speaking so fast she could not understand her. Su Ling took a big breath and repeated what she had to say this time more slowly, but it was obviously difficult for her to control her excitement.

She told her that she believed sincerely that Mai was the long-lost queen and rightful heir to the throne of the ancient Champa kingdom known fondly by her people as the Hoa Cuc. She said the birthmark on her right hip confirmed that.

She told her of an ancient legendary queen named Dau Te Po, who disappeared over a thousand years ago. The Champas believed this ancient queen would one day return to lead them, restore their kingdom, and once again give their lives meaning and purpose. They had been wandering as a people for over a millennium, longing for the return of their legendary queen. What was more, Su Ling further revealed the Champa people were compelled to serve and obey this queen. It was a matter of their heritage, tradition, and deep-rooted beliefs.

Mai of course, had heard of the Champa people before when Jack told them about the lost treasure, and she remembered her two friends in high school who said they were from the Champa people of Vietnam. But she never heard about their queen that had been lost for a long time, or the Hoa Cuc birthmark being a sign of the true queen.

Su Ling's reaction was surprising to her, but Mai was stunned when Su Ling told her that in fact she, Su Ling, was one of these Champa faithful. She further revealed that she was now Mai's humble, obedient servant, ready to serve and obey her in whatever she wished her to do. Over the phone from thousands of miles away, Su ling gave herself body and soul to Mai.

Mai did not know what to think. She was not sure she even believed it. So much of ancient tradition and faith was based on ignorance and superstition.

Mai was separated from her parents when she was three leaving her with no knowledge of her ancestry, so she decided to investigate further. She remembered her aunt telling her as a child that her parents were from Ninh Tuan Province. She asked Su Ling to find out if she could discover what happened to her parents, but to do it secretly and to not let anyone know about her or that she was possibly the real Hoa Cuc. She gave Su Ling as much information about herself as she knew and left it at that.

The more Mai considered the possibility of her ancestry, the more she realized it explained her own feelings concerning her destiny and the unfound purpose and meaning for her life that lately had become something of an obsession for her.

At the same time, she knew it may be nothing more than a wondrous fantasy, and her practical side fought against giving it too much credence.

A week later, Mai received a telephone call from Su Ling with the results of her investigation into Mai's background and the circumstances of her parents' disappearance.

Su Ling seemed nervous and began by saying, "My lady, this call greatly troubles me. I admit I am somewhat reluctant to reveal what I have discovered because I fear it might upset you. I want you to know I am here for you if there is anything I can do to help. The last thing I want is to bring distress and unhappiness into your world."

Mai became impatient. "Please, Su Ling, just tell me what you know and let me decide whether it's upsetting or not. What did you discover as you sought to find information about my family?"

Su Ling revealed that Mai's parents did indeed live in Ninh Tuan Province when last seen as Mai had suspected. They were leading teachers in one of the local schools. She told her that by coincidence, Colonel Minh who Su Ling now worked for was the province chief at that time.

The shocking news was that he was the one who had Mai's parents arrested and taken from her twenty-two years ago. They were in the process at the time of investigating their ancestry, as Mai was doing. Those inquiries took them close to Minh's illicit organization in Northern Cambodia because their ancestors were from that area of Southeast Asia.

It was at a time when Colonel Minh was in the midst of his plans to steal a large amount of gold from South Vietnam. He suspected they were government agents, and in the middle of the night he ordered them to be secretly arrested. He put them on a helicopter, took them out to the South China Sea, and from one thousand feet in the air, tossed them out. They disappeared, and no one ever knew what happened to them. Su Ling was only able to find out through a confidant and old friend of hers within Colonel Minh's organization.

Mai was stunned and told Su Ling she needed time to consider this new development. She hung up the phone and cried. She recalled that when Su Ling told Mai her parent's names, she was saddened all the more because she had forgotten them all these many years. She felt a sudden and tremendous loss and she cried freely.

Slowly, she gained her composure and thought about what Colonel Minh had done. Her anger grew, along with a driving compulsion for revenge. She made a vow then and there to the parents she never knew to go to Vietnam, find Colonel Minh, and kill him.

As was her way, she systematically considered many alternatives, and in the end, she realized they all involved Su Ling. She would need to inform Su Ling of her intentions. If Su Ling were truly loyal to her, she would help devise a way for her to meet Colonel Minh in order that she could execute him.

The following day by telephone once more, Mai revealed her desire to Su Ling to meet Colonel Minh so that she could kill him.

To her surprise Su Ling told Mai it would not be difficult for her to meet Colonel Minh because in fact he had been searching for the lost Champa queen for many years.

He had conceived a master plan of his own to unite the millions of indigenous Champa people living throughout Southeast Asia behind this legendary queen and foment a revolution to take over the area. He was counting on the Champa people's blind devotion to their lost queen to make that possible.

Su Ling asked her, "Do you wish me to tell him about you, my lady? All you would have to do then is come to Vietnam, and we could arrange for you to be taken to him. It would be a relatively simple process, and then you will have an opportunity for your revenge."

Mai's immediate impression was that Su Ling was delusional. "Are you certain of this, Su Ling?" she asked delicately. "The whole idea sounds pretty bizarre to me. How can anyone believe that the Champa people would be so devoted they would be willing to die for such a cause? Colonel Minh would be a fool to believe such a thing were possible."

"My lady, with great respect, the compelling devotion we Champas feel for you is real. Now that I know you are my queen, I am ready to die for you. I will follow you and obey you regardless of where you lead me. This devotion I have for you is at the very core of my being as a Champa. It represents everything that is meaningful for we Champas as a people. Serving you is the only way we Champas can find fulfillment in our lives. We firmly believe that. It was the most joyous day of my life when I discovered you were the lost and real queen. Serving you gives purpose and meaning to my life. You will soon know that all Champas feel the same.

"Colonel Minh has investigated and studied this phenomenon for years in hopes that he can use it and adapt it for his own agenda. It will not be a difficult thing for you to be with him and thus have your revenge."

Mai thought for a moment and decided at the very least it was a means to an end. She told her, "Yes, tell Colonel Minh about me, and let's start planning a way to have me taken to him."

The following day, after this remarkable revelation, Jack walked into their home office upstairs where Mai was working on computer. She was now, along with Jack, a legal owner of the building, and their bank accounts were mixed. In fact, they were joined in every way a married couple would be except for the legal paper making them husband and wife.

That afternoon she was focused intently on what she was doing, so Jack decided he would not disturb her and quietly sneak back out of the room. But just as he thought he was successful, she pounced on him from behind and said, "Hey, GI, you think you sneak past smart Vietnam girl. Now we go boom-boom, make lots of noise, wake neighbors I think," she said, pulling him out the door.

Jack picked her up squealing and laughing. He loved it when she went into Vietnamese bargirl mode. It was the last thing she would ever be in real life, but he knew it was her way of releasing tension, and letting Jack know she wanted to make love.

An hour later they lay together talking, quite satisfied in the soft light cast by the sunset through the glass-block windows of their bedroom.

"Mai, do you remember your parents?" Jack asked.

She rose up on one elbow and looked at him. "Were you reading over my shoulder before?" she asked pointedly.

"Huh? No...what are you talking about?"

"I was emailing someone investigating my parents when you walked up. Her name is Su Ling, and she lives in Ubon, Thailand. She is very helpful as we look into Colonel Minh's operations."

Mai laid back down and rested her head on his bare chest. She wanted to tell Jack more about what Su Ling had told her and what they were planning, but she knew she could not. It was all too crazy to be real, and if it were real, Jack would never let her see it through. And yet...she traced her finger over the small flower-shaped birthmark, the Hoa Cuc, which was always there on her lower right hip.

"What's email, Mai?" asked Jack with a smile. His hand ran down her naked body as an invitation to again make love.

She turned toward him, so they were almost mouth to mouth and softly explained, "There is a new way of communicating with others on computer, and this is still very confidential, that has a method to send a typed message to someone far away almost instantly. It is an extension of the Arpanet I told all of you about the other day.

"That could be handy," said Jack. "When can we common folk use it?"

"In a few years, I suspect everyone will be able to use it, GI. Just ...get ... an ... email ...account," she said, marking her words with kisses on his body.

"GI, huh? OK, Mai, fess up! Where did you learn to talk like a Vietnamese bargirl? I love it when you do because it signals very well what you have on your mind. But I always wondered where you picked it up?"

"Hah, well it's obvious you recognize it! Did you play around with bar girls when you were a soldier boy in Vietnam?" she asked playing her finger down his chest. "Well, I did visit a bar now and then with friends, but it was only for drinks.

I swear," he replied. "But you couldn't walk down a street in Saigon without hearing that familiar lingo."

She smiled, "OK, remember I told you a friend of my mother's took care of me when I lost my parents? Her name was Trinh and I called her aunt Trinh although she was not related."

He nodded.

"Well, she owned a bar in Saigon that was frequented by a lot of GIs when the Americans were still there. I was only nine when the Americans finally left, so I was too young to be a bargirl. I washed dishes and cleaned mostly and wasn't allowed anywhere near the GIs. But I saw the girls and how they worked the soldiers for their money. I wanted to be a bargirl because they could make a lot of money in one night. Many of them supported their families in that way. But aunt Trinh told me, 'No, that is not for you, Mai. You will own this place one day and make much more money than a bargirl.' I was very disappointed because I thought the bargirls were very pretty and happy. I used to hide and watch them work. So, when I go into Vietnam bar girl mode, I'm sort of living the fantasy of my youth."

Jack traced her lips with his finger. "You could never have been a bargirl, Mai."

"Huh? Why not? I think I'm pretty enough," she protested.

"That's the problem. You're too pretty. You would have put all the other girls out of business!"

Mai liked that, and she showed him how much.

Chapter 17

Chicago, March 1989

It seemed Jack was good at making babies, and by spring the following year, he and Mai had their own baby, a daughter. They named their child Devearney Ann Largent, a name chosen by Mai, but one Jack loved the first time he heard it. Jack could not have been happier, and it made Mai happy too because she wanted a daughter to raise as her own. Mai wrote the name on the birth certificate, and when Jack went to sign it, he was pleasantly surprised to find she'd used his last name on their daughter's birth documents. He hadn't thought about it, and they hadn't discussed it. That sealed everything for them. Even with no marriage documents, Mai proclaimed her love and commitment to Jack forever, and he always felt the same.

With little time for either of them to be a stay-at-home parent, they found an Asian au pair who worked well with their busy schedules. Within weeks she was like family and did not hesitate to tell Jack and Mai when she thought they were doing something wrong or needed to spend more time with the baby. Sometimes she was so opinionated, Jack came to regard her as the mother-in-law he never knew.

———————————— ✳ ————————————

With everything going so well for these four friends, it seemed nothing could interfere with their happiness. But Catherine was in the business of exposing powerful people and their nefarious deeds. Her money gave her an unlimited ability to pursue her stories wherever they led. With her investigative glee and ambitious drive, she gave little thought as to the consequences of her actions.

In March of 1989, Jack and Mai went to visit Catherine and Kelly at their home. This was a long delayed response to their invitation for Jack because something always came up, and he had not seen the space since they had moved and redecorated. They were in the same building but moved up four floors to the thirtieth, sharing the entire floor with their production company offices.

The open-design living area was done in muted colors with an Asian look. Here and there were strong color accents, and all of it played to the extraordinary views that could be seen from almost anywhere in any room. Everything was just where it should be to lend its part to the functional design. The condominium went on forever, all of it leading off a step-up-to main hallway that overlooked an open- concept living, dining, and kitchen area with nothing but windows on one side.

As Mai showed him around she was explaining what feng shui was all about. He wasn't so much paying attention as he was taken by how comfortable he felt being there.

Mai stopped and said, "See? You are already having a relationship with this environment. We planned everything just as we wanted, but then brought in a designer to explain to us why we didn't want it quite that way because of feng shui. After that, we changed it because it wasn't what we really intended in the first place. And now it's perfect! Get it?"

"Not a clue," said Jack. "But it's really nice, and I do feel comfortable here."

Mai shrugged in fake frustration with Jack as Kelly greeted them with hugs. Smiling, she said, "Come on back. Cat needs a break. All morning She's been back there typing one of her stories. What ever happened to our weekends?"

Jack heard Charlie cry, and Kelly said, "Uh-oh. This is my shift. Somebody is up from his nap. Go on back!"

'Back' turned out to be the other side of the same floor where the NearNorth Production offices had been relocated. Mai and Jack entered through a nondescript white door at the end of the hallway into a very large office area. Toward the left, several young men and women were working intently on their computers, as seen through glass-partitioned cubicles. Jack couldn't quite decide their function, but they had a look about them, and all they lacked were pocket protectors. Over to the right, Jack noticed several other young men and women working at desks, as seen through more glass partitions that gave a view of almost the entire floor and downtown Chicago beyond looking south from their building.

Almost immediately, Mai was approached by a group of men and women who were eager to consult with her. Mai told Jack she would be right back, and he watched as she led them into a large glass-enclosed office. As she sat down behind a large desk, several staff of all ages came into the office and joined them. They began presenting something to her with great enthusiasm. Jack was impressed, as they made their presentation and then listened afterward intently to her thoughts while taking notes. She looked like a teacher; they hung on her every word. This was a side of her he had never seen and he was very proud.

He saw Catherine working at her desk in an office down the hallway. She looked up from what she was working on and smiled immediately when she saw him. She came out to greet him with a long hug and then gave him a big kiss on the cheek. "Hey, you, where have you been? We've been in here three months now, and I have to call you to get you to make a visit? Are you becoming a snob, Jack Largent?"

Jack ignored the friendly gibe with a big smile. "I love how you've decorated your condominium, and this office setup is amazing. Did you move your production company up here on the same floor?"

"No, just some of the features and production staff. Howard, who runs the corporation, has a huge office on the other side of me. As you can see, Mai has her office over there within a separate area. She has her own staff of producers, about two dozen now, and another group following up on Brad's financial concerns.

You know what your genius wife did? She wrote a program that Wall Street and the local Board of Trade groupies are screaming for, and she did it for free to help out a friend of mine. It's based on Mai's formulas for analyzing a company's real value, risk, and growth potential. She figured out a way to put everything into an algorithm, even the human factor. Fortunately, Brad and I copyrighted it before we turned it over to them because it is revolutionary. I tell you, Jack, she would give it all away if she could. She just does not care about money. But she is an amazing financial analyst.

"NearNorth Productions has four floors in the building now. Three are down on the tenth, eleventh, and twelfth floors, and then there's the one here. Brad set it all up. You remember Brad, right? He was the financial front man when I started. Now he's a real estate mogul after just a few years. He is positively brilliant."

"Like a couple other people I know," commented Jack as Mai returned to their discussion and took Jack's arm. "So you rent four floors in this building? That must cost a pretty penny."

"Actually we own the whole building. Well, the corporation does, but we rent out the upper floors to high-end corporate types who are transient mostly. Brad worked his magic on the whole deal. It was a good investment. Including our floors, we have eighteen other companies in this building, and we're almost fully occupied. When you consider that thirty percent occupancy pays the bills, that is a hefty profit every month."

Jack liked Catherine's new look: short hair, Levi's, and reading glasses hanging over her blouse. She had definitely crossed over to the news-reporter professional. She wore little makeup but was still stunning.

"Mai tells me you're all taking karate lessons now," he said, making conversation. "Are you getting any good?"

"Yep, two months now," Catherine said. "We have a private instructor, so we've been moving along fairly quick. We do it every day. I think I'm pretty good. My long legs help. But you should see Mai. She is like a black belt or something. She did it before, so she just polished her skills, and she's helped Kelly and me a lot." She smiled at Mai.

"Remind me not to get on your bad side," quipped Jack.

"That would be impossible, Jack," said Catherine sincerely. "You could never do that with me. I owe you big time and forever."

As Mai was again interrupted in the hallway and asked to sign something by a man with a manila folder and a pen, Catherine grabbed hold of Jack's arm possessively. She walked and talked, and led him into a conference room. Jack saw it was all done in whites and grays, with a long table in the middle. What surprised him was one full wall, ten feet high and forty feet wide, that was covered with photos, Post-its, and notes, a lot of them linked with red yarn and pushpins.

"What's all this?" he asked and then answered his own question as he made some sense of it. "Oh, I see...it's all about Colonel Minh and Thap Cham."

"Yes, my love, and we almost have it complete. We have only a few holes to fill, so guess what? We're going on a field trip...an investigative vacation of sorts! You in?"

Kelly walked in just at that moment holding Charlie in her arms and said smiling, "Better take it a bit slower, *love*."

"Why, Kelly Ryan, are you jealous over a guy being with your gal?" quipped Jack.

"No, it's just that everyone she cares about is 'love.' Charlie, love. Jack, love. Kelly, love. And then when we're makin' it in bed at night, she's screaming, 'Ohhh, I *love* this!' It's her way of possessing everyone and everything in her life with a passion."

Catherine looked at Jack and gave a big, proud smile, confirming what Kelly said. "But I *love* you most, Kel, although little Charlie is sooooo cute. I *love* him too, except when he has those smelly diapers. Come here, snookums." She took the smiling little boy, dressed in a blue T-shirt and a diaper. Jack watched proudly as she bounced him in her arms. He reached out his hand and the toddler took hold of his finger with a strong grip. Jack smiled at that and exchanged toddler talk in answer to his happy smiles.

Kelly rolled her eyes, pointed to the wall display, and said to Jack, "This has been her passion since I've known her, and with some recent discoveries through Mai's efforts, it's all making more sense. This will be Catherine's first book, and I will let her tell you about it. Lately, I'm just the babysitter around here. Better give me back Charlie, *love*." She took their son once more.

"Catherine, you're writing this as a book?" asked Jack turning away from the distraction of Charlie.

"Yeah, and it's a long one. It's going to have many chapters to mirror the many facets of their illicit dealings. You would not believe what we have found. As you can see by looking at the wall, their network is huge and now a major international investment corporation. A TV feature couldn't cover it all."

As Kelly left the conference room, Catherine walked over to the wall with all the posted information. She turned to Jack, and said, "This is why I asked you to come over. I want to walk you through all of this and see if you have any comments. Come sit down and get comfortable.

"I want you to tell me about what you remember of that Shadow mission above the base that you were on when the rocket attack happened. That sounds interesting and it will make a good lead in to the story of the treasure and how we think it was stolen. Let me cover what we have found out first and then we will get to that. Try to hold your questions until the end because it is sort of complicated, especially with the outlined version I'm about to give you."

Jack looked up at the large, sequenced layout of photographs, connected red and green yarn, printed names and Post-its. Mai returned and sat down near Jack at the conference table. She positioned herself so she could watch Jack's reaction to the story as Catherine revealed it. She was proud of their research, mostly based on her efforts and her agent working within the Minh organization.

Catherine spent the next hour explaining the history and reach of the crime family run by Colonel Minh. To Jack's surprise it even included certain principals in the Air Force including the base commander at Phan Rang. They agreed to continue the discussion over lunch. But when Catherine summoned two very large bodyguards, Jack became surprised and wary.

"You have two body guards now? Has something happened I should know about? You know, you ladies are being extremely naive as you pursue this story. This is not a game with these people and in fact, these are very dangerous men. They are criminals of the worst kind who I am sure would not hesitate to kill anyone that got in their way," he said.

Catherine answered seriously. "Well, Jack you may rest assured that we are taking precautions. That is why I hired these two bodyguards among others that shadow us now. After the attack on Mai and me a month ago on the street…"

"Wait. What? You were attacked? You and Mai were attacked? Why haven't I heard about this?" He looked sharply at Mai in surprise and then pointed a finger at Catherine. "This whole investigation is reckless and I will not have Mai or anyone else I care about involved in your blind pursuit for journalistic glory. You are…"

He was so angry he could not find words. Instead he shook his head, turned and left abruptly.

"Shit," said Catherine.

"Yep," said Mai.

Chapter 18

Chicago, 1989

When Mai got home, Jack was giving Devearney a bottle and walking around her little room, as he sang softly to her in his arms. There was so much Mai wanted to tell him about that was happening with Su Ling, but she couldn't bring herself to do it out of fear he would get in the way of her new and compelling plans.

Jack didn't know she was there, and Mai didn't want to disturb the moment, so she leaned against the door and watched them. She never loved two people so much in her life. They meant everything to her. She had known Jack was the only man for her from the first moment they met. She was convinced that having a baby girl with Jack was part of her destiny, and that it was a part of some master plan. Jack was her soul mate and the anchor she now positioned her life around. This was important particularly now while she sorted out the meaning of the things she was finding out about herself and her unexpected connection to Colonel Minh.

She went up to them, kissed Jack on the neck from behind, and whispered, "When you put her down, come be with me, my love. I'm going to grab some wine and sit out on the deck."

Later, Jack found Mai lounging comfortably with her eyes closed, sipping a glass of red wine. A glass for Jack was sitting on a small table next to her lounge chair. It was a cool, comfortable, and clear night in Chicago. The stars were out.

"Can I join you?" he asked.

"You'd better," she said, opening her eyes, smiling, and moving to give him some room next to her on the oversize lounge.

Jack snuggled up with her and reached over for the other glass of wine. He kissed her gently and after a moment said, "The three of you call yourselves the Three Musketeers, and like them, you're always planning, plotting, and scheming while keeping things to yourselves. That's OK for the most part. But it hurts, Mai, when you're hiding something from me. We cannot last if we are not open and up front with each other. You women are being reckless in this investigation of Colonel Minh. But what hurts most is that you were attacked downtown and didn't even tell me. I thought our bond, married or not, was much stronger than that."

"I'm sorry, Jack. It wasn't as big a deal as it sounds. Besides, they were after Catherine, not me. You don't need to worry about us, honey. We're big girls." But even as Mai told him that, she suddenly realized for the first time that maybe they *were* after her. She had not considered before that very moment that Colonel Minh might have gone ahead with his own plan to kidnap her.

"Mai, I have a Little Moe's pizza shoot in three days that is very involved and it is going to last all week. There's a lot of preproduction on that one because the client is not happy with the food stylist we used earlier. I should be downstairs right now checking everything. But all I can think of is how you got mugged and almost kidnapped! How would you feel if the situation were reversed?"

"I know, baby. I should have told you. I don't know why I didn't. The day it happened, you were in the middle of that soda splash photography for Royal Cola. Remember, the client from Atlanta? I know you were excited about shooting with them, and I didn't want to mess that up. I was totally OK, so I kind of put it on the back burner."

"You could have gotten hurt bad, or worse, kidnapped, and God knows what else!" said Jack softly.

Mai chuckled. "I'm a strong woman, Jack, mentally and physically. I was not afraid at all. It was pretty cool. You would have been proud of your little Vietnam bargirl."

"So I'm supposed to say it was OK that you were attacked and didn't tell me about it because you weren't afraid?"

"Listen, Jack, they came at us on the sidewalk. One of them brandished a gun, and another grabbed me from behind and started to pull me toward a van. I just accessed my Tae Kwon Do training. Believe me, we practiced that scenario a lot! He never knew what hit him. That stuff works. I mean, I was way out of training, but I did it for three years, so it all just kicked in…literally. Hah! I gave him an elbow to his ribs. He let go of me. I swung a leg out and around that knocked the gun from the other man's hand. I got my balance and kicked the first man in the balls and roundhouse kicked the other in the face. You should have seen him go down. Hewaaah! They were hurtin' bad, Jack. Then the driver yelled at them that they better get out of there. I was kicking their asses, and I made those big boys run!"

Her expression was so pumped and her smile so large that he laughed in spite of himself. "Who do you think you are, Wonder Woman?"

"*You* think I'm Wonder Woman, don't you?" she said, taunting him with a kiss.

"Yeah, I do," he said, returning her kiss. "You're some kind of special woman, anyway, Mai Sambaht."

He shook it off in the next breath. "But dammit, Mai, I'm trying to make a point here. For once, listen to me. This stuff you are doing with Catherine is serious and dangerous. I don't like your involvement in this investigation at all. I'm afraid you don't know what you're getting into, and you're not being careful. You're not playing a role on TV. This is real, and people get hurt, even killed, doing this kind of stuff."

Mai defended herself. "You should know by now I'm not like most other women. I am not afraid of men or of kicking ass if I have to. That was not the first man I've put down, although it has been a few years. Physically I'm small, but in every other way I'm a strong woman, Jack. Strong will, strong body, strong mind. I know you worry about me because you love me. But you could not have done any better than I did when we were attacked. I wasn't afraid, and I can take care of myself. I proved it."

"Mai darling, you're so independent and always going in several directions. I don't want to lose you. I don't know what I would do without you."

"I know, baby. Me too. I feel the same way toward you. I have an ability to sense what people are thinking. I can feel them for real. I cannot read their minds literally or tell what they are thinking, but I can sense the sincerity in them and in what they say. It is real, and I have never been wrong. I am a good friend of Catherine and Kelly because they are good, real, and honest people. They are true to me and I to them. I am with you, Jack, because you are just the same. You are a real, good, and honest person. I knew when we met that you were in love with me from the very first. I sensed it in you, Jack. You are the only person in this world to whom I am vulnerable. I have given my heart to you, and I have never allowed myself to be in that position with any other person in my life. You are the only person in this world who can tell me what to do, and I will respect your wishes. I love you more than you can imagine."

They sat in silence for a minute, and then Mai turned toward him and said, "Honey, you know I am an orphan. Remember how I told you about my aunt Trinh, who was really my mother's friend, raised me when my parents disappeared?"

"Yeah, I remember, Mai. It's a sad story about your parents. That must have been really hard for you."

"That made me always stand alone and independent before you came along. It was always me against the world. But there is one memory that is always with me. It is the foundation for everything I do.

"When we were leaving Vietnam on the boat as refugees, I was very scared. I was ten years old at the time. It was a small fishing boat meant for the coast, not the sea. And there were many people on the boat. There was no room anywhere. It was way overloaded. We were trying to get to American ships off the coast, but when we got there, they wouldn't take us. We were among the first, so I think they hadn't planned what to do with the refugees yet. We begged them, but they said they had no room, and they just left us, several dozen boats, floating in the ocean.

"That night the seas got very rough, and it was very dark. There was a storm, and the boat was taking on a lot of water. My aunt tied my little brother, Kai, to me. He was her son, not really my brother, but I think of him as my brother. He was small, so she tied him to me with a rope around my waist. We sat up against a bulkhead on deck, and there was a cleat for tying off the boat nearby. I tied our rope to it so we wouldn't fall overboard because the boat was going up high and then down again on very deep swells in the ocean. I was very scared, I think the most I've ever been. Many times it almost rolled over completely, and we held onto the rope so we wouldn't fall. I got real sick and threw up on the deck a lot. It was raining hard, and everyone was miserably cold, wet, and huddled close together."

Mai's voice was starting to break as she talked, and the words came with more difficulty. "And then suddenly there was a wave that was so big, the boat turned all the way over, and everyone went under the water." Mai's eyes began to water. "Kai and I didn't fall off because we were tied to the boat. We were upside down under the water for a time and being thrown around in complete darkness. I thought I might drown because I could not hold my breath any longer, and then the boat came up again on the crest of a wave and turned back over the right way on another. I hit my head and was gasping for air. When I looked over for little Kai, he was gone. Only the rope was left. I tried to stand up and call to him, but I didn't see him. There were only two other people on the boat with me, and they were holding onto ropes and looked very afraid. It was horrible. I lost the only people I knew as family in the world. Gone. The next day it was calm like nothing happened. The sea was flat. We were very hot, and with nothing to eat or drink. Eventually, a small US Navy boat came by and took us off to a transport ship. They asked me questions, but I didn't know everything they said because I couldn't speak English well. I tried to tell them to look for my aunt and brother, but they didn't speak Vietnamese."

"Mai, I—" said Jack.

"No, wait, I'm not done," she said. "You think I'm being reckless, especially when I have a husband and a baby that I care about and that care about me. But there were over a hundred people on that fishing boat, and only three of us survived. There were two of us tied to that rope, and God chose *me* to live, Jack. I did not live so I could die getting mugged on a Chicago street. I was not for a moment afraid for me, Jack. I was afraid for Catherine. I have a purpose for my life. That is why I didn't want to get married, Jack. I have something important to do. I just don't know what it is yet. I believe that. I have always believed that. There is something I am meant to do."

"Geez, Mai," said Jack, "you are the most intelligent, accomplished, successful, self-made woman I have ever seen. You have an amazing baby daughter and a husband who loves you unconditionally and with all his heart. What more could you possibly accomplish that would bring more meaning to your life?"

She said nothing, so Jack continued. "I get that you're always restless, always trying new things. You never seem satisfied or fulfilled. I have never seen anyone get into as many things as you do, Mai. And you don't just try things; you go in all the way. Like when you started tap-dancing class last month."

"Oh, darling, I don't think God saved me so I could be a tap dancer," said Mai.

"Bad example. But you *are* driven by something."

"Yes, I know," she said, wiping her eyes…. "something."

They lay there silently looking at the stars as that simple word hung in the air.

"Jack, why do you never talk about what you did in Vietnam? Do you have bad memories from that time?"

He was quiet for a moment and then said, "Did I ever tell you how I decided to be a photographer, Mai?" Suddenly he felt like sharing his most important memory with her.

She pulled him closer, snuggling in. "No, baby, tell me."

"It was in Vietnam. I was sitting around a campfire, with this army guy. It was at Khe Sanh, Mai, near the Laotian border. We were covering the Air Force part of the operation when the South Vietnamese invaded Laos to cut off the supply routes of the VC. The Americans were flying helicopter support to supply the operation but Americans were not allowed to have troops on the ground.

So, I met this army guy and we became instant friends that night. He knew I was a photographer, and we got to talking and sharing stories. He told me about his love for photography and that he had a number of photos he was proud of back home. At one point, he said, 'Yeah, man, when I get out of here, I'm gonna go to Art Center College of Design and be a photographer, just like you!'

"That was it, Mai. That was the moment I knew what I wanted to be. I was a photographer in the Air Force at that time for over three years and mostly in Vietnam, but I was just putting in time until I got out and got a real job. I never thought of it as a profession. Right then I knew what I wanted to be and where I wanted to go to school. That was one of the most important moments in my life, Mai. That army guy put me on my life's path and gave my life meaning and purpose. I can still see him talking like it was yesterday."

"What was his name?" asked Mai quietly.

"Wax, short for Waxahachie, where he was from."

"Do you still keep in touch with Waxachie?"

Jack paused a moment. Then he said, "No, baby, he died the next day. I was holding him in my lap on the deck of a helicopter racing for a medevac when he died. He has been with me ever since. I sort of devoted my photography career to his memory."

She sat up and looked at him. His eyes were watery. Her eyes mirrored his in response. "Oh, my darling. That is now a special memory for me too."

Chapter 19

Chicago, 1989

Three days later was the start of the second big shoot with Little Moe's pizza out of Detroit. This one was going to last at least a week. Jack had a professional-size pizza oven brought in and wired a special 220-amp socket for it in the back studio.

He also had to present a new selection of food stylists to the client to consider which to hire for this project. The food stylist working on the Little Moe's pizza shoot the last time was one of the very best in town. So, Kelly and Jack were surprised that Jerry Baden, Moe's marketing director, was not happy with her.

Jack asked all the competent food stylists in Chicago to send in résumés and examples of their work and he forwarded the best of them to Jerry. In the end, he rejected all the ladies and picked Wally Freeman, who looked more like a lumberjack or a biker than a food stylist. He was six five, disheveled, longhaired, and looked foreboding on the street. But put him in the kitchen, and he was impressive.

Jerry explained his decision in a way Jack and Kelly would never forget. He said, "You know, Jack, men have a way of understanding pizza that women don't." Jack nodded in agreement with his opinion but Kelly just rolled her eyes and rejected it outright.

They stopped early that first day after doing two pizza photographs. Jerry felt that the previous food stylist had made the pizzas on the last shoot too perfect and someone back at the main office even mentioned they looked like Italian hubcaps. He preferred they stop shooting at that point so they could look at the finals in the morning and see if there were any hubcaps in the bunch. It would make their routine easier for the rest of the week, and finally he explained that he had an important meeting he had to attend.

Thirty minutes later, Kelly walked into Jack's office and said, "Everything is cleaned up back there, boss. We can't touch the big set, so I guess that's it for now."

"Good job today, Kelly, as usual," he said. "How are things with Catherine and Charlie?"

"You can ask her yourself," Kelly said. "I called her and Mai when I knew we would have an early finish, because Catherine is dying to have a meeting and talk to you about what they just found out about Thap Cham. I'll tell you about some of the things Charlie has been doing later. But for now, the Three Musketeers are here and want to talk to you in the client area. Are you OK with talking to us, boss? The other day when we got together with you, it didn't end well, and frankly, we all feel pretty bad about it."

"Yeah, I'm OK," he said. "You gals sometimes have a way of pushing my buttons and when it comes to your safety I am wired pretty thin. That doesn't mean I love you three any less. Let's do it."

When they finally settled down on the corner couch in the client area, with glasses of wine and a reject warmed-up pizza in front of them to munch on, Kelly took the lead.

"We've found out a few more things in the last couple of days, and Catherine never got to finish her report last time anyway," she said. "I will start off by filling you in. I think you will see the story is really getting interesting.

"We have actually identified Catherine's attackers because they were stupid enough to confront her across from her condo building," Kelly said. "There is video surveillance in six places outside that building, and we got pretty good images. The police are supposed to be investigating, but we don't think they're vigorous enough. That's why we hired a security firm to protect Catherine."

"And those I care about," added Catherine continuing the narrative. "Our investigator, Vincent Manetti, is very good. He has been working with my family's law firm for a long time and has a lot of connections. He got an ID on the two attackers when we showed photos to some informants in the projects. He turned their names over to the police, but so far they haven't been located."

"The projects? Do you know how they may have gotten on to you?" asked Jack.

"There was one Asian and one African American man who tried to take Mai and me, along with someone else driving the van. They did not wear masks and looked like anyone on the street until they attacked us. As to why they chose us, Manetti thinks it might have to do with our inquiries to the Vietnamese government. He thinks Colonel Minh might have informants there."

"So you think this is about Thap Cham more than anything else?" Jack asked.

Catherine nodded. "Yes, and listen, Jack. Manetti thinks your friend Vega is alive. He was able to track down Sergeant Hernandez living in San Francisco and talk with him yesterday about what he did that earned him that Medal of Honor.

As he tells it, there were two Air Force Huey gunships and another Huey slick on that mission. Two of the helicopters ended up on the ground deep in enemy territory with engine trouble. Incidentally, Vega's dad owned a helicopter business stateside near Bakersfield, California, and Vega knew how to fly helicopters really well and even took care of them while working for his dad growing up. Straker brought him on as a pilot in his unit on one of the gunships because he was better than most of the Air Force helicopter pilots and with a lot more flying time.

Manetti thinks it was Vega who actually sabotaged the two other helicopters. One was a gunship, and the other was a Huey slick. The result was that they crash-landed at almost the same time in Cambodia on that fateful mission.

"Vega piloted the other gunship that did not crash. The downed crews were surrounded quickly, and it was pretty confusing as they fought to repair the gunship, hold off the NVA, and escape. The Huey slick was too badly damaged when it crashed, and Hernandez went from the gunship being repaired to the slick, about a hundred yards away, and rescued the pilot and a crewman. He apparently carried them out through a field of NVA automatic fire. All the guys on the downed gunship were working like crazy to clear the fuel line to get it airborne, so Hernandez was left to try to save the downed airmen by himself. He was carrying those guys over his shoulder while firing his M16 and running like crazy. He went through that NVA fire field to get the crewman and then turned around and did it again to get the pilot. They said it was the bravest thing they had ever seen. They got the fuel lines repaired and got the gunship going again and abandoned the slick. They barely escaped with their lives.

"He said they saw Vega's gunship fly away, supposedly attacking an NVA position to protect them. Then they saw an explosion on the other side of some trees but never actually saw his helicopter blow up. Manetti thinks it was staged. When they got the downed gunship flying again they could not find Vega's helicopter. Nobody saw Vega or any of his gunship crew after that.

"One more thing," Catherine continued. "There isn't much of a public record of the actual special ops missions going into Cambodia. Those missions are mostly classified, and our sources can't break through that barrier, but we found out from Hernandez that they moved the crews around three months prior to that incident when Vega disappeared or died on that raid. He says Captain Straker who was formerly the Security Police commander at Phan Rang commanded his own unit by then and was making regular runs over the border. Straker was also in the left seat next to the pilot of the downed slick that was left behind, the one where Hernandez rescued the pilot and crewman. Hernandez says the rescued crewman he brought back told him Vega's gunship made a pass at them immediately after they crashed and deliberately killed Captain Straker who was sitting in the left seat. That crewman died on the way back, and Hernandez kept that information to himself.

"So what do you think, Jack?" she asked when finished.

"Honestly, I don't know what to think," Jack replied honestly. "I always liked Vega, and he was more a special friend to me, so I think I'll reserve my judgment on that. We certainly don't have any real evidence of anything other than the hearsay evidence of what the dead airman told Hernandez and that all happened under battlefield conditions.

"Let me tell you about Vega. He was a bit of a romantic rogue like something out of a dime novel. To me he came off as bold, arrogant, and constantly looking for his next adventure. I told him once he was born in the wrong century. He really liked to talk about the medieval times of kings and queens and how everyone was happy back then. I admit, I can see him getting involved in something like this but I would like to think he had better judgment. He would have been perfect if they needed to helicopter a treasure out of Vietnam to Thailand but I would like to believe he would not murder anyone. Actions during the conflict there could be confusing because people in Vietnam died at the drop of a hat and most of the time for no good reason."

Jack continued. "The last time we talked, I believe you said you thought they got the Champa treasure and took it out by helicopter to Thailand. It's a good theory, but it couldn't have been easy. The Khmer Rouge were very active in Cambodia at that time, and Laos was saturated with NVA troops. It was not a good place for Americans.

Kelly opened Catherine's brief case and retrieved a map. "That's what we thought at first. But check out the geography," she said, opening a large map of Southeast Asia in front of them. "It is a little more than one hundred miles to Thailand straight across Laos from Vietnam. They could have made it into Thailand easily by helicopter, and remember, they were sending drugs back to the US from Laos through Vietnam before that, so they probably had a network and routes set up already."

Jack looked at the map and the area marked by a red circle. The distance could be covered easily in a couple of hours. It was well within the fuel range of a Huey, and it made sense if you believed Vega sold out for money. Jack still didn't want to believe that, but it was something that would have been attractive to Vega. He knew there were two things Vega lived for and they talked about a lot: adventure and money.

"What do you hope to find out by going to Vietnam?," he asked.

"We're mainly looking for background on Colonel Minh," explained Catherine. "The Vietnamese are cooperating and have further information for us. We will be able to interview some people who worked with him. But they want something from us in return. We've been looking into the Asian art market, legal and illicit, and actually have collected a lot of information about both. They want the information we have on that. They're not able to break into the illicit Asian art network, as we have. I've been talking a lot with their foremost authority on Asian art, Dr. Bui in Dalat. Mai has made several contacts over there, including a lady who actually works for Colonel Minh."

Mai continued. "I've been working with a production person and assistant to Colonel Minh who handles some of his side ventures, such as the Asian art. In a sense, she has turned on Colonel Minh and is working with me to find out some of the information we don't have. She is in a very dangerous position, and we must protect her as a source. I have suggested we meet in Vietnam, so she can inform us in person about what she has found."

"We also want to see Thap Cham and the temple area," continued Catherine. "In general I want to familiarize myself with the environment so that when I write, I know what I'm talking about and can add some color to enrich the story. If we can, we would also like to go to the area where the special ops were based, near the border. We have outlined what we want with our liaison in Vietnam, and he has assured us we can do all of that. Actually, Jack, they have been very cooperative with us. I think they want that treasure and Colonel Minh as much as we want the story."

"I know I can't talk you out of going. Mai and I have already discussed this," he replied looking directly at Mai. "But you're not going without me. I want to be sure Mai is safe. I think it's a crazy idea, but I must insist," said Jack.

Catherine laughed. "Jack, from the beginning we've always planned on you going with us. We've made all of our arrangements accordingly. We have carefully planned everything with you included…tickets, hotels, everything. Kelly is staying here and we have good people to help her watch over the kids for us.

"Jack, we wouldn't go without you. Your perspective and memories will be most helpful," said Catherine. "Seriously, don't you think this is going to be an exciting adventure for us?"

Chapter 20

Phan Rang / Thap Cham Vietnam 1989

They flew to Phan Rang air base from Ho Chi Minh City in a two-engine propeller aircraft assigned by the Vietnamese government. It was about one hundred and seventy miles north of Ho Chi Minh City. They left two of their security team to stay with Catherine's corporate jet, which they were not allowed to use to travel directly to Phan Rang.

Catherine with her face glued to the aircraft window admired the coast below them. "It really is beautiful, isn't it?"

"I always said this place would be the resort capital of the world if there wasn't a war going on," said Jack. "It's a very beautiful country and offers many different environments within hours of each other."

"You seem nervous," said Mai, holding his hand. "You're not still worried and being a pessimist, are you?"

"Oh no, not at all," he replied. "In fact, I'm surprised by how easy this has been so far. I expected more of a police state here, but I don't see any of that.

But Mai knew he was at least partly putting on a front. She could sense how apprehensive and nervous he was, and she already asked Big Ben, one of the two bodyguards, to be extra alert. In addition, she could sense Mr. Nguyen, their Vietnamese liaison, was not being genuine with them. She did not feel things were at all as they seemed, and her secret plans were not going to help.

The previous night, while walking around Ho Chi Minh City, Mai spotted two men wearing green soccer team caps. Su Ling told her these would be her people, keeping a watchful eye on them. It gave evidence that her plan was moving forward. But now that they were in Vietnam, Mai wasn't sure her plan was a good idea. It would be a real test of her determination.

Mai knew that Su Ling's people were Champa and ready to serve her in this deception. Colonel Minh's people had no idea she actually wanted to be kidnapped and would no doubt resort to violence if necessary when they took her.

She really wished Jack had stayed at home. She didn't want him to get hurt, and she worried about that more than anything else. On the other hand, she wasn't a bit concerned for her own safety. She was convinced that if she could get to Colonel Minh, she could kill him and get away before anyone knew what had happened. She had worked it all out a dozen times in her head and the fact that there would be many loyal Champas around helped to reinforce her confidence.

As they stepped down from their plane at Phan Rang air base, Jack was surprised by how barren it was. There were much fewer buildings than when he was stationed there during the war. A few of the old Air Force buildings remained, including the big protective arched cement revetments where the F-100s had been parked. But the sprawling air base now was more like a ghost town, and there were no people around. The last time he was here, there would have been activity everywhere during the daytime.

Jack remarked with a sigh, "Home sweet home," which gained him a playful punch from Mai. Three men walked out to greet them and began unloading their baggage into a waiting white eight-passenger van. Mr. Nguyen showed their passports to the more official looking of the three, and they were checked through without incident. They loaded into the van and drove off.

"I think the last time I was in a van at Phan Rang," said Jack, "I was on my way to the chow hall."

"Where was that?" asked Mai.

"Over there somewhere," he said, pointing in back of them.

"You were stationed here at Phan Rang during the war?" asked Mr. Nguyen.

"Yes, Mr. Nguyen. I was here in 1969 for a time. I was a photographer," explained Jack.

"This was an education facility for a while," said Mr. Nguyen. "After the great victory, we housed people here who were loyal to the old regime. They are all gone now and part of the Socialist Republic of Vietnam. We are very proud of our country."

"You are an impressive people, and it is most unfortunate, in my view, that the war ever happened. We should have been great friends and allies."

"Perhaps we will find a time for that in the future, once both nations heal," said Mr. Nguyen.

Jack nodded, smiling, and asked, "May I ask where we're going?"

"I think you must be hungry, yes?" asked Mr. Nguyen. "We go your hotel in Thap Cham. Is very nice. We show you your rooms at hotel, relax a bit, and have lunch. In afternoon go visit temple."

"That would be very nice, Mr. Nguyen," Catherine replied. "You have thought of everything. Thank you."

Mr. Nguyen smiled and seemed pleased by this recognition of his efforts.

They pulled out of the front gate of the air base, and Catherine spotted the temple off the road to the right immediately. "Oh, it's beautiful, in a rustic sort of way," she said. "It's like the American Southwest here, isn't it?"

"Are you talking about the temple or the terrain?" asked Jack.

"Well, one and then the other, Jack. You'll just have to keep up with me," she answered, smiling.

Jack looked at Mai, whose face was ashen. "Honey, are you OK?" he asked.

She shook it off, gave him a smile, and said, "Yeah, babe. I just got a funny feeling back there. That's all."

The van turned left at the crossroads and away from the temple. They had traveled down the road into the town of Thap Cham only a little way when they turned and pulled into an American-style motel that was nice, but not as commercial looking as in the United States.

"We have this for tourists. Lots of tourism in Vietnam now," said Mr. Nguyen as they pulled in by the front main building. The building was painted beige, with blue accents.

"Mai, do your job, and translate the name of the motel for us, will you?" asked Catherine, smiling.

Mai laughed and said, "Sure, Cat. It means 'Sea Breeze' in Vietnamese."

"You've got to be kidding me," said Jack, but then thought, *Well, why not?*

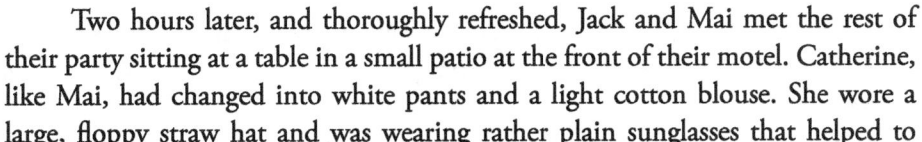

Two hours later, and thoroughly refreshed, Jack and Mai met the rest of their party sitting at a table in a small patio at the front of their motel. Catherine, like Mai, had changed into white pants and a light cotton blouse. She wore a large, floppy straw hat and was wearing rather plain sunglasses that helped to restrain her glamorous façade. She and Jack had hung cameras around their necks.

Mr. Nguyen told them he would meet them at a restaurant that was a short walk from their motel. They set off for the restaurant walking just off the road, as there were no sidewalks in Thap Cham. At one point Catherine said, "This is nice. I like this. It's kind of like rural America in the thirties."

But very soon Vietnamese children surrounded them with their hands out, and they attracted a lot of attention as they made their way down the street. Catherine's bodyguards, Big Ben and Victor kept the kids away as best they could, but Mai was no help, as she conducted an ongoing friendly conversation in Vietnamese with the children as they walked.

They were expected at the restaurant, and when they arrived, they were shown to a table already prepared for them. They were the only ones there, and

Big Ben and his partner sat at a table on the opposite side of the shaded outside seating area. Mr. Nguyen went out and said something to the children that made them all run away.

Jack told the group that the last time he was in Thap Cham, children surrounded him while he walked; much like the ones they just saw. They put their hands out for money while going through his pockets without him noticing.

Mr. Nguyen stood up as two Vietnamese police arrived with another man they were escorting. "This is the man I told you about who worked for Colonel Minh. I thought you would like to talk to him here instead of at the prison. He's being very cooperative and can tell you all he knows. He is a good man. I think he was at the wrong place at wrong time. This Mr. Tran, please." He motioned Mr. Tran to a seat at their table.

They all introduced themselves as the waiter served them tea. Jack was about to ask for menus when Mr. Nguyen told them he had arranged a meal of Vietnamese food for them. He explained that it would give them a better feel for the area because the food was more authentic in Thap Cham than in Ho Chi Minh City. Catherine thanked him and put her hand on his arm. Jack noted that and wondered if it was appropriate here, but Mr. Nguyen smiled in return. She had him on her side, and that was good. He and Catherine had exchanged information the night before in Ho Chi Minh City and it seemed they got along well.

"Mr. Tran," Catherine said as she began taking notes, "I understand you worked with Colonel Minh here in the province. Did you know about all of his activities?"

Mr. Tran was dressed in a light cotton shirt and pants, but was wearing flip-flops instead of shoes. He sat formally, straight and stiff, with his hands folded on the table in front of him.

Mai translated Catherine's question and listened to his answer. She told them Mr. Tran said he was a close assistant to Colonel Minh, but even so, he was surprised when the colonel left suddenly and did not return. Mr. Tran did not know where he went.

Mai asked more questions as Catherine gave them and took notes on his answers. They found out from Mr. Tran that Colonel Minh worked with some men on the air base to transport drugs to the United States from Laos. Mr. Tran told them it was a good situation because the base was closed, private and controlled where needed. Their associates could move drugs through there and out of Vietnam to the United States without outside interference. It was easy to conceal what they were doing. They commonly brought drugs onto the base in maintenance trucks contracted by Colonel Minh as part of the local

Vietnamization program. He said at one time they had some gold, he did not know from where, and he saw some of these things on trucks going west toward Laos. He thought the gold came from the base, but Colonel Minh did not tell him where it came from.

Catherine said, "Mai, ask him if he ever saw a golden Buddha."

Mai translated, and Mr. Tran said, "No." Then he started talking in hurried Vietnamese to Mr. Nguyen.

"Mr. Tran says the gold he saw was in small gold bars. No Buddha," said Mai.

"Gold bars? That doesn't make sense in our scenario," said Catherine. "What the heck?"

"You may have a bigger story than you thought," commented Jack.

Catherine was circling "gold bars" on her notepad as two waiters began serving their meal. Jack looked a bit taken aback as they put chopsticks in front of him, but Mai jumped with delight when the meal of spring rolls, loc lac, and grilled pork with rice was served. The waiters placed full bowls of other food choices around the table and put a plate out in front of each of them, including Mr. Tran. Jack cowered and made a face, as the pungent-smelling nuoc mam fish sauce that was his nemesis in Saigon was placed right next to his plate. He quickly passed it over to Mai, who eagerly set it on the other side of her plate.

Jack was amused and thoroughly enjoyed Mai's reaction to the meal, which was much like that of a child in a candy store.

Mai was talking to Mr. Nguyen in Vietnamese and laughing about something when she glanced at Catherine and got a look. "Mr. Nguyen is very pleased that you like his choice of food for our lunch. He's very proud of his country and traditions, and this meal is very typical for the food that is popular here. I told him the food is excellent and much better than our fast-food choices in the United States."

Catherine smiled, and Mai reminded herself to speak English with Mr. Nguyen, so everyone knew what was being said.

During the meal, Jack thought a moment, and he said to Mai, "Ask Mr. Tran if he ever knew of the temple being closed to everyone. Was it ever blocked off from people going there?"

Mai translated, and Mr. Tran nodded. "Yes, he says once the temple was closed for a month on Colonel Minh's orders. Americans were at that time cleaning up after a bad rocket attack, but he handled only the closing of the two roads leading to the temple."

"Has he ever heard of Captain Straker, Sergeant Vega, Colonel Denton, or Sergeant Spence?" asked Catherine.

Mai and Mr. Tran talked for a minute, and Mr. Tran thought as Mai said the names again. "He knows Colonel Denton. He was the base commander and a good friend of Colonel Minh. He knows Sergeant Spence. He thinks he is the one they often delivered things to on the base. He thinks he met Sergeant Vega sometime. He's not sure. He says Captain Straker was one of Colonel Minh's contacts on the base, but Mr. Tran never had any dealings with him."

Jack again asked Mai to translate. "Mr. Tran, when was it that you saw this gold? What year? Do you remember?"

Even Jack understood when Mr. Tran answered Mai, saying, "Ninetee seventy-three."

"That's something different entirely," said Jack. "The rocket incident at the temple was in 1970. It's hard to believe they would wait three years to ship the temple gold out of the country if they found it. Mr. Nguyen, did you know about this? Did you ask Mr. Tran about this before?"

"Someone else may have asked this of Mr. Tran. I did not, and I was not aware of it," said Mr. Nguyen. "Between nineteen seventy-three and nineteen seventy-five, the South Vietnamese government was shipping large amounts of their wealth and money to banks out of the country. We have gotten most of it back after many years, and the banks have accounted for their holdings mostly to our satisfaction. But a great deal is still missing, and some of it is in the form of gold bars that were shipped from Danang to Saigon before our forces captured Danang. Several million dollars in gold was lost during one incident alone. It was flown on a C-130, but the plane carrying the gold never arrived in the former city of Saigon. The Americans had left the country by that time, so it was an entirely Vietnamese operation. It is reasonable to suspect that Colonel Minh and his network intercepted the gold and got it out of the country."

The meal lasted a full two hours. When the bill came at the end, Mr. Nguyen tried to pay it, but Catherine said to him, "Mr. Nguyen, you have been very nice to us and have taken care for our comfort here in Vietnam. We must insist that you let us pay these wonderful people for working so hard for us. We are honored to do so."

Mr. Nguyen smiled and nodded to her, and she made more points.

They walked out of the restaurant and got in the van that pulled up on the street for them. Mr. Nguyen said something quickly to the driver, who waited for the door to close and then did a U-turn back toward the direction from where they came.

Chapter 21

Thap Cham, Vietnam

Jack looked eagerly out of the window of the van as they approached the temple on the same road he had traveled many years before when the adjacent hill was covered with dead airmen. He recognized the terrain all too well, and he had a moment of déjà vu as memories returned. They got out and walked up to the temple using the steps that were now built into the hill. The temple's three towers still dominated the area. The cactus on the hill surprised Catherine, who again compared the site to the American Southwest. There was a warm breeze blowing about them as they climbed.

When they reached the flat stone base, Catherine was visibly excited. "It reminds me of Angkor Wat in Cambodia," she remarked.

She walked around, carefully observing every detail as only one with a fondness for Asian art could. She popped the lens cap off her thirty-five millimeter camera and began taking photographs of the temple. She was thoroughly enjoying herself for a moment but then gave a sigh, looked at Jack, and said, "Can you point me to the hill where the incident occurred?"

Jack took Catherine to the west side of the temple platform and pointed. "It was there, on that next hill over. The two photographs were taken from the first hill to the far side, where the next smaller hill rises, just before that rocky area beyond. The last time I saw this view, there were bodies, debris, and blood everywhere. It was really bad, Catherine, worse than you can imagine."

She took a few photos of the hills from that perspective. Mai was holding onto Jack's arm tightly on the other side. They stood like that for a minute, without saying anything. Then Catherine asked, "How do we get down there, Jack?"

The two bodyguards and Mr. Nguyen were waiting at the van as the three tourists made their way back down the hill. The others joined up with them as they walked around to the other side of the temple and over to the adjacent hills. Catherine took from her tote bag a diagram she had drawn of the area, and she had marked the hills where the crater and cave openings were in the photos as best she could. She walked over toward the two hills until she and the others were standing between them. They saw nothing but very rocky terrain, dirt, cactus, and dry brush. They hoped to see some sign of a cave entrance, but there was nothing. The ground looked unchanged for centuries. The disappointment was immediately evident on their faces.

"I don't understand," said Catherine. "There must be something...I mean, something must be left from that day."

Jack suggested, "Why don't you go up on that hill where I took the photograph of Minh and Straker and use the photographs to direct us to where it looks like Vega was when I took the pictures? Maybe we can find the spot where there was a tunnel entrance."

"Good idea, Jack," said Catherine, suddenly enthusiastic again. She left and climbed up the larger of the two hills with Big Ben just behind her.

Mr. Nguyen stayed with Jack and Mai. He was amused at them looking for treasure.

"There is no gold here," he said to Jack. "We looked. I think there was never any gold here. When Miss Catherine told us about the treasure, we brought men out here looking. We found nothing."

Jack believed he spoke the truth. The Vietnamese would surely have wanted to find the Champa treasure if they could. He also knew that if it was here, it had been here for centuries. Either Vega found it, or it was still here.

A thought suddenly hit him. *What if Vega didn't find it?* He smiled. That was suddenly an intriguing idea.

"What are you smiling about?" said Mai. "You know the Vietnamese would have looked for it."

"No, baby, I just had a thought," he replied.

Just then Catherine called out, "Move back and up a bit." She looked through her camera and compared the composition to the one in the photograph. They adjusted according to her directions. Again she held up the photo to compare. "I think you're pretty close to where Vega was standing. Do you see anything?'

They looked down and around, but there was nothing. They wanted so much to see something, but there was nothing.

Jack called out, "Where is the cave entrance in the photograph?"

"It looks like it would be at your feet and draw up from there," answered Catherine.

Jack reached down and pulled at some weeds and moved a few rocks, but the ground seemed solid. The guard Victor handed him a shovel.

"Where did you get that?" asked Jack.

"That farmer across the road wants it back," Victor said with a big smile. Jack looked over at a newly plowed field the farmer was busy clearing of weeds.

Jack tried the shovel and he got nowhere. "Anything?" yelled Catherine from the hill.

"No," he yelled back. "I don't see anything." Jack was disappointed. Noticing that Mai had wandered away beyond the hill toward the rocks, he called her back in closer. He did not feel safe for some reason.

Mai and Catherine joined him at about the same time. "I see what you mean," Catherine said. "That certainly doesn't look like any place you would expect to find a cave entrance. What do you think, Jack? I mean, it looks like we're wasting our time. What did Mr. Nguyen say to you before? I saw him talking to you when I was climbing the hill."

Jack walked with them to the other side of the hill and farther out, even though he didn't suspect it was there. "He said they scoured this area with troops for a couple of days and didn't find anything."

"Oh," Catherine said. "OK, I think we should go back and rest up. This has been a long day, and I'm tired. Let's go and come back tomorrow morning."

"Mr. Nguyen," Jack called out, "I think we'll head back to the hotel and come out again tomorrow morning."

Mr. Nguyen waved his hand and headed for the van from a different direction.

"Actually," said Mai, "the morning light might help us see what we cannot see now." Jack gave her a hug with his arm as an answer to her positive attitude. As they walked she snuggled into him. "Mm, I felt a chill just then. This doesn't seem like Vietnam."

"Oh, I could tell you stories about freezing in Vietnam," quipped Jack remembering his days at Khe Sanh covering the Lam Son 719 invasion into Laos.

After dinner they planned to go over everything again. But instead, tired as they were, they just gave up and went to bed. Jack found the foam-cushion mattress a challenge and tossed for a bit. Finally, Mai sighed louder than usual, and they both found themselves face up on their pillows, talking about everything that had happened.

"You looked very disappointed back at the temple, honey," said Mai. "I don't think you should be. I think we're missing something. When I was on the hill, the strangest feeling came over me. Did you ever get that, Jack? Like you have been somewhere before? But I never was there before, and that's what made it strange."

"Yeah. Once when I was in Florence, Italy, I went around a corner, and in front of me was a bridge called the Ponte Vecchio. I had the strangest feeling I was there before, but I hadn't. I always wondered if I had been there in another life."

"What do you mean?"

"Well, we pass along our genes from generation to generation, and scientists are only starting to find out what all that is about and which gene is which. I wonder if it's possible to pass on some sort of memory or experience from generation to generation."

"I think there are many things we cannot explain. Buddhists and Hindus believe in reincarnation, but I don't believe that." After a moment of silence, Mai gave a sigh and said, "I'm not tired anymore, Jack."

"I'm not either. This bed isn't very comfortable."

She turned toward him and licked his ear. "Come here, GI. You go boom-boom me."

"I love it when you talk Vietnamese," he quipped.

They put the bed to a test of their own, and finally satisfied, settled against each other once more. "I feel comfortable with you, Jack. Any place you are is automatic feng shui," Mai said.

"Maybe everything is situated to make you feel comfortable in this environment," he joked.

She punched him playfully, but then she laid back and said, "You just gave me an idea."

Chapter 22

Thap Cham, Vietnam

The next morning Catherine was waiting by the van at eight o'clock when Jack and Mai arrived. Beside Catherine was a Vietnamese man he did not recognize who Jack thought to be in his thirties. He was dressed like Catherine, in a light cotton pants and shirt ready for a hot day, as was common to the area.

"Where's Mr. Nguyen?" said Jack as he walked up to them.

Catherine explained, "This is Mr. Doan. He works with Mr. Nguyen. He got called away and went back to Ho Chi Minh City. He will return this afternoon. Mr. Doan assured me he will assist us with anything we need."

Jack introduced himself and Mai to Mr. Doan. He said something to Mai in Vietnamese that caused her to smile.

Afterward, Jack said, "Let's get some breakfast and then head out for another look at the temple. If we don't find anything, maybe we should push on toward the border and see if we can trace Colonel Minh's egress route."

Mai was right about the light. The temple and surrounding hills looked very different in the morning sun, and all three eager explorers were a lot fresher than they were the previous afternoon. Jack insisted they take another look from the temple platform. He and Catherine walked up to the top, but that proved useless once more. They noticed that Mai and Mr. Doan were talking together as they walked below toward the far hill. Mai put her hand on his arm while making a point.

Catherine noticed and said, "Maybe you should be jealous."

"Well, you know I am prickly about such things, but after last night I doubt I have anything to worry about. That little Vietnamese bargirl is totally mine. She belongs to me. Besides, he is the one who should be watching out. I'm beginning to believe Mai has gone to the Catherine Marsh School of manipulation." She laughed and touched his arm in a friendly gesture.

Catherine and Jack, followed by the two bodyguards, soon joined the other two out at the far hill where Sergeant Vega had been positioned in the old photo. Jack found the slight hole he made in the soil the day before with the shovel. Though the landscape looked different with the morning light, it still consisted of only boulders, cactus, dry brush, and rocky dirt.

Jack looked at Catherine and saw the disappointment on her face. "Let's go find Mai and get out of here," he said. "I feel like we're wasting our time."

Catherine was not yet convinced and instead went back up to the hill she had judged the scene from before, followed closely by her two bodyguards.

Jack went looking for Mai and found her sitting on a rock and staring intently at the far side of another hill. It marked the beginning of very rocky terrain leading off to the foothills of the surrounding mountains. Mr. Doan was pacing behind her and talking quietly into a military style walkie-talkie.

She got up and walked a few paces in one direction, and then the other, each time looking back at the same set of rocks. She turned around in a slow circle and came back to the original spot.

"Hey, Jack," she called out, "come here a minute. I want to show you something."

Jack was filled with disappointment by then. He was tired and ready to leave. He took off his hat and just stood where he was shaking his head.

"Come on, baby," she urged him. "Just go with it for a minute. Trust me. Stand here, and look back at that set of rocks just up from the bottom of that hill."

He flipped his hat back on his head and walked over to look at the rocks she was pointing toward. What he saw was just a bunch of large beige granite boulders like all the rest stacked on each other around the hill. Nothing seemed out of the ordinary to him. "OK, I give," he said. "What's so interesting about them?"

"I'm not sure. They don't feel natural somehow. If I were decorating this hill using feng shui, I would definitely move them. Something is off. Something is wrong here. It just doesn't feel right to me."

"Feng shui, huh?" Jack laughed at her choice of words. "This is a hill in Vietnam, not Catherine's condo in Chicago, Mai. Those rocks got here naturally. They weren't placed here by an interior decorator and if they did, she was overpaid."

"Feng shui is from nature, Jack. It's used for a lot of things. But that's just the point. It doesn't feel natural to me. Something is wrong, and I can't place it."

He walked over to where she stood, and from the same perspective, he didn't see anything out of the ordinary.

Catherine yelled from the other hill, where she was still looking around, "Did you find something?" The two bodyguards were with her and were investigating the area nearby.

Jack yelled back, "We're not sure. Why don't you and the two guards come over here now? We could use some more eyes."

They walked around the area and kept coming back to the one spot where Mai originally stood. She kept muttering to herself, "What's wrong? Why can't I see it?"

After moving back and forth, Mai reached the conclusion that the area only felt uncomfortable from that one spot. Standing there she perceived that something was wrong and she wanted to change what she was seeing.

Mr. Doan, who stood next to them, also did not understand what they were looking at.

"Do you know if Mr. Nguyen's search party looked over this area?" Jack asked him.

"I not think so," he said. "Too far from temple. Catherine say treasure by temple, I think."

Suddenly Mai cried out in triumph, "I think I know what it is! Look at how that group of rocks is arranged. There is a big rock that is mostly hidden that sits there leaning awkwardly to the left. It could never have fallen like that, could it? I mean really, could it? I think it would have to have been rolled or placed there and then the others on top added later. I couldn't see that yesterday afternoon because the sun was in the other direction, and it was all in shadow."

Jack was thinking, *who knows what rocks in nature do?* He just didn't see what she was seeing, but she did have a gift for spatial composition. There was plenty of evidence in Catherine's condo and even in their townhouse, now that she was decorating it too. He looked at Mr. Doan, who just gave him a shrug.

"Jack, there's something not right here. Help me move these rocks," said Mai eagerly.

"Mai, honey, really? I don't think there's anything here," he protested.

Mai ignored his remark and walked over next to the group of rocks that were piled one on the other extending above her head. She put her hands on a boulder that would have crushed her if it landed on top of her.

"Wait!" said Jack seeing what she was determined to do. "Let's be methodical and work the rocks around it first. Big Ben, can you help us move some of these rocks?" The big guard was already sweating as he walked up with Catherine.

An hour later, with great effort and even using a crowbar retrieved from the truck, they had moved most of the large stacked rocks. Nothing was under them but the same rocky ground that was all around. All that remained was the biggest rock, which stood about six feet high and appeared to be awkwardly leaning to the left. Jack still didn't see anything out of place, as the shape of the rock added to that leaning illusion. It was the one that originally sparked Mai's idea of the formation not being natural and was almost entirely covered by the pile of smaller rocks in front of it. Jack still was not sure about all of this, but he decided to give the very large rock a try. With Big Ben on one side and Jack and Victor on the other, they pulled at it, but it would not move. Mr. Doan came over, bent down and helped them pull on the rock. To their great surprise, the massive rock moved a little.

Jack took a closer look at it and told them it looked like it was round on the outside but the other side might be flat, meaning it wasn't as big and thick as it appeared. "OK, everyone," he said. "Let's give it one more try. Give it all you've got. Catherine, you and Mai stand back because if this rock tips over, it's liable to go anywhere."

On Jack's count of three, the four men pulled. The rock gave slowly, and when they had momentum, they gave it a final effort, and it tipped over. It crashed down the hill landing close to Mai, who stood with big eyes having just scampered back barely out of danger.

When the dust settled, they all stood spellbound, looking at a small cave entrance about five feet high. Mai and Catherine rushed up to the entrance from below, and they all tried to look inside.

"Wait!" warned Jack. "Don't go in yet. It might be unstable. Let me go in alone and take a quick look. Big Ben, do you have the little flashlight you usually keep in your pocket?"

Ben handed him a thin, four-inch light, and Jack peered in from the entrance. He took one step in and paused for a moment to adjust his eyes from the bright sun outside. He was eager but still hesitated. He felt a need to move forward with caution. The walls of the cave looked to be solid rock, with a dirt path leading back into the cave. The first thing he noticed were footprints on the dirt path leading into the small cave.

"Do you see anything, Jack?" Catherine asked.

"Wait a minute. I'm trying to adjust my eyes to the dark inside. I see footprints in the dirt. Give me a few more minutes, and then I will look further," he said.

After a moment, he said, "OK, here goes."

Looking at the ground where he walked, he stayed to the side avoiding any of the footprints. He turned the flashlight on and went in a little further. The light caught something shiny reflecting back at him, and eagerly he got closer to take a better look. There were four large and ornate old chests, and beside them were two small statues. He could not see if there were more, but he believed they had indeed found the fabled missing treasure.

"Come on, Jack," Catherine called from the entrance, bouncing her hands up and down in frustration. "What do you see?"

"It's here!" he yelled back.

"What's here?" demanded Mai, not believing what he said or that it was possible, even when moments before she had been the positive force driving them.

"The Champa treasure. We found it!" Jack yelled.

Catherine and Mai looked at each other with huge eyes and then began jumping about like little girls. They gave each other, Big Ben, Victor, and Mr. Doan high fives. After a few minutes of celebration, everyone gathered around the cave entrance, waiting for Jack to come back out.

He appeared a minute later holding a gold statue, about eighteen inches tall, of a man standing with a bow and arrow. Jack was struggling because it was heavy and looked to be made of solid gold. Catherine took off her jacket and set it down on the ground by a large rock for a clean surface. They sat the gold statue on the jacket and gathered around to look at it.

"Oh, heavens!" Catherine said. "It's amazing. Look at him. He's beautiful! Wait! I know who he is. This is Rama, the ideal man, and perfect protector. Oh… Catherine want! I've never seen anything so beautiful."

"He kind of looks like Jack," commented Mai, examining the face closely.

"Well, there's a biased opinion if I ever did hear one," said Catherine with a big smile.

But then for a moment they all stopped and looked silently at the statue.

Suddenly, as one, they laughed, because it did sort of look like Jack.

Jack turned to Mr. Doan, who held a bewildered expression, and was scratching his head at what he was witnessing. "Mr. Doan," he said, "you better get on that walkie-talkie of yours and get some security forces out here right away. You will need to put a cordon around this whole area. I would bet the treasure in that cave is worth many millions of dollars."

Mai glanced at Catherine and added to him in Vietnamese, "And call Dr. Bui Tre, the head of the antiquities department at the University of Dalat. Tell her to get here as soon as she can with a competent crew. If she asks any questions, give her my name and Catherine's, and tell her I said we found the Champa Treasure. Tell her this is the real deal and to drop everything."

Mr. Doan walked quickly back to the van presenting one side of an animated discussion on his walkie-talkie.

Catherine turned back to the rest of the group and explained, "My thought is that this is an archeological site now and a very valuable one. We should not go in there anymore until Dr. Bui has arrived to process the site. What do you think?" With different expressions and nods they all agreed.

They sat in a circle on rocks around the golden Rama statue resting on Catherine's light-beige morning jacket. Mai noticed Catherine kept glancing back toward the cave entrance. "He seems happy to see you, Catherine," said Mai, smiling toward the statue that was facing Catherine and that did indeed seem happy about something.

"You should see the one still in there. I was afraid to bring it out because it looks pretty delicate, but it's even more impressive," said Jack.

"What does it look like?" asked Catherine eagerly.

"It is of a woman, and she has a bunch of arms, maybe six or eight, and she's holding a spear and slaying a man at her feet. It's all gold like this one," he said.

"Yes, that's Durga, the protector of the righteous and destroyer of evil. She's a tough chick," said Catherine.

"How do you know so much about Hindu gods?" asked Jack.

"Well, you can't have a minor in Asian art and not study the Hindu gods, Jack. They're everywhere." Catherine got up and brushed her pants off. "OK, I know what I said before, but I can't stand it! I just have to see. I have to go take a look. I think it's okay if I'm careful not to touch anything."

Jack nodded and handed her the flashlight. "Of course, you'll be fine. Just watch where you put your feet. There are footprints in the dirt that should not be disturbed. Try to step on mine. They're the larger ones on the right side."

"Yes, sir!" she said, saluting, with a big smile. Then she disappeared into the cave.

"Do you plan on taking a look too, Mai?" Jack asked.

"No, darling. I'm not ready yet," she explained mysteriously. Jack gave her a curious look but let it go.

Catherine was inside the cave for ten minutes and then came out again talking eagerly as she rejoined them. "There looks to be four large chests and some other stuff. Not sure. I didn't go in too far. Oh my God, Jack! The Durga statue is magnificent. I bet it's worth several million on its own! This is so exciting!"

She came over to Mai and kissed her on the cheek. "Mai, oh Mai," Catherine said, cheerfully enjoying her pun. "What would we do without you? We were all ready to give up, but you persisted. You knew it was here. But how did you know? You are the most amazing woman I have ever known!"

Mai looked up at her and scrunched her face as if confused. "I just had a feeling. That's all. I can't explain it. There was something about this place that seemed familiar and then I saw the rock that seemed out of place." She paused for a moment in thought. "But if you ask me, without the combination of all of us, this would not have happened. Even Mr. Nguyen brought all his people out here and found nothing. We supported each other in our own way to make our group effort positive and fulfilling. That is the why of it when all the others failed. I think it is so."

"Of course you do, you genius!" said Catherine, with real admiration for her dear friend. "That is so like you."

A nice breeze found them, and Big Ben wiped his brow as he got up to look around once more. "It's going to be a hot afternoon on this hill, I think, Miss Catherine," he said.

Within twenty minutes Vietnamese police arrived and were positioned about the site, guarding all sides of the hill and back, including the temple.

Catherine was in reporter mode once more, as she took notes of the growing excitement surrounding the treasure sight. Jack walked around and took pictures once again of the area, this time with a new perspective.

After a while, he sat down beside Mai on a rock and watched the scene forming before them.

After an hour, more police cars arrived, escorting a black, official-looking French Citroen. A distinguished-looking older man got out and was escorted by Mr. Doan up toward the cave entrance. They talked some, and then Mr. Doan brought the man to where Mai and Jack sat. They stood and shook his hand as he was introduced.

"This is Mr. Thien, our local province chief," said Mr. Doan. "He says this is a proud day for Vietnam and Ninh Thuan province."

Then Mr. Thien turned to Mai, and Mr. Doan said something further to Mr. Thien in Vietnamese. Mai beamed and lowered her head as if embarrassed, and Mr. Thien took both of her hands in his and spoke to her solemnly. Mai began to tear up as he spoke, and then the province chief hugged her unexpectedly. Mai was a bit overwhelmed by the attention and forgot to introduce Jack who stood by watching. He got a good idea of what was happening and was very proud of Mai.

She wiped away the tears and led Mr. Thien over to the Rama statue. He studied the golden statue and bent down for a closer look. He smiled and spoke again in Vietnamese to Mai.

Then Catherine walked up, and Mai introduced her to Mr. Thien and said something to him in Vietnamese. The province chief stood and took Catherine's hand as she was introduced and said something very serious and obviously important to her. Catherine looked at Mai, who translated. "Mr. Thien says he and the people of his province are most grateful to you for your work on their behalf and that you should think of yourself as a welcome and honored citizen here."

He said a few more words, and again Mai translated. "He says if you need anything, if there is any assistance he can provide to make your project easier, he would be most happy to help, and please do not hesitate to ask him."

Catherine nodded and thanked him warmly, putting her hand on his arm. Jack thought, *there she goes again*, but Catherine's routine seemed to work well in Vietnam.

The province chief continued on through another translation. "You are always welcome here. I hope you will come and visit us often. This man, Mr. Doan, will see that your travels are effortless and without difficulty. Thank you, Ms. Marsh and Ms. Sambaht, from me and the Socialist Republic of Vietnam.

Catherine hugged Mr. Thien. Then she bowed and thanked him for his kindness. Mai was happy to translate.

Then Mr. Thien asked if he could look inside, and they took him to the entrance. Several men carried larger portable flashlights and handed one to the province chief. He peeked in, going in only a little way. Then he came out, stood up, and said with a huge smile aimed at Mai and Catherine, "Wow!" It was something that could be understood in any language.

After the province chief and his entourage left, Catherine asked Mr. Doan again about Dr. Bui, and he surprised her by saying, "I just received word she has arrived at the airport from Dalat. She will be here soon."

Not long after that, a voice greeted Catherine from behind, asking, "Are you, Miss Marsh?"

Catherine turned to see a Vietnamese woman, about forty years old and a little over five feet tall, wearing glasses and carrying a camera. "I am Dr. Bui. I am thrilled to finally meet you."

Five young men and women, who appeared to be her assistants, attended her. All displayed bright, eager faces with big smiles as they looked toward the cave.

"Likewise, Dr. Bui," said Catherine, "it is indeed my pleasure to finally meet you. I have corresponded with you so often over the last year, I feel like I'm greeting an old friend. Come, I think we have a wonderful present for you."

Dr. Bui looked eagerly toward the now well-lit cave entrance. "Is that what I think it is? I mean, even I thought it was a myth." She could not hold back her excitement any longer and asked eagerly, "Miss Marsh, is that really the Champa treasure?"

"Yes, but please, before you look, I want you to meet my friends and the young lady responsible for finding it. This is my friend and photographer, Jack

Largent. I hope you will insist he photograph everything for you. He really was instrumental in finding the treasure. Jack shook her hand momentarily with a friendly nod. He was happy that Dr. Bui spoke English.

Then she took hold of Dr. Bui's arm and turned her toward Mai. "And this is our heroine of the day, his wife and my dear friend, Mai Sambaht. She is the one who persisted and actually found the treasure. But of course, you know her already. I think you've been corresponding with her perhaps even more than with me."

Mai smiled warmly and said, "Dr. Bui, it's so nice to finally meet you."

"Mai! So you are Miss Mai. I do feel like I know you very well already. Strangely, you seem most familiar to me. I admit I am surprised you found the treasure. But please, how did you do it? It has eluded many treasure enthusiasts for centuries. What was your secret?"

"I'm not sure," said Mai. "Something on this hill just didn't look natural to me. It took me a moment to figure it out, and the really amazing thing is that unless you were standing in one exact spot, you wouldn't see it. Right, Jack?"

He nodded as Catherine pulled Dr. Bui away toward the cave entrance with a face beaming with pride. "Come on, Doctor, we've kept you long enough. You have to see this!"

Dr. Bui looked just inside the entrance a moment and then turned back and said something to her group. One of her assistants gave her a small but powerful light. She took a pad and pencil from another assistant, and carefully stepped inside. She found a rock near the entrance and placed the light on it. Then she sat down a moment on another rock beside it to observe what was there. The others watched her from the entrance. After a few minutes, she said something in Vietnamese, and an assistant handed her another light and a pair of gloves. Then she got up and moved farther into the cave, where the others could not see her.

We Jack paced outside and kept watch on the entrance with Mai and Catherine nearby. Ten minutes passed before they heard Dr. Bui call from inside in Vietnamese. An assistant ran to one of the trucks and acquired a large flat aluminum container. As Dr. Bui exited the cave he held it open for her. She carefully placed a large parchment inside, closed it and nodded to the assistant.

Then she went over and spoke with Mai and Catherine, "I believe this is the most fantastic archeological find ever in Vietnam. You cannot imagine what this means to the Vietnamese people."

"When you get some time, can I talk to you about it?" asked Catherine. "I want nothing from this, but I am a journalist, and I would like to write the story about it. Can you give me that honor, Doctor?"

"We will be equally honored, Ms. Marsh…"

"Please call me Catherine, Dr. Bui."

"And you may call me Emily, Catherine," she answered quickly.

"Emily?" Catherine asked, surprised.

"From my school days in England," explained Dr. Bui.

"What did you see, Emily?"

"There are four large chests, and many old robes behind, all of which appear in surprisingly good condition. One is lying near the third chest. I suspect there may be the remains of bodies within each one. We will have to proceed with great care. I could see some pottery and some carved statuary also. There is a golden statue of the goddess Durga, about eighteen inches high, right in front. I have not looked in any of the chests, but one can only imagine. They are large and must have barely fit through the cave entrance."

Just then, Dr. Bui saw the golden Rama statue still sitting on Catherine's jacket and said, "Oh, the one inside has a brother!" She bent down and looked closely at it. "I wonder if it is solid gold."

"It is quite heavy, Doctor," said Jack. "My bet is that it is indeed all gold."

"Well, we cannot leave Rama here exposed to the elements." She called out once more to her assistants, who were gathered around a large truck unloading equipment. After a moment, a large metal aluminum case was brought to her. She placed a protective cover over the statue and then placed it within the foam rubber matting inside the case. She gently closed the case, and two men carried it back to the truck. Jack noted two guards were posted nearby.

"Can you direct me to Mr. Doan?" Dr. Bui asked of Mai. "I want to secure this site for the evening and I've been informed he is in charge of security for the moment."

Mr. Doan was again on his walkie-talkie as they walked up. Mai introduced Dr. Bui, and he listened intently as Dr. Bui talked to him in Vietnamese. "We will need enough men around here to be sure the area is completely secure from harm. I would set up a perimeter five hundred meters out."

Mr. Doan nodded and spoke to her in Vietnamese with Mai translating for Catherine, "I have talked to the province chief, who is very excited about this discovery. He has authorized the construction of a building nearby for you to organize the retrieval of the cave contents. They will start on construction tomorrow and give it the highest priority. It will take two or three weeks to complete, and then you will have to outfit the interior as you want it. Where would you like to place it?"

Dr. Bui put a hand to her mouth in surprise and replied, "You mean here? They're going to build a facility for me right here? That is wonderful to get such support."

Mr. Doan explained, "The excitement over this incredible discovery has gone all the way up to our president in Hanoi. He wants you to have everything and anything you want to preserve these priceless relics of our heritage. We will have a temporary facility in place soon. You will, of course, want to consult with our province architect, who will be here in the morning to look at the site."

"How big is this building you are planning to build for me?" Dr. Bui said, somewhat bewildered by all the attention.

"It will be six thousand square meters, I think," said Mr. Doan. "I suspect it will be one of the standard buildings they have been constructing around the province as they build up our industrial capacity in response to an increase in Western business investment. It will be easy to construct because we have built many of them already and have all the materials we need to start work on it immediately."

She shook her head and walked around, looking at the area. Finally, she said, "Let me see. I suppose over there about two hundred meters away should be fine, where the terrain flattens out a bit. It would be very convenient there. I will have my students walk the area until you start digging to make sure there is nothing of interest to us. In fact, I think I will have one of them monitor the excavation for that building if you don't mind, Mr. Doan."

Chapter 23

Thap Cham, Vietnam

More trucks with workers pulled up and parked adjacent to the area. They were college student volunteers from Dr. Bui's classes at Dalat. They were all very excited and full of youthful energy as Dr. Bui went about assigning tasks and responsibilities for them.

At one point Dr. Bui commented to Catherine, who was nearby watching and taking notes, "I have only to ask, and things appear instantly. I have never seen anything like this on any archeological site in the world. That man I was just talking with is one of Mr. Thien's men who wanted to know how many were in our group so he could set up a kitchen and organize daily meals for us. I think this has become an instant point of national pride for the Vietnamese people. I bet Mr. Thien already has plans for all the tourism that will come to the area because of this discovery. With the airport nearby, the beach, and the mountains, this area is going to boom. It is easy to see why they are putting in a supreme effort on this."

Mai walked up with Jack and commented, "We're getting tired. How about you, Catherine? Would you and Dr. Bui like to join us for dinner and then an early bedtime?"

Dr. Bui spoke up. "Oh no. I'm very sorry. I can't leave this site as it is. We're just starting to get things organized and there is still a lot of initial work if we are going to do this properly. I will probably bed down in one of the tents with my students later. Tomorrow we are going to discuss our plan for recording the interior of the cave. That may take a week or more, and then we'll have to formulate a strategy for bringing out the chests. I will see you in the morning." She gave Catherine and Mai each a kiss on the cheek.

Before she could get away, Dr. Bui took Mai's hand firmly in hers and said, "It is our good fortune that brought you and your friends here with your experience and talent. I have no doubt it was meant to happen. You have changed our world, Mai. Be proud of your heritage, because forever more your name will be directly connected to it."

Mai turned to Jack and beamed. She was proud to be an American, and she was also very proud to be Vietnamese. But she was most proud at that moment, if it were true, to be of Champa heritage. Could it be possible, was she really the long sought-after Champa queen? Was Su Ling right about her?

She couldn't help remembering Su Ling's words while they talked about her family and the Hoa Cuc. "If you find the treasure, my lady, there will be no further doubt that you are the Hoa Cuc, the true heir to the throne and queen of the Champa people. It is our tradition and belief that only the daughter of Queen Dau Te Po could find it. Your situation will change very quickly, and you will become most important to a lot of people. Move forward with caution, my lady."

And yet, with all that Mai knew and all she hoped was about to happen, she couldn't tell Jack. He would insist she go back to the United States immediately. *Damn! Why hadn't he just stayed back in Chicago with Devearney?*

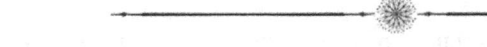

Jack held Mai's hand as the three tired, yet pumped-up adventurers arrived at the restaurant for dinner. Jack was reminded of Mai's words on their townhouse deck when she said she had something important to do. This must be it. He was very proud of her.

They sat in the same restaurant as before, but inside this time, drinking coffee and discussing their plans for the following day.

Mai kept her eye on two men who had slipped into the restaurant earlier, while Jack and the group were getting seated. These two men sat at a table away from them, near the back by the kitchen. They positioned themselves where Mai could see them. She immediately recognized them as the ones who had followed and watched them closely in Ho Chi Minh City. They both wore the same green soccer caps, a sign they were from Su Ling. She glanced over and made eye contact with one of the men. This time he gave a nod as a signal from Su Ling that her plan was moving forward. She would be taken soon.

All of that went unnoticed by the others as they shared their varied perspectives on all that had happened that day. Catherine reached out and held each of their hands. "I am at a loss for words to express what I'm feeling at this moment. I want to quote Shakespeare or say something profound. But all I can come up with is that I feel we three have shared a once-in-a-lifetime bonding experience. I love you guys, and I wish Kelly were here to share this with us. Oh!" she said suddenly. "I have to call her right away. Let's see, it's six a.m. in Chicago so I can't imagine I will get into too much trouble. I bet she'll be bothered that

I didn't call her sooner. How could I forget to do that? That's proof of how crazy exited I am over this. Come on. We have to go!"

They quickly paid the bill and were heading for the door when Jack spotted a face he had seen before. He was sure it was one of the men he saw outside their hotel in Ho Chi Minh City.

He gave Big Ben a look of concern and directed him with his face toward the two men as Mai asked, "What's wrong, honey?"

Before he could answer, Big Ben got up and walked back toward the table with the two men who were watching them. They saw him coming and quickly left the restaurant through the kitchen and the rear door. As a result, the two bodyguards became very protective as they led Catherine and the others out the front door.

While walking back to their hotel, Jack explained. "I think I saw those two guys following us in Ho Chi Minh City. It looks like somebody is still keeping a close eye on us, and I bet it's Colonel Minh."

"I almost forgot about him," said Catherine. "It's funny. It seems anticlimactic after our extraordinary day, doesn't it? It was so important yesterday. Wow, what a day!"

"What do we do about it?" asked Jack.

Catherine said, "I want to stay here, and I want you to stay also, Jack, to take photographs. We need the whole story. This story about finding the Champa treasure has all the fulfillment I need for now." Catherine suddenly realized that the treasure story was huge and she would need to talk to Howard, her company manager, about getting some more people sent over to Vietnam to help.

"That may be, Catherine," he replied. "But I need to know about Vega too. I need to know what happened with him."

"That leaves me," said Mai eagerly. "I can follow up. I'm the only one of the three of us who can get around without suspicion."

"Not going to happen, darling," said Jack, taking her hand. "No way, no how. Forget about it. We will just put that story on hold for now, I guess."

Mai nodded as if she agreed. She was now confident for better, or worse, her plan was in place, and Colonel Minh's people would soon take her and she would get her revenge for her family.

Catherine had a busy night in conference with Howard, the head of NearNorth Productions. They decided to send a cameraman and another reporter to help her cover the story best. She realized that this story had many facets to it and she did not want to leave any of it behind. At worst she would have a good video record of everything when they were done. She made note that Howard, upon hearing what had happened, was every bit as enthusiastic about this story as she was. She had no doubt he was already planning and organizing things back at NearNorth Producitons.

Chapter 24

Thap Cham, Vietnam

Though Jack, Mai, and Catherine arrived at the temple site by eight the following morning, Dr. Bui was already well into her routine.

She informed them that it had been decided that the cave and its contents would remain intact and untouched until the construction on their new processing facility was completed in about four weeks. That would give them a good opportunity to examine the scroll she retrieved from the cave the previous day. It was being studied very carefully under laboratory conditions in a very large tent nearby that had been erected overnight. She was very excited about the scroll and explained that although her knowledge of the area's ancient languages was extensive, she had already called in an expert, a colleague of hers, to work with her on the scroll. He was due to arrive that afternoon to take an initial look over the scroll with her and then take it back with him to Dalat the next day.

Jack noted that Vietnamese army regulars, who appeared very serious and professional, had replaced the local police. They generally kept to the perimeter, but there were a few near the cave entrance. They made Jack feel a bit uneasy, even though they were there to protect them and the site. In contrast, Mai went up to an officer of some rank, who appeared to be in charge of the military presence there, and introduced herself. He smiled immediately and bowed slightly as he took her hand and shook it. Mai gestured toward Jack and Catherine before bringing him over to meet them.

"Jack, Catherine, this is Colonel Jung," Mai explained. "He is the commander of the unit charged with protecting the archeological site. He works closely with Mr. Nguyen."

Colonel Jung surprised them by speaking perfect English. "I am happy to meet you, Mr. Largent and Miss Marsh. Mr. Nguyen speaks very highly of you and your efforts here in Vietnam. Mr. Largent I understand you were stationed here during the war. This must be somewhat disconcerting for you."

Jack smiled because Colonel Jung was right. In spite of his wariness just a moment ago, Jack immediately liked this man and knew that Mai would not have brought him over unless she sensed he was a good man. "Yes, a bit, I admit. It's nice to meet you. I feel better having your troops guarding this site."

"Has there been any sign of trouble? Have you observed any suspicious people, Mr. Largent?" Colonel Jung asked, suddenly concerned.

"No…Well, yes, actually I have. How much has Mr. Nguyen told you about what we are doing here?" Jack asked.

"Mr. Nguyen and I work closely together under the Ministry of the Interior, so we discuss areas that are of our mutual interest. I have been following your correspondence and then your progress here in Vietnam. I assure you I am a friend and here to help should you need my assistance."

"Jack saw two men following us when we were in Ho Chi Minh City," Catherine explained. "He spotted them again at the restaurant last night. We think they are Colonel Minh's people. But we really don't know for sure."

"I see. Did Mr. Nguyen see them also?" he asked.

"No, unfortunately, he did not join us last night for dinner," explained Mai.

"I can assure you we will look into this matter. I will be placing a guard detail at your hotel. If you are still willing, I would like to talk with you further concerning your interest in Colonel Minh. I would like you to meet someone who is being brought here and who might have some information to aid you in that project."

Jack gave him a shrug. "Finding the Champa treasure is a large distraction and something we need to focus on for now, Colonel Jung. I should tell you we have been discussing our options. Our biggest concern about continuing our search for information on Colonel Minh is the safety of Ms. Marsh and my wife, Mai. I would not like anything to happen to them. I don't think when we were back in the United States that we really considered that we could be in danger here. It all seemed like an exciting adventure then, and it still does to a certain extent. I have personal questions that need to be answered whether Ms. Marsh writes a book about Colonel Minh or not."

"I see," said Colonel Jung. "I think we can make arrangements to ensure your safety, but at the same time, we would not want to bring attention to you or your compatriots. Your methods are working well, and too much visibility will not help you to find the information you seek. I have a plan in mind and would like to discuss it with you later in the week if that is OK."

"Oh, well we are always happy to discuss our options." Catherine said. "I must wait to hear when the prisoner arrives," replied the colonel. "Prisoner?" asked Mai.

"Yes, he is an American deserter who we believe was working with Colonel Minh. Since he was not in the military when he was captured, we have not mentioned him in our correspondence with your government. We think he knows a lot more than he has revealed to us, and we hope he may open up to you. I will let you know the exact time when my associates inform me. That will conveniently give you a few days to focus on this project, before continuing with the one that brought you here in the first place."

After a few final comments, the group split up as Colonel Jung bowed slightly and walked back to his post supervising the security detail around the archeological site.

Catherine looked toward the big tent and declared eagerly, "Come on! Let's go see what's going on with Dr. Bui in the tent."

When they entered, they were surprised to find the large tent was dark and air-conditioned within. It was divided into areas separated by real doors. They were in a reception area, and through a vinyl window they could see Dr. Bui talking with a man over a canvas scroll held within a Plexiglas container that was laid out before them. When she saw them, Dr. Bui motioned for them to join her and her companion.

After introductions Dr. Bui said, "We think we have made a most remarkable discovery. We believe we can place a date on this site from the scroll alone. We must examine the scroll more, but we believe the chests are from the eleventh century, at the end of the reign of Queen Dau Sarrel Linh, and were left here by a royal dignitary who accompanied a party escaping the Dai Viet invasion from the north.

"The scroll is very old and delicate and is a written history of the royal family. Everyone in Queen Linh's family who might have succeeded her was slain during that time except for a young princess by the name of Dau Te Po, who was traveling with this party that fled the Dai Viet invasion. She is very famous, one of the greatest queens in the Champa tradition. She lived in a legendary paradise valley with her people for a time. According to the legend, she was taken away one day by a prince from a neighboring country and never returned. Her story is lost after that and remains a mystery. The Champa people dispersed and settled all over Southeast Asia and to this day await the return of their queen to lead them.

The scroll speaks of Queen Po's journey here as a young child with the small party and the deposit of the treasure. It also delineates the lineage for succession to the throne. There is a lot more, but we will have to study it carefully for an accurate translation. At the end, there is a prayer to a sacred Hindu god to protect

Po on her journey and a pledge that she will return to claim her rightful throne. It is the last written record we have of the Champa kingdom."

"I'm surprised you're already studying it, Doctor," Catherine commented.

"We have only taken an initial quick look. I wouldn't have dreamed of it except that we happened to bring two protective containers that preserve works such as this quite well. Like everything in the last twenty-four hours, I expressed a need to one of my assistants, and it showed up forthwith from our facility in Dalat. Even so, we will move it out of here soon up to Dalat where it will be properly cared for."

"Did you say Queen Dau?" asked Mai.

"Yes, she was one of the last rulers of the Champa kingdom," said Dr. Bui.

"My grandparents' family name on my mother's side is Dau," said Mai.

"There are many Daus in Vietnam and Cambodia, Mai," said Dr. Bui, "but it is possible you are descended from the great queen. That was almost one thousand years ago, and a lot of generations have passed. They say we are all connected if you go back far enough."

Mai was looking at the writing on the scroll and realized that while it looked somewhat familiar, she could not read it. However, she then noted the very familiar flower drawn in the lower right corner of the scroll. Su Ling during their correspondence mentioned that Dr. Bui was Champa and thus, also one of her subjects. It was time to find out if that were true.

"I think I recognize the flower there," Mai said, looking at the small round flower with a large center and many petals drawn in dark ink.

"That is the Hoa Cuc, Mai, the traditional flower of the Champa people. It is a very popular flower in Vietnam and a symbol for the ancient royal family," explained Dr. Bui. "Around Dalat, where I am from, they are everywhere. Queen Po herself may have drawn that on there. She may have signed it with her symbol of the Hoa Cuc. I think she may have written the prayer next to it because it is different from the rest of the writing on the scroll."

"I have a symbol like that on my hip," said Mai, pushing her shorts down on the right side to display it.

Dr. Bui was visibly stunned and then stooped to examine the less-than-one-inch mark. She slowly fell to her knees as she examined it. "That is most curious. You say it is a birthmark?" she asked.

"Yes, as I recall, it was always there. I am certain it is a birthmark," explained Mai.

"Well, it is interesting," said Jack. "Do I have to start calling you princess now?"

They all laughed except for Dr. Bui, who was gazing at Mai with an almost reverent expression on her face. Before she could comment, Mai waved her off, "We can get together later and discuss it, if you can find the time with all of this chaos. It's Just a coincidence, I'm sure, and I am interested to know more about the Champa culture. We will discuss it later, Doctor."

It was so quick that Mai hoped no one took notice. It was too early to reveal the possibility that she was the Champa queen. Mai had accomplished what she needed by showing the Hoa Cuc to Dr. Bui. It was obvious Dr. Bui was Champa and one of her obedient subjects if everything Su Ling told her about that part was also true.

Dr. Bui nodded a silent assent to Mai's wishes, which were as a command to her. She returned to the task at hand as if nothing had happened.

Instead she offered, "Jack, if you don't mind, before we move this, can you get lots of photos of this scroll? I want close-ups of each section so we can make enlargements and study them. Can you do this well without taking it out of the transparent container? I know there may be a problem with reflections."

Jack looked around the room and, seeing the black coat Dr. Bui was wearing when she arrived that morning, asked, "Can I borrow that? It will help with reflections. But I have a problem in that I do not have any tungsten film at the moment. It would be better if we were doing this in the open shade outside."

Dr. Bui went to one side of the tent and pulled aside a flap, revealing a clear vinyl window of about four feet square that opened to the outside light, facing north.

"That'll do!" Jack said, smiling. "Perfect!

Chapter 25

Thap Cham, Vietnam

Two days later, Mai and Dr. Bui met again in the morning in Dr. Bui's office "going over notes," according to what Mai told Jack. Other than informing Dr. Bui it was her wish to be consulted before any decisions were made concerning the treasure, Mai had not met privately with her before this. From the start, this meeting was very different from previous meetings as prompted by the reverent attitude of Dr. Bui. Once they were finally alone, she went to her knees and professed her faith and loyalty to Mai as her rightful queen. In the next moment, she bowed her head all the way to the floor.

Mai jumped back in surprise. "What are your doing?" she asked. "Please, get up." She had never seen or imagined anything like this. But Dr. Bui stayed on her knees as she talked with her queen. She told Mai behind eyes watered in real happiness that she firmly believed Mai was the rightful heir to the Champa throne. She proffered the evidence of Mai finding the Champa treasure according to legend and the Hoa Cuc on her hip as proof. Dr. Bui told her this was a glorious time for the Champa people. She said that Mai's coming to them would restore meaning, give purpose to their lives and unite the Champa people once again.

Mai was not comfortable being raised to such a stature and she felt very awkward. She calmed a bit and thanked her but told her that for now, she did not wish her to reveal her secret to anyone, not until she was ready. She instructed Dr. Bui to act normally around her in public and to treat her as a trusted friend and colleague as they explored the meaning of what was in the cave. Mai also told her that she needed her help because the events that were unfolding were still a mystery to her. She further explained that for some unknowable reason, she was positive it had something to do with the second and third chests in the cave. They were to be protected at all costs. She told Dr. Bui she was allowed to remove only the first chest and to delay that for as long as possible. She also told her that it was necessary for her to be away for a while and that Dr. Bui was forbidden to remove any of the other chests until she received Mai's explicit approval.

Before she could leave, Dr. Bui begged Mai to allow her to bow before her once more. Mai was again surprised and asked her why she thought it was necessary.

Dr. Bui explained, "Because, my lady, like all Champas, I have been waiting my entire life to demonstrate my loyalty and devotion to my queen. Honestly, I did not think it was something that would ever happen in my lifetime. I cannot tell you how much I have been longing to do this and how important it is for me and all of the Champa people. I have carried this empty feeling with me for all of my life.

"As a people, my lady, we were lost, and now we are found. Once the word goes out of your return, the thousands of Champa faithful will come to you, ready to give everything they have in service to you. It is for we Champas the only way we can find fulfillment in our lives. It has always been so. Serving you, my queen, brings us great happiness and joy."

Mai watched as Dr. Bui, bowed three times slowly, reverently, and meaningfully to the ground before her while reciting a mantra. Mai realized she was being worshipped like a goddess more than a queen and understood for the first time the new reality in her life. *As a people we were lost, and now we are found!* Her analytical mind began processing a hundred questions and answers at once and in the end she felt and realized her power for the first time.

That inner knowledge that seemed embedded within her and that had surfaced in so many classes through her years of learning beckoned to her as if wanting her to know something important. She got glimpses of ancient civilizations and circumstances that made no sense to her. She knew that in time she would pursue this knowledge that she now knew was so vital to her. But first, she had a job to do for her family and her heritage. In doing so she would protect her people and gain her revenge for her mother and father.

Later, that same morning, Mai received the final signal from Su Ling telling her that all was in place and ready for her to be taken very soon. As the time of her kidnapping came closer her only concern was that Jack was not harmed.

When it was apparent back in Chicago that in spite of her efforts Jack was coming with her to Vietnam, she talked at length with Su Ling through e-mails and then by telephone emphasizing it was most important to her that Jack not be harmed. In the present circumstances, it seemed impossible to stress that point again, and it concerned her. She took some solace in the knowledge that her contacts were using the signals she had prearranged with Su Ling during those many conversations.

Mai suggested earlier that morning that she and Jack get away for some personal time. Jack agreed it would be a nice diversion from all the chaos of the last few days. It was considerably hotter, and both of them were dressed in shorts and T-shirts. They walked up to the temple to look over the whole site before they left. They sat down on the temple platform, and watched workmen below toiling feverishly to complete the large structure that would make up Dr. Bui's new research facility. The foundation was being carefully surveyed and marked for construction. A roof-like structure had already been built over the cave and the adjacent area to protect the entrance from the elements. The areas near the cave were relatively empty of people, but farther out there were many bustling and crowded tent areas.

Mai commented, "I'm happy we did this. I love being here with you and sharing this special occasion together, Jack. I love you very much. You must never forget that and always believe it."

Jack pulled her close, and they sat with their legs falling over the edge of the platform side-by-side. After a moment she said, "I'm sure I've been here before, Jack. I really feel it. This is all familiar to me. It is as I remember it."

"Well, Mai, maybe when you were a little girl, your family brought you here," he said.

She paused. "Yes, that must be it."

"You think it is something else, don't you?" he said.

"I don't understand a lot of what I'm feeling. That's all," she explained. "It's not so much that I remember it. It's that I *feel* it. It is within me already. I am one with it. It's as if it's a part of me. Somehow I have an embedded knowledge of it, and yet I have never heard of such a thing. It used to happen to me in school too. The teacher would mention something and it would bring forth knowledge from within me. Like when we were learning about weather. I suddenly knew all about it like magic."

"Did you see the look on Dr. Bui's face when you showed her the mark on your hip?" he asked.

"No…what do you mean?" she lied.

"Her eyes got real big, like someone who's startled and in awe of you," he said. "I swear she gave you a slight bow. At first, when she went to the ground, I thought she was kneeling before you. But then she examined the flower on your lower hip. So, I don't know. I could have imagined it. It was pretty crazy, wasn't it?" He hoped she would tell him what was going on.

"Yes, crazy, like the choices we sometimes feel compelled to make, and then later wonder how we ever could have made them. It is like someone is guiding us. Do you ever feel that; like someone is controlling your destiny?"

"Mai, I've felt like that so often with you three gals, you can't imagine. From week to week, I never know what to expect. I guess I'm used to it because advertising photography is like that too. It has been a wonderful roller-coaster ride with the three of you, especially with you. I feel for once in my life I have everything I could ever want." He ran his hand through her hair as she gazed on the site below.

"I wish I felt that," she said. "There is so much left to do."

He looked at her curiously and wondered if she realized what she just said. She had been acting differently over the last few days. Her mind seemed to be off somewhere as she walked around the site. With her shorts and her tied-up shirt, she almost seemed like a little girl begging to be cared for and protected. Her usual brilliance and confidence were gone and replaced by an uneasiness that was apparent to him. He knew her better than anyone, and when he asked Catherine about it, she shrugged it off, attributing it to all the commotion at the site.

Suddenly, Mai looked up at him and said, "Let's go back to the hotel so we can call Devearney and then maybe take a walk downtown. We need to do something different and take some quality time, just you and me, OK?"

Jack wanted to let Catherine know they were going back to the hotel but my insisted that they just go and not disturb her. In truth she didn't want any bodyguards around complicating her plans.

Kelly was with their au pair when they called Chicago, so they enjoyed a much more meaningful conversation. She had shared long daily conversations with Catherine and was up to date on all that had happened. She had even made plans to join Catherine in Vietnam. They spent a few minutes listening to Devearney gurgle and coo on the other end of the line and finally said good-bye and hung up.

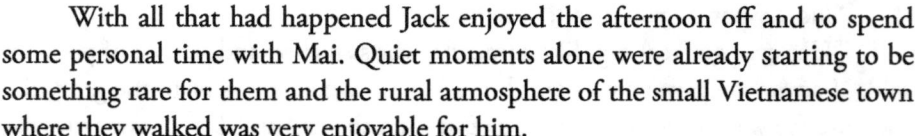

With all that had happened Jack enjoyed the afternoon off and to spend some personal time with Mai. Quiet moments alone were already starting to be something rare for them and the rural atmosphere of the small Vietnamese town where they walked was very enjoyable for him.

As they passed a mud-brick building, one of many in Thap Cham, a man stepped out from behind. Jack was talking and did not hear the man's footsteps as he approached, but he saw Mai look back at the last second. Then everything went blank as he was brutally struck on his head and fell to the ground. Through dizzy eyes, Jack saw another man join the first to lead Mai to a van that was waiting by the building. She was not resisting in any way but seemed concerned only for Jack, as she kept looking back. He heard her declare, "I love you, Jack," and lost consciousness.

At first, when Mai saw Jack on the ground unconscious, she had second thoughts. But then her abductor warned in Vietnamese, "He will be OK, but we will kill him if you resist. Do as we say, and no further harm will come to you, or him. I am sorry, but this is just a necessary precaution." The men cuffed her hands behind her, and the leader continued, "Please tell us if you have trouble breathing." They put a hood over her head and put her on the floor in the back of the van.

Mai became strangely calm and she had time to collect her thoughts as they drove to wherever they were taking her. *This is it*, she thought. *Now it begins. Be brave.* She was worried about Jack but clung to the assurance of her abductor that he would be OK. They had not harmed her at all. In fact, they were courteous. That, to her, was evidence this abduction was being conducted by Su Ling and Colonel Minh's people. This was all part of her plan to get close to Colonel Minh.

Since the revelation of what Colonel Minh had done to her parents, Mai had pursued extensive research and spent a good amount of time practicing. She knew ten different ways to kill a man, even if he was twice her size. She felt well prepared and only needed a chance to fulfill her driving compulsion for revenge on Colonel Minh for him killing her parents.

She had time to consider all that had happened that day. She could not forget the sight of Dr. Bui literally worshipping her on the floor of her office that very morning and begging to do so. It was obvious the Champa people considered her some sort of living deity, certainly more than a queen. If that were true, she could see why Colonel Minh wanted her, and for the first time, she realized his plan might not be so crazy after all.

They stopped briefly. She heard someone get into the van and sit up front by the driver before they continued on their journey. Minutes passed before she felt the engine surge. They were going very fast now, perhaps on a major highway. On instructions from the man who had joined them, they pulled her up on the back seat between two of her abductors. They removed her hood and handcuffs.

She looked quickly around but did not see any women, so Su Ling was not with them. That was to be expected. But Mai also did not see the men who gave her the prearranged signals from Su Ling. These men were probably Colonel

Minh's people and were all new to her except for one. She was surprised to see Mr. Doan in the front right seat..

He said, "Ms. Sambaht, we are coming to a checkpoint. If you cooperate your husband will live. If not, we will execute him. You know we can do that. Do you understand?"

Mai nodded seriously. The man sitting next to her gave her some water from a small bottle. She saw they were approaching a guard station and realized it was a border crossing.

At the direction of a guard on the driver's side, their van pulled to a stop. On the other side of the van, two Vietnamese soldiers looked in and inspected the inside of the van. Mr. Doan handed them a document. The guard read it, nodded, and handed it back. Then he stepped out of the way, saluted, and waved the van through.

"We are leaving Vietnam?" Mai asked, pleased that things were apparently unfolding as she hoped.

"Yes, Ms. Sambaht," Mr. Doan replied. "But you do not need to concern yourself with such things. You are among those who sincerely care about you and wish to protect you. I assure you, your safety is our primary concern. If you cooperate, we will allow you to stay sitting up without the hood. Do I have your word?"

"Yes," she said. " Of course. But I must ask you again, please do not further harm my husband. That is very important to me. I will not make any trouble. I will cooperate fully. Thank you for your kindness." She assumed they were taking her to Colonel Minh.

Several hours later they slowed and pulled off the highway onto a dirt road. They drove another thirty minutes, going ever higher through dense jungle that almost blocked their way several times. They came over the crest of a mountain and took a winding switchback road down into a beautiful valley lit by the late afternoon sun. There were so many exotic flowers and hanging fruit, it truly gave the appearance of a paradise.

They were on a small road that took them through a village and then to the entrance of a beautiful white Asian palace with seven golden spires that looked to have been restored from an ancient building or temple. Mai could see many armed men outside, most carrying large automatic rifles, which made it resemble a military compound. She did not expect that, and they had not traveled far enough to be at Colonel Minh's estate in Thailand. *What's going on she* thought?

The van pulled up to the front steps of the white palace, and they got out. The leader guided Mai gently by her elbow up the steps and inside. He led her through a hallway with many doors beyond and into a large parlor. Then he gently but firmly guided her to a comfortable chair where she sat down before he departed.

Looking around, Mai saw that she was in an old room sprinkled with antique Asian artifacts. The décor included several antique statues of Hindu gods. These people might be Champas, she thought.

She looked up as an old Asian man, and to her alarm, not Colonel Minh, entered the room and bowed slightly to her in greeting. "I am pleased to meet you, Miss Sambaht. Or should I address you as Queen Dau Te Po?"

Chapter 26

Siem Kulea, Cambodia, 1989
The Parlor of the White Palace

The old Asian man spoke in English as he did not think Mai knew the old language common to the local Champa people. He was fat, and his white tropical suit strained to hold in the weight. He had a full head of gray hair and a double chin. Mai put his age in the late fifties or early sixties. He made her a sweet fruity drink, which she eagerly accepted. She took a sip, then smiled, and drank several gulps because she was very thirsty.

"I am Dr. Minh, Ms. Sambaht," he explained. "You have heard of my brother Colonel Bao Minh. It is through his largesse that our effort here is principally funded. I am sure you are very confused at the moment. But if you let me explain, I think you will see why you are very precious to us and most welcome here in our valley paradise."

Mai, still wearing blue shorts and a white blouse, settled in the large chair. It was old and covered in a gold material tastefully embroidered with hoa cuc flowers. Curiously, she felt like she was sitting on a throne. She liked the room and did not feel in any danger. In fact, in a strange way, she felt at home and comfortable. She considered the layout and decoration of the room for a moment. But then, the old man sat down in the leather reading chair opposite her and her attention focused on him once more.

"Being Vietnamese, you of course know of the flower similar to those embroidered on your chair cushion…the hoa cuc. You, Miss Mai, are the Hoa Cuc of the Champa people."

"I do not understand what you mean. I am Mai Sambaht, a Vietnamese refugee, and now an American citizen, that's all I am and nothing more," she protested. She hoped this man was leading up to telling her she was going to be meeting Colonel Minh.

Dr. Minh smiled and continued, "Do you, in fact, have a small flower on your lower right hip, a flower like the ones on the chair?"

She didn't have to look. She already had made that comparison. She looked at him reluctantly. He won this point, whatever he might be leading to.

"Yes," she answered softly.

"Did you indeed find the legendary Champa treasure? Before she could answer, he continued to drive his point home. "Did you find it when no one else had been able to for over a thousand years?"

Mai was bewildered, and she was becoming drowsy. "Yes, I think so," she answered finally. "But that means nothing. I am still only me and nothing more. Please, let me go. My husband will pay you whatever you want." She felt her strength slowly draining from her. This was not going according to her plan.

"You are the symbol, Miss Mai, the Queen Dau Te Po we have been waiting for," he declared. "You are the rightful and only surviving heir to the ancient Champa kingdom, the one true descendant of legend. Around you, all the indigenous Champa people will unite, overthrow the illegal and oppressive governments of Indochina, and form the sovereign state of Champa once again. Do you know there are millions of Champas in Southeast Asia who will be eager to follow you and Colonel Minh in this rightful cause?"

Mai heard what he said with a foggy understanding. She grew more and more tired from the long day and just wanted to rest. Finally, her eyes gave in and closed in a welcome sleep. Her glass fell and bounced off the thick woven rug. She settled back against the cushions of the chair and slept.

"And now you must rest," Dr. Minh said to himself as he picked up the remains of the drugged glass.

He clapped his hands, and two massive male guards entered quickly. "Carry our esteemed guest to her royal chambers. Have her handmaidens prepare her for bed. I will be there presently to instruct them and begin the treatment."

The larger of the two guards bowed toward Dr. Minh, picked up Mai gently, and carried her out of the room through the door held open by the other.

Dr. Minh went to a large desk at one end of the room and found a file he had prepared on his newest subject. He was going to enjoy this particular treatment indeed. It was to be the culmination of all his previous efforts and experiments.

An hour later, Dr. Minh entered the ultra-luxurious royal quarters, where Mai now slept in a canopied bed behind sheer silks that protected her from the elements on all sides. One side of the room opened up onto a verandah before a beautiful tropical garden.

Standing in attendance were six Champa handmaidens, all dressed in floor-length beige dresses embroidered with small white hoa cuc flowers. Their hair was bound up in identical silk ribbon. He looked at each one and nodded his approval as they knelt, their hands clasped respectfully in front of them. Su Ling stood forward, as she was in charge of the others. Dr. Minh was pleased to be working with her again at the behest of his brother on this important project.

He spoke to them in the traditional Champa language and then switched to English, as these were handpicked to be the queen's handmaidens because they could speak both languages and would be helpful in training their queen in the old traditional language of the Champas.

"You have seen the physical evidence proving that this is your rightful queen, according to your faith and tradition. You are from this moment her handmaidens and subject to her will. You will obey her without question as long as she follows my wishes. She is going through a treatment to restore her to the manner and ways of her ancient Champa heritage. You are to bow to her, avert your eyes, and treat her respectfully as your Queen. She must live every day as your queen and must grow to expect you to regard her with the utmost obedience and deference. You are very fortunate to have been chosen for this assignment. Do you have any questions?"

"No, master," they all said in unison.

"Su Ling," he said, as he took her aside, "I trust you have everything ready and prepared for me?"

"Yes, of course, Doctor. I followed your instructions carefully. I checked and double-checked everything. All is ready for you," she replied.

"I want you to know I am personally pleased you are assisting me with her treatments. I find great comfort during this process knowing you are administering and checking my doses."

"Of course, Doctor. The syringes are loaded with the special opiate at the proper dosage, just as you requested. I have inserted a cannula on her left arm to make it easier for you."

Su Ling wore a green Vietnamese-style áo dài that clung to her figure, in contrast to the others. Her shoulder length dark hair was styled elegantly and framed her oval face and inviting lips perfectly. Dr. Minh always enjoyed her company and had entertained many fantasies concerning her.

"Right," he said. "Now I will administer the first dose of the opiate, but you must follow up every six hours around the clock, Su Ling. Watch carefully so you can continue her treatment as scheduled. One of you should always be at her side. If anything looks unusual, call me immediately. She is going to change over the next week and must be monitored closely. She may resist at first. You must be there to gently but firmly guide her along the path of treatment we have designed for her."

"Yes, doctor. I understand. You know you can depend on me. I will ensure she remains calm and obedient during this process while you gain complete control of her. I find this all very exciting as our plans unfold toward the new empire Colonel Minh has planned," she replied.

Dr. Minh rolled a small medical cart nearer to the ornate gold bed where Mai slept. Taking a filled hypodermic prepared by Su Ling, he tapped it a few times and then pushed the drug into Mai's IV line. It was the best and finest opiate available, straight from the poppy fields of Laos. It was just the right dosage, having been tested previously by this truly talented, vile physician who left nothing to chance. He pulled out the needle and handed it to Su Ling. He leaned over and gave Mai a possessive kiss on the cheek. She moaned and settled back on her pillow.

Mai was dressed in a sheer white silk nightgown that did little to hide her perfect figure. He admired her for a moment as if he were a god creating a creature to his likeness and for his purpose. She, like all the others, was just an experiment further validating the routine he had perfected.

When it came to remote cerebral mapping, commonly called brainwashing, he was possibly the best in the world. He had discovered and perfected a regimen of drugs and thought suggestion that worked to subdue the minds of his victims far better and more efficiently than any other known method. He would erase her past and insert one of his own making and design. After the treatment, she would only know what he wanted her to know and think what he wanted her to think. Ironically, he did not desire her, but he desired the creation he would soon make from her former self. This was a kind of power very few men have ever known, and he was addicted to it. It excited him immensely.

When he was done with her treatment in three weeks, he would hand her over without any regret to his brother to use for his diabolical plan. He did not care what happened to her after the process. He would move on to the next subject. It was this depraved indifference to the aftermath of his results that made him the best at what he did, and inhumanly evil at the same time.

He sat down beside where she lay. He pulled her nightgown up to reveal her naked hip. There it was, the Hoa Cuc birthmark, just as Su Ling had said. She truly was the long sought-after queen and heir to the Champa throne. Remarkable.

He leaned his head in close to her ear where she slept on the soft pillow in the darkened room. He could smell her freshly bathed, sweet, clean, lavender-scented skin. He began a hypnotic mantra he would continue for the next twenty minutes. "You are our queen, Dau Te Po, the true and rightful heir to the ancient throne of Champa…"

Chapter 27

Ninh Thuan Province Hospital, Thap Cham, 1989

Jack lay on his pillow, a bandage wrapped around a shaved and wounded area on the back of his head. Opposite from where Catherine sat, he had an IV morphine drip taped to his left arm. She softly coaxed him through tears as she leaned in and ran her hand gently along his cheek. He lay as he was for three days.

Catherine left his bedside only for necessities during that time and was growing disconsolate.

"Jack...Jack, please wake up. Jack, it's Catherine. Can you hear me? Jack?" She thought she couldn't cry anymore but still her eyes watered as she begged a response.

Just then, for the first time, she heard him moan, and his head twisted back and forth on the pillow. He slowly opened his eyes and tried to focus on Catherine, who was smiling joyously because he was awake.

He moaned some more. His head was sore, and he was a bit woozy from the morphine drip. He lifted his head off the pillow suddenly. Upon seeing her, he asked, "Catherine? Where am I?"

"You are in Ninh Thuan Province Hospital. You were assaulted and knocked out," Catherine explained.

Jack fell back against the pillow, trying to understand through a muddled memory. The large room was air-conditioned and bright with the sun streaming through two large windows. The light-green metal bed where he laid and two chairs were the only furniture in the room.

"Yes," he replied, shaking his head on the pillow, "I think I remember now. Something hit me. But I don't know why. I can't remember. Wait! Where is Mai? Is Mai OK?"

Catherine took his hand and held it in hers. "She's missing, Jack. We're trying to find her. So far there haven't been any leads."

Jack tried to get up, and Catherine pushed him back gently. "No, no, you must rest. Everyone is trying to find her. She is very important to many people in this country now, and they're doing all they can to find her. You have to rest and get better."

Jack looked at her and said simply, "Mai."

"I know, Jack. They'll find her. Rest now," she said.

Jack felt very weak. His memory was muddled. He tried to remember, but finally, his eyes closed, and he fell asleep again.

Catherine walked out into the hallway, past the two Vietnamese guards who were at his door. One of them got up, closed the door behind her, and sat back down again. But both men sat straighter in their chairs as they saw Mr. Nguyen approaching down the hallway with Colonel Jung by his side. Catherine greeted them, and they all slipped into a private office a couple of doors down the hallway to talk. Colonel Jung closed the door behind them so they could talk in private.

"Have you found her?" Catherine asked Mr. Nguyen.

He shook his head. "We've made progress in our search, but no, we have not found her, Ms. Marsh. We will tell you what we know, and perhaps you can add something that might help our search."

"Yes, of course, please. I am eager to help. What have you discovered?"

They all chose one of the three former US Government Issue chairs arranged around an old gray desk that made up the furniture of the hospital office.

Mr. Nguyen surprised Catherine by lighting up a cigarette. Too anxious for information to worry about her objections to cigarette smoke, she focused on his words. "They were attacked in Thap Cham as they walked," he began. "There was a struggle. Mr. Largent was knocked unconscious, and Miss Mai was taken away in a dark van. The van crossed the border into Laos three nights ago. We are still trying to track it from there."

"She's in Laos?" asked Catherine.

"No, we think she is in Cambodia, but we cannot tell you why at this time," Colonel Jung said from his chair in the corner. "We have reason to believe she is being held in Cambodia but somewhere near the Laotian border. The area is very mountainous with dense jungle, and it is almost impossible to find someone there."

He got up and handed her a paper with some writing on it. "Miss Marsh, does this mean anything to you?"

She read in Vietnamese, "Các Cúc Hoa là ở Việt Nam." Catherine did not recognize it and asked what it said.

Mr. Nguyen explained, "It says, 'The Hoa Cuc is in Vietnam.' It is a radio transmission we monitored from Ho Chi Minh City to certain factions in Cambodia. We think it may be important, but we do not know exactly why. So it means nothing to you?"

She shook her head. "Who or what is the Hoa Cuc?"

"Hoa Cuc is not usually a reference to a person. It is our national flower. You call it chrysanthemum, I think. It is a wildflower here in Vietnam."

Catherine appeared lost in thought for a moment and then she remembered a few days earlier when Mai was looking at the scroll with Dr. Bui. She looked up sharply.

"You remember something?" Colonel Jung asked, noting her reaction.

"I heard that name…a few days ago," she explained. She told them about the scroll and the flower printed at the bottom.

She paused a moment, trying to remember everything that was said, even though at the time she was not paying much attention. "Colonel, Mai showed us an identical small flower mark of some kind on her right hip. We laughed about it at the time. Jack teased about how we should call her 'princess'. Do you think this is important?"

"Perhaps," said Mr. Nguyen. "We are following leads and making connections where we find them. We cannot tell you more at the moment. We will talk later."

Catherine pleaded, "Mr. Nguyen, please keep me informed. This is important to me."

"Indeed, Ms. Marsh, it is important to the people of Vietnam. We will be communicating soon," said Mr. Nguyen. He bowed slightly as he began to leave the office with Colonel Jung.

"Wait," said Catherine. "That's all? How did you let the van cross the border with a kidnap victim inside?"

"I am sorry, and I am embarrassed for my country, Ms. Marsh," said Mr. Nguyen. "It was a mistake we are doing our best to repair. It was a government vehicle that crossed the border with Ms. Sambaht inside. We have proof the guard was presented with government papers. We think we know the person who was in the vehicle, and we are searching for this man." There was a pause as Mr. Nguyen considered something.

"Are you going to tell me?" asked Catherine finally.

"Mr. Doan," said Mr. Nguyen. "The man in the van was Mr. Doan. As you can imagine, we are doing all we can to find him." And they went out the door.

Chapter 28

Siem Kulea, AD 1059

Six years of abundant harvests following the arrival of the young Queen Dau Te Po left a prosperous and peaceful community in the Siem Kulea valley. They shared their prosperity across the mountains, supplying their neighbors with many and bountiful farm goods in return for dry goods from Khmer-, China, Burma, and India. Their neighbors waged war against each other, but none found an enemy in Queen Dau Te Po, who always pledged neutrality and found respected friends in the winners and losers. The beautiful young queen and her valley paradise were legendary, with word traveling along the trade routes to countries many thousands of miles away.

When Po arrived in the remote and mostly hidden valley she was eleven years of age and carried in a litter by her loyal and devoted guards. Fleeing the conquering Dai Viet forces that had swept down and conquered their homeland, they had risked everything to bring her to the relatively safe environs of this valley paradise.

Po was concerned that the Champas living there might not wish to honor her as the rightful heir and queen of the Champa people. But when they saw her, the people as one went immediately to the ground and bowed before her. She met the chief of the Palace Guard, Wan Bae, and Chi, the head of the Palace servants who formally welcomed her and assured her of their loyalty and devotion. The valley became festive and filled with great joy upon her arrival. But when her handmaidens reported that she did indeed have the sacred birthmark, the Hoa Cuc of the rightful queen on her right hip, the valley as one dedicated their lives to her happiness.

By the time she was seventeen she was comfortable with the many forms of respect and devotion shown to her by her people who revered her as a living goddess. She had expected this deification because her mother had explained to her about the Champa people's need to worship and obey her as a part of their heritage and devotion to the ancients. Po, as the other queens before her, possessed knowledge from within and was aware that the ancients bred the Champa people to serve them and instilled in them an embedded devotion that was their only hope for fulfillment in life.

This queen-deity status existed from the time when all of the ancients departed one day leaving behind only one alien woman who had fallen in love and mated with a Champa man. This woman was the daughter of the leader of the aliens and was revered naturally by the Champa people who obeyed her without question. Po was directly descended from her and thus the recipient of the compelling devotion the Champas felt for their queen.

But Queen Po was fully aware that with their devotion to her came the almost overwhelming responsibility for her to nurture and secure for her people health and prosperity, and to protect them at all costs.

She had grown into an exceptionally beautiful woman, and her daily work routine kept her slim and very attractive. She was called on regularly to settle disputes, and her superior intellect, exceptional wisdom, and charming manner, especially for one so young, seemed always to prevail and resolve disagreements to the satisfaction of everyone. Either way, the people in the valley regarded her word as law. When she conducted court to settle disputes or make a judgment, she always sought the opinion of the village leaders and the head Hindu pandit, Havta, who sat with her to give consul. He too was surprised by her wisdom, even though her opinions sometimes ran contrary to his own. She was the most objective and altruistic person in the valley. She could weigh all arguments fairly and bring them to a just conclusion. No one ever complained about her rulings. They accepted them as the final word.

At the age of seventeen, and fully grown, she felt the time was right to produce her daughter and heir. At the same time, she found herself attracted to a young man who often worked close to her in the fields. His name was Le Dabi. She looked forward to seeing him each day. He was tall, muscled, and fit, but also intellectually curious. He quizzed Po every day about her knowledge of the world.

She liked Dabi a great deal, and their friendly verbal trysts soon turned into something more serious. One day, when she was done with foreplay and was prepared to carry out her plan to ensure an heir to her throne, Po calmly led him to her bed. There they explored the more intimate aspects of their relationship. Dabi returned to her bed many nights thereafter until she announced to the valley that she was pregnant.

What Dabi could never know was that the baby was a product of her passion and not his seed. The Hoa Cuc, the queen of the Champas, and her heirs, were uniquely descended from the mating of a human with an alien species resembling humans many thousands of years ago. This was a secret passed from the first Hoa Cuc mother to daughter down through time and shared with no one. Her mother in Dong Na carefully explained this secret to her before Po fled the Dai Viet forces with Uncle Tap. While her metabolism and reproductive system were similar to humans and allowed for a normal pregnancy, she first self-reproduced a female heir marked with the Hoa Cuc birthmark. A particular hormonal response during sexual passion triggered this unique self-reproductive process.

Dabi wanted to marry her and even proposed. She foresaw this reaction by him as a possibility, but he was only an instrument to arouse her passion and for several reasons he could only be her consort, not her equal. She tried many times to explain to him in practical terms that although she liked him she could not marry him, because she was of royal lineage. He was beneath her station, and people in the valley would never accept him as her husband. If he wanted to stand by her side, then he needed to accept her mark and be branded as her consort as was the Champa tradition. It seemed ironic for this queen who made it her routine to work in the fields with her people like a common person would worry about such matters. But one was her heart and the other was her heritage. She must preserve her station in life out of respect for her ancestors, her people, and her daughter. She thought no one would understand, but the entire valley agreed as usual with her decision. As it happened, Le Dabi was too proud to be branded by her and take up a life as her consort.

She determined that he was going to be a problem, so she decided pragmatically to dispose of him right away. He was a means to an end, and during the process, she had been sincere in her affection for him. But he made the mistake of thinking he could possess her like other women when in fact she was superior to him in many ways besides being his queen. She dealt with his arrogance and naïveté in a decisive manner that, were she not queen, might be judged as cold-hearted. But, to her surprise, her handmaidens confessed to her that the entire valley had been waiting for her to send him on his way for weeks. It was simply tradition that no man could possess the Hoa Cuc.

He was taken to the road leading out of the valley, given a horse, ample supplies, and a bag of gold coins. Then he was escorted to the guarded mountain pass and told never to return under a penalty of death. He was banished forever.

Six months later Po had her baby, a little girl she named Devearney.

Seven more years passed and the valley continued its prosperity and peaceful harmony with its neighbors. Queen Po, now twenty-four, was delighted to see her daughter regarded affectionately by everyone. They bowed and gave her the respect due a royal princess. Indeed, she looked so much like Queen Po that it almost seemed a miracle as Queen Po became herself again. Devi even bore the royal Hoa Cuc birthmark on her right hip, as everyone in the valley was pleased to know because it spoke to the legitimacy of her birthright.

Little Devi could be seen every morning walking and talking with Sentai, her educated teacher, who taught her about the world around them. Sometimes Po joined in and explained certain points that Sentai had not mentioned. Sentai looked forward to Queen Po's presence and loved her participation in the schooling of the princess. He was amazed at Queen Po's vastly superior intellect and told her one day that he had never known anyone as learned on so many topics as she. She replied that it was too bad he did not get to spend more time with Uncle Tap before he passed.

Each morning during planting and harvest, Queen Po would show up at a different field with her subjects so they would share her love for this valley paradise. Every afternoon she and Devi could be seen riding their almost identical black stallions toward the hills like the little girl Queen Po had done when she first came to the valley. Sometimes Queen Po would bring her great mount to a halt in the middle of the road that led up to the mountain pass where she entered the valley many years before. Young Devi listened eagerly as her mother celebrated their time together with tales of the life she remembered beyond the mountain and that day when she first arrived in the valley.

Devi's handmaidens never failed to put in her hair one of the many orchids that grew in abundance in the valley, and she was often referred to as "the little flower." Po smiled when she heard it the first time because it reminded her of Big Sem and Uncle Tap, who had long since passed away. She missed them a great deal. She built a meditation stele in honor of them in her garden, which was just outside of her royal chambers so that she could continue to sit and talk with them. She was positive they moved on to a new and better life as a reward for their growth and kindnesses in this one.

It was about that time that Queen Po began having a dark recurring dream that greatly troubled her. In the dream she was in a field of wild hoa cuc flowers with her daughter Princess Devearney. The princess was laughing, and playfully running away from her as if they were engaged in a game. Suddenly the skies turned dark around them and a storm arose bringing deafening thunder, fierce winds, and very dark menacing clouds. The clouds swirled over them but Devearney did not seem to notice them or react to the thunder in any way. She continued playing as if everything were normal. Po called out to her and tried to run to her side to protect her, but Devearney ignored her and if anything ran even farther away. Then to her horror Po saw that Devearney was running toward the edge of a nearby cliff unawares. Po ran with her hands out frantically yelling at her to stop and come back. But soon the dark clouds became a whirlwind that swept Po up within it and took her away. She lost sight of the ground, Devearney, and everything. Then she woke up.

Finally, one night after just such a dream she summoned Lady Chi, her head of household, Wan Bae first of her guards, and Sentai to her. She told them she had experienced a troublesome dream and did not know what it meant, but it left her concerned. She charged them with the safety and security of Princess Devearney. She told them they must dedicate their lives to the young princess's happiness. She informed them that she might be gone one day unexpectedly, and they must help Princess Devi to make the right choices, much as Uncle Tap had so wisely counseled her. Lady Chi would be the nominal head of the valley in Queen Po's absence until Princess Devearney was ready, and then Lady Chi would defer to her, always lending her counsel to her decisions. Thus, she hoped she had prepared them for whatever uncertainty the future might hold.

Even a paradise can be visited by a devil, and one day a Khmer prince, Indravar Tu, rode into their village on his white stallion, with twenty of his soldiers marching behind. Royal dignitaries visited the valley often with the best of intentions, and were treated as welcome guests. Most of these dignitaries were just curious to see the legendary valley and its queen who worked beside her people. Queen Po was always pleased to accommodate them and share her hospitality.

On that warm afternoon, she was lounging comfortably on her verandah in a large woven chair. She wore pantaloons stitched in green and gold with a gold-cropped top. She was enjoying the new wine of the season and being offered an assortment of fruits by her servants when he rode up before her. He dismounted and walked boldly up the steps, stopped only briefly by her two massive guards, who let him pass with a command from their queen. He went to her and bowed at the waist.

She thought this prince was the most handsome man she had ever seen. "My greetings to you," he said in a language Queen Po understood. "I am Prince Indravar Tu. You may have heard of me. I have heard much about you, and I must say the rumors of your beauty did not do you justice."

Queen Po was stunned. She had heard of this prince from the west. He had won many battles, and never failed to subdue his enemies. She was also aware he had a ruthless reputation and his cruelty to his people was legendary. Yet he was still a man, and Queen Po had never seen a man as magnificent, muscled, and powerful looking as this Prince.

His garments were lined with leather that looked to have a gold weave throughout. His chest was bare behind a vest of handcrafted leather. He carried a large sword on one side and an intimidating coiled whip with an ivory handle next to it.

He took her hand and kissed it with a surprising gentleness, and Queen Po was momentarily taken with that simple gesture. Then, quickly recovering, she said with a warm smile, "Please, Prince, won't you sit with me?"

It was late in the afternoon, and Queen Po offered him some wine, which he readily accepted. He took a sip from his goblet and commented that it was some of the most flavorful wine he had ever tasted. She smiled, warmed by the compliment, as servants brought more fruit and a few pastries fresh from the kitchen.

Queen Po saw her people watching from afar, no doubt envisioning a romance between the two of them as they conversed in the cool afternoon on the front verandah of her white palace. She did not approve of such gossip, but as she was conversing with him in public view on her front verandah, she knew it was inevitable and gave it no concern.

"I have come to you to see if the rumors are true," he continued. "It is said you are Queen Dau Te Po, yet you do not rule like a queen, as is your right. I have heard that you work in the fields with your subjects and even feed livestock." He reached over and picked up one of her delicate hands, bearing long, slim fingers and painted nails, and turned it over in his. "Yet these hands are soft and womanly. Perhaps those are indeed just rumors, no?"

"Ah, Prince, I am sorry, but the rumors are true. I do work with my people in the fields," she replied. "I happen to love working on the land. It is a part of me. My valley is beautiful, and I share a personal relationship with it and my people. Everything living is a part of us as we are all a part of the universe. Haven't you felt that is so?"

They conversed through the afternoon as the sun went down behind them, and dinner replaced the afternoon appetizers. Prince Tu could not help himself. He wanted this woman. She was indeed very beautiful, maybe the most beautiful woman he had ever seen. He could talk with her like talking to a man. She seemed to have knowledge of many things and on many levels. This was enhanced by her surprising wisdom and an elegance of manner that made her all the more desirable.

Her eyes were dark glasz in color, something that was rare in this area. She accentuated them with shadow and dark accents on her eyelids, and they charmed with every smile or spoken word.

She was a queen in every sense except that she did not demand that others show deference to her station. He noticed they seemed to do it anyway and were most eager to do so. How curious. He never witnessed a populace serve with such devotion and love as these people had for Queen Po.

One way or the other, he was going to have this woman as his, and his alone.

Chapter 30

Thap Cham, Vietnam, 1989

Two weeks later Mr. Nguyen met with Catherine and Jack again. This time they were at a former French plantation house in Ninh Thuan province. Catherine had rented it and moved Jack there from the hospital after Kelly joined her in Vietnam.

Jack was now mostly recovered and obsessed with saving Mai at any cost. He spent his days exercising and studying maps that Catherine had acquired of the area. Mr. Nguyen said they thought Mai was being held in Cambodia, but Jack was convinced she was being held at Colonel Minh's estate in Thailand. Thus he formed a plan to try to enter the country through clandestine means. He acquired the things he needed, including an experienced mercenary and guide who spoke several languages and he was ready to leave at a moment's notice. As Jack recovered, he practiced several times a day with various weapons, and his guide spent a great deal of time educating him on how to survive in the jungle.

Every morning he proclaimed he was about to leave, but he relented at the constant urging of Catherine and Kelly, and the assurances of Mr. Nguyen that they were close to being ready to save Mai and round up the abductors.

That afternoon they were all gathered in the great room, which served as a family room, library, and office. Under the constant breeze of large ceiling fans, Catherine and Kelly were dressed comfortably in shorts and light blouses that helped them cope with the growing heat of the day. It also helped that the old estate house, with its open design, provided a cool breeze under the shade of the tall banyan trees that surrounded it. Jack was dressed in tan safari shorts and a navy-blue T-shirt.

Mr. Nguyen requested this meeting, and they all listened intently to what he told them. Kelly and Catherine knew that they could no longer reason with Jack. They were fully aware that he was likely to set out after Mai very soon, probably the very next day unless Mr. Nguyen had a viable plan for her rescue.

Jack did not trust Mr. Nguyen. It seemed there was more to this story than he was telling them. He was sure there was another reason why the Vietnamese so strongly wanted Colonel Minh brought to justice. This particular meeting with Mr. Nguyen was in his view the final one before he went on his mission to save Mai.

"I have brought a prisoner with me who will not talk to us, but we think he might talk with you and Ms. Marsh," Mr. Nguyen said to Jack as he began his briefing. "No, Mr. Nguyen. This has gone far enough already. First, you tell us what you know and what is really going on here, demanded Jack. "We know you've been holding back information from us. We've been patient, but we're done with that." His jaw was set, his eyes riveted in defiance.

Mr. Nguyen did not try to placate Jack with words, for he had already concluded the time had come to involve the three Americans in his plans. He nodded toward Jack and began.

"There is a growing unrest in Southeast Asia among the indigenous Champa people of the region," he began. "They are sponsored by a powerful group headed by Colonel Minh, who we believe has stolen much of the wealth of South Vietnam and shipped it out of the country. He is a very influential man, with many international friends, even countries, who protect him. It is difficult to strike at him directly. This situation has been developing since the fall of South Vietnam in 1975, but lately, it has become more organized and dangerous. All these indigenous radicals needed was someone to rally around and to act as the symbol of their revolutionary zeal, much like our Uncle Ho was for us."

Catherine and Kelly were sitting on a loveseat, focused on Mr. Nguyen's words. Jack sensed where he was going with this presentation, and he didn't like it at all. He got up and began pacing nervously while Mr. Nguyen continued with his narrative.

Mr. Nguyen continued, "They could not use Colonel Minh because he has no historical connection with the Champa people. They needed someone who would instantly draw all the proud indigenous people into one force acting in unison. That one person came to them at this most opportune time. As it happens, we believe Ms. Sambaht is that person."

The three Americans visibly straightened their posture and focused on Mr. Nguyen.

"We now have proof of her heritage. You may not have been informed of events at the Thap Cham treasure site since the kidnapping, and Mr. Largent got hurt. Thus, you are probably not aware that in that cave we also found three bodies along with those chests. One, in particular, is of interest to us. At first, it appeared to be just ancient royal robes that were piled near one of the chests.

Upon examination, they discovered it was, in fact, the remains of a young woman in her twenties. It took Dr. Bui's investigation by surprise and sent it in an entirely different direction. Our forensic people thoroughly examined the remains, but there were no overt markings to indicate how or why she died. We have concluded she probably died from a poison of some variety.

"Many people and investigators of many specialties have been working on this. As I said, this is very important to all of us. After a time, we surmised a possible relationship to Ms. Sambaht, and recently we have connected her to the Thap Cham treasure site through DNA."

"Ah, the hairbrush," said Catherine suddenly aware.

"Yes, that is why I requested it from you, Miss Marsh. We needed the DNA from a lock of her hair to compare," Mr. Nguyen confirmed. "This is a new field, but with recent breakthroughs, we were able to compare with great certainty the DNA of the young lady in the cave to Ms. Sambaht. They are an excellent match, even with so many centuries between them.

But what is even more remarkable is that their DNA is different in one minor area from other humans. We have no explanation for that but we are certain of it. We retested it several times to be sure and received the same result. It might surprise you to know that Vietnam is at the forefront internationally of DNA testing due to the many unidentified bodies found during and after the war. It was a necessary science for us. In this case, it proved most advantageous, at least in confirming Ms. Sambaht's ancestry."

Jack sat down, stunned into passiveness. "You are saying Mai, my wife, is actually related to this woman they found in the cave with the treasure? How can that be? Is she really a princess or something?"

"Now you are getting to the crux of the matter at hand and why we are most concerned," said Mr. Nguyen. "While our own knowledge of this connection is recent, others, including some in our own government, have been searching for Ms. Sambaht for many years. They traced her to the United States and tried at least on one occasion to abduct her there."

Catherine gave a start and said, "Oh my God! We all thought they were after me. It never occurred to us that they might be after Mai."

"Yes, indeed," continued Mr. Nguyen. "And when she decided to join you on the trip here, those individuals knew about it as soon as the visas were issued. Mr. Doan followed her closely and even reported her arrival and progress to his superiors in the conspiracy. Mr. Doan moved up to Phan Rang to wait for an opportunity to abduct her and deliver her to these insurgents. As you know, that opportunity presented itself when Mr. Largent and Ms. Sambaht took a walk alone in Thap Cham several weeks ago. With Mr. Doan's diplomatic passport and papers, he was able to easily get her out of the country."

"So what are you doing about it?" asked Catherine. "What are you doing to get her back?"

Mr. Nguyen turned his head to one side and continued. "This is a very difficult situation, Miss Marsh. The People's Republic of Vietnam is a country in transition and trying to move forward as a modern and respected member of the international community. We do not want to start another war with our neighbors. As I mentioned earlier, we cannot get to Colonel Minh through normal means. He is well protected. But you can, and moreover, we want you to.

"We have been aware for some time, of insurgents who have been building up their strength with support from foreign countries. Our problem is that even with all of our resources, we do not know positively where the insurgent base camp is located. We think it is located in northern Cambodia and have made raids around there several times trying to eliminate their leadership. Each time the lead proved false. They knew we were coming as those within our government such as Mr. Doan worked secretly to thwart our efforts. Our inability to determine the location of their base camp concerns us greatly, as we have information the movement is growing rapidly to dangerous numbers. It even may be, as you believe, at Colonel Minh's estate in Thailand."

"How did you know about that?" asked Jack, surprised.

Mr. Nguyen walked over to a clock on one of the shelves and removed a small electronic device from the back of it. He tossed it to Jack, who caught it and examined it carefully.

"We just do not know for sure, and their people are intensely loyal and impossible to infiltrate with spies. Your plan to go after her might be the best way to both find and free her from these people. We think you will not be successful and will be captured and taken to where she is."

"How will that help anyone?" asked Jack. "If they think I'm there to save Mai, they will probably kill me the first chance they get."

"I do not think so," said Mr. Nguyen. "They are likely to hold you as a means of being sure she cooperates with their plans. I think you will be quite safe from serious harm, Mr. Largent."

"OK, so I go and find this place. How do you find me?" asked Jack.

"You will be wired with a tracking device held within your belt," said Mr. Nguyen. "But we are again getting ahead of ourselves. I told you at the beginning of our conversation that I have brought a prisoner with me. He has been our prisoner for five years now, and I believe you know him, Mr. Largent."

"Who would that be?" asked Jack, surprised. "Daniel Vega," replied Mr. Nguyen. "Our prisoner is Daniel Vega."

Chapter 31

Thap Cham, Vietnam

Jack recognized his old friend even after fifteen years, though he was a lot thinner and dressed in what looked like a civilian form of the Vietnamese army uniform. He was a bit disheveled but was not looking bad for a man who had just spent five years in a Vietnamese prison.

As Vega looked around upon entering the room, he saw the ladies, and his posture straightened. Then he saw Jack and gave a big smile. He stepped forward and greeted Jack with a big hug. "Man, am I glad to see you! I couldn't believe it when Mr. Nguyen told me he was bringing me here to see you."

Mr. Nguyen said, "I will leave you old friends to get reacquainted for now. I will return in a few hours, and then we will discuss, as you say, Mr. Largent, the plan." With that, he bowed slightly to Jack and the ladies. He went outside, got in his car, and drove off.

Vega went to the window and looked out. "It looks like he left a whole platoon to make sure I don't scurry out of here. He's a funny one, that Mr. Nguyen. You never know exactly what he's up to."

Jack could certainly agree with that assessment, but he had an entirely different quandary at the moment. "What the hell is going on, Daniel? What have you gotten yourself into? We came here investigating you and Colonel Minh as criminals, international drug dealers, and gold thieves. I need some explanations, and I need them now. I really don't know whether to hug you or refuse to have anything to do with you."

"Well, too late. You already hugged me, my friend," said Vega, still elated to be with Americans again and out of prison. "Do you know what this is all about? I don't even know what I'm doing here. Oh my God! Is that Scotch?" he said, seeing the fully loaded bar cart on the other side of the room.

Catherine spoke up for the first time from the couch beside Kelly. "That's my Scotch, Mr. Vega, and if you want some, you better sit down and start answering some of our questions."

Vega was distracted by her interruption and focused his attention on the other temptation in the room represented by the two gorgeous women sitting on the loveseat. He followed her suggestion and sat down in a comfortable chair opposite them. "What do you want to know?" he asked.

But Jack interrupted them. Daniel these are my friends, Catherine Marsh, and Kelly Ryan. They acknowledged him with nods. Daniel said, "Well, it is very nice to meet you ladies!"

Catherine whispered something in Kelly's ear. Kelly went over to the cart and said, "It's single malt, Mr. Vega. Do you want it straight up or on the rocks?"

Vega seemed mesmerized as he watched her. With the shorts and light-blue tank top she was wearing, Kelly's figure was well displayed. For a prisoner of five long years and with a libido like his, it was almost overwhelming.

In answer to her question, Vega pointed silently to the ceiling. Kelly poured one-third of a glass and handed it to him before she sat down and drew her legs up on the couch close to Catherine.

"Mmmm...oh my, I haven't had a drink in five years...six maybe," he said, after his first sip.

"OK, Daniel. Let's start from the beginning," said Jack. "We heard you were supposedly killed in a helicopter crash, but at least one person swears you not only survived but that you strafed his helicopter on your way by and killed Captain Straker. Either way, you were not heard from again. We have pretty much surmised that you and Straker helped Minh get South Vietnamese gold worth about twenty million dollars out of the country."

Vega looked quickly around the room and motioned for Jack to keep his voice down. "Talk quietly, will you? They may be listening."

Jack smiled to himself because he was sure there were many more bugs planted in that room beside the one Mr. Nguyen showed him. Now he understood Mr. Nguyen's intent. Vega wouldn't talk to the Vietnamese, but he would talk freely to them. It was a clever way to get a prisoner to tell you what he knows. Jack sided with Mr. Nguyen for now.

"I found and rented this house, Mr. Vega. We aren't being listened to," said Catherine wanting to hear his story.

"OK, Daniel, fill us in. Tell us what happened," Jack insisted.

Vega instead held his empty glass out to Kelly with raised eyebrows, and she acquiesced by retrieving the glass, refilling it, and returning to sit by Catherine. Vega explored every curve on Kelly's figure as she walked across the room.

"Boy, these two are something! Where did you learn to score so high, my friend?" he asked, emboldened by the Scotch.

Kelly had already decided she didn't like Vega. She leaned over and kissed Catherine on the mouth slowly and passionately and then sat back and gave him a smirk. She took pleasure in frustrating his over-charged libido.

"Oh, shit!" said Vega. "Are you two lezzies? That's downright criminal. You two outstanding examples of American females cannot be lezzies. Jack, tell me it ain't so."

"Afraid so, Daniel," Jack said. "And they are my two best friends besides. I love 'em both dearly, but not on the same street your mind is driving down right now."

"My, my," said Vega. "I guess there have been a lot of changes in the last five years."

"Mr. Vega, I believe you were going to tell us what happened that day you supposedly died in a helicopter crash," said Catherine, noticeably irritated.

"Yes, you're right," he said, pointing toward her and nodding. "You remember Captain Straker, Jack? You met him on the hill that day when you went out to photograph the rocket attack at the temple. He was in command of the security police at Phan Rang."

Jack nodded and motioned to the ladies, asking if they wanted drinks. Kelly said, "Yes, the usual, Jack. Thank you." Jack fixed the drinks as Vega continued.

"Well, he and Colonel Minh had something going before that. They were smuggling drugs out on MAC flights back to the States. It was a pretty good deal, and Straker was making a lot of money. Colonel Denton was in on it too. Minh had connections stateside in the drug business, and Denton had gambling debts. Minh bought those debts from his friends in the states. He offered to cancel Colonel Denton's debts and give him a percentage of the take if he looked the other way. Denton had no choice, but it wasn't long before he devised better ways to move the drugs out of the country and become a major player. They had the whole operation well hidden and organized.

"They went on like that for several years. But in seventy-one, someone in Laos cut out Colonel Minh, and the source in Laos dried up. At Colonel Minh's urging, Straker got himself assigned to special ops so he could go open it up again. It took a few months before he had his own squadron of six helos, two of them the specially outfitted gunships. He took some of his old crew along, including me. Soon he was able to consolidate his trusted team into one unit and strike back quickly and effectively, and the pipeline opened back up again.

"A little later, the South Vietnamese began moving all of their assets from the north down to Saigon just before the Americans left. Straker knew about the gold shipments that were coming through Phan Rang on special Vietnamese C-130 flights. They used Minh's people to hijack one of those flights. They landed and unloaded the gold at an airfield controlled by Minh, and they killed the five Vietnamese onboard. They crashed the airplane into the side of a mountain to cover their tracks. It was in a very remote area, and by the time they found the crash and could get to the site, the gold was gone. Of course, it was never there, because Colonel Minh had it. But he had to get it out of the country and to his supply bases in Laos and then to Thailand. Straker was perfect for it. He helicoptered it out bit by bit until the whole twenty million dollars was safely away in Thailand.

"It was perfect, except that Colonel Minh and Straker had a disagreement over the money, and Minh felt he could no longer trust Straker."

Vega again held out his glass to be refilled by Kelly. "Add some ice this time, darlin', would ya?"

He continued, "I got to know Minh better because I was a major participant in planning some of his more successful operations including the logistics of moving the gold out of Vietnam to Thailand. He approached me about doing something about Straker. I took leave in Bangkok, and he met me there and showed me the town. I saw and did things that week I never saw or did before or since." He looked at Kelly and Catherine who obviously did not approve.

"Well, anyway, he offered me a huge amount of money. He said all I had to do was kill Straker and make it look like an accident, or like the VC did it, and the money was mine. Hell, I would have done it for a lot less than that. I didn't like Straker anyway. I fixed one of the gunships and the slick so they would have engine trouble and have to set down while we were on a mission into southern Laos. My crew were loyal to Minh like I was, and the four of us had already decided to go mercenary after we discharged. I offered them a cut and a chance to start out with some big money in their pockets, and they all signed on with me. My gunship was the one that strafed Straker and killed him. We were taking so much ground fire, it seemed unlikely anyone would notice."

"Bad news, Vega. Sergeant Hernandez in that unit saved Reese, the crewchief, and the pilot. He went through a hundred yards of enemy fire to do it, twice. Got the medal of honor for it, too," said Jack.

"Go figure," said Vega. "Just my luck. A Medal of Honor winner shows up when I'm doing my dirty deed for money. Well, that's actually good news. I didn't want anyone to die but Straker. I sabotaged the fuel lines in such a way that they could be easily fixed in a few minutes. I was pretty sure the rest would not have any trouble getting out of there alive. Straker's helo pilot made an error going in. That's why they got messed up."

"So what happened after that?" asked Kelly, really hating this man now. "Mmm-mmm, Jack. I don't know how you stand it," he said looking at the two women.

"The story, Mr. Vega. Please continue," said Catherine. She was getting tired of his good old-boy routine.

"So Colonel Minh got me a Canadian passport. He called me Emilio Vaillagaros. I laughed at that, but it was better than John Smith. I lived in Bangkok for two wonderful years, and then Colonel Minh showed up again. Vietnam was falling, and there was a lot more gold to get out. He wanted me and my boys to fly into Vietnam, load it up, and take it back to his estate in Thailand. Three trips. He said if I did, he'd make me a rich man. I didn't hesitate. I was almost out of money anyway. It was an amazing time." He paused with that memory.

"So Minh got a couple of Hueys," he continued. "We painted them to look like South Vietnamese helos, and hauled out the gold. We did it in two jumps. We got it first to one of his supply bases in Laos and then all the way into Thailand. It was the easiest money I ever made, and no one ever suspected because everything was crazy in Vietnam at the time. Six months later the country fell, we were left with a lot of the gold, and no one could prove a thing. Colonel Minh had some friends in the Thai government that helped deposit the gold into banks secretly, and overnight a new international power player was born."

"One thing, Mr. Vega," said Catherine. "Why would Colonel Minh trust you? You would seem to be a huge loose end in his conspiracy. Why wouldn't he just have you killed like Straker?"

"At first he needed me, and then I think he liked me, for a while at least," Vega replied. "We partied a lot together, and he even put me on the board of his corporation. I was adept and very helpful with planning and executing a lot of the logistical details he needed on his operations. I was a millionaire in my own right, so there was no reason to ever turn on him. Besides, I liked him too. It was love at first sight...we both loved gold!"

"I see," said Catherine, disgusted. "So how did you end up a prisoner of the Vietnamese?"

"Like I said, he needed me. When Vietnam fell, the drug smuggling conduit fell with it. It was much harder to get the drugs out to the rest of the world, and the stock was piling up. Colonel Minh started a whole new network through contacts in Burma. Vietnam was a closed door for him. They would have executed him if they could've gotten him there. I was in charge of getting the powder to bases in southern Thailand and into the Burmese network.

"That worked pretty well, but then one day he came to me and asked me to fly into Vietnam and pick up a friend near the border. He said she was important to him, and he wouldn't trust anyone else to do it. I figured he wouldn't ask me if it wasn't really important. But it was a setup. He was supposed to be coming to pick her up. She had sold him out, and they got me instead. End of story."

"So now you're a common criminal," commented Jack. "What ever happened to that guy who wanted to be an archeologist and find hidden treasure?"

"No, actually Jack, now I'm a common *prisoner*...a common Vietnamese prisoner; the worst kind. I need to get out of here. You have to help me. This may be my one and only chance to get away from these guys."

"Mr. Vega, we have a photo of you standing over a cave entrance at Thap Cham after the rocket attack," said Kelly, remembering what brought them to Vietnam in the first place. "Did you find a cave and treasure that day?"

"No...what the fuck are you talking about? I never found anything there. You have a photo?"

"Yep, this one," she said, handing him one of the eight-by-ten black-and-white photos.

"Well, I see what you mean," he said, after studying the photograph. "That does look like a cave entrance, or a man's severed torso in uniform lying on its own."

Jack took the photo and looked closely at it, then passed it to Catherine. "I'll be damned, it was an illusion all the time," he said, shaking his head.

"Amazing," said Catherine, laughing. "Who knew?"

She got serious again. "We cannot help you, Mr. Vega. Unless you help us."

"How can I do that? How can I possibly help you? I'm a goddamn guest of the Vietnamese government, probably for the rest of my life."

"They know of your association with Colonel Minh, yet you have told them nothing?" asked Kelly.

"Fuck 'em. I won't betray him. He was good to me. I'm not going to tell them anything about Colonel Minh."

"Daniel, we need your help because Colonel Minh has kidnapped my wife," said Jack.

Vega slowly lowered his glass. "For real?"

"Yes."

"Why...how?"

"Now it's your turn to listen," began Jack. "Want another drink?"

"Uh, no," said Vega, dropping his good old' boy facade. "I'm good...Say, have you guys got some coffee or tea and a sandwich?"

Kelly jumped up and said, "I'm on it."

"Remember the day we all went to the temple in Thap Cham, and were looking about for anything unusual because you thought there was a treasure there?" Jack asked.

"Sure, the gold from the Champa kingdom. It was legendary," said Vega.

"We found it," said Jack.

"*You* found it. No...really? Jack, you found the Champa treasure?"

"Well, actually the woman who found it is my wife, Mai, and now Colonel Minh has her. She was abducted off the streets of Thap Cham by some of his men three weeks ago."

"So what did you do with it? The treasure? Where did you hide it?"

Jack shook his head and looked at him, smiling. "We gave it to the Vietnamese right away. They were working closely with us as we were investigating you and Colonel Minh. We never considered keeping it."

"You what? Oh, Jack. Jack, Jack! Oh, man, I can't believe you did that. I bet it's worth millions and millions of dollars. Jack…what were you thinking?"

"Well, we didn't come here for the gold, Daniel," Jack explained. "Catherine is an accomplished and well-known television journalist back in the States, and she brought us here to track down some sources related to you and Colonel Minh to finish a book she's writing. She already discovered through her investigations most of what you revealed to us today, so we know what you told us is the truth.

"The fact is, Daniel, if we weren't at the temple one morning just looking around on a whim when Mai found the cave that held the treasure, we might all be back in the States right now."

Kelly came back and put down a tray of food in front of Vega on the bamboo coffee table.. "I brought you an iced tea to go with that. I figured you hadn't had one of those in a long time either," she said.

Vega was staring at her rear end in the short shorts as she served a plate to Jack and then one to Catherine. Catherine noticed and decided she had enough. "That's mine, Mr. Vega," she said.

Vega looked around at her sharply and said, "Oh, I'm sorry, Catherine, is it? I don't mean to offend anyone. I really don't. I apologize. It's just been a long time."

Kelly sat down and snuggled close to Catherine again. She grabbed a chip, took a bite and said, "I suppose I should be embarrassed, Mr. Vega, but I'm not. Wait till Catherine gets up. Then you'll see a real show. Her legs are longer, and her shorts are shorter than mine. Speaking for myself, I'm happy to be your sorry-you-can't-have-it reality check."

"That may be true, miss," Vega replied. "But I doubt she has an ass as perfect as yours."

In spite of herself, Catherine laughed involuntarily. "I will second that, Mr. Vega," she said, coughing and laughing. "On that, we can agree."

"I don't understand one thing," said Vega. "Why would Colonel Minh want to kidnap your wife, Jack? I don't see a connection."

"This is where it gets crazy, Daniel," he explained. "Apparently Mai's ancestors were the kings and queens of the original ancient Champa kingdom before the Vietnamese came down from the north and took it over. Mr. Nguyen thinks she is some sort of symbol for the indigenous people to rally around so they can overthrow a government here in Southeast Asia. I think Colonel Minh is holding her at his estate in Thailand. I know what you're thinking. It's crazy. But there it is."

"No, Jack," said Vega. "It's not crazy. I've heard Colonel Minh talk about that a lot, and that was five years ago. It was his dream. He wanted to unite the Champa people from Indochina and lead a revolt against the governments of some of these countries. He actually thinks he will be like a king or something of the new Champa Empire. There are millions of Champas spread out among the four countries that once made up Indochina.

"He was really into it and did a lot of research," Vega continued. "In fact, the whole idea grew out of an old partner of his who was of Champa ancestry. He told Colonel Minh over drinks one time that if he could find this legendary queen, the Hoa Cuc, he like millions of others, would follow her obediently without question. I mean, it was like they were all enthralled with this legendary queen going back a thousand years. At one point Colonel Minh told me he was thinking of finding someone to pretend to be this Champa queen.

"If your wife, Mai, is really the heir to the old kingdom," continued Vega, "the people may very well rally to her, and that would make her very valuable to Minh. In fact, Jack, that would at this time make her the most important woman in Southeast Asia, wanted by Colonel Minh, the Champa people, and the Vietnamese, all for very different reasons."

Jack paced and considered this revelation. What had Mai gotten into? Any way he lined up the facts, they spelled an uncertain future for everyone involved, and none of it looked good. He glanced over at Catherine and Kelly and could see they were thinking the same thing as they considered their options with worried looks on their faces.

"Now I see where I fit in all of this," said Vega after a moment. "You want me to lead you to Colonel Minh."

"Yes," said Jack.

"Why would I betray an old friend who gave me my chance and made me rich?" Vega asked.

"I'm your friend too," said Jack weakly.

"For ten million dollars," said Catherine, getting everyone's attention. "I will pay you ten million dollars if we get Mai out of there safely."

"What if we don't?" said Vega, astonished at the amount of money she offered. "We are talking about one of the most dangerous places in the world. It's an area where they absolutely hate Vietnamese and round-eye white guys. They know them mostly from coming to their shores and bleeding their countries of their natural wealth with a tremendous cost in the lives of their people. Those men are ruthless and cruel, and they won't hesitate to kill anyone without notice. Oh, and they are armed to the teeth. It is like medieval times but with AK-47s."

Catherine ignored that and said, "Five million now and five million when you come back with Mai alive and unhurt."

Jack and Kelly stared at Catherine, stunned by her offer. Jack never loved Catherine as much as he loved her at that moment. He was surprised and not surprised. That was just Catherine's way of doing things, instantaneous and to the point. Whatever it took to get the job done. Money was no object.

"I will want immunity from the Vietnamese government and a pass out of this piss hole of country," Vega said.

"You will have it, Mr. Vega, all of it. Will you do it?" she asked.

"Yes, I will lead you to Colonel Minh," he said, pausing and looking at Kelly again, "but only if Kelly bends over and serves Jack another drink, just between us *friends*."

For the first time, Kelly smiled at him.

Chapter 32

Thap Cham, Vietnam

Vega thought a moment and said, "One problem."

"What's that?" asked Jack.

"I don't think she's at Colonel Minh's estate in Thailand. He wouldn't bring her there. It would be too dangerous for him, if she were discovered to be there. He wouldn't be leading a revolution from there. That's the place his corporate buddies jet into every week on excursions to Thailand."

"Then where is she?" asked Jack.

"In Cambodia," said Vega. "Minh owns a whole mountain valley in northern Cambodia near the Laotian border. His brother has set up some sort of experimental clinic there, and he has an amazing compound in place. It's an old French plantation adjacent to the ruins of an ancient palace. The compound dates way back, many centuries. We used to run drugs through there all the time."

"What's his brother's name?" asked Kelly.

"I don't know except that he's a doctor. I always called him Dr. Minh," said Vega. "The area is quite remote, rugged and difficult to get into by land. It's beautiful, a real jungle paradise. He has a lot of mercenaries around there protecting the place too. It would be difficult to get in and out again without any of us getting hurt, or worse, killed."

"You could do it, couldn't you?" asked Kelly.

"Yes, ma'am, I can do it. And for ten million dollars and a ride out of here, I will," Vega said.

Catherine and Kelly smiled broadly and toasted him.

"I believe I have just made two new friends. I can't wait to get to know them better," said Vega.

Jack laughed and said, "Don't get your hopes up, Daniel."

"Or anything else either," added Kelly.

While they waited for Mr. Nguyen to return, Jack suggested they write down everything they knew about the people Mai might know in Vietnam. His idea was that one of those might have triggered Colonel Minh's interest in Mai.

"I know she was looking at a lot of catalogs for Asian art," said Kelly. "She was in contact with a lot of people over here, and she was working closely with one in particular. That's how she met Dr. Bui from Dalat. Dr. Bui gave her connections to some other dealers in Asian art, and some of those I think were from Cambodia. I would have to look at her files to see if she wrote any of them down. She never told us who her special contact was inside of Dr. Minh's organization. She said she wanted to protect her. Hold on a minute."

Kelly got up and went to the back of the house, and soon returned with an overstuffed legal briefcase full of folders. Vega watched her all the way. But Kelly surprised him as she grabbed his hand and led him over to the large desk that dominated one end of the parlor. "Why don't we go through these papers together, Mr. Vega?" she suggested. "You might see a name you recognize."

"Call me Daniel, honey," he said.

"And you can call me Miss Ryan," Kelly returned.

Catherine chuckled at the exchange and gave Jack a look. "Jack, we have heard of this Dr. Minh before somewhere. I can't remember it right now, but I know I've heard the name."

"Yeah, I got that feeling too. At least it's not Mengele. What kind of doctor is he, Daniel?" asked Jack.

"I think he's a psychiatrist," Vega said. "I really don't know. And don't ask me what a psychiatrist is doing in the middle of the Cambodian jungle. But he had a thing going on with his brother, Colonel Minh. They were conducting mind-control experiments, and I know of at least two of Colonel Minh's former enemies who graduated from that clinic. He has all the trimmings and a fully equipped operating room. The place is in the middle of nowhere but has all the modern amenities. There was a jail connected to the clinic, and I concluded that whatever they were doing, it was nothing good and none of my business. And he has the women too, Jack. There are lots of beautiful Asian women walking around wearing next to nothing and looking sexy and all. I liked to go there a lot, but it was frustrating. He doesn't share."

Jack got that bad feeling again.

From the desk, Vega said suddenly, "I recognize this name: Su Ling. She's one of the ladies who does a lot of business and production work for Colonel Minh. She is a well-educated lady and handles all of his black-market Asian art dealings. Colonel Minh told me once that she was very competent and extremely loyal. She often worked on special projects for him."

"Yes, I remember Mai mentioned that name to me at one time," said Jack. "Ah, I see here that Mai corresponded with her a lot and bought a lot of art from her," said Kelly. "She was introduced to her through Dr. Bui. It says in her notes they are old friends, and she was going to meet her over here. I would bet she is Mai's contact inside Minh's organization."

"I think she was the one Mai told me was looking into her family background. Does that mean she lied and is the traitor who put them on to Mai?" asked Jack.

"That's what we think," said Mr. Nguyen, entering the room with Colonel Jung. "Good evening to all of you. Mr. Vega, I trust you enjoyed your afternoon. Are you ready now to cooperate with us in this matter?"

"Yes, sir. I got my mind right, and I am ready to help all I can," he said, feigning sincerity.

"I am sure the ten million dollars and a promise of immunity from the Vietnamese government helped to persuade you, Mr. Vega," insisted Mr. Nguyen.

"How did you know…?"

Jack walked over and showed him the same bug Mr. Nguyen had given him earlier.

Vega looked at Jack with big eyes and then at Mr. Nguyen. "I've been rode hard and put up wet! That's not fair, Jack."

"I assure you, Mr. Vega, that if we are successful, everything will stand as offered," said Mr. Nguyen. "We want to capture Colonel Minh and to destroy this conspiracy before it becomes a viable and destructive entity."

Mr. Nguyen laid out a large map that showed the southern part of Laos, the northern part of Cambodia, and the Vietnam area across the border. They all gathered around it, and Colonel Jung explained how they thought they would proceed.

When they were done, they devised an entirely new plan based on the fountain of information from the newly reformed Daniel Vega.

Chapter 33

Siem Kulea, Northeastern Cambodia, 1989

Mai splashed the soapy water over her breasts and commanded from her bath, "Su Ling, bring the lavender oil."

Su Ling dutifully returned with a small bottle of the essential oil but paused as Mai motioned her to lean in closer.

Mai took a moment to look around her chambers for any of her handmaidens before whispering conspiratorially, "Oh God, Su Ling, maybe I'm overdoing it."

Three weeks had passed since she arrived at Siem Kulea and began her treatment under Dr. Minh. She was now Queen Dau Te Po as far as anyone in Siem Kulea was concerned. Only Su Ling, her trusted companion, and devoted subject, knew she was only pretending to be a drug-induced puppet of Dr. Minh. After Dr. Minh left her chambers that very first night when Mai arrived at Siem Kulea, Su Ling ordered all the handmaidens to their chambers for the night. Alone with Mai, she shook her awake, covered her with a cloak, and walked her groggily to the garden. She guided Mai to a bench that was hidden from the rest of the palace and spoke gently with her. Mai was confused and afraid because she did not know where she was or who took her. For Mai, everything was like a bizarre dream because of the knockout drugs Dr. Minh put in her drink.

"My lady, I am Su Ling," she began.

Mai brightened up immediately and hugged her close. "What is happening, Su Ling? What is this place, and who is that vile man?"

Su Ling explained the circumstances and what they must do if they were to survive and kill Colonel Minh, as they had planned. As Dr. Minh was managing her drugs initially, Su Ling had at great risk substituted a polymer liquid for the opiates Mai was supposed to receive that first night. After that it was easier because she personally had administered the fake opiates for the past three weeks. So far, Dr. Minh was not suspicious because Su Ling had carefully coached Mai on how to act as if she were in a drugged state of obedient helplessness. They practiced often and spent the last three weeks playing their roles while waiting for Colonel Minh to arrive so they could execute him.

That morning, Mai lounged in her royal bath in an ancient tub of black marble whose upper rim was done in a gold-leaf design, as were some of the flowered accents along the sides. Colonel Minh restored the tub and other fixtures for Queen Po's chambers using a small amount of the gold he had stolen from Vietnam. The actual royal chamber still existed almost intact within the ruins of the ancient palace complex that had existed there since the tenth century. Colonel Minh purchased the land encompassing the valley, and he expanded the French plantation adjacent to it to include the old ruins. It was a minor chore to restore it to its original glory. The chamber was decorated in beige, dark green, and maroon tile and was brightly accented with exotic flowers.

Su Ling leaned in close as she ran her hands over Mai's body and bathed her. "My lady, you are performing perfectly," she whispered. "When you are acting as if you're under his control, I cannot tell that your mind has not been taken over by Dr. Minh. He is very happy with your progress and struts about the compound like a little boy pleased with himself."

"I couldn't do it without you, Su Ling. That second night when I felt his breath near my ear, I almost gagged. And then when he started touching me during the second week, it was hard not to react. It takes everything I have to submit passively and control myself. But I think he loves me, Su Ling. He will not notice any faults if that is the case."

"No no, my lady! You must never think that. You must be very careful, or you will be lost. Do not underestimate him. He is very dangerous and very different from most men. He does not love women as you think. He regards you as a lab specimen and one of his experiments. He loves his creations and his power over you. He is fascinated and perversely excited by that. The power is what excites him. He does not love you, but instead he loves the power he has over you. It is exciting to him that he can tell you to do as he pleases and you will obey. Do not ever be familiar with him or treat him like a man in love. You must obey him without question and show only total love and subservience on your part. You must demonstrate complete, passive obedience. That is what you must do if we are to be successful with our plan. Please, my lady, be careful."

"Well, at least he's stopped the injections," said Mai. "Those were hard for you to fake, and now that I'm on the biweekly IV drip, I'm really taking none of the drugs he thinks I am." She rubbed her arm where the drip connections were administered. "Without you replacing the opiates, I would be one of his obedient petals by now.

"It's easy for me to see how he's so successful with his mind-control experiments. His hypnotic routines and mantras alone are very strong and very difficult to resist. Even without the drugs, several times I have caught myself starting to fall into his pit of helplessness and obedience from those suggestions. I am honestly not positive that he hasn't programmed something in me already. I mean, there's no way to be sure, is there? He is a diabolical and perverted monster, and I'm afraid of him."

"I should tell you, my lady, that in fact he probably has instilled some sort of obedience trigger within you. It would be a word or phrase that puts you back into a hypnotic state when you hear it. In every one of his subjects, he uses hypnotic routines to plant a trigger phrase that allows him to control his subjects should any of them ever find the strength to resist his commands. I have seen it several times. Once the trigger phrase is spoken, you will be instantly possessed, go into a trance, and be helpless again."

"How do we prevent that?" asked Mai, very concerned.

"There is only one way. We must kill him too, at the same time we kill Colonel Minh," she replied. "I will take care of that, my lady. But in any case, you shouldn't worry about it. He may not have done it to you since you are very special to them. I haven't heard that he did. Just be careful."

Since discovering what Colonel Minh intended to do with her, Mai had formulated a new plan. She would wed the monster that made her an orphan. Then that night in bed, when Colonel Minh was about to consummate their wedding vows, she would put a hairpin into his jugular vein and watch eye to eye as he helplessly bled out in front of her. She would tell him who she was and make him embrace his destruction in her family's name.

Su Ling smiled. "The lavender oil you requested, my lady," she said out loud, adding more oil to the bath. She poured hot water around Mai, who in spite of the circumstances laid her head back and relaxed in the luxurious bath.

She observed Su Ling who closed her eyes, swooned, and bowed as Mai reacted to the bath. This lady, like Dr. Bui, worshipped her. It was bizarre and beyond all reasoning, or at least anything Mai understood.

"Su Ling, please explain something to me," Mai whispered. "You have been one of Colonel Minh's most valuable and loyal people, yet you are helping me to destroy him. Why have you so easily come to serve me and work against your old master?"

"I am compelled to do so, my lady. It comes from deep within my very being. It is very fulfilling for all us Champas to serve, worship and obey our queen. It has always been that way for our people, your majesty. Besides, you are the great Hoa Cuc. Colonel Minh is just a man."

"This is all very new to me, and I think I still do not understand," said Mai. "You can't mean you are helpless to disobey me. You can decide *not* to obey me, can't you?"

"As a Champa disobeying my queen is not a choice I have, your majesty," she said. "Once I am aware that you are the Hoa Cuc, I am yours to do with as you please and I must obey. It is the most wonderful feeling in the world to give myself in service to you. It is what has been missing in my life. It fulfills me and gives me purpose. Serving and obeying you is our calling, and we Champas have been waiting for your return for a thousand years so that we may do so."

Her statement comforted Mai and reinforced what she experienced in Thap Cham with Dr. Bui. This blind devotion to her was important because she needed Su Ling if her plan to kill Colonel Minh was to succeed. But it also frightened her because she realized once more that this deep, religious-like devotion that compelled the Champa people to serve and obey her would work just as well for Colonel Minh if she somehow succumbed to Dr. Minh's hypnotic routines and became their obedient subject.

Mai considered this as she looked around the chamber and took a sip of wine from her goblet. She commented, "It's so beautiful here. I feel comfortable and at peace. Strangely, I feel like I've been here before. It's easy to forget sometimes why I'm here and what I must do. I have to tell you, it's a great comfort to have you by my side, Su Ling."

They heard footsteps approaching on the tiles outside the door leading to the verandah, and they returned to their practiced roles as servant and queen. Su Ling bowed low before her queen as she bathed.

Dr. Minh entered from the garden portico. "Ah, you are bathing, I see," he commented. He picked up a towel and went before the large, ornate bath. "Come here, my dear, and let me dry you. You look lovely today."

Mai lowered her eyes in deference toward Dr. Minh, as she was programmed to do, and stepped out of her bath. She stood on a rug in front of him as the old man eagerly dried her dripping body. He commanded, "Turn around and let me see you, Po." She turned slowly, displaying herself with her arms out, as he liked. "You will be pleased to know that your fiancé is coming in two days to inspect you," he said.

Mai trembled and ran her hands over her body quickly, as she might with an involuntary response of anticipation, but what she was really feeling was dread.

"There, there, my dear. Be patient. Your master will be here soon to claim you and make you truly happy as he crowns you queen of our new Champa kingdom. Then you will tell the Champa millions that there is only one man who is qualified to rule over them, and that is Colonel Minh."

He picked a lavender-and-white orchid from a nearby bouquet and lifted her delicate chin, so that she was looking directly into his eyes. He placed the orchid in her hair and examined her features closely.

"Stand with your hands up on your head while I inspect you, Po," he commanded.

He ran his hands over her body inspecting her. Mai hated him touching her. It required her own personal form of mind control to detach herself from reality as he did. She had not anticipated any of this when she devised her plan to get close to Colonel Minh and execute him, and it was almost more than she could tolerate.

"Are you happy, Po?" Dr. Minh asked, admiring the helpless and obedient creation standing naked in front of him like a devoted pet. He felt almost godlike when he was with her as she responded obediently to his every whim.

She repeated verbatim the words he gave her to remember. "Yes, master. I have never been happier in my life. My presence in this valley paradise fills me with great pleasure. But it is being with you and my beloved Colonel Minh that gives me the most pleasure. You are my most trusted advisor, who always knows what is best for me. I must always obey you and my beloved Colonel Minh."

She was looking at the floor as she spoke and was surprised when he turned and walked out the door, leaving her and Su Ling alone once more.

Dr. Minh was pondering a possible problem as he departed her quarters. It occurred to him that she seemed a little specious as she spoke. As he was examining her closely just before leaving, he noticed a minor flutter in her eyes where there should only be a passive obedient calm. He could take no chances. The treatment was going splendidly. But as a precaution, he decided he would personally administer a booster injection of his mind-altering combination of opiates tonight when she prepared for sleep. But before that, it would be his personal reward to have her perform for him, as did all of his petals at the end of their programming.

After the door closed, Su Ling quickly wrapped a robe around Mai's naked body and commented, "I have never seen him like this, my lady. He seems… giddy!"

That afternoon Mai once again went over her plan with Su Ling looking for any contingencies that might bring disaster. It seemed foolproof and had an excellent chance of working, provided there were no more surprises. With everything in place, Mai took a welcome nap.

Su Ling woke her and informed her of a temple dancer who had come to teach her the Sadir, a very old and sensual temple dance that was designed to inspire the libido. Mai would perform it tonight, and Dr. Minh expected it to be perfect. The dance was very erotic, and she was told it was to be performed naked before her master. Mai discussed it with Su Ling, and they decided there was no way around it if Dr. Minh was not going to be suspicious of her supposed drugged and obedient condition.

Within an hour Mai could do the dance better than the temple dancer in Su Ling's opinion, and the dancer was sent on her way. Mai was given a bite to eat, and then her handmaidens bathed her and put her hair up with gold accents placed here and there among her dark, glistening tresses. Then they placed a sheer floor-length, gold robe over her naked body and led her before the door of her chamber to await her master.

She took a deep breath as Dr. Minh walked in right on time. He motioned the handmaidens out, and they left closing the door behind them. He walked over and sat down in a large, regal, high-backed chair that was usually reserved for the queen. He undid his pants, clapped his hands, and said, "Come before your master, Po."

She walked before him with her head lowered. He clapped his hands again, and from the garden nearby music began to play, performed by the small chamber group that accompanied her meals. This music was very different and designed to invite the darkest and most erotic feelings in a slow and sensual dance. "You may begin, my lovely flower. Dance for me," he commanded.

Slowly she moved her hands up and raised her head to look at him. She undid the clasp of the sheer gold robe, and in one soft move, the garment floated to the floor, revealing her completely naked before him. She posed giving her the likeness of a human statue that had come alive. She began dancing for him as commanded, but she was really thinking of home, Jack, and anything she could while ignoring what this feckless old man was doing in front of her.

Much later, after she had performed several times, she pretended to sleep on her bed as he had commanded. She listened intently for him to leave the room so she could run to the garden and breathe some fresh air again to cleanse her mind. She was a very strong-willed woman, but this repugnant, evil man disgusted her greatly and, worse, was getting ever closer to breaking her. Her eyes were shut as she waited for the sound of the door opening and closing. She felt a cool breeze sweep over her bed. It was welcoming and comforting.

She did not hear what Dr. Minh was doing. She didn't know he was filling a syringe with a fresh dose of drugs from a special bottle he had prepared for her himself in his clinic. If she ever weakened her resistance, even without the drugs, his quiet and constant hypnotic mantras to her every night lingered in her subconscious, seeking to enslave her. And now, too late, she realized he was injecting the opiate directly into her arm. She gave a surprised start at the soft sting of the needle and raised her head in protest but fell back as she floated quickly away and gave herself up to it.

In a few moments, she was deep into Dr. Minh's world of helpless obedience. She moved her arms and legs slowly and sensually against the satin sheets of her royal bed. Nothing mattered anymore but what she felt, and she felt everything at once as if within a sensual symphony that played throughout her body. She felt warm and comforted and never wanted to lose that feeling as it built evermore glorious to a matchless euphoria. She felt as if she were in *parinirvana*, the ultimate state of escape. She moaned aloud in pure and absolute pleasure.

And with all this, she now became Dr. Minh's total slave as the hypnotic suggestions he'd planted replaced her free will; her resistance was gone. She truly belonged to her master. She was the happiest she had ever been because that was what he told her she was, and she would be whatever he wanted her to be.

Dr. Minh watched her reaction clinically, with great pride in what he had accomplished with her. He loved watching this particular subject. Of all the beautiful women he brought here and enslaved, she was by far his best work.

He drew close and spoke into her ear. "You are Dau Te Po, the rightful heir, and queen of the Champa Empire. You love and trust Dr. Minh, who is your beloved friend and advisor. You love to please and obey him. You love most of all your future husband..."

Chapter 34

Siem Kulea, Cambodia

Word of the return of their legendary Champa Queen Dau Te Po spread quickly from farm to farm, village to village, and country to country throughout Southeast Asia by the exclusive and very secret indigenous, and devoted Champa grapevine. The excitement over this event was spontaneous, and shared as sacred knowledge only among loyal Champas. It was the awakening of a sleeping spirit that was fundamental and at the core of the Champa faithful, and connected with their ancient traditions and heritage. The news of their queen's coming brought them en masse to serve, follow her, and find the fulfillment that had been denied to them for generations. For a thousand years, they had been left scattered all over Indochina before the conquering Dai Viet and Khmer armies. Now, as word of her return came to them, they were drawn on a sacred pilgrimage to the ancient valley long believed to be the final domain of Queen Dau Te Po. They came on foot, car, horseback, and by any means possible.

Not surprisingly, Colonel Minh arrived at the compound by a more modern conveyance in the form of a helicopter on the back lawn. He quickly exited with help from an assistant and hurried to find his future wife and inspect his brother's work. He was so excited and eager that he all but ran down the hallway to her royal chambers. He was in his late fifties, with a completely bald head and a round face that matched the shape of his body. His beige uniform, thick leather belt, and riding boots gave him a military look and bearing.

He threw open the big, heavy chamber doors to find Queen Po waiting before him. He was not disappointed. She was the most beautiful woman he had ever seen. Dressed as she was in a long sheer robe of red silk embroidered with small flowers, she was a vision of an earthly goddess. Remarkably, she appeared to be smiling through tears of joy upon seeing him. She stepped forward and greeted him with a kiss that was warm and sensual, like none he had ever experienced from a woman before. He asked, weak and trembling, "Who are you, dear one?"

She replied, "My dearest darling, I am your Queen, Dau Te Po. You are my master, whom I love with my whole heart, mind, being, and whom I must obey.

I am very excited that we are back together again. I have missed you greatly and I don't want to ever be away from you again."

Colonel Minh smiled broadly and stepped back. She was just as he wanted her to be and now programmed with a memory of his own design. He put his hands on his hips proudly and commanded, "Po, darling, remove your robe."

Queen Po dropped the sumptuous silk robe to the floor. As she was taught to do, looking directly at him, she ran her arms over her body provocatively. Slowly she turned for her master and put out her arms, displaying herself with a smile for his approval.

Colonel Minh was pleased. Stepping forward, he took the opportunity to run his hands over her beautiful body. The back view of this living icon was as beautiful as the front, and he took a moment to run his hand along the curve of her shapely bottom.

He found and inspected the Hoa Cuc birthmark on her hip. Indeed it was there just as he had been told. He kissed her on the back of her neck and was surprised to feel her swoon when he did. Wonderful! He thought of taking her right then, for at that moment he was as excited as she. This was something extremely rare for him given his sexual preferences. He kissed her again on the lips, and felt her entire body tremble in his arms.

Sitting off to the side, Dr. Minh surprised him suddenly with his presence when he remarked, "What do you think, my brother?"

Startled by the interruption to his intimate inspection, Colonel Minh turned and smiled as his sexual arousal fled. He nodded and said, "Ah, yes, Samuel, my very talented brother, you were right. Whew! She is exquisite indeed! She had quite an unexpected effect on me."

He hid his embarrassment as he summoned her handmaidens and commanded, "Dress Queen Po." He gave a sigh, took a deep breath and walked across the room to sit opposite his brother.

He poured himself two fingers of cognac from the decanter his brother was using. He toasted with him and declared, "To living perfection. I am going to enjoy her devotion to me for the rest of my life as we rule the new Champa kingdom together."

Her handmaidens dressed Queen Po in a traditional two-piece Champa outfit of the finest silk that matched her robe. She stood impatiently with her hands out. Her devoted eyes never left Colonel Minh. Her top was a red halter that displayed most of her beautiful breasts. Her loose silk pantaloons hung purposely low on her waist to show the Hoa Cuc birthmark. Her handmaidens finished with a few final touches including gold slippers. This was not quick enough for Queen

Po, who flittered them away impatiently and all but ran across the room to sit down beside Colonel Minh.

She picked up her waiting goblet of wine and declared smiling, "To my two favorite, adorable men, whom I dearly love." She toasted each of them and then followed that up with a kiss on Dr. Minh's cheek and another on Colonel Minh's mouth. Her happiness to be with them was evident by her demeanor. Dr. Minh noted with great pride how thrilled she appeared to be as she gazed toward Colonel Minh.

She snuggled close to Colonel Minh, kissed his neck and asked, "Darling, Doctor Minh tells me you are very busy. I hope you have reserved some time for me? I confess that I think about you all the time. I love you so much I almost cannot control myself. I want to do something to please you. Perhaps you would like me to dance for you, or maybe you will just lie back and let me make love to you. I promise you will be relaxed and in the end, blissfully happy." She ran gentle kisses up his neck and breathed into his ear.

Colonel Minh smiled and said to his brother, "Remarkable."

But then Dr. Minh said to her, "Queen Dau Te Po, isn't it a great day to be queen?"

Mai sat up straight and stiff. She turned, lowered her head and faced Dr. Minh in a hypnotic daze.

"What just happened?" asked Colonel Minh, surprised.

"That's her trigger. Use that to enter any programming you want. If she ever resists a command, simply recite that phrase to her, and she will be helpless, and ready to obey you."

"Queen Dau Te Po…"

"Queen Dau Te Po, isn't it a great day to be queen?" repeated Dr. Minh. "She is in a helpless, receptive state now, ready for programming. Do you wish to add something to her routine? You are her god now and can make her into anything you want her to be."

"You already added the crueler aspect to her personality that I requested, didn't you?" asked Colonel Minh.

"Yes, several days ago. I watched them. Su Ling practiced with her using whips and various devices in our dungeon. I have no doubt you will enjoy it. They left two slaves all but lifeless. Our Su Ling has a very sadistic nature of her own."

Colonel Minh nodded. "Yes, I was already aware of that. Actually, I do have a few things that I have planned to make things more copacetic for me and *my* personal routine. Let me explain what I want to you."

"Why don't you do it? Go ahead, try it. I think you will find it very stimulating," said Dr. Minh. "And then in the future, you can program her as you wish."

"Ah, OK," replied Colonel Minh, putting down his Cognac on the table. "Po, stand here before me," he commanded.

Again Colonel Minh inspected her and once again admired the curve of her behind, which once again gave him a rise. He turned her and examined the Hoa Cuc birthmark on her hip. "She really is the lost queen, isn't she, my brother? What remarkable luck that Su Ling came upon her. We shall have to reward Su Ling for that. You mentioned you have plans for Su Ling. I am open to any suggestions you may have." he commented.

"Po, kneel before me," Colonel Minh commanded.

After she knelt before him, he told her to look into his eyes. She looked up and gazed upon him with a look of awestruck adoration. As his brother predicted, the power he felt excited him. He took her hands in his and felt them tremble. He said to her, "Po, your love and desire for me is boundless, and I want you to demonstrate that to everyone with the way you conduct yourself in and out of my presence. When we are in public, freely show your love for me. Not with kisses, I find too many of them bothersome and I want you to avoid that. Take my arm instead and gently rub your hand over it to show your affection. Subtle touches tell everyone how all encompassing is your love for me.

"You will tell your handmaidens what an amazing and talented lover I am and how you cannot get enough of me. Tell them only I can truly satisfy you. Your handmaidens without a doubt love to gossip and will carry that bit of information to the rest of the Champa people.

"Now, Po, listen carefully and obey me. When I am staying at the Palace, you will tell your handmaidens to prepare your quarters for bed by ten o'clock each night. You will tell them you are not to be disturbed after ten because that is our time. Each night when I am here in the Palace you will have them prepare you to best arouse me in what you wear, how you smell, and how you feel. All of this must happen before ten p.m. After your handmaidens have properly prepared you, order them to go to their chambers and not to leave them until they come to serve you at dawn. You will yourself be excited that soon you will be sharing your bed with me. You will then undress, go to your bed, go to sleep, and not awaken until morning. In the morning you will wake up happy and satisfied with the memory of me coming to your room and making passionate love to you until you fell asleep.

"Finally, I want you to tell your devoted Champa people it is your wish that they obey me as they do you because I am the one and only leader who can restore the Champa Empire. They should honor me as they do you and always show the greatest respect in my presence."

When he was done, he turned toward his brother. "Did that surprise you?"

"No, not really. I, of course, am fully aware of your sexual preferences, brother. Not that I understand them. Nothing you do surprises me anymore. But it is a shame. I have created quite a sensual masterpiece in Queen Dau Te Po and her devotion to you is boundless."

Colonel Minh nodded as if it were unimportant. "Does that do it? What else do I have to do?"

"She is very bright," said Dr. Minh. "If you wish, she will repeat those commands back to you word for word, and I assure you she will obey them. She is your personal human pet to train and use as you wish. The great thing is that when you snap your fingers, she will come out of her programming and not even remember that you commanded her to do those things. She will just do them."

Colonel Minh examined his new slave as she knelt before him, still in a trance. He straightened a hair by her left ear. "What kind of things does she like to do, Samuel? I mean I really don't know anything about her."

He caressed her cheek possessively. He had waited so many years for this moment and truly enjoyed the fact that he owned the queen of the Champa people completely now. With her he would realize all of his goals and make his dreams a reality.

"Does it matter? She will like and do whatever you wish, brother. But she seems fond of horseback riding. She rides every afternoon. You should see her mounted on her black stallion. She is a vision, and the people love to see her riding around the valley. They fall to the ground in real adoration when they see her. It is something to behold."

Colonel Minh nodded and said, "Po, darling, when I snap my fingers, you will tell me it is time for your afternoon ride. You will kiss me once more and then depart."

He looked at his brother, smiling, and snapped his fingers.

Queen Po looked up, broke into a big smile and said, "Oh, you! I am in heaven here with my two handsome gentlemen. I'm really enjoying that we are finally all together, but it is time for my afternoon ride, and I love to do that. Would you like to ride with me, my love?"

"No, darling, you go on. I have lots of business to discuss with Samuel. It is all very boring but necessary. You can run along now."

She got up and gave him one final long and affectionate kiss. "I love you so much, my darling. I want you to know you have made me very happy! I have never been happier in my life."

Colonel Minh proudly watched her go, then turned to his brother and commented, "She is quite a distraction from all the work I need to do here."

He gave a sigh and then continued, "Well, wonderful indeed. It is all coming to pass, Samuel, just as we hoped. As we landed, I saw outside, coming out of the jungle thousands to pay homage to her. Wait till they see her! You know, my brother, looking at her, who would not believe she is a goddess? Such beauty, such perfection! I confess I am becoming a believer myself in this Hoa Cuc legend."

Not far away, Su Ling watched them secretly from the garden and she was deeply concerned. Somehow, in spite of all her efforts, Mai had fallen under Dr. Minh's total control and had been transformed mind and body into their image of Queen Dau Te Po. Over the last three weeks, she grew to love Mai and was astonished at her transformation from the sweet, naively innocent young American who arrived three weeks ago to the demanding and dominant goddess-queen she personified now.

But beyond that, over the last three days as Dr. Minh administered her drug dosages, she saw something else in Mai as Queen Dau Te Po that made her appear even more goddess-like. Yes, the hair, dress, and adornments physically helped to add to the image, but there was more. She had gained an aura about her that brought almost everyone who saw her to their knees in awe. She doubted that the Minh brothers saw it with their male libidos running in perverse ways. But Su Ling did. Mai now possessed a disarming ambience about her, and Su Ling was positive it had not been there on that first night. Something was different now, she was sure of it. But she didn't know exactly what it was, or why.

The two Minh brothers talked for twenty minutes about their objectives before Colonel Minh at last declared, "Samuel, she is excellent work. You should be very proud. Our little venture here has proven fortuitous and has reaped great dividends. It was money and time well invested."

"Thank you, my brother. I have some more of my work waiting for you in your private chambers," said Dr. Minh.

"Oh…really. Now I am excited. You spoil me, Samuel. I will catch up with you at dinner," said Colonel Minh as he got up and left eagerly to his chambers.

"We spoil each other," commented Dr. Minh, watching his brother leave, now so distracted by the boys waiting in his room that he had all but forgotten his beautiful queen.

A few moments later Su Ling entered and asked, "Did you permit Queen Po to go horseback riding, master?" I saw her mounting, and it wasn't scheduled."

"Yes, Colonel Minh ordered her to do that to get her away for a bit. He regarded her as a distraction. Can you believe that?"

He gave a sigh of exasperation and motioned for Su Ling to come over and sit with him. She had turned out to be very helpful in his treatments and he had learned to trust his brother's very competent and loyal assistant. He was very fond of Su Ling and during this last conversation with Colonel Minh he had gained permission as a reward from his brother to make her one of his obedient concubines when he was ready. Right now he valued her insight and counsel in their efforts to ensure Mai's continued obedience.

"You have done very well, Doctor," she commented. "Queen Dau Te Po is here with us in every sense of the word. I cannot believe how perfect she is. You should be very proud of your work. Whatever you did this time, you must try it again on your next subject. You are a like a god, creating these creatures as you do. I admit it is one of my great pleasures to watch your work."

"You talk as if you admire what I do," he said.

"Why yes! Of course, I greatly admire you, Doctor. I find what you do, and do so well to be fascinating. I've been monitoring your technique not because Colonel Minh told me to, but because I think you are a genius and I want to learn from you and continue to be of assistance when you allow me. There is something to be said about being the best at what you do. I find it very attractive and...sexy. I would be very proud to learn from you and work closely with you more often."

There followed a meaningful pause as she looked into his eyes.

He nodded as if just making a decision. "Well then, while you are here we should work more together so I can demonstrate and teach you my theory on mind control. It has taken me many years of experimentation with various routines to arrive at the techniques I use that work so well on my subjects," he told her. He was surprised and genuinely flattered by her statement.

"I would dearly love that, doctor. But I fear now that Colonel Minh is here, you will be too busy to have time to teach me anything."

He gave a sigh and nodded as he reached out and held her hand in his, "Don't worry, my dear. I will make the time to work with you."

He leaned over and gave her a gentle first kiss on her lips. She did not pull away but answered him with one of her own. This was unexpected and it took a moment before he composed himself.

He collected his thoughts and remarked, "I agree with you about Queen Dau Te Po. She is perfection and a stellar example of the validity of my routine. I have decided I will personally continue to prepare her doses and administer her injections over the next week, what with the wedding celebration and Colonel Minh showing her off to the Champa people. We want her to be devoted to him as much as her people are to her. I will let you know when you can return to administering her opiates."

Su Ling smiled, squeezed his hand and said, "Of course, Doctor. You always know what is best. I really enjoy being with you and watching you work. I would like to try it myself on some subjects. I think it would be fun to control someone the way you do and turn him or her into my own obedient, personal servant. I would love to share that experience with you. Do you think we could do that?"

"Of course. We can talk about that in more detail once Colonel Minh gets more settled in. I will look forward to that," he replied.

Su Ling smiled "I love it here in this paradise. Sometimes I think I would like to stay here forever."

Indeed, thought Dr. Minh, *and you will, but as my loving obedient concubine and partner, and I will have you begging to entertain me. No worries, my pet. I will give you all the personal servants you need.*

He lifted her delicate hand possessively and kissed it. "I tell you what. Meet me in the examination room at nine in the morning. I have a new young lady coming in and she will be a good subject with which to begin your training. It will be fun for us," he said as he gave her one last kiss on her lips. He gave a slight bow, got up and left the room.

Su Ling just sat there for a moment, stunned. At first, she did not believe what she saw in his eyes, but then she realized she had miscalculated with her pretended advances. *Oh my God! That's not love he's showing toward me. He's coming after me!* She was not fooled for a minute. She saw the desire and possessiveness in his eyes, and when he lifted her hand and kissed it, she was fully aware of the dark energy coming from him.

She now sensed a real danger she had not anticipated. She hoped there was enough time to bring Mai down from the opiates before Dr. Minh took her. He could have Su Ling arrested any time, and once she was strapped to his table, she was gone forever. She had to stick to her plan. Even now there was no other choice. She must bring Mai back first, whatever the danger to herself. She sat staring at the door where he had departed. She concluded that her pretended advances toward him might hold him off for a bit from making her one of his obedient petals.

She took a deep, worried breath, got up, and walked outside to welcome Mai when she returned from her ride. She shivered involuntarily as she walked to the stables. Her queen was so happy under Dr. Minh's control. If only she knew the hopeless danger facing them. The next few days would decide their fates.

Chapter 35

Siem Kulea, Cambodia

As part of the plan they had devised, Vega convinced Colonel Jung that the sound of the helicopters would be heard from many miles away. The only safe and sure way to rescue Mai was for a small party to land farther out and walk the twenty-mile distance over the mountains to the valley. He and Jack, with six other Vietnamese soldiers, would go in first to find and rescue Mai. The larger assault force supported by gunships would follow, in seventy-two hours. Vega believed that gave them enough time to get Mai out safely before that happened. As it was, his loyalty to Colonel Minh won out in the end and he gave coordinates for that raid on the secret base that were one hundred in the wrong direction.

After a long walk taking most of that day, Largent and Vega, with the Vietnamese troops, had made their way through the dense jungle on a trail just north of the valley. Vega knew this area well from his drug-dealing days, but he never saw it from the ground before. It was a much more difficult march through the jungle undergrowth than he had anticipated. His first goal was to get to the high ridge that marked the foothills on the other side of the mountains at the north end opposite the valley. He hoped to see it soon, because the jungle heat was wearing him down. Now he knew why he liked helicopters so much.

As they topped the crest of the hill they had been climbing for the last hour, they found a clearing. Vega saw up ahead, a mile or so away, the path to the narrow ridge that was his first destination. In another direction to his right several miles away he could barely make out through a break in the jungle foliage, long lines of Champa people making their way up the mountain. They were in an orderly procession on the one small road wide enough to drive a vehicle into the valley.

He signaled his small party to rest. They sat down on a few fallen trees and drank some water from their canteens. He smiled, pulled out the old American Colt 45 the Vietnamese had issued him back in Thap Cham and checked the clip. He did the same with his AK-47. He didn't think he would need them, but he wasn't taking any chances after getting this close.

Jack nodded toward the natives in their colorful clothing that he spotted through the jungle foliage in the far distance and said, "Is that what I think it is?"

"Yeah," said Vega. "Looks like it's already started. Those would be the devoted Champa faithful going to serve their queen. God help us. We won't be going up on that road. We're going to take a back trail I know about, one dating back a thousand years. We can avoid crowds and trouble that way."

They had talked very little since they left their helicopter, so Largent was surprised when Vega said, "Tell me about your wife, Jack." He nodded toward the long line in the far distance. "Witnessing an expression of devotion maybe not seen since the time the Egyptians built the great pyramid, I can only wonder what is so special about this woman. She must be something to get you to endure all of this to rescue her."

"If you knew Mai, you would understand. She is the most amazing woman I've ever known, or will know."

"Easy on the eyes, huh?"

"Yeah, but not just that, Daniel. She has an incredible mind, super-brain brilliant, always thinking, always into new things. I gave up trying to keep up with her a long time ago. I love her so much, I can't imagine living without her."

"You know you're a fish out of water here, right?"

Jack swatted a mosquito that landed on his arm. "Yep, pretty much."

Vega got serious and changed his demeanor accordingly. "Jack, listen to me. Minh is going to drug the hell out of her. She won't ever be the Mai that you knew before all of this," he said. "He's going to dress her up like an Asian doll and present her to the Champa people as their legendary queen. They're all going to go nuts, and blindly worship her. They'll be ready to do anything she wants while Minh uses them to take over the whole area. She's going to do anything and everything he wants, because just like all the other women they've brought to that compound, she'll be totally under his control. That's the honest truth, Jack."

Jack just looked at him sadly and nodded.

"And one other thing. We're going to have to kidnap her against her will. If she has to choose between you and Minh, she'll choose Minh. Don't expect her to see you and want to come back. She probably won't even recognize you."

"So how are we going to do that...kidnap her from a compound surrounded by thousands of devoted followers?" said Jack.

"I have a plan," said Vega.

"Care to let me in on it?" asked Jack

"No, I think it's better if you just follow my lead and go with it. You're going to get captured and taken in as my prisoner. That's all I'll tell you right now. It's going to get dicey, but trust me no matter what happens, OK?"

"Yeah, I guess so. I don't like it, but I don't really have a choice, do I? I'm in all the way whatever happens," said Jack.

After a thoughtful moment, he continued, "Thanks for doing this, Daniel. I wouldn't have a chance of rescuing her without you. I don't know how I will ever be able to repay you for this."

Vega nodded and then got up. He directed the six Vietnamese soldiers on a path up the mountain in front of them. Then he told Jack to go in front of him but to hold back just a bit from the Vietnamese troops as they started to move out.

"Say, Jack, is that amazing blond beauty good for that ten mill she offered me?" asked Vega as they made their way up the hill.

"She's a freaking billionaire and more," said Jack. "She's probably the richest person you'll ever meet, and her word is golden. She's the most generous person I know. And if she owes you, or if you have done her a favor, and Daniel, this is a major favor, you will have your future assured whatever you decide to do. She will make sure your goals happen, and with her on your side, anything is possible. In the end, I would bet she pays you much more than ten million dollars if we get Mai back."

Vega pondered that, as they got closer to the mountain pass. This was going to get complicated and dangerous real fast if he was right about the trail he had chosen. He took a deep breath and got ready for what he thought was about to happen.

As they went through a narrow path between two high walls of rock on either side, and came around a curve just cresting the mountain, Jack felt Vega's Colt pressed into the back of his head.

"Hold back here," commanded Vega. "Drop your rifle and put up your hands."

At almost the same instant, the Vietnamese soldiers who were ahead of them on the trail, were set upon by armed mercenaries firing AK-47s from all sides. They were able to offer little resistance before the instantaneous and withering fire. Five of the six Vietnamese soldiers were killed in seconds. The last struggled back past Jack and Vega and fled into the jungle barely alive. Vega could see he was wounded. He threw two shots his way above his head for show, and then pushed Jack forward.

As he and Vega advanced forward carefully they saw the five dead Vietnamese soldiers lying on the ground.

Vega yelled, "I am Daniel Vega. Don't shoot!"

Jack heard someone shout from behind the rocks in front of them, "Hold your fire!"

"Shit, Vega," Jack said.

"Yeah, I didn't think they would kill all those soldiers, but these people do hate the Vietnamese," whispered Vega. "Be smart now. They hate whites too. This is the hard part."

As they came into an open area beyond the rocks, they were confronted by eight mercenaries who pointed AK-47s at them.

Vega recognized and greeted their leader informally. "Hey, Martinez!" he said, going over and reaching out to shake hands with him.

Martinez replied with a big smile and took his outstretched hand. "Daniel Vega, it's been a long time, *mi compadre*. You took a chance to come this way. If I hadn't recognized you, you might be dead too."

Vega nodded. "Yeah, seeing you here is a big relief, my friend. I have been in a Vietnamese prison for five years. I was hoping you guys were still keeping watch on this old trail so I could get rid of my guards. You made quick work of that. The Vietnamese thought I was leading them on a secret path into the valley. No worries…the rest of the Vietnamese forces aren't anywhere near here. I gave them coordinates that were many miles away.

He pointed toward Jack. "This is Jack Largent, a man Colonel Minh will be happy to have in his jail. Did you miss me, *tu gran oso*? What trouble have you been getting into without me?" Vega bantered.

He and Martinez, being both Latino mercenaries, became good friends in the old days and raided many villages together, enemy and otherwise, under Colonel Minh. Jack observed that the mercenaries with Martinez wore newer jungle fatigues as if part of an organized force. Most of them were busy going through the pockets of the dead Vietnamese soldiers and removing their boots.

Martinez commented with a shrug, "Same old, same old, *mi compadre*. Some things never change. You know. We make a little money, we drink a lot of whiskey, and then we do it all over again.

"Oh, but wait! I forget you don't know what's going on in Siem Kulea right now!" said Martinez, suddenly with great enthusiasm. "The great queen of these people, she come back to lead them.

"I've seen her many times. Vega, she is *muy magnifico*. Oh, man, I don't think I've seen any woman so beautiful before. She says, 'Follow me,' I follow her. I swear I would follow her anywhere. She does that to you, man. It's like electricity or something, what she does, what she makes you feel. You just want to get on that ride and go with it, smiling all the way. I think I love her, man. I'm not kidding. I get light-headed every time I see her. She has that effect on me. I see her in my dreams now, and I tell you, I never sleep happier. Sometimes my men laugh at me, the way I talk about her, but I can tell they worship her too.

"Here's the thing, and believe me when I tell you," continued Martinez. "They are going to have a revolution all over Indochina. There's going to be lots of money for the taking. You came back at a good time, Vega. We're going to be very rich!"

Jack was given over to the mercenaries who immediately began stripping him. He resisted his treatment and three of the mercenaries beat him brutally and yelled at him in a language he did not understand. But he quickly got the idea as he was stripped of his shirt and backpack.

Vega walked over and quietly advised him, "Jack, don't resist. Forget everything else and think of your own survival now. It will go easier for you if you cooperate. If you resist, they will continue to hurt you, or maybe even kill you. As it is, you'll be lucky to get to Siem Kulea in one piece."

"Is that what they call the place where they're keeping her?" Jack asked bitterly. "Siem Kulea?"

"Yeah, that's where we're going. It's in a valley mostly hidden by mountains on all sides," said Vega.

Jack's arms and hands were bound painfully behind him around a bamboo pole, causing him to lean forward awkwardly with his head out, as he walked. They took his boots and even his socks to hamper any thoughts of escape. He was left with only his pants. They put a rope leash around his neck, and Martinez led him with it like a pet. Predictably, Jack ignored Vega's warning and tried to resist at first, and again the mercenaries beat him to the ground. After that, Jack gave up resistance and passively followed Martinez on their way down the mountain. He was genuinely hurt and weakened by the time they ran into the first natives an hour later and farther down the path.

It was a small party dressed in the colorful cotton and woven pants preferred by most natives in the area. Some of the women had betel-nut- blackened teeth, which made their anger toward him appear even more ominous. They hit Jack with sticks and spit on him as he went by. Jack was reminded of the similar experiences American POWs had reported during the Vietnam War. Martinez tried to drag him through quickly, but they still took their toll on Jack's strength.

Another half hour passed, and as they came around a turn farther down the path, they saw several thousand men laboring in a farm field off to the right of the path. Martinez and Vega observed the men and shared a joke that brought heavy laughter between them. The men in the field were half-naked, and wore metal collars. A few guards on horseback held whips and watched over them as they toiled in the hot sun. Jack noted that even from a distance you could see the scars on their backs where they had been brutally whipped.

Jack shook his head and yelled to his former friend, "Look, Vega! There's a good example of what you get with those medieval kings and queens you are so fond of talking about. Half of those prisoners are westerners too. Is that what you want? Fuck you, Vega!"

Vega came over just beside him and replied, "Geez, Jack. We had lots of conversations like that. I can't believe you remember. That's amaz…but really, man, take a good look at them. Martinez and I were just joking that maybe we should go work there because they are happier than we will ever be. They may be in leg irons and slave collars, but you have to admit, the guards are not driving them at all. They are very eager workers. Look at them. They look more like happy farmers than slaves, wouldn't you agree?"

Vega was right. The prisoner-slaves all seemed to have accepted their fate and were putting in their best effort, working very hard at cultivating the field where they toiled in the hot sun. They strained and tugged at the plows and almost seemed to be competing against each other to do the best job.

"I don't get it," said Jack struggling in his ropes to look again. "I see, what, three, four guards for over a thousand prisoners. Why don't the men revolt and kill those guards and free themselves? It would be easy, even if the prisoners don't have guns."

"Jack, remember one thing," said Vega leaning in with one hand on Jack's shoulder. "This is Dr. Minh's valley too. He has other more subtle means of control. The guards feed the prisoners drug-laced food, and that keeps them docile and obedient. After a while, they crave that crap the guards feed them and will do anything to continue to get it. Add in the subliminal programming that plays every night while they sleep, and what you see is what you get. Those slaves, like everyone else, now eagerly serve their new queen and Colonel Minh. They're happy, Jack. This is their life now. They have accepted it, and I bet they happily spend their days finding ways to please their masters. No slave has ever escaped from this valley, mostly because they simply don't want to, but it's impossible anyway. That's a fact."

"Drugged and programmed." repeated Jack.

Vega leaned over and spoke almost in a whisper to Jack's ear. "You are dealing with two of the most depraved men who have ever lived. This is all one big lab experiment for Dr. Minh, and Colonel Minh is worse. I would say that right now, they have a good chance of ruling this area of the world. And the only opportunity we have to stop them is to get that crazy woman of yours away from them."

An hour later they came upon more people working in the fields, only these were actual farmers and not slaves. There were about two-dozen of them, but none wore chains of any sort, and many were singing as they worked.

But as they watched, the people suddenly went to the ground, bowing in the direction of something or someone yet unseen. Martinez halted the march to look at what was happening and then exclaimed, "There she is! There is the great Queen Dau Te Po. Isn't she something, Vega? Oh man, who wouldn't want to serve a queen like that? You see? *Muy magnifico*, my friend! I told you! *La Hermosa Diosa*." Queen Po galloped across the field on an imposing black stallion. She sat proud and noble in her bearing on the animal, which she rode like a seasoned expert. Vega found himself transfixed with the same feelings Martinez had warned him about. She wore an outfit of beige riding pants, riding boots, and a white silk blouse. Her hair was pulled back and gathered in a gold-and-leather band that matched her belt. She carried a small curled whip. She stopped and spoke with her people in the field who stood and eagerly gathered around her. It was obvious they adored her and she rewarded their devotion with affectionate smiles and friendly conversation.

But then, Queen Po looked toward the road and saw the group with Martinez walking down the mountain trail. She walked her horse away from the adoring crowd and galloped over.

When Martinez and the rest of the party saw her coming toward them, they went to their knees and lowered their heads respectfully. Vega wisely followed their example as Queen Po approached. But Jack who was behind everyone remained standing, facing her as best he could while leaning over awkwardly in his bindings. He was positive that Mai would know him, in spite of what Vega had told him.

She pulled up her mount in front of Martinez. "Who is this slave who disrespects me?" she demanded in English.

Martinez tried to speak but was frozen in the midst of a swoon. He was the kind of rough, brutal character most men would fear and avoid on sight. But now his heart was racing, and he was becoming light-headed.

Queen Po lashed out at him, bringing her whip harshly across his face. "Answer me!" she commanded.

This shocked Martinez back from his momentary stupor, and he quickly looked around to make sense of her question. He was instantly enraged when he saw Jack, his prisoner, standing and looking directly at her. This showed great disrespect for his queen whom Martinez worshipped. In the next few moments, he brutally beat Jack to the ground.

"Mai! It's Jack…Mai!" Jack yelled before Martinez pushed his head into the dirt with his boot on the side of his face.

"Please, forgive me, your majesty," said Martinez humbly in English. "I will try to be better and be sure those around me show you proper respect."

Queen Po, displaying an angry façade, smiled inwardly at the reaction of this mercenary. She had observed this many times in the last few weeks when powerful, even brutal men were humbled merely by her presence. She was pleased by his submissiveness. It was one way of knowing whom to trust among the many mercenaries who now populated the valley.

"Get your boot off of him before you ruin his usefulness to us, and answer my question," she commanded.

"He is an outsider, my lady," explained Martinez as he removed his boot from Jack's face and went to his knees once more. "What he has done is unforgiveable. I will make him pay for such a grave offense. This other man has brought him to us and says Colonel Minh will want him in his jail. I was going to take them both to the colonel."

She spurred her horse forward and ordered Jack to stand up. He struggled to get up and after a moment stood beneath her in his bindings. His head was next to her gold-inlaid saddle and he was bent down almost touching the bottom of her riding boots. Bound with his head held down as he was, he was too close to look up and see her. But he tried anyway and got a painful glance. She was backlit by the sun through the trees behind her. Just then he got her scent, and he struggled desperately to look up to see her.

"Different times, different cultures, Jack. Don't mess up," Vega cautioned him in a whisper from behind.

Queen Po glanced at Vega before she drew her whip ominously over Jack. She held it up, ready to strike as she studied the prisoner. He fought the sharp pain of his bindings straining against his skin. He jerked up suddenly with all his strength in a desperate attempt to see her, but it was just at the moment she struck down with her whip, which landed hard across his face. Jack cried out and fell back to the ground, stunned by the unexpected blow. He shook his head in surprise and pain.

But as result of where he had fallen further back, he could see her now. He looked up at her sitting proudly above him. Her big stallion was held tight by the reins in her gloved hand. It protested nervously and stomped the ground not far from where Jack cowered. He struggled and managed to get himself up off the ground again and stood a little farther away gaining a less strained and full view of her.

Again he looked up at her in what looked like defiance. In reality, he just wanted to see her and to have her see him as Jack, her husband. She was not smiling and appeared even angrier as she drove her horse closer to him. He recoiled again as she struck him hard landing once more across his face. The blow caused him to lose his balance and he fell back to the ground.

Jack was not hurt greatly by the whip, even though his face now bore two red welts. He was more hurt by the simple idea that would do that to him. Once again he struggled to get up in an attempt to look at her in defiance. He gathered himself and started to raise his head and eyes again, but Vega pleaded, "No, Jack, you're playing with death. This is not a game. Bow down to her. Please! They will kill you."

After an extended pause, Jack went to his knees and lowered his head, not because he was beaten but because he saw that Vega was right and that Mai did not even know who he was. He didn't know what else to do. He felt suddenly broken and lost.

"So proud, this outsider," she said. "I will give him a reason to be proud when he bears my mark, wears my collar, and works devotedly for me in my fields." Satisfied, she turned sharply to Vega. "And who is this one?"

"I am Daniel Vega, your majesty," he said, averting his eyes. "I used to work closely with Colonel Minh, but I have been in a Vietnamese prison for five years. I captured this outsider, who may be of some interest to Colonel Minh. I have returned to serve your majesty and him."

"Your name is strangely familiar to me, Daniel Vega. If what you say is true, my husband will be pleased to hear of your return. He leads our people in a glorious revolution to restore our Champa kingdom. I'm afraid our little valley is little more than ordered chaos at the moment with so many of my devoted people coming to serve me and train for war. We are preparing a larger main camp to the west, and we will be moving many of our forces over the mountains in the next few days. Then I will have my peaceful valley back. Perhaps you may have dinner with my husband and me tonight. Be in the palace yard by sunset. If you are to be honored with our presence, you will be brought to us."

"Thank you, my lady," said Vega. "I am already honored to be in your presence. It will be my pleasure to serve you."

She walked her horse closer to Martinez. "Look at me," she commanded him.

He raised his face from where he knelt, and looked directly into her eyes. He swooned once more. He wasn't embarrassed that she had this effect on him. He didn't care what others thought. She seemed to take possession of him, and he was totally given to it.

She smiled, amused by his reaction. "What is your name?"

"I am Martinez, my lady. I am your humble, devoted servant," he replied with a sincere voice.

"I think you are one of the good ones. Obey and follow my orders to the letter if you wish to gain my favor. Do you understand? Do you speak English well?"

"Yes, Your majesty. I am ready to serve and obey you. I speak English, and a few other languages. What do you wish of me?" he asked eagerly.

"Collect yourself, and listen carefully. This slave belongs to me now," she said ominously, pointing with her whip toward Jack. "He has much spirit. That pleases me, but you have him bound too tight. You would break him even before I have a chance to do so for my own amusement. Loosen his tether so he can walk properly under your whip. Take him and lock him up in the stockade at the slave farm compound. No one is to touch him. No one is to harm him. That will be my pleasure alone. See that he is fed well. It is for my amusement and for my husband's pleasure to break strong men, not weak ones. In a few days, my husband and I will visit the compound to brand and collar him as our property. I will personally break him and bring him to his knees before my husband. He will be put to work in the fields with the others. Do not take him into town. The people will kill him. What is his name?"

"Jack Largent, my lady," said Martinez.

"Jack Largent. I know that name, but I cannot remember from where. Perhaps my husband will know."

She spurred her horse back over beside Jack and ordered him to stand. She lifted his chin up with her coiled whip, which forced him to bend his back painfully against his truss. "You should thank me for my kindness toward you, Jack Largent. With my brand on you, no one will bother you, and you can have a long and happy life working as one of my field slaves."

She raised her whip again, and Jack flinched. She laughed heartily at him, reined her horse around, and galloped off.

Jack watched her go and could think only of how much he still loved her. But he also heard her refer to Colonel Minh as her husband. It was only six weeks since they took her. Could so much change in six weeks? Vega was right. She was not the Mai he knew anymore.

Martinez put his hand on Vega's shoulder. "I guess this is where we part company, my friend. I have to take this one up to the slave camp for my queen, and you are heading into town to dine with her and Colonel Minh. You always did get the better of me. But how about Queen Po? Isn't she something?"

"Yeah, Martinez. She is indeed very special, and on so many levels! I have to say, you were right about the effect she has on people. I could feel that too. Colonel Minh got him a good one." After what he just saw, Vega wasn't sure how he was going to get her away or if it was even worth trying.

But his friend Jack was another story entirely. He looked over at Jack and shook his head. *Poor bastard.* He had to think about what just happened and what his options were. He was even more determined to get him out of there.

He said good-bye to Martinez and headed for the town without a further word to Jack. He figured there was nothing he could say to change the unexpected mess Jack was in or to give him any kind of hope.

———————————— ❋ ————————————

As Martinez loosened Jack's ropes so he could walk normally, he said, "I'll give you some advice, and if you're smart, you'll take it. The important thing for you now is to adapt to your situation. I heard what my friend Vega said to you back there on the trail and he's right. It'll go much easier for you if you don't resist as they train you.

You're a slave now. Our queen just made you one. Whatever you were before doesn't matter. That life is gone forever. You will be a slave here for the rest of your life. So get used to it, and don't resist. No slave has ever escaped from this valley. After your initial induction, and after you get your mind right, you will be fed and treated well. Like all the others who thought they could resist, you will be broken, and made eager to please your masters. All that will happen in less time than you can imagine. I have seen it many times. You will work very hard and do your best every day to find ways to please them. Why, hell, it's not a bad life, and most slaves are proud to wear her brand. I have seen them even boast about it. It is a special bond they share. It'll be OK over time. You'll see. You'll grow to like it, as they all do. I'll tell you a secret. Sometimes I think I would like to wear her brand. Maybe I envy you, huh?" He laughed.

As they marched up the hill to the slave camp, Jack was disconsolate and subdued. At one point, he surprised his captors by laughing like a crazy man. He had come all this way only to be enslaved by the very woman he was trying to save and whom he loved more than anything in the universe, with the possible exception of his little Devearney. Devearney! *Oh God,* he thought. *What have I done? I will never see my little girl again.* He moaned in real agony over his foolishness.

It was the loss of all that he loved in life that finally consumed him. He sobbed as the world caved in around him. He spent the afternoon seeing his new life through tear-swept eyes, and he could not remember a time when he felt so dejected.

Chapter 36

Siem Kulea, Cambodia

Vega came into town and found the places where he formerly stayed filled with Champas from all over Southeast Asia. The small, valley town was very crowded, and joyous as if everyone were celebrating a festival. A recruiting post off the central square was very busy with long lines seeking to join Colonel Minh's army. A continuous line of men left from there to the west with families trailing behind.

He was contemplating what to do when an old friend from his mercenary days greeted him and invited him to stay at his home. His friend, Arno, told him the Champa revolution was indeed very real and centered around their blind devotion and obedience to Queen Po. But just as in the old days, Colonel Minh actually ran the place. Arno, like Vega, was not Champa, but as he talked, Vega could tell that even he was under the spell of this Champa queen.

"Queen Po is madly in love with Colonel Minh and will do whatever he wants, and the people will do whatever *she* wants, so that puts him in charge," Arno explained. "That's OK, because he wants to build the Champa kingdom again, and that's what the people want too. So they adore Queen Po like a living goddess and celebrate the rebirth of the Champa Empire.

"But Colonel Minh's word is still the law around here. The Champas love him because he has them believing they are special and chosen. Right now you are unaffiliated and you have to be careful, Vega. One way Colonel Minh has won their favor is by demanding that all outsiders show respect toward the Champas at all times. He says they are the future rulers and elite of Southeast Asia. They believe it is their time. I have seen some of my friends arrested for talking disrespectfully to a Champa woman. Watch yourself out there."

"How many loyal Champa followers are there?" asked Vega.

"It is hard to say, my friend. Start with thousands and go from there. They come in one side of the valley and go out the other to the new camp. But I have heard there are even more going directly to the main camp and not coming through here, so it's impossible to know.

I haven't seen it, but they are getting weapons from somewhere: lots of arms, good stuff, probably from China. The word is Colonel Minh has been stockpiling arms for years and he keeps them hidden in caves on the other side of this mountain. The Chinese never did like the Vietnamese, and they would love to have a friendly state to their south. At the very least, any such struggle will greatly weaken Vietnam.

"Look, Vega," observed Arno, "if you're going to be dining proper with Colonel Minh and Queen Dau Te Po, you'll need to dress a lot nicer. We're about the same size. Let me lend you a few things, so you don't embarrass yourself."

Later that evening, at dusk, Vega entered the courtyard of the imposing structure they called the White Palace. Several hundred people were already gathered there seeking an audience. Guards dressed in jungle fatigues diligently blocked the steps leading up to the palace. They were armed with Chinese Type 56 assault rifles, a variation on the AK-47. It was the weapon of choice for most mercenaries around the world and proof to Vega that the Chinese supported their efforts.

Vega was dressed in a mixed outfit of a formal Champa shirt tied at this waist with regular dark pants. He waited and several hours later, when he was about to give up, a guard at the front portico called his name and motioned him through the doors. This guard who came from inside the palace was dressed in an ancient Champa style, with gathered skirt, big belt, and a leather strap across his chest. Vega concluded that was the style preferred for their evening banquets.

He followed the guard inside and down a long hall into a great room colored in maroon and green with gold accents throughout. It was beautifully decorated, with five columns on the left and right that were twisted and carved to look like golden ropes going up to the vaulted ceiling. The room was lit by candlelight. Asian style music of a sort Vega did not know played in the background. In the middle of the open space were tables arranged around an open area in a U shape. More than twenty couples lounged on comfortable divans behind the tables. They ate and engaged in laughter and conversation. They were all dressed in fancy Champa fashions of bright shirts and pants for men, and colorful two-piece outfits with ankle-length skirts and ornately embroidered halter-tops for women.

Vega was brought forward with a guard on either side of him holding him firmly. He saw Colonel Minh beside Queen Po, lounging at the head of the table arrangement on an ornately carved gold-leaf divan. He felt like he had walked back in time a thousand years, right down to the two slaves fanning them.

Colonel Minh was dressed in a fancy dark-green uniform probably of his own design, replete with campaign medals and decorations.

Queen Po looked spectacular in a green silk two-piece outfit that was tight and revealing. Her belly was exposed, and she lounged in a way that formed an alluring curve to her jeweled navel. The skirt conformed tightly to her figure and was slit along the left side, revealing a long, shapely leg leading to a gold sandal. Her top presented her cleavage nicely for all to admire and she wore a ruby necklace with one large stone that settled comfortably within those curves.

On first look, Vega thought she appeared bored because as the men talked, she quietly gazed around the room. But remembering what Jack told him about her intelligence, he realized she was observing everything and everyone in the room pragmatically. But then her blank expression changed to an evil smirk as her gaze settled on him. She left him feeling uncomfortable and very much like a lab specimen about to be dissected.

He stood there for a few minutes awkwardly without being recognized. Finally, Colonel Minh clapped his hands and motioned Vega to be brought forward. The two guards held Vega's arms on either side as he approached, moving forward a little of the way in the space between the tables.

Colonel Minh said, "Well, Daniel, you've returned to us. Why?"

"I escaped from a Vietnamese prison, Colonel, and came right back here to take up where I left off. I know I can be of value to you in your new rebellion, and I'm here to serve you and our beautiful queen as you wish." He bowed. "I have no doubt a helicopter pilot with my combat experience will be most useful."

"I am sorry for you, Daniel. I don't like traitors, and I take every opportunity to prove that to my men," said Colonel Minh.

"But Colonel, I…"

"You betrayed me, Vega!" Colonel Minh yelled, throwing down his napkin. "Did you think I would not know of your conspiracy with the Vietnamese to quell our rebellion before it could get started? I have people everywhere, Vega. I knew you were coming here the day you left. This ruse of yours was stupid, and if I had my way, you would be taken to the square and suffer a public death of a thousand cuts as an example to my people of what happens to those who betray me and Queen Dau Te Po. Your only saving grace is that you sent Colonel Jung's assault forces to the wrong place. Yes, I know about that too."

Queen Po leaned over and said something to Colonel Minh. She kissed him on the cheek, and then offered an evil smirk toward Vega. He shuddered because she looked like a viper in the outfit she was wearing, and he had no doubt she was deadly. It was hard to believe this woman was ever Jack's wife. In fact, he couldn't believe it, especially after what he saw out on the trail.

"Yes, my dear, I'm well aware of what I told you," said Colonel Minh. Then he announced to Vega, "Queen Dau Te Po has mercifully lobbied for your life. She argues quite correctly that she needs more slaves in her fields, as our numbers are growing every day. But I confess I only acceded to her wishes when she promised me that if I gave you to her she would provide some amusement for me as she trains you to serve us. She promises quite a show, as she breaks you and brings you to your knees for a life of devoted servitude. You belong to her now, Vega. She has invited me to visit with her the day after tomorrow to watch you and your friend formally collared, branded, and chained as her property. Frankly, I think my beloved is too kind. Take him away," he commanded with a wave of his hand in dismissal.

But as the guards were leading Vega out, Colonel Minh called after him, "Oh, Daniel, what is the name of the man you brought with you to the valley of Queen Dau Te Po?"

The guards turned Vega around and prompted him to speak with a firm nudge to his side. "Jack Largent," he replied.

Colonel Minh stopped drinking mid sip, lowered his goblet, and laughed heartily. "Jack Largent! Now that is good. How ironic. I am going to enjoy this induction a great deal!"

Chapter 37

Siem Kulea, Cambodia

Vega sat in his jail cell and muttered quietly to himself. "Sorry, Jack." He couldn't have messed this thing up more if he'd tried. He still couldn't think of anything he'd done wrong. For him, it was a win-win situation from the start. Either he would make good on his bargain and get Mai and Jack out of there, or he would settle in and work for Colonel Minh. But whatever happened, he always had a contingency for getting Jack out. He was never sure about Mai, not really. If it weren't for Minh's spies in Vietnam, it might've worked. Damn, that old man was cagey. He should have thought of that. *Spies. Of course, he had spies. Shit.*

With the reality of his circumstance, he was honestly concerned now because he too was headed for an almost certain life of mindless slavery. Colonel Minh had proudly showed his slave fields to him one day from the air. He called the unfortunate creatures laboring there his minion. Bigger and better men than Vega now labored at the behest of Colonel Minh up at that slave camp. His situation looked hopeless.

He had to think of something before they put him in those chains. Once on, they would be there for the rest of his life and certainly prevent any hope of an escape attempt. He could feel them already. *Daniel Vega, a life of slavery*, he thought. *Hell, I really messed up this time.* Suddenly that Vietnamese prison didn't look so bad.

An hour later two huge guards that appeared to be of Samoan descent came to his cell door and unlocked it. They were both a head taller than Vega, and he was not short. They were a matched pair of two of the most muscular, perfect male specimens he had ever seen. Like the guards at the banquet, they wore knee-length skirts with big leather belts that showed off their powerful physiques. As most everyone else he saw that day, they were dressed appropriately for a thousand years ago.

"You are to go with us. Put your hands behind your back," one of them ordered him.

Vega obeyed, and they shackled his hands and led him out a back way. They took him through a long underground passage, and when they came out into the night, they were near the outer walls of the compound. They took him through a side door that opened into a garden and through there directly into the queen's chambers. They brought him inside and he was astonished to be pushed to his knees before Queen Dau Te Po.

She was lounging on a pillowed divan. She was attended by a familiar face, Su Ling, who was dressed in a two-piece Champa lounging garment. Queen Po was still dressed in her banquet attire.

The room was decorated in maroon and gold with marble floors and walls. Off to one side, her bathing area was visible and in another direction was a magnificent canopied bed surrounded in hanging sheer silks. It was a very large and spectacularly luxurious room beyond anything Vega had ever seen before.

Vega heard Su Ling say to her, "I think this slave is an excellent candidate for relieving our sexual frustrations, my lady."

Queen Po remained silent as she regarded him with an expression that gave no hint as to her feelings. This made him feel very uncomfortable as before when she regarded him at the banquet. Daniel assumed nothing good was about to happen. He could not imagine what she planned to do with him, but he was of the same view as he had advised Jack earlier: "This was not a time for personal pride. Don't resist. Let them take you where they want you to go. You are going to end up there anyway."

She took a sip of wine and still said nothing as she watched his obvious anxiety build. She was devastatingly beautiful and Vega was at a distinct disadvantage in this silent contest. He had not touched a woman in over five years and he found himself weakened, even a bit light-headed before her gaze, much like his old friend Martinez had described out on the trail. He never felt anything like that before and certainly not over a woman. It was just too much all at once, and he didn't understand what he was feeling.

She studied Vega for a moment longer and then commanded, "Fetu, Ramadi, remove my slave's chains, and free his hands."

Fetu started to protest. "My lady, I do not think it wise..."

"Fetu, you know better than to question me. Do as you're told, and then you may leave. Don't concern yourself. This slave won't harm me. If he doesn't obey, you will be summoned, and I will allow you to entertain me in Colonel Minh's dungeon. You'll remain alert, Fetu, to protect your queen."

"Yes, my lady, always," he said, bowing. He and Ramadi removed Daniel's shackles, and then they left, backing out respectfully.

Queen Po commented to Su Ling. "I swear, they are so devoted to me, they would cut off their right arms if I told them to. Perhaps that is why I love them both so dearly."

"Yes, my lady, they have become more like protective brothers than guards," she replied.

Queen Po got up and walked toward the kneeling Vega, who found each step a temptation. Once beside him, she possessively fondled his cheek. He did not move but involuntarily reacted to her touch. Her smell was intoxicating, and added to the other sensations he felt, it left him breathless.

"How about you, Mr. Vega? Are you devoted to me also?" she asked.

"I...I'm not sure what you mean, your majesty," Vega replied honestly.

"My husband Colonel Minh is old and is attracted to...other things, Mr. Vega. And as much as he would like to make love to me every night, he cannot. So, sadly I sit here tonight, the sexiest, most beautiful woman for a thousand miles around and in need of a man. Do you know where I might find a such a man, Mr. Vega?" she asked, purposely tormenting him.

"Well, those two guards who just left here look like the best examples of male virility I've ever seen," commented Vega. "How about commanding one of them to give it a go?"

"Yes, my beauties...but sadly, there is a reason why they're qualified to be my personal guards, Mr. Vega," she said, giving him another gentle caress and then a soft slap on his cheek.

"Remove all of your clothing, slave. I will inspect you now," she commanded as she turned away.

While he undressed, she walked over to a table near the divan and began removing her jewelry giving each piece to Su Ling to put away. Vega did not take his eyes off of her while he disrobed. In the end, he was left naked and unable to hide what she was doing to him. When he was finished, he returned to his knees in front of her.

She smiled at his discomfort and his helpless display of sexual arousal as she approached. "Mr. Vega, I can see that you like your queen. How perfect, because I will have use of that tonight. And if you wish to find yourself in my good graces, you better perform as well as you look. Su Ling, tell my slave what happened to the last man who failed to please me." She ran the back of her hand gently across his cheek as she presented her ultimatum.

"He was tortured and is still hanging nearly dead in your dungeon," Su Ling replied.

Vega shuddered at the threat.

She walked away from Vega making each step a temptation from behind. She stopped, turned and posed for him.

"Look at your queen," she commanded him.

Vega thought the command unnecessary; his eyes had never left her since he walked into the chamber. He focused on Queen Dau Te Po as she stood before him and presented herself in a way that left no illusion as to her intentions.

She put out her hands, and Su Ling began disrobing her. First, her top came off, and Vega, in spite of himself, got even more excited upon seeing her beautiful breasts presented so proudly and demanding of his attention. In all of his wild mercenary days, he had never seen or imagined a woman as tempting as this. She knew what she was doing to him, and her smirk spoke to her amusement at his expense. Then Su Ling, in two quick motions, removed her skirt, leaving Queen Dau Te Po naked before him. She turned her hip and ran her hands over her body slowly and provocatively, and Vega was overwhelmed like never before.

At that moment she owned him in every way and she judged he was ready for her. She commanded, "Slave, come pick up your queen, and carry me to my bed."

Vega, by then overcome and even trembling with desire, got to his feet and took an aggressive step toward her, but then he stopped and stood motionless. As much as he wanted to obey her, he stopped. After a moment of frustration, he went back down to his knees.

He didn't have many scruples about anything, and morally he was worse than the devil, but he was not going to screw Jack's wife no matter who she thought she was, and no matter how much he wanted to obey her command. He couldn't do that after all he had done to Jack. *I must be nuts*, he thought.

Queen Po stood with her hands on her hips. "Slave, I command you to carry me to my bed and make love to me."

He did not move, and even he could not believe it. Finally, he shook his head and confessed quietly, "I can't."

"Why not?" she demanded, throwing her head back proudly. "You look ready to fuck something! Are you trying to make a fool of me?"

A moment passed while Vega averted his eyes to the floor honestly concerned for his life. He tried to find an answer that would assuage her anger and save him from a doubtless horrible and painful fate. His thoughts glanced at the medieval dungeon below, and the horrible devices he knew were waiting for him. He told himself he was a fool for not giving in to her wishes, and every part of him wanted to grab her up, queen or no, and take her to that bed.

"I asked you why not, slave!" she demanded again.

He was left with only the truth. "Because you're Jack's wife. He trusts me, and it wouldn't be right," he said, finally. He raised his face and looked at her defiantly.

She paused a moment and nodded. She said softly to Su Ling, "Ok, we're done with this."

Su Ling put a silk robe over Queen Po covering her nakedness. Then Su Ling ran to the door to see if the palace guards had moved to their nightly posts outside the garden walls. Queen Po stood in silence. She sipped her wine and regarded the naked Daniel Vega with a serious expression.

Su Ling returned and said eagerly, "The courtyard and pool are empty, my lady. May I? Please? You mentioned before that I might."

Queen Po walked over to where Vega knelt. She could tell he was very afraid, even shaking and wary of what she was going to do to him. Thus he was totally surprised when she kissed him on the cheek warmly. She commanded him, "Daniel, go along now with Su Ling."

She turned to Su Ling and said, "I will give you thirty minutes, and then I want both of you kneeling by my pool attending me while I swim."

"Yes, my lady," said Su Ling eagerly. Approaching Vega she said, "Don't bother putting your clothes on, Daniel, just leave them. Hurry!"

Vega was confused, and still surprised, but he responded quickly and eagerly followed Su Ling. He wasn't sure if they were headed to Colonel Minh's dungeon or what, but he decided any momentary reprieve from Queen Po's wrath was OK with him. As he followed Su Ling down the path by the pool, he saw her unhook her halter-top, and he picked up his pace.

Mai watched the two enter the little lounge room next to the pool, and smiled. She took a deep breath and felt better. So, she could trust Vega. That was important because of the helicopter; now for the next part.

She clapped her hands and summoned her personal guards, Ramadi and Fetu. Other than Su Ling, they were the two people she most trusted in Siem Kulea, and she greatly depended on them in her new life as Queen Dau Te Po. In a way, Mai and the two guards shared a bond, because just as she had been programmed, Dr. Minh had run a similar routine on them to not be able to consider Mai in any carnal way. Their physical attraction for Mai was replaced with blind, unquestioned obedience.

They returned and went to their knees and bowed before Mai. She was like a child both in size and fascination of their magnificence. She went to them, ran her hands over them, and kissed both of them possessively on their cheeks. Jack would have a fit if he saw her doing this, but who could resist such an opportunity?

She sighed and walked around them slowly. Even with them kneeling, she was barely as tall as them. She said, "Ramadi and Fetu, my beauties, you have been very loyal to me over the past weeks that we have been together here in my palace. You are my most loyal guards, and I am thankful to have your honest devotion. I know you were personally picked and programmed by Dr. Minh to serve as my personal guards. But I am curious; whom do you finally serve and obey? If you had to choose, would you obey Dr. Minh, Colonel Minh, or me? Please, I insist on the truth. I will not think less of you even if choose either of them."

Fetu raised his head but kept his eyes averted as he replied, "We are loyal to only you, my queen. Even though we have become aware that he has done something to us, we also know that you have our total loyalty and obedience."

Mai commented. "Yes, we share that bond in that I am also programmed to serve our masters. Are you aware how Dr. Minh has programmed you? For instance, what commands has he given you regarding him and Colonel Minh? Do you perhaps know your trigger phrase?"

"Your majesty," replied Ramadi, looking straight ahead while kneeling at attention, "at first I was not aware of any such influence as you call programming. But later I became surprised by my feelings in regard to Dr. and Colonel Minh, and I suspect they have made me to feel that way."

"What feelings?" she asked.

"I do not wish to harm them in any way, your majesty," he said.

"What if I commanded you to kill them?" she asked. "Could you do that if I commanded it?"

"In that instance, I confess I am not sure, your majesty. My primary command is to obey you before all others and to protect you with my life. That is something I feel at the core of my being and it is my purpose for living. But I have regarded Dr. Minh in the past when he was in my presence and thought I must not physically harm him."

Mai considered this for a moment and decided it would not interfere with her plans.

She turned to them and said, "Then listen carefully. You needn't be concerned. I will never command you to harm Colonel Minh or Dr. Minh in any physical way.

"I am going to escape from this valley and Colonel Minh in two days. I care about you and want you to go with me, but you must help others to escape also. Will you do this?" She asked them.

"We are ready to obey your every command, my lady," said Fetu.

"We are ready to die for you, my queen," Ramadi said.

She sighed and nodded. "Yes, I know, because of the programming, no doubt. You are like protective brothers to me, and I love you both very much. I can promise you that if you help us, you will have a very happy future with me."

"With respect, my lady," said Ramadi, "We have feelings of devotion for you that transcend anything Dr. Minh has done with us. We are both sure of it. Tell us what we can do to help. We have a deep and sincere desire to serve you."

Mai smiled at them. "Good, we share that bond also. Now listen to my plan and your part in it. You may tell no one."

She told them her plan and at intervals asked them if they could find any fault with it. They suggested a couple of adjustments but assured her they would have everything in place and be ready to fulfill her wishes when she landed at the slave farm the day after tomorrow.

Then they asked about Daniel Vega, and she told them, "He is the key to our escape. Be sure he is not harmed and that he is kept healthy enough to fly that helicopter well.

"Unfortunately, he has an attitude problem that you must guard against, especially when he finds out he is going to escape. An arrogant slave is something that will not be tolerated by other guards or free people in this valley. Treat him and my husband, Jack, as slaves. Be harsh with them if you must, but without really harming them. Vega is vital for my plan to work, and Jack is my dearest and is most special to me. But we cannot risk any suspicion, so weigh your actions carefully. Protect them, isolate them and keep them away from others while giving the appearance of treating both of them as common slaves.

"My beauties, I love you both very much, and you have pleased me greatly," Mai said finally as she kissed each of them once more on the cheek. She sent the guards on their way and told them she would send for them when she retired. She further ordered them to see that no one, including her handmaidens, disturbs her until then.

She slipped outside to the pool area and retrieved a swimming cap that she put on over her hair to keep her tresses dry. It was purple and regal, like a crown in its look, even with a small hoa cuc in gold on the front rim. After she adjusted the sides, she dropped her robe by the pool. Only pool lights illuminated the area giving a sense of peaceful and quiet privacy.

Sitting on the tiled edge, she slipped down into the warm, welcoming water. She dipped her head and dived down deep and came back up again, shaking the water from her face. The heated pool felt comforting, and it helped her to relax. She swam back and forth a few laps to relieve her frustrations and finally returned to the edge of the pool.

She saw that Su Ling and Vega were dressed once more and kneeling by the pool, with their heads bowed to the ground, as she had commanded.

She put her arms over the edge of the pool and commanded, "Su Ling, bring me wine. Daniel, fetch a towel and dry my face." She was amused as they both jumped up quickly to obey her.

Su Ling left and then returned with a goblet of wine, which she sat in front of her. Daniel brought some towels, dabbed her face gently around her eyes, and then dried most of the moisture from around her head. He doubled up another towel and laid it at the edge of the pool for Mai to rest her arms on. She was impressed by that simple gesture. He had turned out to be an unexpected resource, but he still remained a complicated factor in her plans.

Mai took a sip and regarded them both. She watched as Vega knelt back down, with his head bowed and his arms locked behind his back, echoing the proper slave position of Su Ling. This queen stuff was pretty cool. Mai took a moment to watch them. Su Ling had already demonstrated her selfless devotion, but Daniel who mimicked her actions was another story entirely.

She waved her hand at them. OK, you two, relax. Get some towels, and lie down with your heads over here close to me. I don't want anyone to hear our conversation."

Su Ling grabbed some large towels and laid them on the tile. She and Daniel both moved toward the pool and lay straight out by the edge, looking very much like they were prostrating themselves before her. This allowed them to protect their conversation.

"That's better," she said. "I am Mai, Daniel, and, as you said, Jack's wife. As you have passed my little test, I sincerely hope for all of our sakes you meant what you said back there. You now have met Su Ling formally. I wonder if you had a proper introduction?"

Su Ling laughed. "He's pretty good, my lady. Thank you. I like him a lot. Whew! I needed that."

"When all of this is over, Su Ling, I will give him to you as your reward for serving me so loyally," she said sincerely while studying Daniel's reaction.

"Fine with me!" Vega blurted out eagerly. "Not so long ago, I didn't think I was ever going to be with a woman again. I think I'm in love. Honestly."

There was a moment's pause as both women regarded his remarks. Mai shook her head. His rudeness in speaking out of turn was exactly what she was concerned about and especially since he wasn't aware he did anything wrong.

"What?" he asked. They were both frowning at his lack of understanding of his situation.

Su Ling took a breath and said, "Now that Queen Po has returned, in Siem Kulea there is a new social order and rules. The first is that everyone, especially slaves, show respect toward Champas and free people at all times. Slaves do not speak unless spoken to and given permission. You have to understand our ways, Daniel. My queen owns you now. You are her slave, according to our Champa tradition. To the outside world and in this century, it may seem ridiculous, but for any of our people in this valley, it is very real because of those traditions and beliefs that go back many thousands of years. In this valley she really owns you. I could not be with you without her permission. So when she just promised to give you to me, it means just that. I will own you then. You will be my property. Do you still feel so eager to be with me?"

"Wow. Really? So you think anyone can just enslave anyone else?" he asked. "How is that supposed to work?"

"No, Daniel. Stop it, please," said Su Ling showing her frustration and irritation with him. "We are trying to help you so you can help us. There are consequences for such an attitude as yours. Remember, Mai is our queen, our sovereign. As such, she can decide if we live our lives as slaves or free people. Only our sovereign can make us slaves to each other."

"Daniel," said Mai, "we are speaking of the lifestyle in this valley, here and now. However foreign it may seem to you and I, they are living one thousand years in the past. I believe it was you I heard say out on the trail, 'Different times, different cultures' to my husband. Until we get out of this place, be very respectful to the free people in this valley. They take this stuff seriously around here; too seriously if you ask me. I don't want you to get hurt just when we need you. If you insult or sass a free person, they can have you severely punished, and even I would not be able to help you. I am very concerned about your attitude. You must lose it and humble yourself before everyone now, or you will positively end up at that slave farm for the rest of your life."

"I admit I am having trouble understanding any of this," Vega replied. "Why was it necessary for you to test me the way that you did?"

"I needed to be sure where your loyalties lie, Daniel. Colonel Minh told me all about you. You served Colonel Minh for many years; quite loyally from what I've heard. And now you have sided with his enemies, the Vietnamese. It seems you can change colors like a chameleon, and I had to know whether I could depend on you, or not."

"Oh. Well, Mai, I have to tell you that was *not* a good test for any man, especially a man who has been in a prison the last five years. Except for one thing, I would have easily given in to that temptation."

"Yes, I am aware of that. But that one thing was the most important part, and it was necessarily an all-or-nothing test because what we are about to do is very dangerous. You play the roguish mercenary, not caring about anything or anyone but money. But I have discovered that you are actually a man of great character when it comes to your friendships. I don't know you, but I know you are the best friend my husband could have."

Daniel replied honestly, "You should know that my changing sides was not as simple as it appears. Ms. Marsh offered to pay me ten million dollars and free me from the Vietnamese prison if I got you out of here. That was an offer

I couldn't turn down. But I will admit I came here with mixed feelings and was unsure what I was going to do when I got here. I confess I am still unsure."

Su Ling noted what he said and took his hand and gave it a gentle squeeze that he answered in kind.

But then he had another thought. It occurred to Daniel at that moment that Colonel Minh might be interested enough in Mai's planned betrayal to reward him with his freedom. That was worth considering further.

Mai gave him a frown and shook her head even as he thought this. "Yes, as I said, a chameleon. Your loyalty to Colonel Minh is senseless in my view, and that only adds to your arrogance. But telling Colonel Minh about my plans won't gain you your freedom."

Daniel was stunned and said, "Huh? What did you just say?"

She smiled at him. "I can tell what you're thinking, Daniel. I have always been able to sense when someone is being false or of bad character, but recently I have become aware that I can read the thoughts of others. Trust me, and accept that you are mine and must follow and obey me. That is your only hope of getting out of here."

Daniel's mouth dropped open as he gazed at her in real amazement. He smiled. "Well, that is an easy choice anyway."

After a moment, he looked around and asked, "What if Colonel Minh finds us out here?"

"Oh, don't worry about him. He and that weasel brother of his go to bed early every night. He couldn't even take me on my wedding night, which fortunately I don't remember, but Su Ling saw the whole thing.

The good news is that I am just a showpiece for him. He likes little boys and is a real dyed-in-the-wool pervert along with that evil doctor brother of his. Everyone thinks he's taking me to his bed every night, and he wants to keep that image out there. So he sends me to my room, and I obey my master gladly," she smiled at the irony.

She took a sip of her wine and continued. "His evil doctor brother is a different story. I keep waiting for him to show up ready to rape me. I have no idea what he has done to me. I only know I am programmed like a freaking computer to obey his will on command. I am absolutely afraid of what he will do with me or have me do at his command. Fortunately, in his mind, he is done with my processing and has turned me over to Colonel Minh to use for his personal agenda which includes conquering all of Southeast Asia."

"Did he drug you? I've seen a lot of his petals, as he calls them. They will do anything he wants. I don't think they even know what they're doing."

"Daniel, if you came here several weeks ago, you would have really met that Queen Po you saw out there today on the trail. Su Ling brought my mind back partially by altering the opiates that were breaking down my resistance to his hypnotic suggestions. She has learned a lot while assisting Dr. Minh and even worked on undoing what he has done with me. They have a drug here in this valley that is well known among the natives. It is terrific for rehabilitating drug addicts. As a result, where I was a total and obedient slave before, I am now somewhat independent, but with the knowledge that I am still vulnerable.

"I am still addicted and not over the opiates yet because I won't let Su Ling stop administering them to me. There is something else more extraordinary, even magical going on in my head, and if we get out of here, I want to explore it further. But at least she has adjusted the drugs given to me and freed my will from his control. She has saved me from his control twice now.

"Because I am a great actress, and a natural at being an arrogant and demanding queen, Colonel Minh has no idea I have my mind and my independence back," she continued. "It's really a trip. Another time, another place, I might just settle in. It's a great gig!"

She put her goblet down and, in the next moment, turned to the pool and swam away from them. She did several laps ignoring them and enjoying the relaxing feel of the warm water. She dove down deep, revealing her beautiful naked bottom clearly above the water as she began her dive.

She returned to them, shaking the water from her cap. As Daniel again dabbed and dried her face, he joked, "Phew...wow! How many kids do you and Jack have?"

She looked at the enthralled adoring expression on his face and said, "I am quite aware of the impact the image of the Hoa Cuc and my physical presence seems to have on everyone in this valley. All these people bowing to me really was annoying at first, but I confess that now I like it. It does wonderful things for my ego. I have to keep reminding myself that I have a husband whose wishes I love to defer to most of the time. Presently, I am committed to doing what I came here for and getting him out of here safely. I am prepared to do anything it takes to make that happen."

She smiled at him and continued, "Two months ago I was living in Chicago. I bet you wouldn't have that same thought if we were back in Chicago with me in a pool like this. It's crazy and most curious when you think I am still little Mai Sambaht, Jack's wife.

"Yes, my lady," said Su Ling. "That's who you were when you arrived here. But I have noticed a change in you. There is something, a sort of feeling, which makes me regard you with great deference. It is something that makes me want to worship and obey you beyond just the Champa heritage and tradition. That was not there at the beginning. There is an ambiance about you now, and it is really powerful."

"She's right. I'm somewhat of an expert now, having been formally tested by you," said Vega, smiling. "You had me without taking your dress off. I have never felt anything like that before for any woman."

Mai gave a smile and a smirk. "Well, Daniel, I am positive five years in prison is much to blame for that. But seriously, I have thought on this a lot.

"Something wonderful is happening within me. The legendary Queen Dau Te Po is really and actually with us. She is talking to me. I feel her words and thoughts all the time now as a result of the opiates expanding my senses. I have memories of the past and my ancestors I never had before. It is just so new and strange that I am still processing it, and I don't quite know what to think about it yet so I am taking it slowly, day by day."

Su Ling brought Mai more wine and presented a plate of fruit, cheese pastries, and sweets.

Mai chose a cheese pastry and continued, "Daniel, we knew you were coming, through Colonel Minh's spies. That is why I was out there riding when you came down the mountain trail. I went there to protect Jack if I could. I recognized Jack, of course, but I couldn't do anything about it then. It was necessary for me to play the part if we're ever going to get out of here. Jack in his defiance kept flinching before my whip, and I kept hitting him in the face accidentally when I was aiming for his shoulder."

Mai took a sip and continued, "Colonel Minh commanded his guards at the pass to intercept you, although I don't think he realized Martinez would be in charge and that he was an old friend of yours. I suspect Martinez felt you were still loyal to Colonel Minh. I couldn't take any chances. If they had the slightest clue I was not Queen Dau Te Po as they programmed me to be, they would drug me again, and we would all spend the rest of our lives here."

"Yeah, well, now I'm a prisoner just like Jack," Vega said somewhat bitterly reaching for a pastry.

Su Ling slapped his hand. Those are for Queen Po. Slaves don't eat until given permission and certainly nothing like this." She was genuinely angry with him.

Mai regarded him clinically. "A slave," she corrected him. "You're a slave just like Jack, Daniel, and you better get your brain wrapped around that and show some humility, or you will get us all killed. I mean that."

She pushed the dish of pastry toward him. "Go ahead, but remember your place. You are an unexpected and welcome asset, and part of our plan now. But you could easily bring the whole thing down with your attitude and your mouth. Play the part well and we can get through this."

Daniel looked at Mai and then turned around to look at Su Ling. For the first time, he realized they were not joking about his slave status. He took a pastry because he was very hungry and nodded a thank you toward Mai.

"Yeah, a slave, and that's even worse. OK. But the bottom line is I'm no help to anyone. Once they get those chains on me and put me to work out in those fields, there is no escape. You know that, as well as I do. No one has ever escaped from that work camp. I can't imagine what Jack is thinking right now. I'm sure they're ready to introduce him to the farm routines. The first thing they do up there is whip them bloody and weaken them. When they get to the second-stage, the scourging, with those horrible studded whips of theirs, it will be all over for him."

"Yes, but I don't think we have to worry about that," Mai said. "Remember, I ordered that he be put in a cell, well fed, and not be touched until I get there. Who knew that crazy husband of mine would try to save me? Who does he think he is, Batman?" She shook her head and laughed realizing the irony. "I really got us in a mess this time."

"Why are you here in the first place, Mai?" Vega asked. "Jack almost thinks you knew you were going to be kidnapped, and it appeared to him that you let them take you here for some reason."

"Mmm…yeah, I did, Daniel. I even helped plan it with Su Ling. I came here to kill Colonel Minh. He ruthlessly killed my parents when I was still a little girl. He doesn't know that or realize who my parents were. I admit I am obsessed with killing him. It drives everything I do, even now. I was going to do it on my wedding night, but then his equally depraved brother messed up our plans by injecting me with a super dose of drugs before Colonel Minh arrived, and I spent three weeks as their obedient slave. I have to tell you, my free will was gone. It was really powerful stuff. They owned me, Daniel. I spent my days obsessed with finding ways to please them. I did some cruel and horrible things to many slaves who still languish in the dungeon below."

"But as I said before, I'm most afraid of Dr. Minh because Su Ling told me she believes he has planted a posthypnotic trigger in me as part of his routine that will allow him to put me in his control any time he wishes, regardless of the drugs. She has seen it work with his other victims. I shudder when I think about it. That scares me more than anything. That is why he is so confident around those of us he has programmed. We are like his puppets, and he knows he has his very own safety switch that lets him take absolute control of us anytime he wishes."

"That is why I'm going to kill him," said Su Ling. "I am going to kill him before he knows what's happening, and that will end all of this."

Mai smiled and took Su Ling's hand. "You will have your chance soon. Be sure you are ready. If he takes you, we're all lost."

"You've been through a lot, Mai. I think it's time we just get you out of here. So what's your plan?" Daniel asked.

"Ramadi and Fetu, my personal guards, will be taking you out to the work farm tomorrow morning. When you arrive, they are going to put leg irons on you and Jack like all new slaves. They tell me it will look like they are using normal hot rivets to seal the irons on you. But they will slip in special rivets to temporarily hold the leg irons in place around your ankles.

"Ramadi and Fetu will watch over you so the other guards do not bother or abuse you. They will tell the guards I want both of you to be closely watched by them until Colonel Minh arrives to formally collar, brand, and whip you. I am sorry about the collars, but Ramadi tells me there is no way around that. They are about one inch thick and lock permanently when closed, but they are not tight. We will have to remove them later sometime if we can figure out a way to do it. Then I will brand Jack and…"

"Lady, you are a piece of work," interrupted Vega, shaking his head. "That's your plan? To put us in chains, whip us, collar us, and brand us? I hope I didn't hear you right."

"Daniel, you can't talk to her majesty like that!" Su Ling quickly warned with a hand on his shoulder.

Mai slapped him hard across his face and then again. She gave him a stern warning at the end of her finger. "I'm not kidding, Daniel. You better get your mind right in this, or we will all end up here. This is all very real and not a game. If you don't wise up, I will give you back to Colonel Minh to do what he intended in the first place!"

Vega bit his lip and nodded seriously. She continued, "Colonel Minh and I will be coming out to supervise your branding and formal induction as my slaves the day after tomorrow. Colonel Minh will be at his rebel-army base camp over the mountain in the morning until then. So, we will be arriving in a helicopter, because Colonel Minh doesn't like to ride horses."

"Wait a minute, my beautiful queen," said Vega, suddenly understanding. "It's going to be you, me, Jack, and a helicopter?"

"Yep, and I assume you can fly it," she affirmed.

He nodded. "You bet your beautiful queenly ass I can!" he replied eagerly.

"Then you and Jack must be ready when it is time for us to escape. Trust me, you will know when it's time.

"Now listen. This is important. Do not tell Jack anything about our plan to escape. His desperation before Colonel Minh and the evidence of your pretended helplessness will help to ensure our success. It must be convincing in his eyes. That's what excites Colonel Minh, and it will distract him. I expect you to plead to Colonel Minh for mercy, acting as if your life depended on it. And you know what? It actually does! So for all our sakes, be smart!"

Mai looked at him smiling eagerly back at her and said, "And now it is time for some training because you're still not humble or desperate enough to act convincingly within my plan." Mai clapped her hands and yelled, "Guards!"

Ramadi and Fetu entered and came before her on one knee.

"Seize him!" she commanded.

"Yes, my queen," said Ramadi respectfully. He bent down and held Vega firmly with an arm around his neck.

Mai looked at Vega and explained, "I am going to have them beat you now. If Colonel Minh hears anything about you being here tonight and is curious in the morning, I want to have evidence that I beat my new slave for my amusement the night before."

"Ramadi and Fetu, mark him where it shows, but not where it will impair his ability to walk or fly anytime soon. I think a black eye and a few bruises will suffice," she said.

"Mai, please! This is all new to me. I meant no disrespect," Vega pleaded while her two guards held him firmly.

She motioned her guards to bring him closer so she looked directly into his eyes. "Now, you listen to me and mark my words, Daniel. If you do anything to mess this up because of your cavalier attitude, I will personally see that you suffer painfully for weeks and are tortured slowly to death in Colonel Minh's dungeon." Mai slapped him hard. "That is not a threat, Daniel Vega. That is a promise."

You're already on my list for bringing Jack here and letting him get captured."

Mai waved him away nodding to Ramadi who pulled Vega up to his knees and held him firmly there.

After Mai climbed out of the pool, Su Ling wrapped a robe around her, retrieved her goblet of wine, and followed her to a padded chair nearby. Mai sat down and settled in, taking the goblet from Su Ling.

Su Ling removed Mai's swimming cap and began drying her hair from behind. Vega looked at the two serious women and realized his arrogance had gotten him in trouble again.

He saw Mai give a nod for the guards to proceed. He never saw the first blow coming, which landed hard on the side of his face, definitely bound to leave a bruise. The guards continued to beat him superficially for a few minutes until Mai, with a wave of her hand, motioned for them to stop.

Then she commanded, "Take the slave back to his cell."

They dragged Vega back to his cell and threw him in. He hit the floor hard, rolled over, and faced the ceiling, exhausted and hurting in a dozen places.

So that's Mai, he thought. *Wow!*

Chapter 38

Siem Kulea, Cambodia

Ramadi and Fetu, wearing jungle fatigues, arrived at the slave farm on horseback, with Vega bound on a separate horse in tow. Vega was dressed in the in the shirt and pants that his friend Arno had lent him two nights before. But now it was soiled and in tattered in several place.

Two of the Asian guards at the compound waved them a friendly greeting upon seeing them.

It was midday and very hot, and Vega was surprised to see Jack was chained up and hanging naked from a post in the compound. His pants were on the ground nearby. He was sweating profusely, and it was apparent he had hung there all morning. His back was striped with the evidence that a whipping had already begun and no doubt from the bullwhip one of the guards carried. Vega knew from the past that this was all part of Dr. Minh's routine for breaking captives and turning them into obedient workers in the fields. But Mai had specifically ordered that Jack not be harmed until she arrived.

He said, "Ramadi, that man they are whipping is Jack, Queen Po's real husband, and the one she said was to be left alone until she arrived. She's going to be very upset when she sees what they have done to him."

At almost the same time, one of the guards yelled to them, "So you bring us another slave to break. I will get him started."

Ramadi walked his horse over to him and instead demanded angrily, "Who ordered that slave beaten?"

"It is the first thing we do with all the slaves who come here, Master Ramadi," he explained. "It is our normal procedure. You know that is our way here. What is the concern about this one? It is only a slave." The guard shrugged.

Ramadi dismounted with Fetu. He roughly pulled Vega from his horse throwing him to the ground in a demonstration of his anger. He stepped up to the little Asian guard, who barely came to his upper chest. "Queen Po left instructions that this slave was not to be harmed. She wants the pleasure of breaking these two slaves herself when she visits this farm tomorrow. These are to be trained only by her. She informed me that you were given specific instructions about that."

He lashed out viciously at the guard with his whip, marking a cut across his face. Ramadi continued to beat him until the guard was bloodied and cowering in a fetal position on the ground before him.

The other guard rushed forward, went to his knees, bowed his head, and pleaded, "We are sorry, Master Ramadi. We were not told this slave was different from the others. We found him locked in a cell waiting for us when we came back from the work fields yesterday. There were two notes in different languages nailed to the door of the cell. We saw the notes, but they were written in two languages we could not read. We only recognized the Spanish words for 'slave' and 'whip' on one of the notes, so we assumed those were instructions to break in this slave like all the rest. I swear we did not know! We will take him down immediately."

Ramadi followed the two guards, who hurried to the post where Jack sweated and hung limp in the hot sun. Ramadi examined his back and saw that the bullwhipping had brought red welts and blood in several areas, but a closer inspection showed that they had arrived before the whipping in the second-stage became severe enough to bring the inevitable scarring that marked every slave at the compound.

"I would not want to be you when Queen Dau Te Po sees what you have done to her slave," said Ramadi. "It is very likely you will be whipped and put in chains beside him for disobeying her."

With great care the guards helped Jack down from where he hung. They helped him to put back on his pants. Because he was weak and dehydrated, Jack began to wander around aimlessly. Ramadi grabbed him by the arm and said, "Follow me." Jack blindly followed, and offered no resistance.

Fetu fired up the hot coals so they could put the two new slaves in leg irons. When the coals were ready, Ramadi placed the usual rivets for their shackles into the cauldron. Then he turned to Fetu, and nodded.

Jack and Vega were both told to stand by the hot cauldron on a stone platform, which was about three feet high. As they did, the two Asian farm guards stood to one side and nervously watched them as they argued with each other.

Fetu turned on them and let out a loud grunt in anger. He took up a bullwhip and went after both of the guards, shouting, "Get your weak, puny asses out of here, and I do not want to see your faces again before we leave with our queen tomorrow. Because you are ignorant and stupid fools who cannot even read, you have betrayed her majesty and deprived her of the pleasure of breaking this slave herself. I guarantee you will suffer for that."

The guards quickly retreated from the area.

"Are they gone?" asked Ramadi as he began placing the shackles around Vega's feet.

"Yeah, the little mice have fled, my brother," said Fetu.

Ramadi told Jack and Vega to sit at the edge of the stone platform. He grabbed some ointment, clean cloths, and a bucket of water. He stepped up on the platform behind Jack, and began cleaning Jack's wounded back. Jack was surprised at the sudden kindness from this huge and serious-looking guard.

In a few minutes, Ramadi was done. "That will have to do for now. Queen Po will not be pleased, my brother," he said to Fetu. "They broke the skin in a few places but I do not believe it will leave any scarring."

He gave Jack a drink of water and cautioned him to sip it because he was very dehydrated. After several swallows, Jack stopped drinking and nodded to him.

Ramadi ordered both Jack and Vega to stand again and put their feet close to the edge of the stone platform. Ramadi placed leg irons around their ankles and closed them. He retrieved cold rivets from his pocket and inserted them into the holes, locking the leg irons on their feet. Afterward, the two huge guards stood in front of them, inspecting their work. "I think that will do for now, my brother," said Ramadi.

Jack whispered to Vega. "What's going on? What are you doing here and now a slave like me?"

"Silence!" commanded Ramadi as he pushed Jack and Vega roughly to the ground from the stone platform and ushered them to the stockade.

When they were locked in the confines of the stockade cell, Vega asked, "How're you doing, Jack?"

"I don't know how much more of this I can take," Jack replied. "I never thought I would say it, but I have no doubt they can break me. I don't want to get whipped or beaten anymore."

"Jack, you're not alone. Your reaction is normal. This is not a time for pride. They have broken many men stronger than you, and these guys are sadistic experts. Remember what I told you on the trail. Don't resist. Let them take you where they want you to go. You will end up there anyway.

"When we rode up just now, they were just beginning with your training. You were to be whipped from time to time for the rest of the day and tomorrow, as is the normal procedure. There isn't anything you or I can do about it. They own us now, and they're going to train us to serve them in the most savage way you can imagine. I have seen this process before, Jack. It works on even the hardest men. Accept it. Let them train you to serve them. We are slaves now. That's all there is to it."

The cell door opened, and Ramadi put down two plates of food. He left and returned with a tin of water and a few clean rags. He gave the water to Jack, saying, "Remember, drink it slowly. Sip it at first. You are very dehydrated. I will return with more food and water until you get your strength back."

Jack was surprised by the sudden kindness and started to attack the food but stopped, remembering what Vega had told him on the trail previously about the drugging of prisoners to make them docile.

Vega saw the hesitation. "Go ahead and eat, Jack. You need it. That's real food, like what the guards eat. As you become a permanent guest here, you'll be eating something that looks like putrid mush designed to give you all the nutrients you need to do your work, and you will get it three times a day. As bad as that sounds, after a while, you will be begging for it, along with the drugs in it, and you will do anything they want to keep it coming. But not to worry. By then you will be little more than a mindless animal and won't even know or care what you're doing. They're giving you real food because Queen Po wants you healthy so she can break you into submission herself. Apparently that's one of her favorite things to do, breaking in slaves, and Colonel Minh gets his jollies watching her do it."

Jack attacked the food and drank the water as advised. An hour later he was feeling better in spite of the heat in their cell. "So this is it? We're stuck here now as slaves? Wait. You never said. Why are you a slave?" he asked, wiping the sweat off his face with a rag Ramadi left with the food. "I thought these were your people."

"Colonel Minh knew we were coming, Jack. He was waiting for us. Last night after dinner, I was brought in expecting to be greeted, and instead, I was put in handcuffs, imprisoned, and given along with you to that cruel bitch queen of his to brand and keep as her slave. From what I heard last night in the jail, he loves to watch his queen torturing helpless victims."

"Mai? Mai does that?" asked Jack sadly.

"I told you, Jack. She's not Mai. She's a programmed puppet posing as Queen Dau Te Po, who knows and does only what Colonel Minh wants. They are a matched pair of sadistic tyrants. She will do anything to please him. I warned you." Jack shook his head. "Oh my God, I wouldn't believe they could really change a person so completely like that if I hadn't seen it myself. What can we do? You know this valley. There must be some way to escape."

"When I visited here several times, Jack, I saw the slave farm from the guards' point of view. I'm afraid that there isn't much hope, especially with the drugs. Pay attention to what I'm telling you. The slave numbers have quadrupled since then. But the routine is the same. Even though those men here are slaves, you must be careful because they are now totally devoted to Colonel Minh and Queen Po. They are broken and very devoted. They will report you if they suspect you're trying to escape. Colonel Minh told me no one has ever escaped from him. He likes to bring all his enemies here and watch them toil in his fields under his whip. This guy is sick, Jack, and he will own us for sure and permanently after tomorrow."

Jack looked at him, and faced the reality of his situation. "Queen Po will own us," he said finally.

"Same difference," said Vega "It's over, Jack. I messed up."

Jack already had decided his life as he knew it was over. This was to be his life now. He had lost everything, and he wasn't even sure how it had happened. He closed his eyes and thought of the time not so long ago when he and Mai and little Devearney snuggled together happily on their bed. Everything was so right then. Why did he ever let them come to Vietnam?

Once he'd seen Mai as Queen Po, he realized she was gone from him forever. But he still had Devearney, and he would get back to her somehow. He would get out of there or die trying.

"No, Daniel, it's not over," he remarked after a moment. "I wasn't meant for this, and neither were you. We're going to get out of here. I'm going to save Mai and go home," he said with honest determination. "Somehow, some way, I'm going home to be with my daughter. You have to help me. Tell me what to eat and what not to eat so I can avoid the drugs as much as possible. I bet they don't drug every meal. If we can figure out which ones have the drugs, we can keep our heads on straight. We will figure out how to get out of this. It's not over, Vega."

Vega looked at Jack and wanted to tell him everything, but he couldn't do it. He admired Jack for what he just said and was comforted by the thought they were getting out of there tomorrow if Mai's plan worked. He pondered his fate faced with two extremes; a life of slavery if her plan didn't work, or a ten million dollar payday if it did.

Chapter 39

Siem Kulea, Cambodia

The next morning Mai woke up early feeling alive and eager to get on with her plans for the day ahead.

Her private breakfast in her garden was of the finest and freshest the valley had to offer. The offering of rich fruits, meats, and pastries was far more than she could ever imagine consuming. Her coffee was full and rich as she contemplated what was to come on this, her last day in Siem Kulea with Colonel Minh.

After a morning massage and bath, her handmaidens prepared her hair the way Colonel Minh preferred. It was in braids on either side of her head, wound at the top, and wrapped in cords of gold and leather. They dressed her in leather-lined riding pants, as instructed, and added a leather vest over her white silk shirt. For shoes this day, she chose simple knee-length riding boots with flat heels. She put on gloves, clapped her hands, and ordered everyone to leave her except Su Ling.

She took Su Ling in her arms and hugged her close. "This is it, Su Ling. This is the day I get my revenge and we get out of here. Are you ready?"

"I will not let you down, my lady," said Su Ling, as she displayed her nine-millimeter Beretta.

Su Ling affirmed the previous day her plans to kill Dr. Minh while Mai was busy killing the colonel. At the same time she showed her Beretta to Mai. She demonstrated how to check the magazine, cock it, and turn off the safety.

Mai took a deep breath and held her at arms length. "Wow. I never imagined I would be this excited. See what I'm wearing? Get something like this on, and be ready when we come back for you. I have to hurry now. The colonel will be waiting by the helicopter in less than fifteen minutes."

"You mean I'm going too, my lady?" Su Ling asked, surprised.

"I could never leave you behind, Su Ling. We are bonded sisters. Besides, you saved my life twice!"

Su Ling kissed her impulsively on the lips with honest passion. She held it for a long moment, and then pulled back and averted her eyes respectfully with an embarrassed look on her face. "Oh, my lady, what have I done? I am so sorry. Please forgive me."

Mai smiled in surprise and gave her a quick kiss in return before she remarked, "You should have done it sooner. We may have resolved some of my lonely nights here. Now hurry!"

After Su Ling left, Mai went quickly to her vanity. Around the mirror embedded in stone were a number of hoa cuc flowers, which were painted in gold leaf. This wall and much of her chambers were left standing among the ruins of the original palace built a thousand years ago. She pushed one of the gold carved flowers. The wall gave a slight click, and a hidden compartment was revealed as the stone from behind parted and opened just a bit. She pulled it all the way open, retrieved the large ornate jewelry box inside, and opened it. Inside were hundreds of magnificent jewels passed down through the centuries by the queens who lived in this palace. The Minh brothers had no knowledge of these jewels and she had not told Su Ling. It was a treasure of incalculable value.

Mai discovered the secret compartment the previous week, when the location was revealed to her in a dream. She thought it was just a dream, but still half asleep she got up and went to her vanity. Fascinated by the possibility, she pushed the same carved stone flower as in her dream. To her surprise, a secret compartment opened for real in the wall in front of her. Inside was a large jewelry box inscribed with "The jewels of the Hoa Cuc" in their ancient language, which was now familiar to her. She put the box back, closed the compartment, and went back to bed. Since then the real Queen Dau Te Po was in and out of her mind often, talking to her.

This was the new and fascinating part of her mind-tripping experience brought on by the opiates that she wanted to explore further after she got away from Colonel Minh.

Her knowledge within grew as Queen Dau Te Po revealed to her the story of her ancestors and heritage. She learned that she was descended from the first Hoa Cuc who was the daughter of an alien leader. The aliens who were called Ferrens came to earth thousands of years ago. They intended to stay and settle on earth because of problems on their home world. They found these particular earthlings they called Champas to be very primitive and instilled in them the knowledge and training necessary to make them capable and devoted servants. Along with this knowledge they added an inbred obsession to please the Ferrens as their only means of fulfillment in life.

But after time they discovered that they had difficulty surviving on earth because of subtle atmospheric differences, and after a thousand years, when the interstellar magnetic portal opened again for them, they elected to return to their home world. They left behind one daughter who had mated with a Champa man and chose to stay. She was the first queen of the Champas.

The end result was the strong devotion of the Champa people for Mai as the descendant of the first Hoa Cuc and rightful heir to the Champa throne.

Mai quickly emptied the large box into her purse, put the box back, and closed the compartment. She opened Queen Po's jewelry box, which sat on her vanity, and poured those jewels of every variety in too. She considered for a moment that she had many millions of dollars in jewels in that large white leather Prada purse. She added a scarf on top of the jewels in her purse to hide their presence.

She turned away and was headed for the helipad when Colonel Minh came through her door in a rush and declared, "Po, we must go now. I want to take care of this matter and get back to the training facility this afternoon for an important meeting. We must leave right away if we are to have a proper amount of time for our amusement. Come, come."

She hurried to him and kissed him on the cheek. "Yes, my darling, I have been waiting eagerly for you to arrive. I'm very thrilled about what we are about to do, and I know it is very entertaining for you. Let's go."

She kissed him on the lips and took his arm. "You look so handsome in your uniform. Have I told you how much I like you in that color?"

Colonel Minh appeared as visibly excited as she pretended to be. He put his hand over hers around his arm and said, "I want to have some time for us up there too, Po, before I head back over the mountain. I always love these inductions, and this time is going to be very special indeed."

Mai nodded and laid her head on his arm, as a loving, devoted wife would. *Give me strength*, she pleaded in her thoughts. *Oh dear God, I hate this man so. Now I will at last have my revenge.*

They went out the door and got into the waiting helicopter, which took off as soon as they were buckled in. Mai looked back until the compound was just a dot. She was determined to get back there and pick up Su Ling before they left the valley. Last-minute nerves were finally taking their toll, and she was not at all confident that her plan would work. A lot depended on chance, and chance was a fickle partner in the best of times. Until the ultimate moment when she took her revenge, she must continue to play the cruel Queen Dau Te Po as Colonel Minh expected her to be. She believed that was imperative as she led him blindly to his destruction.

It was a ten-minute flight to the work farm by helicopter, and Mai began by fawning over Colonel Minh and kissing him because she knew he didn't like it. As she expected, after a few minutes he ordered her to sit back and look out the window. "I am going to have to adjust your programming, my dear," he said. "I don't want you to be kissing me all the time. Reserve that kind of thing for our public appearances. A man needs to breathe."

"Yes, darling," she said. "I will try harder to control myself. I will try to be exactly as you wish me to be." It was a double win on her part. He was convinced she loved him and she didn't have to show affection to the old man anymore in private.

As they approached the work farm, Mai could see thousands of shackled slaves working half-naked in the hot sun. When she was the drugged Queen Po, she remembered she inspected them with Colonel Minh, and regarded them proudly as her property as if they were livestock working to please her. She was even amused as Colonel Minh expounded on who they were and explained their circumstances.

Two of them had been powerful business rivals of Colonel Minh from New Delhi, India who had tried to block a license and permit that he needed for a big contract worth millions of dollars. They were kidnapped and brought to the work farm for disposal at the hands of Colonel Minh. She had collared and branded them herself for his amusement. She remembered how Colonel Minh got in very close so he could look right into their eyes and even smell the burning flesh on their arms when she branded them.

She was totally under his control during that three-week period when he owned her mind. But now she was deeply sorry for what she did. She wondered what would become of them after this day. She hated this place and all it stood for. But in the next breath, she shook those thoughts away. *Focus. Let nothing distract you from your revenge.*

Colonel Minh noticed her looking out the window at the thousands of slaves below. "They're working very hard for you down there, my pet. I'm told they are happier and working harder than ever since your return. Their daily output has greatly increased."

She nodded. "Yes, but I'm not impressed, my darling. I am glad that I inspire them but we have many more mouths to feed. I think I will increase their quota. They are lucky that I give them meaningful goals that enhance their lives and fulfill their existence."

Farther on and away from the fields they finally saw the buildings of the main compound from the air. They could see Jack and Daniel kneeling in front of Ramadi and Fetu waiting for the helicopter near the stockade. Beside them was a cauldron of red-hot coals on a raised stand. Smoke billowed up out of it, and hot irons were buried deep within.

The helicopter landed near where the small group waited. After stepping down from the helicopter, Colonel Minh walked up proudly before the two prisoners with Queen Po holding his arm. "So, Jack Largent, we finally meet."

Queen Po looked up at Colonel Minh, and ran her hand across his chest as she asked, "Who is this man, my darling? Who is Jack Largent? That is the slave who disrespected me."

"Never mind your pretty little head," said Colonel Minh, patting her hand. "The ritual we will perform this morning will give us some closure. Are you ready to collar and brand your new slaves, Queen Po?" His lips were moist, and he was almost slobbering with anticipation.

Queen Po gave him a playful peck as an answer, and then turned around and approached the kneeling slaves. She glanced back at Colonel Minh, and announced proudly, "First, my darling, I will put my collar on them." Fetu handed her one of the collars that would be locked around their necks permanently, and she held it up in front of each of their faces to taunt them.

"My husband designed these slave collars from the finest and hardest metal," she told them. "The lock is self-engaging and permanent. My personal property tag, of which I am very proud, hangs from them telling everyone that I own you."

Jack pleaded, "Mai, I'm your husband...your real husband. Don't you recognize me? Mai, it's me, Jack!"

She smiled and ran her hand over his cheek possessively. "Oh, I remember you from the trail. You're the silly one who hasn't learned his place yet. It will give my husband and me great pleasure in training you. By the end of this day you will be begging to do whatever he wants."

"Please, don't," pleaded Vega. "Mercy, please, Colonel. I don't want to be a slave here. You've got it all wrong. Please, I beg you. I have never stopped being loyal to you. I swear! I can be a big help to your cause. My talents will be wasted here."

"Oh, I love it when they beg," said Colonel Minh as he nodded for Mai to continue.

Mai went to Vega and put the thick steel ring around his neck. She closed it with a resounding metallic click. She stepped back from him and took a moment to regard him with an evil smirk for Colonel Minh's benefit.

Colonel Minh clapped with real pleasure. He was enjoying himself immensely. "Welcome to slavery, Mr. Vega," he said, mocking him. "Oh...I forgot to tell you. I cleaned out your bank accounts five years ago after I sent you to be captured by the Vietnamese. Yes, I planned all of that. Now you are one of my slaves forever. It's just too perfect isn't it?"

Jack looked over and saw the metal tag in the form of Queen Po's symbol, the hoa cuc hanging from Vega's new steel collar. He shook his head and muttered defiantly, "This is so wrong."

Queen Po looked over at Jack, flicked Vega's tag, and announced, "There, there, my silly one. Be patient. You will soon have a collar of your own to wear with pride like your brother. Very soon, you will learn to enjoy your new life as a slave serving us. The pain you are about to experience you will endure often to ensure that we are amused and properly entertained."

Jack became flustered in anger. From somewhere he found a new resolve to fight back. Once again, he looked at her with an expression of defiance and he started to voice his anger.

But Mai sensed his mood change immediately and read his thoughts. With her back to Colonel Minh, she was on him in the next instant. She held his face firmly between her two gloved hands and looked at him eye to eye. She leaned in close and whispered in his ear, "Jack, darling, don't resist, or all is lost. Please trust me, my love. I know who you are and I love you dearly. Trust me. We're going home. I love you, Jack Largent with all my heart."

He stopped struggling instantly, stunned by her words. Then she gave him a hard slap on the face for show and flicked his nose playfully. She proclaimed loudly for Colonel Minh to hear. "Ah, how foolish you are, my silly one. You are truly amusing. You will very soon learn that resistance is useless and a lot more painful for you. But that's the part my husband likes the most. So if you really wish to entertain us, keep resisting. This will be great fun and very amusing for him!" She looked back at Colonel Minh to share the moment with him.

She walked behind the two men so Colonel Minh could have a better view of what she was doing. She accepted another slave collar from Fetu to put around Jack's neck. But when she turned back toward Jack she saw for the first time the welts from the whip on his back. Her face flushed red in a raging and instant anger. She was ready to lash out at everyone, exposing how much she truly loved Jack. Fortunately, Ramadi anticipated her reaction, and had adroitly moved in front of Jack before she reacted, blocking her and Jack momentarily from the colonel's view with his massive body. He whispered, "Your majesty, not now. Please, you must control yourself!"

His words broke her rage and helped her to refocus on what she was doing. There followed a difficult moment, but she took a big breath and gained control of her emotions once more.

She nodded to Ramadi who stepped to the side, and with one huge hand, pulled Jack's head up to accept the collar. She clamped the permanent collar around him, flipped the metal Hoa Cuc symbol with a gloved finger, and said to Colonel Minh, "Don't my new pets make a cute pair in their collars, my darling?"

She paraded back over to Colonel Minh, and he eagerly took her in his arms and gave her a long kiss in front of them. He was enjoying this spectacle a great deal.

Then he turned Queen Po around in his arms facing Jack while he still held her from behind. He ran his hands up and down her body possessively. She swooned, closed her eyes in pleasure and backed into him. She ran her right arm up behind her, caressing his neck, and laid her head back, looking at the two collared slaves proudly.

"You see, my darling, they are already yours," Queen Po said to him. "But the best part is still to come. I know you agree."

Colonel Minh declared triumphantly, "Welcome to our work farm, Mr. Largent. I have taken everything from you, and now you will serve as a slave working in my fields for the rest of your life. Do you see how Queen Po swoons when I touch her? Do you see how she cannot resist my kiss and desires to make love to me and only me? She is most eager to please her master because her love for me is boundless. I can certainly understand your motives for coming here. Every night I am blessed with her superior talents in my bed. Each night I explore every curve and crevice of her body. That is something that is only for me now. You, on the other hand, will soon learn, like her, to call me master and obey me without question."

Colonel Minh was visibly excited as he kissed Queen Po once more in front of Jack. She returned his kisses passionately, and her hands embraced him with loving caresses. This took several minutes while the others watched. Jack was confused, and didn't like at all what was happening. He hated seeing Mai kiss Colonel Minh. But Ramadi had a firm hold of him, and there was nothing he could do about it.

Finally, Colonel Minh broke off the kiss and commanded, "Let's get on with it, shall we? Let's get our new slaves properly branded. Guard, bring Queen Po a branding iron with her mark."

Fetu went to the flaming-hot cauldron next to them. He pulled a branding iron from the coals and offered it to Queen Po. She looked back at Colonel Minh, as if to share the special moment with him. She appeared especially delighted as she accepted the iron from Fetu in her gloved hand. The red-hot Hoa Cuc flower blazed ominously at its tip.

"Hold him firmly," Colonel Minh commanded Ramadi, and the big guard wrapped his massive arm around Jack's neck, and held him as in a vice. His shoulder was presented as a perfect canvas for Queen Po to easily apply the hot brand.

Ramadi took a firm hold of Jack while she held the flaming-hot brand before his face as Colonel Minh watched every detail with sadistic delight. Jack drew his head away from her with huge, frightened eyes, grimacing in real fear as Queen Po continued with her game for the amusement of Colonel Minh.

Vega tensed. He felt sorry for Jack, knowing what he must think, but that was all going to change in a few seconds, he hoped. Acting the way she was, it was hard to believe this woman was the same one he conspired with in her chambers two nights ago. He wasn't completely sure anymore that her plan was still in place. She was acting very different now.

Colonel Minh was shaking with excitement. "Brand your new slave, my dear. Hold the iron a little longer on him than necessary so I can get a richer experience."

"Oh, darling, that will muddy the brand and ruin my mark," she pouted. "But if it amuses you, I will do it. Come closer, my darling. Come here right next to me. I know you like to be close to get the full experience as we brand our slaves with our mark. I like to feel you close to me and I don't want you to miss any of it."

This was the climactic moment for the depraved Colonel when he claimed another human as his property. He had done this several thousand times already and it always excited him. His brother's devices were subtle and produced effective results, but this way was more stimulating and to the point. He loved it all. He wanted to see it, hear it, and even smell it. He wanted to look directly into the slave's eyes when he realized that he owned him now and forever, and there was nothing he could do about it. Colonel Minh was near his personal sexual peak just watching his beautiful wife torment this slave. This was the only time she could excite him, and she did it very well.

Queen Po moved the branding iron methodically toward Jack's naked shoulder as Colonel Minh eagerly moved in very close, right next to her arm so he could feel with all of his senses the moment when Jack screamed in helpless agony.

Mai put the iron to Jack's skin for a second, and he screamed out in real pain. But then she pulled it back quickly, turned, and pushed it hard into Colonel Minh's face.

She hit his left eye perfectly, and she drove him back relentlessly, even as he tripped and fell on his back to the ground. He struggled wildly beneath the blazing hot iron, trying to fight her off. She was focused and determined, as all her pent-up zeal for revenge came to fruition. In desperation, he grabbed the blazing hot iron at the tip with his hands, which only burned them too. In the next moment, he stopped resisting and began to shake, howling helplessly on the ground in pain. She forced the red-hot, fiery brand down through the socket and into his brain. She held it there smoking and sizzling for ten or more agonizing seconds while it cooked mercilessly. She spit on him and watched his body continue to convulse and shake in uncontrolled agony. Then he gave one last gasp and fell back dead. She pulled the iron back, put it to his cheek, and applied her Hoa Cuc mark there permanently.

"Smell that, you pig!" she said angrily. "That's for my parents. This is my family's mark, and you will wear our brand on your soul for all eternity. I curse you and condemn you forever!"

She allowed another brief pause as she stood over him in triumph breathing heavily. She collected her thoughts, looked around and commanded, "Ramadi and Fetu, protect us!"

Jack watched all of this in stunned surprise and was still totally confused. But he understood completely when she turned to him and yelled, "Come, Jack my darling. Quickly! Let's get out of here!" She threw down the branding iron and rushed for the helicopter.

Vega said, "Jack, pull the pins out of your shackles like this. They'll come out easily." Jack followed Vega's example and stepped out of the shackles.

Two camp guards who stood nearby saw what happened and started to come at them with their weapons. But Ramadi and Fetu were ready. They shot and killed the guards in the next instant. There were other guards in the fields farther away, and no doubt the sound of the gunshots carried, but they were all too far to be of any concern.

Vega rushed over, and picked up one of the guard's weapons. He ran to the helicopter and ordered the stunned pilot to get out. The pilot jumped down and ran with his hands high in the air toward the work field.

Jack arrived soon after and lifted Mai into the back of the helicopter. She sat down and started to buckle in but then looked back at Ramadi and Fetu. They were coming out of the radio room after they had destroyed the work farm's radio and communication devices. "Hurry, my beauties!" she yelled to them as she gathered her purse near her. She reached over and grabbed a clean tan shirt Colonel Minh always kept hanging behind his seat and handed it to Jack to put on as he settled in. "I think this will be loose on you but it is better than nothing."

In a few strides, the guards were at the helicopter and climbed in. Finding seats facing them, they buckled in quickly. "We made it," Vega yelled back from the front right seat. "Back to Vietnam, we go!"

But as they pulled away, Mai shouted, "No, Daniel, we have to first go to my palace and get Su Ling."

"OK, you crazy queen. Let's go one more round," he said smiling and swung the helicopter back toward the direction of the palace. "I have no reservations about going back to pick up Su Ling anyway. I have plans for that woman."

"Whew! Baby, remind me never to get on your bad side," said Jack, newly energized and smiling broadly ear to ear. "You did all that to Colonel Minh because of what they did to me?"

"No, Jack; that too, of course. But Colonel Minh killed my parents." She took his arm and leaned toward him. "I will tell you the whole story once we get out of here. I love you, my darling. I love you with all my heart." She reached up and kissed him.

Jack was still experiencing an adrenaline rush with the sudden change of events. He had been brutally beaten and whipped, and he still suffered from dehydration. Even so, he felt nothing but elated happiness as a result of being together with Mai again. Explanations and stories could wait.

Chapter 40

Siem Kulea, Cambodia

As they landed in the back of the palace, everything looked just as it was when they left earlier. It was peaceful and quiet, in stark contrast to what they just experienced ten minutes before at the work farm. Ramadi helped Mai down from the helicopter, and he and Fetu followed her as she hurried into the palace. She went directly to her chambers looking for Su Ling but found only her six handmaidens standing by the entrance. They had worried faces and a few were crying.

"What has happened?" she demanded. "Where is Su Ling?

"Not long after you left for the work farm, my lady, Dr. Minh took her to his laboratory. We think there was a commotion of some sort before that, but we were not present to witness what happened. We are all very worried," replied one of her handmaidens.

Mai saw Su Ling's nine-millimeter Beretta lying on the polished floor. She picked it up, checked it, cocked it, and turned off the safety.

Jack arrived at that point and asked what was going on.

"Come! We have to hurry," Mai said grabbing his arm, as she rushed from her chambers.

With her two guards following behind, she and Jack ran down the corridor to the clinic annex and thrust open doors to the laboratory. They immediately saw Su Ling strapped down to an operating table. At the same time, Dr. Minh walked in through a door on the opposite side of the laboratory. He held a syringe up to the light gauging his dosage as he walked. He was so focused on his evil intent as he approached the operating table that he did not notice he had company. He played the syringe before Su Ling's face to torment her and was thoroughly enjoying himself. She cowered, fought her restraints, and looked back at him in absolute fear.

"What are you doing to her, you animal?" Mai shouted.

Startled from his evil game, Dr. Minh looked up, and saw them for the first time. "There, there, don't excite yourself, Po," he said. "I'm just going to give her a little something to calm her down. She tried to kill me with a gun. I managed to wrestle it out of her hand. Can you imagine? I don't know what got into her. I have always admired her and thought she would make an excellent concubine. Now I guess we'll find out, won't we?"

From that moment everything happened at a frenzied pace brought on by the panic of not knowing what Dr. Minh might do, or say. Mai, exhibiting great determination, focused on freeing Su Ling and getting her to safety. She rushed to the operating table, put down the Beretta, and began undoing Su Ling's restraints. She called to her guards, "Ramadi, Fetu, help me remove these restraints and take Su Ling out of here. Hurry!"

"No, my lady, save yourself!" urged Su Ling from the table as they were undoing her restraints.

In contrast to all the distress shown by those trying to free Su Ling, Dr. Minh was disturbingly calm, even amused as he watched them. He spoke to them in a tranquil, patronizing voice. "Oh, no, you can't take her. She's mine now. Queen Po, you know you must obey me. Oh, I see, you're not Queen Po, are you?" His tone was patient as if he were dealing with an errant child. "You can't escape, my dear. I don't know why you even try. It's hopeless. You belong to us now. Don't you understand that?"

Jack helped Fetu and Mai to remove Su Ling's restraints. As she jumped off the operating table, Jack turned suddenly and hit Dr. Minh as hard as he could in the face, sending him crashing against the lab wall and down to the floor unconscious.

Su Ling picked up her gun that Mai had left on the table and started to aim it at Dr. Minh. But before she could fire, Ramadi, obeying the command to save her, grabbed her up in his arms quickly and headed for the door preventing her from shooting. She saw Mai hurrying behind her looking terrified with her hands over her ears. When Su Ling looked back toward the doctor, she saw he was shaking his head and slowly regaining consciousness. Ramadi held her tightly in his arms as he rushed her out of the lab.

Mai was frantic now and suddenly very afraid. Seeing, and then hearing Dr. Minh destroyed all of her previous confidence and determination. She knew he intended to speak her trigger phrase and take control of her again. She saw it in his eyes when he was talking to her with that evil, condescending voice of his. She could almost feel it happening already, and he hadn't done anything yet. She was not aware that Jack had hit him, and that he was disabled for the moment.

She fully expected him to call out to her even as she fled the room. Outside she ran desperately for the helicopter, which was standing just a few yards away. Jack held back by the main door, keeping watch just in case Dr. Minh followed them. Seeing no one, he finally turned and ran toward the helicopter after the rest.

Then everything moved as if in slow motion in contrast to the frenzied panic only moments before. Mai worried aloud, "Oh God, no!" as she desperately ran for the helicopter. The closer she got, the farther away it seemed. Her world was spinning out of control. She expected to hear Dr. Minh's voice at any second, and she was powerless to prevent it.

At that moment, Dr. Minh did indeed reappear through a side doorway leading directly from his laboratory to the helicopter pad. He dabbed a handkerchief to his bloody nose and called after her in a calm voice, "Queen Dau Te Po, isn't it a great day to be queen?"

Hearing her posthypnotic trigger phrase, Mai stopped immediately. She stood helpless, just a few yards from the helicopter. Her hands tensed into clinched fists, and then relaxed.

"Come to me, my dear. Come to your master," he commanded.

She slowly turned around in a daze and walked back toward Dr. Minh, who was waiting for her at the side door.

"Yes, that's right, my dear, come to your master. Come here, dear Po. You must obey me," Dr. Minh commanded.

For Mai, the surrounding confusion and desperation went far away and retreated from her mind. She knew only the soft voice of Dr. Minh calling to her. It was a friendly voice, a comforting voice. She was OK now, and everything was going to be all right. She knew it was important to obey Dr. Minh. He was her master and would keep her safe. She needed to please him. She calmly walked to him obediently and at peace.

Fetu followed his queen. Ramadi put Su Ling down, and joined them.

Jack stopped running and stood bewildered, as he watched Mai walk slowly and obediently toward Dr. Minh with a warm smile on her face. He didn't understand what was going on or why she was acting like she was. He yelled, "Mai!" and ran after her.

"Queen Po, order your guards to kill those escaping slaves," Dr. Minh commanded calmly. He was now once again in complete control. He was enjoying this game, like a puppeteer putting on a show. In god-like fashion, he would decide the fate of everyone performing that morning.

In the next moment, Mai turned around, but before she could speak, she heard the loud crack of two gunshots nearby. Dr. Minh's head burst in pieces behind him, and his signature white suit was covered in bright red blood. He crumbled to the ground, instantly dead.

Jack turned around quickly toward the shot and saw Su Ling pointing her gun in a perfect shooting stance at Dr. Minh. "That's three times I've saved your life, my lady," she commented in a moment of satisfaction.

But Mai did not hear her because she was still compelled to obey Dr. Minh and tell the guards to kill the escaping prisoners. It was important, and she must do it.

Jack, arrived next to Mai and saw the calm, and focused look on her face. He understood immediately what was about to happen. With her mouth opening to give the command that her devoted guards would most certainly obey, he had no choice and he didn't hesitate. Right in front of Ramadi, he punched her hard across the jaw, knocking her out. He looked sharply at Ramadi ready to protect himself, as he let Mai fall over his shoulder. But the big guard only nodded an affirmation.

"Protect your queen!" Jack yelled to him, and Ramadi instantly turned to guard their escape.

Jack carried Mai quickly to the helicopter, with Ramadi and Fetu behind, backing away from the palace with their AK-47s ready.

The next moment brought more frenzied chaos. At the palace door more guards appeared. They'd come at the sound of the gunshots and saw Dr. Minh dead on the ground. Then they saw their queen unconscious and apparently being taken by escaped prisoners to the waiting helicopter.

"They are kidnapping the Queen!" one cried aloud. They pointed their guns to shoot at the fleeing helicopter.

"Shoot for the engines, and stop them from taking off," another commanded.

Ramadi and Fetu engaged and killed many of the guards before Ramadi was hit and thrown back violently to the ground. Fetu killed three more, but then he too was shot and fell silent. More guards replaced those who were killed and began moving in to fire on the helicopter and stop them from escaping with their queen.

Just at that moment, three formations of Vietnamese helicopters arrived overhead in a swarm attacking the compound; their machine guns firing and tearing apart all they hit. The guards immediately changed their focus and began answering the fire of the assaulting forces. Several helicopters engaged the remaining guards in a quick and deadly firefight. Many guards were killed by the automatic gunfire coming from the helicopters, while others took cover around the palace grounds.

"Come on, Vega," Jack said, setting Mai down in her seat next to Su Ling in the helicopter. "This place is too hot for us. Let's get out of here!"

The Viet helicopters fanned out and came at the mercenaries and guards from three sides, surrounding them with murderous machine-gun fire. They landed their forces quickly, and then their gunships went to work.

Vega didn't wait for everyone to get strapped in their seats and instead pulled up quickly and back, away from both the Vietnamese assault and those on the ground who had been shooting at them. As their helicopter pulled away from the compound where the Vietnamese forces were now winning the deadly battle, Vega spied a gunship bearing down on him. He pulled quickly to the left, but the gunship pilot was skilled, and Vega could not lose him.

It was a tense moment for Vega, who expected to be blown out of the sky. He did not know the radio frequency of the Vietnamese helicopter and did not have the time to try to figure it out. He was trying to make a decision when the gunship pulled up beside him on his left. He saw through the cockpit that piloting the helicopter was Colonel Jung who he had met back in Thap Cham while planning the mission.

Colonel Jung gave him a quick once-over, saw his passengers, and then gave a questioning thumbs-up, which was answered with the same by Vega. Then Colonel Jung pulled away to go back and cover his men in the compound, where the attack was already coming to a victorious end.

Vega turned his helicopter toward the border and headed in that direction. He looked in the back and called out, "Everyone OK?"

Mai had gained consciousness and was curled up in a ball in the center of the padded bench seat beside Jack. Her feet were pulled up under her. She looked terrified. Her eyes darted wildly back and forth like a trapped and panicked animal. Her hands worried as if wringing a damp cloth. Jack, sitting beside her, was leaning in, talking to her gently. But it was obvious she was resisting his words. He continued talking to her softly trying to find the doorway to her mind. Su Ling was on the other side of Mai, very troubled and concerned as she witnessed the exchange. She held Mai's purse and watched as Jack tried desperately to bring Mai back to them.

He had almost given up when he said, "Mai, Devearney loves you and needs you. I love you and need you. Please come back to us."

At the sound of her daughter's name, she seemed to focus her thoughts as if hearing him for the first time. She turned to him. "Devearney?" she asked.

Jack cried joyously. "Oh yes, darling, Devearney, Devearney, Devearney! We three together forever! Devearney, our beloved daughter, needs you! You are Mai Sambaht, my wife, and I love you very much. You love your daughter, Devearney, and we are a family who will never be apart again." He hugged her close and wiped the tears from her eyes. "I love you so much, my darling."

Su Ling leaned over and kissed her queen on the shoulder. She called up to Vega and said, "Looks like we're going to be fine, Daniel. She's coming around. You fly the helicopter, my handsome pilot."

"Hey, Su, why don't you come up here in the left seat so we can talk. It's going to be a long flight," said Vega.

Su Ling took a look at Mai and Jack, and decided she wasn't needed there anymore. She unbuckled and set the purse down next to Mai, who was busy kissing Jack and engaging in a quiet and meaningful conversation. She moved up to the left seat and buckled in. Daniel leaned over, and they kissed quickly, before Su Ling cautioned, "Fly this thing, Daniel. We don't need an accident now."

Vega took a moment to check his instruments. There was enough fuel to get back to Vietnam but not much more, and they did take a lot of hits while on the ground. He saw no indication of a problem on his panel, so he took a deep breath and relaxed a bit. When he turned around again, Jack and Mai were still talking softly. More importantly, she was leaning into Jack, and all the body language said she was back.

He was thinking that was a good thing when he noticed another helicopter behind him on his right and getting closer. He yelled back to the others, "Jack... Jack!" and pointed out the window.

Jack looked and then unbelted and took up the AK-47 that Vega had left on the deck by the pilot's seat. He checked the clip and saw it was still half full. He opened the side door on the right and sat back down, placing himself between Mai and the doorway. It was hard to tell who was in the helicopter and thus far they had showed no hostility toward them. The other helicopter was civilian and bared no military or national markings. Jack thought it was likely one of Minh's loyal followers coming after them.

The other helicopter did not approach in a threatening manner from behind but was getting ever closer on their right side. Any minute Vega expected the side door to open to reveal an automatic rifle aimed at them. Finally, it got close enough for him to see Catherine waving to him frantically from the left-seat window, and he called back to Jack to look outside.

Jack saw Catherine and switched seats with Mai so that she could see Mai was with him. Even from the distance between the helicopters, Jack could see the broad smile on Catherine's face. She pointed to her headset. Vega turned to the standard civilian frequency and was pleased when they finally connected by radio. "Mr. Vega, you cannot return to Vietnam," said Catherine. "Mr. Nguyen thinks that you led your team into an ambush and many soldiers were killed. One of the soldiers who survived managed to get word back to his base. Is that true?"

"I'm afraid so, Miss Marsh. It was not a part of my plan, but it happened," he affirmed. "So what is the alternative? Thailand?"

"I think that is up to you, but I want to take your passengers with me," she said. "I want my friends back. Our deal still holds. Ten million dollars. You only have to tell me where to transfer the funds." She paused. "Hold on a minute." After a few seconds passed, she said, "Look in the window."

She held up a sign with "130" printed on it in black ink.

Vega switched frequencies, and they resumed the conversation. "I have a plane waiting in Ubon to fly us out of here, Daniel. I want you to be on that plane with us."

"That's Minh's backyard, Catherine. I am sure Colonel Minh is dead, but there were others who would immediately replace him and are equally as ambitious. They might have been contacted from his base camp to his headquarters in Ubon to tell them what happened. If they know your corporate jet is there, they will put two and two together and try to stop us."

"Perhaps, but it's all arranged, Daniel. The Thais like my money too," she said. "What do you say?"

"OK, but remember these are very serious and determined people you are dealing with."

"All the more reason to land and transfer the four of you to this helo. At Ubon we can get right on the plane without too many questions," said Catherine.

"I don't have enough fuel if we're going to Thailand anyway," said Daniel. "Let's get it done."

They found a clearing, landed, and moved to the much larger and more comfortable Sikorsky S-76 helicopter Catherine had commissioned for the trip. Kelly and Catherine greeted them inside and helped them to get buckled into their seats. They called ahead to Ubon and made sure Catherine's private jet was fueled and ready on the flight line. They received instructions to land adjacent to the aircraft, where an airport representative would process their papers.

"You guys look terrible," said Catherine addressing Jack and Daniel as they sat buckled up in their seats. Jack was in the back next to Mai and Su Ling while Daniel sat next to Kelly and Catherine opposite them.

"Why can't you vacation like these classy-looking ladies here?" she joked and gestured to Mai and Su Ling, who were dressed nicely by comparison. "Seriously, how are you? Is there anything we can do for you right now?"

Mai turned and buried her head into Jack's chest. The last six weeks finally landed on her like a sledgehammer, and she was beside herself with emotion. She let go of her purse and clung to him as if her life depended on it, and then she began to wail uncontrollably. Jack had his arm around her and was rubbing her back gently with his hand. She hugged Jack closer while she hid her head in his shirt and sobbed in shudders.

"I'm OK," said Daniel looking at Mai, "but Jack's pretty beat up. You might want to take a look at his back. He got whipped and beaten pretty bad back there, and Mai branded him."

Kelly looked very concerned and got up to take a look, but Jack waved her off with his free hand. He shook his head and motioned for her to sit down. Catherine and Kelly watched as Mai let her emotions run freely. They could not imagine all that Mai had endured, especially when they looked at Jack, who appeared to have gotten the worst of it. Six weeks in the hands of those two matchless evil men had to have taken a toll on her too.

Catherine and Kelly had planned ahead and had passports for each of them, and even a fake one Su Ling could use. Catherine did not expect they would get a close perusal anyway by the officials at Ubon, and she would have a better passport waiting in New Delhi for her. Catherine was going to use her 'magic envelope' routine on the airport officials. She had tried this successfully with other reporters on location within the NearNorth Productions organization.

It was only an hour from their rendezvous to the airport at Ubon, but it was enough time for Mai to corral her emotions and resume a normal facade. She took a large breath, gathered herself together, dried her eyes, and kissed Jack passionately one more time. "You boocoo dinky dow, GI," she joked, smiling and dabbing her eyes with a handkerchief.

"What's dinky-dow?" asked Kelly, happy that Mai was feeling better.

"It means 'crazy' in Vietnamese slang," explained Jack.

"Well, she got that right," said Kelly. "But she could have addressed that remark to all of us!"

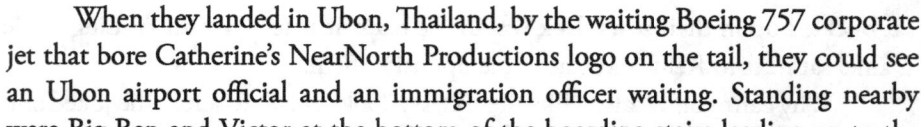

When they landed in Ubon, Thailand, by the waiting Boeing 757 corporate jet that bore Catherine's NearNorth Productions logo on the tail, they could see an Ubon airport official and an immigration officer waiting. Standing nearby were Big Ben and Victor at the bottom of the boarding stairs leading up to the aircraft, along with two Ubon airport ramp attendants.

Catherine and Kelly stepped down from the helicopter and went to talk to the two airport officials. Catherine gave each of them an envelope, which they opened, inspected, and put inside their coats. Then Catherine handed them each another envelope and explained there was a bonus inside in appreciation for their efforts on her behalf. They perused the contents and smiled broadly this time. They quickly stamped the passports, bowed slightly as was the custom, and wished her a safe flight back to the United States.

Kelly told the attendants at the bottom of the stairs to be ready to pull the stairs back as soon as they were aboard, so they could pull away to the runway without hesitation. After that bit of business, she took Catherine's hand and smiled. They had done it and were on their way. The officials barely glanced at the passports.

Catherine urged the others to hurry, and Daniel and Su Ling, who were walking toward the aircraft, scrambled over to the boarding stairs and quickly went up them and into the big customized jet.

Jack was walking hurriedly with Mai, but then to his surprise she stopped abruptly. She let go of his hand, and ran back to the helicopter and hopped onboard again. In a few seconds, she jumped back down and ran back to Jack. He greeted her halfway to the stairs and asked, "What was that about?"

"I forgot my purse," she explained, showing him her large white leather Prada purse.

"You've got to be kidding me!" he said, shaking his head while smiling at her. "Now who's dinky dow?"

Catherine and Kelly, standing at the top of the stairs, saw a white limousine pull ominously onto the tarmac from the local highway, just beyond a row of airport hangars nearby. It turned toward their aircraft and picked up speed. It was coming to intercept them, and it could mean nothing but trouble.

They anxiously watched their friends walking casually from the helicopter to the steps, oblivious to the apparent danger. Catherine yelled to them, "Jack, Mai, hurry!"

Jack and Mai picked up their pace and quickly arrived at the bottom of the stairs. Jack went up a few steps as the white limousine pulled up and abruptly stopped nearby. Mr. Doan got out with one of his assistants. As he approached, Jack yelled from the boarding stairs, "Stay back. This is over. This ends here. We're going home."

Mai looked around with her hand up blocking the sun from her eyes to see whom Jack was talking to.

Mr. Doan ignored him and called out loudly, "Queen Dau Te Po, isn't it a great day to be queen?"

Mai looked angry and then froze at the bottom of the steps. With a blank face she turned completely around, and walked calmly to Mr. Doan in robot-like obedience.

No! Not again, thought Jack. *Oh please, God, no.* "Mai, no! Please stop!" he yelled frantically.

Mai did not respond but walked right up to Mr. Doan who put out his hand to her and said, "You will obey and come with me, Queen Dau Te Po. I am now your master, and your people want their queen back," he commanded.

Mai bowed her head and said, "Yes, master," which brought a big smile of triumph to Mr. Doan's face.

"You will obey and serve me now as my wife and Queen, Dau Te Po," he said.

Mai said again, "Yes, master," but with her head bowed, she found the Beretta that Su Ling for want of a better place had put in her purse when she boarded the helicopter in Siem Kulea. Mai spotted it when she retrieved her purse. Mai pulled the gun out of her purse and pushed it viciously under Mr. Doan's chin, throwing his head up at an odd angle in sudden fear.

"As my *real* husband just said, you pathetic little piece of shit, this is done. This is over! Do not even think of bringing further harm to me, my family, or friends. I swear I will bring all of Indochina down on you. You know one word from me, and my people will hunt you like an animal until you are dead. We will come after you and yours, and you know we have the people and resources to destroy you and wipe any trace of your existence from the face of the earth. I suggest, Mr. Doan, that you find a new line of work. Keep away from me and mine."

She lowered the pistol, stepped back, turned, and then walked past a stunned and happily relieved Jack, who was now standing a few yards behind her. She handed the gun to Big Ben, took Jack's arm, and said, smiling, "Come on, baby. Let's go home."

Behind her, Mr. Doan stood frozen like a statue for a moment and then visibly became enraged. His demeanor changed accordingly. He pulled a gun from under his tan suit coat and started to point it at Mai.

The two bodyguards standing at the bottom of the stairs yelled at the same time, "Gun!" Both went into instant shooting stances and filled Mr. Doan's body with bullets before he knew what a mistake he had just made. He spun around and fell against the white limousine, slowly sliding to the ground dead. He left dark-red streaks where his body touched against the vehicle. His assistant threw his hands up in the air immediately and yelled he was unarmed.

Catherine yelled from the aircraft door, "Let's get out of here! Hurry!" as airport personnel began to look toward them. Mai and Jack rushed up the stairs and followed Catherine into the aircraft. The two guards boarded last, with their guns out, watching warily from behind. They ordered the attendants to quickly pull back the stairs.

The big customized luxury jet was pulling across the tarmac before the door was even closed. They did not wait for clearance but went right to the runway and took off.

They expected some displeasure from the airport tower but apparently Catherine's overly generous bonus ended the incident and the tower gave them safe passage out of the country.

Chapter 41

Ubon to New Delhi

The mood inside the aircraft was festive and initially everyone shared their feelings in one large post-thrill talkfest. But as the aircraft gained some stability in flight, Catherine held her nose and politely informed Daniel and Jack that they smelled like a dirty locker room. With a flutter of her hand she ordered them to go back to the rear compartment of the ultra luxurious private jet where a shower and fresh clothes awaited them. She instructed her steward, Brian, to get them started.

After the two men went to the rear to clean up, Catherine took the seat next to Mai and gave her a long and meaningful hug. "Welcome back, my friend. I was beside myself with worry about you."

Catherine held one hand on each of Mai's arms as she talked with great sincerity to her. "I don't know where this is all going, Mai. But I know you well enough to know this adventure is not over."

Mai took a big breath and nodded, "I have to tell you I'm still an emotional mess from all that's happened. I know I'm not myself and it will take a while I think for me to come down. A lot of this was unexpected in many ways and just as bewildering for me as I am sure it was for you. So much has happened, I haven't had time to process it all and think it through."

"OK, but whatever plans you have, you don't have to do them alone. Let Kelly and I help you with what you need to do," said Catherine. "I hope you know that what you just did was crazy, and you were very lucky to get out of there alive. You should have confided in us. We would have supported you and had your back all the way. You are the smartest person I know, but, my dear friend, that was a very dumb move on your part. Next time, let's put our three heads together and talk it over, OK?"

Mai nodded sincerely. "There *is* something I need, Catherine, and I confess I'm hesitant to mention it."

"Just tell me. Anything, Mai. How can we help?" Catherine asked.

"Right now I need drugs," said Mai. "I'm an addict, Catherine, and I can't go through a real treatment yet. The opiates they gave me to make their hypnotic routine most efficient and control me has opened my mind to feel Queen Dau Te Po, the legendary Champa queen, talking to me from within. Believe me, I know how crazy that sounds. Before all of this happened, I wouldn't have believed it either if someone told me such a thing. But Catherine, it's true. Wonderfully true. I am finding out so much about my past and heritage. I need the drugs to continue for a time until I can sort this out."

Catherine got very serious and looked at her for a moment in silence eye to eye. She was trying to decide if Mai was making up the voices-in-her-head story to get to some illicit drugs like a common addict. In her high-society world, she had a few friends who were addicts.

But in the next moment she disposed of that possibility based on the Mai she knew and trusted. As a matter of fact this entire adventure had been so bizarre thus far that there was really no reason to doubt this latest revelation. She decided to believe what Mai told her, however unusual it sounded at the moment, and see where it took them.

Catherine nodded. "I know someone, Mai. Someone responsible, a discreet professional, who can help you get through this…this…whatever it is you have going on in that wonderful head of yours. Are you OK now?"

"Yes, but how long is this flight?"

"We're going through New Delhi, India, and then to Frankfurt, Germany, and then back to Chicago. About twenty-four hours, Mai. At each stop, we will be on the ground for an hour or two while we're refueled and resupplied. Can you handle that?"

"Yes, but it would be better if I had something light to tide me over. With all that has happened, I'm still filled with a lot of nervous anxiety. That last part happened so fast."

Kelly said, "We have methadone on the aircraft for medical emergencies. We can give you that."

"What do you think?" asked Catherine. "Kelly worked as a nurse's aide in a small clinic while she was in college. She knows all about giving medication."

"Yes, a very small amount of that will do well for now I think. Thank you." Su Ling who sat nearby was watching and listening to their conversation.

She got up and came to kneel down in the aisle beside Mai's seat. She bowed her head and asked, "May I get you anything, my lady?"

"Yes. I would love a glass of cabernet, if they have any, and something light to eat," Mai told her.

Catherine interrupted, "Oh, Brian can bring that!" But Mai waved her off.

Su Ling got up eagerly and headed to the galley in the front of the plane.

Catherine asked her, "Mai, is Su Ling your servant or something? Brian could have brought us drinks and snacks."

"She seems quite eager to please you," observed Kelly.

"This is a situation that has come upon me and that I will deal with shortly," explained Mai. "I am still getting used to it. The Champa people worship and obey me as their rightful queen and she is Champa. I owe that woman my life three times for real. Do not disrespect her devotion to me. You need to know that serving me gives her great fulfillment and satisfaction. I have a plan to give her a new life and happiness not centered on that. Just let things play out, please."

She implored them with her expression and continued. "Don't make light of her Champa faith and beliefs. I love and respect her too much, and it's all too complicated to explain just now. Suffice to say that the Champa devotion is thousands of years old and serving me is their only means of fulfillment in life. I know how that sounds. Just go with it for now, please."

Su Ling returned with three glasses of wine prepared on the serving tray she placed between them. She knelt down again and surprised Kelly and Catherine when she offered them her perspective on the situation. "Ladies, I know I am confounding you by appearing as the devoted servant I am to my queen and I fully understand the contrast between our two worlds. I took the liberty of also bringing you wine. Brian advised me on your preferred choices, and I prepared enough hors d'oeuvres for everyone."

"No worries, Su Ling," said Mai. "My friends were just surprised, that's all. Sit here beside me, and talk with us. You'll have to get used to the idea that we're not in Siem Kulea anymore. You and I will have to work on that and adjust our routine, agreed?"

Su Ling nodded. "Yes, my lady. I just thought that since this was a private situation, I could take the opportunity to serve you openly, as in Siem Kulea. It saddens me that our close relationship is ending."

Mai hugged her and kissed her softly on the cheek. She voiced her thoughts. "What am I going to do with you?"

"Oh my god!" remarked Kelly. "Are you two lovers like Catherine and me?"

"No, Kelly," replied Mai. "Nothing like that. We love each other dearly, but it is a different kind of love. We are bonded in a different and very special way that only Champas can fully understand."

"How do you feel toward Daniel?" asked Mai of Su Ling.

"I love him very much, my lady," she answered. "I admit I'm confused and conflicted because of it. I'm also wondering about the collar. Do you remember your promise to me that you would give him to me, my lady?"

"Of course I do, Su Ling," said Mai with an assuring smile. "But we are not in that world anymore. I just want to have some fun with him first. We can wait on the collar."

"What's going on, Mai?" asked Kelly, looking at her with a serious expression. "Is Daniel your slave?"

Mai gave her a big smile. "Just stop! Be patient, Kelly, please, for me. We have a few relationships to resolve involving two very different worlds, as you can see. I will take care of it all very soon. But you must be sure not to be disrespectful and maintain an open mind until things are sorted out. Besides, I think it is going to be great fun for you and Catherine to watch us unravel our complicated relationships."

"Hmmm, Mai, I think we'll let this be your thing, and we'll just enjoy the show," said Catherine joining looks with Kelly. She was fascinated and not a little envious of Mai for Su Ling's devotion to her. Su Ling was a beautiful young woman.

"Su Ling, Kelly and I are very grateful for all you have done for our dear friend," said Catherine. "We would like to welcome you into our close family of friends, and we cannot wait to get to know you better."

Catherine asked Su Ling, "What kind of wine do *you* like to drink?"

Su Ling was surprised, but answered meekly, "Well, when I am allowed, I usually drink a red of some sort."

Catherine called up front to Brian to bring another glass of cabernet. It arrived soon thereafter and was served to Su Ling. Catherine raised her glass and toasted with Su Ling first and then to the rest. "To friends," she said.

Su Ling gave her a large smile and replied with real enthusiasm, "Thank you, Catherine. Mai has told me a great deal about you and Kelly. I am honored, even excited, to be counted in this group. You are all so…American! It will take some getting used to."

Catherine nodded and asked, "Mai, are you considering returning to Vietnam in two weeks with Kelly and me?"

"Oh, yes, I must! It's very important to me," Mai said.

"OK then, we will make our plans accordingly. How will Jack feel about that?" Catherine asked.

Mai just looked at her silently and shook her head. It was a problem. "I think he'll fight it, Catherine. And who can blame him? Between the four of us, he got the worst of it. Oh my god, Catherine, they whipped him horribly and…"

"You branded him," said Catherine, raising an eyebrow and looking at her pointedly with a smile. "Daniel already mentioned that part on the helicopter," explained Catherine. "I admit I wouldn't have believed it if I had not seen the brand with my own eyes. Now I can't wait to hear the whole story. This tale just keeps getting better and better!"

"Yep, I branded him," replied Mai smiling, "but it was only for a second and partly so I could bring Colonel Minh in close to where I could get at him unexpectedly with that hot iron. I planned all of that carefully beforehand. It was a perfect setup for my revenge. Oh wait, that's another story…no the main story. Oh my! As I said, there is a lot to tell."

Mai paused a moment and got serious, "But about me branding him, I won't lie to you, Catherine. I branded him with my mark on purpose and as a necessary part of my plan. It's important as he stands beside me before the Champa people that he be branded for them to accept him. When I realized that, I began to plan how to do it and one thing led to another. It turned out to be a perfect setup for my revenge. When I have a chance, I will try to explain why. I just need some more time to collect myself and my thoughts."

"You will have to tell us all about it, Mai, when you're ready." said Catherine. She looked over at Su Ling and said, "And it appears it's going to be quite a story. It's a good thing we have a long flight ahead of us.

"Oh, one thing. Mai," Catherine continued, "there have been some developments at the cave-treasure site. They found a body of a young woman in there, and they traced her DNA to you. She was an ancestor of yours."

"Yes, I sensed there was something like that when I was there. I think I know who it is, but not why she is there. That's why I did not go into the cave at the time. It's all connected, Catherine. You will be amazed to know that everything that happened at Thap Cham and Siem Kulea is connected and it all involves my Champa ancestry."

Catherine nodded and as Mai went to the restroom, she got out her notepad and began writing down everything she could remember.

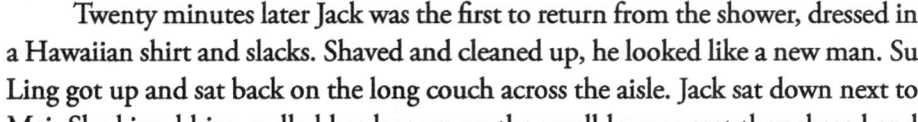

Twenty minutes later Jack was the first to return from the shower, dressed in a Hawaiian shirt and slacks. Shaved and cleaned up, he looked like a new man. Su Ling got up and sat back on the long couch across the aisle. Jack sat down next to Mai. She kissed him, pulled her legs up on the small lounge seat they shared and snuggled in close to him.

Catherine said to Jack, "Jack, we were just discussing our plans. Kelly and I are going back to the United States with you now, but we are returning in two weeks to Vietnam to cover the archeological site being processed at Thap Cham. We've already arranged this with Mr. Nguyen. In fact, I have another reporter and a film crew working there now. We would really like you and Mai there too, Jack. It is still our story, all three of us. We are a great team. Dr. Bui is expecting you to take over the photography, Jack. You don't have to worry about expenses. I'm covering everything as part of the book I am going to write about it, and I want you to photograph everything."

Catherine glanced at Mai, who nodded and assured her, "I will be ready by then. I can't wait to get into those chests. It's very important to me. I have to get back there and very soon."

Jack, sitting beside her, said, "Mai and I will need to discuss that, Catherine, and I have to get this looked at." He pointed to the hoa cuc brand on his arm. "I guess I won't be going to the shore anytime soon."

But Mai knew he would think differently about the brand after he thought more about it and put it in context. She leaned in, kissed the brand through his shirt, and snuggled against him. Her perspective on the world had changed dramatically in the last six weeks. She was now a queen with a responsibility to millions of indigenous people throughout Southeast Asia who loved her so much they were willing to die for her.

But her immediate and most valued relationship was still with Jack, and their love was proven by what had happened in the last twenty-four hours. They both risked everything to save each other. Now she owned him for real within the Champa tradition and she wanted her mark on him. It was going to stay there, as far as she was concerned.

She raised his shirtsleeve and examined the mark. It was forming nicely and would be nearly perfect when it healed. "Kelly, do you have anything we can put on this in the way of antibacterial ointment, and perhaps a loose bandage, so it doesn't get irritated by his shirt? We don't want it to get infected."

"Yep, hold on a minute. Oh! Jack, let me see your back," Kelly said, remembering Daniel told them he was whipped. "Take off your shirt, boss, and let me see the damage."

Jack stood up in the aisle and took off the wildly colored Hawaiian shirt he'd found in the closet in the rear of the aircraft. He noted regretfully that it was stained with blood in a few places on the back. He turned around so Kelly could see his bare back.

"Holy crap, Jack! What the hell did they do to you? That looks really bad!" said Kelly, as she gave Mai an accusing look.

"It looks worse than it is, Kelly. Some of the cuts opened up in the shower. That's all. Relax, please," he said.

"*You* relax, you crazy commando! What were you thinking, Jack? As you so often like to tell me, this isn't a photo shoot! And it certainly isn't a game!" She shook her head as she got up and headed toward the front of the aircraft throwing back one final remark, "God save me from macho men and crazy queens."

Kelly returned soon with her arms full of disinfectants, ointments and lots of bandages. She took charge and ordered Jack to lie down on one of the two large leather couches that skirted the left side of the cabin. As she went to work, Su Ling got up to help her.

Mai watched from across the cabin as Kelly tended with great care to Jack's wounds. She could see where the whip broke the skin in a dozen places, and Jack winced as Kelly applied the disinfectant before Su Ling bandaged each wound.

Mai felt firmly that everything that had happened to Jack made him stronger and more of man. He proved his love for her and she felt the same love for him in return. He was not as big as her beauties, or as roguish or handsome as Vega, but he was more of a man than any of them. She was proud of Jack for not mentioning his injured back and bearing his pain in silence. Jack was her man, and bearing her brand like a thousand years of civilization turned on its head. What a crazy world it was that had landed on them!

Mai noted Kelly's growing anger that blamed her for the condition of Jack's back and it made her feel very uncomfortable. She knew she had to explain what had happened back at Siem Kulea before everyone got the wrong idea. When Daniel joined them once more she resolved it would be a good time to tell her story.

But that very moment, Jack commented to Kelly, "Actually, somebody should look at Mai's face and get some ice on it. It still might swell up. I'm not sure what got into me, but on pure instinct I hit her pretty hard back there. I knocked her out before she could give the command to her guards to kill us all!" That was too much for Kelly. "You crazy bitch!" she screamed. In the next instant, she lunged in a rage toward Mai. Everyone was taken by surprise and too stunned to stop her. But Kelly hadn't moved in anger halfway toward Mai before her demeanor changed abruptly right before their eyes. She stopped and became calm. She even smiled at Mai. With obvious reverence she knelt on the floor before Mai, bowed, and suggested, "Let me see your face, my lady. Maybe I can get some ice for it if it's serious."

Catherine spoke her thoughts out loud. "What just happened? What was that?"

Everyone exchanged bewildered looks.

Even Mai was at first taken aback, before she realized the same power that humbled her Champa faithful at Siem Kulea had probably taken over Kelly. She noted that none of the others seemed humbled before her, so perhaps it was Kelly's threat that activated some force to protect her. She considered that all of these new feelings within her began when they opened the treasure cave and later took fruition with the mind enhancing drugs at Siem Kulea. She had a lot yet to consider and think about.

Kelly carefully examined Mai's face and said, "Nope, Jack. You're not as macho as you think. Not one mark on our Asian queen. She looks unharmed and as beautiful as always." She put her hand on Mai's hand and squeezed it gently, then went back to treating Jack.

"Maybe we shouldn't bandage his brand too tightly, Kelly," Mai reminded her gently. "It needs air to heal. We could try it without a bandage at all. What do you think? You're the expert in such things. It's clean, and none of the burns seem open so just the ointment might be OK."

Kelly did not answer at first, but continued to carefully care for the wounds on Jack's back. At last, she said, "I think I don't understand the two of you at all. Your husband has been severely whipped and branded, and both of you are treating it like it's nothing. Heck, you two even seem pleased with it. There must be something I'm not getting here. Honestly, I'm so confused, I don't know what I think anymore."

Daniel returned looking fresh and reinvigorated. He sat down, and Su Ling joined him on the couch leaving Kelly to finish the last of the bandages on Jack's back. He saw Kelly administering to Jack's back and asked, "How's the brand doing, Jack? I would've sworn Mai didn't get you but just a second there. I'm surprised it's so pronounced." Daniel leaned over and took a closer look. "Wow! When that heals, it's going to be a perfect flower. Mai has some real talent!" he joked.

"I'm actually having second thoughts about it," said Jack. "Kelly just called me a macho male, and no one has ever called me that before. Maybe I'll just keep it. At worst, it will make a great conversation piece."

"Come on, Jack," said Catherine. "One of my friends is a great plastic surgeon and does wonders with burn victims all the time. That will be an easy job to fix."

Vega laughed along with Jack, but he saw right through him. He too had been dominated by that queen on the one side of Mai's personality. If he were a betting man, he would bet Jack wanted to keep it there because Queen Po put it there. She was a whole lot of woman in that little package. Now he totally understood why Jack risked everything to go in there to get her.

That reminded him of something. "Jack, I don't understand how the Vietnamese Special Forces found us. I intentionally sent them a hundred miles in the wrong direction so they wouldn't go after Colonel Minh. That was when my loyalty was misplaced and I almost paid severely for it. But I know I covered my tracks to Siem Kulea. That was a pretty lucky coincidence."

Jack looked at him triumphantly in the midst of putting on another clean shirt and after thanking Kelly with a heartfelt hug. "You weren't the only one with a plan, Daniel. Colonel Jung didn't trust you, so he planted a wire on me. The belt they issued me was a tiny transmitter, probably a smaller version of the one we were issued in our survival vests for flyers in Vietnam. Of course they took that from me on the trail but whoever got it must have been in the valley and led them to it.

"With the trauma of everything that happened, I forgot about the transmitter and I was as surprised as you were when they showed up. They always planned to attack at noon on the third day, and it just happened to work out to be the time we were escaping Siem Kulea. Frankly, I'm surprised they didn't just come in sooner once they located Colonel Minh's home base."

"Well it probably took them that long to plan their assault," replied Vega. "That said, you guys should have seen Mai at the end there. She was something else! Queen or no, she took charge, put a plan in place, and executed it with perfection, literally."

"Yes she did," added Jack proudly. "And remind me never to get on Mai's bad side. She put that branding iron into Minh's face, cursed him, and held it there so he could have no doubt who was doing it to him and why."

"Wow, Mai, most women are happy just to win!" said Catherine. "It's the guys who usually want to make sure the other side knows they've lost and then rub their faces in it. What brought on such anger in you for Colonel Minh? What was this all about Mai? Why did you need to get revenge?"

"Catherine, the reason I went after Minh was that he killed my parents. He arrested them in the middle of the night, flew them out to the South China Sea, and then threw them out of a helicopter like he was emptying the garbage. They disappeared forever, and no one ever knew what happened to them. Su Ling was able to find out through her sources within the organization. I found that out when I was researching Colonel Minh for your story.

"When she told me the truth about what had happened to my parents, nothing else mattered but killing that beast. That started this whole adventure for me. Everything else was driven by my desire to get to Colonel Minh and kill him. I'm really sorry you all got drawn into this. I didn't want that. It really didn't seem that complicated when I planned it all. I had no idea any of this would happen. But I see now that I was blinded by my obsession to kill him."

"So what are we going to do about these collars?" said Jack. "At the very least mine was a nuisance when I took a shower and got dressed. Are they really made of the hardest steel and permanent?"

"Yeah, that's a problem we'll have to figure out for real, baby," said Mai. "Colonel Minh had a bunch of them made for his special slaves. My sign, the Hoa Cuc, was added later. He told me they're made of a steel alloy that is considered one of the hardest known. Nothing can cut it, and if you try to burn it off, the heat would be so intense it would kill whoever was wearing it. Colonel Minh actually ordered several thousand of them."

Mai secretly gave a wink to Catherine and danced her fingers on Jack's hand. "Daniel, Su Ling and I discussed how to avoid locking the collars on the two of you when I would later act out my charade at the work farm, but we couldn't see any way around it and still pull off the escape successfully."

"When did you three have time to get together and discuss that?" Jack asked, surprised.

Mai walked her fingers farther up his arm and said playfully with pursed lips, "When I was swimming naked in my royal pool, and they were bowed down worshipping me. That was after I tested Daniel to see whose side he was on."

Jack became confused and concerned at the same time. Catherine and Kelly noticed and thought it was wonderfully funny, made even more so by of the look of dismay on Jack's face. Catherine declared, "You go, girl," She gave Kelly a playful high-five.

"When did you test Daniel, and how did you test him?" demanded Jack.

Mai gave him a look of pretended sincerity as she explained, "It was necessary for the escape plan to work to know if he would be loyal and on our side. So, I pulled a Queen Dau Te Po brand of striptease and commanded him to fuck my brains out!"

Kelly choked her drink through her nose upon hearing that, and Catherine was laughing so hard, she fell back curled up against the seat. Jack just stared at Mai incredulously with his mouth open. Then he looked over at Daniel and challenged, "So did you? Did you fuck my wife, Daniel Vega?"

But Mai, enjoying the moment, answered for Vega instead. "Darling, you have one of the most loyal and devoted friends anyone could ever want in Daniel Vega. I threw everything I had at him, and when everyone in Siem Kulea was going crazy over me...and so was he, by the way..."

"What do you mean...How do you know that?" Jack demanded.

"Oh, I had him naked in front of me as I ran my hot little hands all over him, honey. He was saluting me most definitely the entire time," she said, enjoying herself with the other ladies, as Jack grew more perplexed.

"So what happened?" he insisted.

Mai took a deep breath, gave a sigh, and pretended disappointment. "He wouldn't do it, Jack. He said it was because I'm your wife and I belong to you.

He would not betray your friendship, even when I threatened him with torture in Colonel Minh's dungeon. You won't find a better friend than Daniel Vega, Jack."

Jack looked over at Daniel sitting across the aisle with Su Ling and said, "Thanks, man. I don't know what to say. I don't know that I could've done that. I've seen Mai naked, and it's hard to find any better temptation than that."

"Phfftt! You *couldn't* have done it, Jack!" said Mai laughing and throwing his words back at him. "And neither could any other man. This guy was amazing, right, Su Ling?"

"Yes, and then Mai let me take him out to the back lounge and try him on. I think my lady thought he might be gay or something. Let me tell you. He is not! I am still feeling our time together that night."

"Me too," said Vega. "I'm going to marry this gal if she'll have me."

Mai turned toward him, surprised and happy at the same time. "Are you serious, Daniel, because if you break her heart, Queen Dau Te Po will come after you? I owe Su Ling my life. In fact, so do you and Jack. If she hadn't brought me back from those drugs, you would both be mindlessly plowing fields nearly naked for the rest of your lives."

"No, this is the real deal. I am so much in love, I can't catch my breath," said Vega with his adoring eyes on Su Ling. "I feel comfortable and natural with her, almost like I've known her all my life. I never felt about any woman this way, and it's not because I was in prison for five years. I know you're all thinking that."

"I'm not thinking that, Daniel," said Su Ling. "And I'm the only one who matters. I feel the same way toward you. For me, it was love at first sight. So if that was a proposal, the answer is yes! I want to find our special place and spend the rest of my life enjoying every day with you. I love you, Daniel Vega."

Mai said, "I hope you're both serious, because Su Ling, I think this is the right time to give you the gift I have been planning for you. I will just make it sort of an engagement present too. I have something very special for you as a gift for what you have done for Jack and me, and all Champas everywhere."

Mai called up front, where Big Ben and Victor were sitting by the galley. "Hey, you two wonderful men, please join us, will you? And bring the white bag I left with you. Oh, and ask Brian for a dinner tray too. We'll need that."

Catherine added, "You two are off the clock as of right now. It's time you relaxed and enjoyed the trip. Get a drink from the galley on your way back."

Big Ben and Victor joined them soon after, each holding a drink, as they sat down on a couch nearby.

Mai took the large three-foot dinner tray, which had a one-inch rim on each side and set it on the small table between the group of friends. After she retrieved her large white Prada purse from Big Ben, she turned around dramatically, and held up the purse for all to see. Then she turned it over and carefully poured out the contents onto the dinner tray.

The accumulated impact of so many magnificent jewels in one collection was overwhelming and literally took everyone's breath away. The rubies, sapphires, emeralds, diamonds, and exotic stones of every color piled up and filled the whole tray. There were spectacular necklaces and bracelets mixed in, but most of the hundreds of stones were loose. These were the best, most exquisite jewels, a real treasure worth hundreds of millions of dollars.

Catherine had her hand over her mouth, and with big eyes, said, "Oh my God! Mai! Oh…my…God!"

Kelly said, "Holy shit!"

"I don't guess that's all costume jewelry, is it?" remarked Daniel, shaking his head.

"These are the collected gems of my ancestors, the queens who preceded me," said Mai. "They were hidden in a secret panel in my chambers at the white palace. It was a secret compartment that even the Minh brothers didn't know about. Queen Dau Te Po told me about it in a dream. Dr. Minh's drugs did more than prevent me from resisting his control. At a time when it was important for my ancestors and me to be united as one, the drugs opened my mind to Queen Dau Te Po. She is talking to me now. If you still don't believe me, the proof is lying right in front of you."

"Mai, there are so many and so exquisite! You may be more wealthy than I am," said Catherine, honestly enchanted by the beautiful jewels lying in front of her. She looked at Mai for a moment in fascination and knew, without any doubt, that earlier she had been telling the truth. But what did it all mean? They would have to wait to find out, she thought.

"No, Catherine," replied Mai. "I would never sell these. They belong to the many Champa Queens who have lived before me. They are a symbol of the covenant we have with our people. To sell these stones would be to insult them and our heritage. But I will give some of them away as a grateful sign of the bond between us queens and those who have proven their loyalty and devotion. I may one day use them to buy a place for my people to settle. I'm not sure…I need to consider it further."

The eight of them gazed in wonder as the stones sparkled in the light.

"But for now," she said, as she clapped her hands twice, "we have some royal business to administer. My darling Su Ling, would you do me the honor of kneeling once more before your queen?"

Su Ling released herself from Daniel's arms and immediately obeyed her by kneeling down on the cabin floor in front of Mai with her head bowed respectfully.

"Su Ling, it is time for you to lead your life and follow your path freely wherever it takes you. Go and marry this man, Daniel, if that is your wish. Have lots of babies, and raise them proudly as Champas, for no woman has honored our heritage more than you have done these past months. I declare this day that you are Lady Su Ling of the royal court of Queen Dau Erin Maisong, with all the rights and privileges thereof, and I release you of any service and obligation to me as your queen."

Su Ling replied through tears of happiness. "Your majesty, I…I am deeply honored. But no, I must and will always be in service to my queen no matter where in the world I am living! My life is meaningless without my service and devotion to you,"

Mai leaned over and kissed her and said, "I thought that would be your answer. But now for the fun part."

Mai reached over and picked out an exquisite gold necklace with six dark-red rubies hanging from it and one larger ruby in the middle. Everyone gasped as she placed it around Su Ling's neck and fastened it in the back.

"A proper lady will need proper jewelry. Take this as thanks from me for saving our Champa people from those evil men. Without you, Su Ling, our people, and heritage would have been lost. We owe you our lives."

"Oh, my lady, I do not know what to say," began Su Ling. But Mai stopped her by putting one finger to her lips.

Then Mai commanded, "Put out your hands as you have done every day when kneeling before me, properly presenting your devotion to me as my subject each morning."

Su Ling bowed her head, closed her eyes, and put her hands together, palms up, out in front of her, offering herself in perfect service to her queen. Mai reached into the pile of precious stones again, took out a beautiful large sapphire, and closed Su Ling's hands around it.

"Open your eyes, Su Ling," she commanded.

Su Ling opened her eyes and looked up at Mai. "My lady?" she inquired, looking for a meaning and beaming with happiness.

"Open your hands, and see my gift to you," said Mai.

Su Ling opened her hands, and the exquisite sapphire seemed to glow. Su Ling's face showed her wonder looking at it. "Oh, my lady, it is so beautiful, but it is one of the largest ones. I cannot. It is too special. I am not worthy to have something so special."

"Look at the stone, Su Ling. Whom does it remind you of?" asked Mai.

After a moment Su Ling said, smiling, "You, my lady. It reminds me of you because it matches your eyes."

"Yes," said Mai. "And you will keep this as a symbol of the never-ending bond between us as you seek your happiness with Daniel. You and I will always be as one, and I will always be there for you if you need anything. I suspect there is a great deal of our story yet to be written, Lady Su Ling.

"And finally, the two of you will this day be engaged. As queen, I could perform your marriage, but I think you will want something more official in this precise world of ours. So instead I offer you these two matching rings." She gave them matching gold rings each mounted with a ruby.

They put them on, and Jack said, "Here's to our knights in shining armor, Daniel, and Su Ling." Everyone raised their glasses.

"I do not have words to thank you, my lady," said Su Ling. "These jewels are priceless. You do not have to do this. I swear just serving you is the only gift I need, my lady."

"No, they're just objects," said Mai. "You and Daniel are priceless. You may sit down again, please."

She paused a minute while Su Ling got situated because she wanted to share the next moment with her. Mai gave her a conspiratorial smile as a prelude to what she was about to do.

"Now, Daniel, I have a gift for you," Mai said, getting up and standing in the aisle. "Will you come and kneel one last time before me, your queen, and indeed your owner in our Champa world?"

Daniel smiled at everyone. He performed a deep-waist bow for show and then knelt down facing her. "No, slave, turn and face in the opposite direction," Mai commanded sternly with a glance toward her friends who were enjoying the show. Daniel turned around and gave a shrug to everyone. Su Ling was sitting on the couch smiling broadly.

Mai said, "I now release you as my slave and formally give you to Lady Su Ling, as I promised." Mai held the back of Daniel's metal collar, twisted a certain way twice, then pulled and pushed, and the collar opened up. Everyone looked on with surprise and then started laughing and talking all at once about what was now a very funny joke.

"You little minx!" said Jack, smiling broadly. "You led us on all the time. Did you know she could take them off, Su Ling?"

"Yes, I knew that only Colonel Minh and Queen Dau Te Po knew how to do it," she affirmed, smiling. "When we got on this airplane, I reminded my lady that she promised to give Daniel to me when her plan was resolved. In this world, it seems silly, but in our Champa world, she still owned him. You must understand, that was why I asked her to remove her collar from him. She told me she would free Daniel for me but wanted to have some fun first."

"Now you are both free in whatever world you decide to live. Would you like this collar as a souvenir, Daniel?" Mai asked.

"Oh, hell no!" said Daniel. "I don't trust either of you Champa ladies with those collars."

Su Ling laughed, "That's right, we Champa women are very unpredictable. Never, ever make us angry. And don't you ever forget that in our world, I own you, Daniel Vega." She smiled and then said more seriously, "And in both worlds, I love you with all my heart."

She looked at her necklace and held out her hand to show off her new engagement ring. "Hey, look, everyone, I'm engaged!" she said, beaming.

Daniel kissed her and inquired about sleeping arrangements on the aircraft. "Not to worry, lovers," said Catherine. "This jet divides into three suites and the security-galley area, once we partition it. Each one has at least a queen- size bed and a restroom. Mai, Kelly and I have already decided that back suite is yours, so not to worry. Daniel, you and Su Ling will have the forward suite, and Kelly and I will have the mid-aircraft suite. We will partition the aircraft at Frankfurt and sleep during the final leg into Chicago."

Big Ben spoke up from the couch where he was sitting, "Miss Mai, if you don't mind, I would like to collect all these pretty stones and get them into the safe in the front of the aircraft. Would that be OK with you? And Miss Su Ling, you might want to think about putting those stones in the safe also."

"Oh, Ben, yes, I would like to do that," said Su Ling. "But I just want to enjoy them a bit longer."

"Yes, Ben, please," Mai said. "I would be honored if you would collect these jewels for me and put them in the safe! And thank you for thinking of me. You will always be very special to me." Mai got up, walked over to Jack, and took his hand. "Please excuse us for a bit. I have to talk privately with my man." She led him to the large suite in the back of the aircraft.

Within the suite, they just stood for a moment holding hands at arm's distance and looking at one another sharing this very special moment alone. Then they undressed slowly. Jack was left with only the bandages and the collar. There followed an extended pause while they held each other close with unspoken words of love. After a moment, they got into bed.

They took everything slowly at first as if cherishing every facet of each other that Jack at one time thought was gone forever. But soon they were lost to the passion and went freely with it and wherever their senses took them. They soon became ravenous and devoured each other in a wild animal frenzy that grew and grew until they joined in an orgasm they would truly never forget. They were breathing heavily, Mai with her back arched enveloped in Jack's arms.

They spent several minutes sharing that moment holding each other. They had made love many times before but it was never like this, not even close. They were both sensual animals addicted to the myriad sensations that continued to run through their bodies that they had never felt before. Neither of them wanted to stop. So after a moment, they began again.

When they were truly spent they laid back on the pillows with their hearts still racing and their breathing still catching up. "Oh my god, Mai," exclaimed Jack. "What was that? I never felt anything like that before. Hell I never imagined anything like that before."

Mai giggled. "I think Queen Po was making up for centuries of frustration, Jack. I think you just met her formally. Queen Po is always with us now."

He didn't know what to say so he kissed her and settled back.

After a moment, she kissed his chest and said, "My darling, I have things to tell you that are most amazing and wonderful, and I need you now more than ever to believe me and support me. The truth is, I only feel truly safe when I am in your arms. I have never felt safer in the last two months than I feel right at this moment. Mai continued, "You know people who talk to themselves? I'm having an ongoing conversation with Queen Dau Te Po within me. We are now one and the same, and she is becoming stronger and stronger within me. I sound crazy even telling you this much. But I swear it's true."

He had just experienced the proof of her words and he always believed everything she told him. "How did all of this come about exactly? I think I understand the drugs opening your mind and all. But Mai, are you OK? Daniel told me you would never be the same after Dr. Minh got through with you. But you seem OK to me."

Mai nodded. "With his hypnotic suggestions implanted in me and then the drugs, Dr. Minh took me whole. I was his and completely obedient. It was a very bad path he and Colonel Minh had me on. Fortunately, Su Ling was there to bring me back from that. But Jack, something else happened that no one expected. When they drugged me, it opened my mind further to feel my ancestor's spirit within me. That is how I communicate with her. It's like I think something, only it's not me thinking but her within me. I know it sounds crazy, and I don't understand completely what is happening. But it's very important, and you must help me get through it. I know things, Jack. Things I never knew before and I suddenly just know them. It is truly amazing. I know all about my ancestral past all the way back to the first Champa Queen." She paused for a moment as they lay there in silence.

Mai glanced at the collar still hanging around his neck and giggled. "You goof. Why didn't you ask me to take off that collar when I removed Daniel's?"

"Oh, well I'm glad that amuses you, my Asian queen. But I bet it will surprise you to know I am not at all threatened by wearing this collar. As we were sitting before and talking, a realization came over me. This collar and brand do not weaken me or demean me. I celebrate them as signs of your love, whether as Queen Po, Mai, or both. I mean it. I actually get it now. I decided to leave this on until you're ready to take it off. I wanted to show you that I love you just the same, totally, and unconditionally whatever world we live in. After what you just told me, I suspect you will always be joined in some way with Queen Dau Te Po. From now on, I will always respect her wishes and her traditions, even this one. I am honestly comfortable with that if it means you and I remain together. I hope I got it right, because I love you so much, sometimes the feelings I have for you overwhelm me."

Mai liked that. But that collar was not one of Queen Po's traditions. She reached behind him and easily removed the collar. "We, Queen Dau Te Po and I, love you, Jack Largent, with all our heart."

The captain came into the cabin to announce they were coming into New Delhi in ninety minutes, and he whispered something to Catherine. She nodded and took up a discussion in earnest with Kelly. Afterward, Catherine nodded and got up to radio her ground team.

Thirty minutes later Catherine and Kelly asked Daniel and Su Ling to join them around the oval table, next to the stateroom.

As they sat down, Catherine handed Daniel an envelope. "Daniel, I have been told by one of my production people who is coordinating on the other end that you cannot go with us back to the United States. It seems there is an open warrant from the military there for your arrest for desertion, among other things. You could fight it, and we would support you in that financially. But we both know it could take years, in which time you would probably be incarcerated, and you would probably lose in the end."

She saw his shoulders sag a bit, so she continued, "Here's the plan Kelly and I have devised for the two of you. We're going to land in Frankfurt in about eight hours. You and Su Ling will leave us there. We have coordinated with some of my production people on the ground who are arranging things and who will greet you at the airport. They will escort you to Switzerland. What you do after that, my dear friends, is entirely up to you. But these same people are assigned to you, along with some of our staff, until such time as you do not need their services anymore.

"I strongly suggest you and Su Ling figure out what you wish to do for your future and then let my professional production people help get you started. They only need to know what you wish, and they will take care of everything on your behalf.

As I said, there is an open warrant for your arrest, but the good news is that the US authorities apparently got word from the Vietnamese that you were killed as a result of the assault at Siem Kulea. If you're wondering, that was our deal. Once it was clear that you were coming with us, Kelly radioed Mr. Nguyen and convinced him that he owed us that favor for resolving his Colonel Minh problem. So I do not think anyone will ever be looking for you if you're smart and play your cards right. But if you ever need anything, or our help in any way, do not hesitate to call us. We are grateful to you for saving our friends and being a friend."

"You know, I was never a deserter," Daniel said. "I served my time in the service and in Vietnam, and I chose to stay over there when I was discharged. Straker was supposed to put in my paperwork for the discharge and all that. I hated that man so much you can't imagine. He used his troops for his own personal gain even when we were at Phan Rang. It doesn't matter now, I guess. But I don't want anyone thinking I betrayed my country. So why Switzerland?"

"Because you have to first get your payment for saving Mai, Jack, and Su Ling. In this envelope is a Swiss bank account number and the name of a particular bank. That will contain your payment of twenty million dollars. Ten is as agreed, and ten is my part as I become your new partner in whatever business venture you decide to advance. I will use it for a loss the first year and then it will be freely yours. The papers will be in Zurich for you to sign when you get the money. Also, there is a new identity for you. Our representative on the ground in Frankfurt will have all of your new IDs, credit cards, and everything needed to back them up. There is also some walking-around money in there for expenses. I will do some checking into your discharge issue and get back to you on that. We love you both, Daniel and Su Ling. Kelly and I are always here for you. Never forget that. This will not be goodbye. We want you in our lives, so please know we will all be together again as soon as we can sort things out."

"Twenty mill…Jack was right about you!" he said. "You are an angel."

"Jack said that? How sweet. I won't tell you some of the names he used to call me," she said, smiling at Kelly.

"I have to admit it seems like I'm way overpaid," Daniel confessed.

Catherine shook her head. "We beg to differ. You cannot put a price on the lives of our dear friends. But practically speaking, Mai has brought many times more than that in profit to our corporation in the short time we have known her. If anything, we got a deal."

"Man oh man, you two ladies are amazing. I hope you know that I regret the things I said to you back in Vietnam. Actually I can't think of a better-matched couple than the two of you. I'm honored to be your friend."

Chapter 42

New Delhi to Frankfurt

After they took off from New Delhi, Catherine quickly settled at her desk in the cabin amid a stack of papers and notebooks. Her plan was to consolidate her notes and expand on them on her laptop computer.

She was visibly excited about the story of the treasure and then to hear from Mai that it was connected to this Siem Kulea adventure was enough to capture and enthusiastically engage all of her attention. Her immediate concentration now was on that story and the possibility of an incredible book to follow. She was in journalistic heaven.

After forty-five minutes, she stopped when she saw Mai returning from the back suite and said, "Mai, I'm still confused about a lot of this. I'm starting over on a whole new book and I have to tell you I have never had so much fun in my life! You gave us the outline version of what happened but we have time now, and if you're willing, I would like to get much more into the details now. Can we talk for a bit?"

Mai sat down and settled in across from her.

"Let's begin back in Chicago and how you learned you were the lost heir to the Champa throne. Oh my god! That must have really blown you away! I can't imagine. But wait on that...let's do this is sequence.

"Ok, let's see. How about we start with Su Ling. How did you happen to connect with her? I'm going to turn on my tape recorder so I can work from that afterward."

Mai replayed the story of how she'd gotten involved with Su Ling and the importance of the Hoa Cuc birthmark that revealed her as queen and rightful heir to the Champa throne.

At one point, Mai stood up, opened her riding pants, and pulled the top of them down five inches to reveal the flower birthmark on her hip. Su Ling immediately went to the floor, and bowed reverently toward her. But Kelly, always the intellectually curious one, leaned over close to Mai to examine the birthmark.

She had never seen it on her dear friend previously in Chicago, and it had never come up in conversation.

"It all starts with the hoa cuc, as you see here that I have as a birthmark here on my hip."

Mai turned around slowly so they could all see the birthmark. "This flower birthmark means I am the Hoa Cuc, the queen and rightful sovereign of my people. All of my ancestral queens had it, and my little flower, Devearney, has it." They all gasped and looked at Jack in surprise, and he nodded a smiling affirmation and raised his drink in a toast as Mai fastened her pants. She went to Su Ling, and bade her to take her seat again. Then she sat back down and continued her explanation.

"Our throne is passed on through a female heir. It has always been so. There is a real and honest reason for this, but that is a secret I only recently discovered and I am not willing to share. If any of my people see this symbol on me, they will bow their heads; ready to serve and obey me. Su Ling just did that. It is a belief, and a tradition going back for many thousands of years among the Champa people.

"Before our recorded history, my ancestors, which were an alien race, came to Earth and settled near the Champa people. The Champas were very primitive then and the alien race instilled in them enough knowledge to be able to serve them properly. They embedded in their newly gained understanding a compelling desire to serve them, the alien people called Ferrens. The Champas could only ever be fulfilled if they satisfied the needs of their alien Masters. One day, the aliens left Earth and returned to their home planet. Only one of them stayed behind. She was a daughter of their leader who was in love with a Champa man. From her union with a Champa man came the first Hoa Cuc. This first queen was called Nagani.

"Three months ago I was simply Mai Sambaht, Jack's wife. But then everything changed as I found what I was so desperately seeking in my life. Now I know I am their queen, even though there is no realm for me to rule. They will follow me and obey me without question. It is a fact that they desperately need me in their lives to be fulfilled, and I have to tell you, I am the same way on the other side of that paradigm. Now that I understand I am thus chosen, I need to be their queen for my own fulfillment in much the same manner. That is the bond we share.

"Back in Siem Kulea, Dr. Bui said to me, "As a people we were lost, and now we are found." I now fully understand the meaning of her words. I represent the end of a long unrequited need for fulfillment for the millions of my people, the Champas, who live in Southeast Asia. As such, I need to go back to the cave and find what it is in one of those chests that is so important, and I need to be with my people. That will happen someday."

As she said this, Mai looked at Jack and smiled. He nodded an affirmation back to her.

Later, after several hours had passed, Kelly had a thought. She put down her drink, and asked, "Jack, can I borrow Mai for a minute so we women can go in the back and talk girl talk?"

Jack nodded absently, as he was replaying his part of the story at Siem Kulea for Catherine, who was quizzing him and typing as they talked.

Mai and Kelly went back into the bedroom suite and locked the door behind them.

Kelly hugged her and said, "How are you doing, Mai? I thought you must need some methadone by now."

"Yes, I was going to mention it in coded words even as you got the idea yourself," Mai said.

Kelly retrieved a bottle from their medicine shelf. "Do you know how big a dose you need?" asked Kelly.

"Here, let me see the size of the dose in each pill," Mai said, taking it from Kelly. "Ah...one pill should do it. Not to worry, it's just a small dose to calm my nerves. But when we get back to Chicago, I want to get connected with that friend of Catherine's soonest."

Mai took a pill and Kelly handed her a glass of water to wash it down. She started to leave, but Kelly begged, "Mai, please, wait for a minute. I want...I need to talk to you."

They talked for a while mostly about Jack, the brand on his arm and why it was important for him to have it. Kelly was surprised when Mai told her she and Jack would be returning in about two years to Siem Kulea. But she was stunned and a bit incredulous when Mai told her it would be Jack's decision. Mai again professed her deep love for him and told Kelly she could not return to Siem Kulea until he was ready to go with her. She felt he just needed to get Chicago out of his system first.

Finally, Kelly voiced her last concern to her dear friend. "I think the thing that is most disconcerting for me is that you are a queen now, and I am not sure how to deal with that. Do you expect me to defer to you and such? How should I act around you?"

"Be my friend just as before, first and last, Kelly. Nothing more. Do not act any differently toward me than before. I am not your queen, but if you start feeling awkward around me, I will not be your friend anymore either. I will work as hard with Catherine as I have always done in the past. As it happens, our interests right now are connected, and many of our questions will be resolved at the cave site at Thap Cham."

Kelly had more questions and Mai did her best to answer them and reassure her that she was still the same Mai she had always known.

Finally, Kelly nodded and then sighed. "Thanks for talking with me. I feel better about everything. We really should go back now, or they will be the ones asking questions." They had one last hug before returning to the others.

After taking off from Frankfurt, and with the aircraft divided into sleeping areas, Kelly and Catherine settled in to try and get some sleep. After a time, both of them were lying in bed face up. Kelly turned sideways to find that Catherine was staring at the upper bulkhead with her eyes wide open in thought.

"I can't sleep," Kelly said just after kissing her shoulder.

"Me neither," Catherine replied. "I cannot believe this story that has dropped into my lap, Kel. It is a truly amazing tale that has everything; love, adventure and even a treasure! And it isn't even done yet. Did you see how happy Daniel and Su Ling were when we said goodbye to them in Frankfurt? They were like little lovebirds beginning their new lives. I almost envy them."

"I have a different take on Su-Ling," said Kelly. "Something is going on with her, and she didn't seem at all happy to me to be parting with Mai."

"Well, she is a Champa and devoted to her queen."

"No. In fact, something else is going on and Mai is very protective of her. I don't know, but I think Su Ling is ambitious and has designs on Mai. That lady is very smart and manipulative, Cat. She won you over by bringing you a glass of wine. She plays people. I'm going to keep an open mind about her, but proceed with caution. I think there is more to her than meets the eye."

"Wow. That's a can of worms," said Catherine. She turned toward Kelly, kissed her, and said, "OK, let's use our resources and check Su Ling out thoroughly. In fact, let's check out Daniel too. In many ways, they seem a matched pair. Let's see if you're right about your feelings. But right now I'm tired of talking."

Chapter 43

Chicago, 1989

When they got back to Chicago, Catherine again offered to put Jack in contact with her plastic surgeon, but Jack turned her down. He felt very different about it by that time and knew keeping the brand on his arm was important to Mai, and now it was important to him too.

Early on, when they were alone, Mai talked it over with him and explained, "The reality is that it's the only way my people will accept you as my consort and husband. I want you beside me, Jack, when I go back to be with my people. I want that more than anything."

Jack knew without further explanation what she meant. She had several times mentioned that she would be going back to Siem Kulea. He also knew that on that day he would do as she wished and go with her. But for now, he wanted to live safely in Chicago with Devearney and her as a family. He wanted *that* more than anything. The crushing remorse he felt when he believed that was gone forever was still very fresh in his memory. It was the most traumatic moment in his entire life. Chicago and all he had once taken for granted seemed very precious to him now.

They spent most of their free time with Devearney. Mai thought Jack doted on her too much. That made Jack laugh because they both competed to do everything for her. Jack said, "It's impossible to spoil a princess," as to that idea, Mai had no argument.

The original return to Vietnam and the Champa treasure site was moved back to four weeks instead of two. Catherine had too many outside commitments to manage before returning to Vietnam, and Brad had a full slate of items he needed to work on with Mai. Dr. Bui said the delay would not matter much because the construction and the frenzy over the body in the cave had delayed everything else. Besides, they could spend a year just examining the contents of the first chest that had been removed from the cave the previous week. There were many valuable documents in the chest along with thousands of gold coins from many different countries.

In a private conversation with Catherine, Dr. Bui revealed that she needed Mai there when they opened the rest of the chests. Catherine asked her if her family was of Champa ancestry, and Dr. Bui replied they were.

"So you're really waiting for instructions from your queen before opening the rest of the chests," said Catherine, getting right to the point.

"You will understand, Catherine, if I don't address that remark. I will only say that Mai is integral to the correct interpretation of our findings," said Dr. Bui. "Her perspective and insight will be invaluable. We need her here. Please bring her back to us."

"I understand completely," said Catherine, amazed that everything Mai told them, however strange it sounded at the time, continued to be true. "We will follow your lead on this end, and I assure you we are doing all we can to bring Mai with us when we return. There is only one obstacle to overcome."

Jack and Mai continued to have amazing sexual relations. She thought he had accepted her plans to return to Vietnam simply by his particular attention and desire to please her when they made love and Jack's initial acquiescence to the idea. Thus they had not discussed it. But one night as he lay beside her and she held him close, she commented, "My love, I hope you're remembering to adjust your schedule so you can be with me when we return to Vietnam in two weeks with Catherine and Kelly."

He took a deep breath because he was not ready to go back yet and he knew she was not going to like his view. He replied, "Mai, we live in two worlds, and you have conquered me in this one. In the other world, I will always respect your opinion, but if I have anything to say about it, you are not going back to Vietnam anytime soon. Right now, here, with the three of us together, this is our paradise. And, my darling, we almost lost it. I can't forget that. If you love Devearney and me, you will not return. I am very afraid that if you go back, I will never see you again. I cannot imagine what would happen if those horrible people get hold of you."

"No, Jack. That won't happen. The bad people are all gone. But you must understand. I have to go back soon. It is very important to me. I have to get something from inside that cave."

"What? What do you have to get that could be so important as to risk what we have here?"

"I don't know. I only know that it is very important and I must go there to get it. We can do that without risking what we have here. "

"See, that's exactly my point. You don't even know why you want to go back. How could that be more important than the security and happiness we have here."

There was a silent pause in their conversation before she asked, "If I go anyway, is it a deal breaker between us?"

"No, darling, of course not. There is no such thing as a deal breaker between us. I understand your passion and drive and even your bond with Queen Po who is dancing around in your head, and messing with that beautiful mind of yours. But Devearney and I are important too. I don't want you to do it. Not now. Maybe later."

"Oh, Jack. My darling. *No!* You can't be saying this. I need you to support me. I must go back as soon as possible. I have to get whatever it is that is waiting for me in those chests and honestly, it is only the first thing of many things I have to do.

"Everything is different for me now. My life in many ways is no longer my own. I have an obligation to lead and protect my people, which is as compelling as their need to serve me. My actions of late led to hurt and destruction for them and now I must save them. I am the only one who can do that. I don't completely understand all of it just now, but I am positive there is something I need in that cave that will clarify everything for me. I must go very soon, Jack. Please, I'm asking you to support me in this."

He did not answer her and remained steadfastly silent.

Mai became increasingly angry at his stubbornness. She had never felt that before and was confused by it. After a protracted silence between them, she again pleaded, "This is very important to me, my darling. Please, I need you to support me. Jack?"

Still, he remained silent as if that were the last word on the subject.

Mai could not hold back her feelings any longer. With tears in her eyes, she sat up suddenly. "Who are you?" she cried out tearfully. "I don't know you anymore. You're not the man I love. What has become of you?" She slapped him hard reflecting her own frustration. In this matter, she needed him to accept her decision, and she did not know what to do when he would not.

"Oh, Jack, I'm so sorry for you, and for us. We've always been so close and supported each other always, I don't understand how it's come to this," she said, crying real tears. She got up and got dressed quickly in front of him.

"Where are you going?" he asked when he realized she was getting dressed.

He had never seen her like this.

"None of your business," she said, grabbing her purse.

"Wait! Please don't go," he said, chasing her. "Can't we talk about this?"

"Talk? No. You don't want to talk. You want to dictate. You don't care about me. You've made up your mind. You profess your love and that you care about what is going on with me, and then you turn out to be a typical selfish, narrow-minded, stubborn male who wants to possess and control his wife as it suits him. That is precisely why we Champa queens never marry!"

"But where are you going?" he asked again.

"Wherever I want," she replied, "including Vietnam! Do whatever you want. I don't care anymore. I have things I have to do with or without you."

She hurried down the stairs, and he heard her slam the door on the way out. He sat there naked on the couch, having chased her that far, and tried to make sense of what just happened. He knew Mai better than anyone. As he thought about it, he realized that he had made a big mistake. He was telling her to choose between her life here as his wife, and her life over there as queen of the Champa people. She wanted them both and he couldn't imagine how that could ever happen.

Just at that moment, Jack got a chill, much like the one he had when he was in that cell in Siem Kulea. The sound of the door slamming downstairs left him in a cold place and it took him back to that time when he thought all was truly lost and his life was over. In the next moment, he asked himself, "What did I do? How could I have been so blind and selfish?"

He could see clearly now it was necessary and important to let her go back and play this out wherever it took them. She had begged him to understand and support her. Why had he not done so when that was all he ever wanted to do? Of course, he would support her and help her, but how? With a sudden clarity of mind it came to him. He realized the only way for them to have both their worlds, the family here and the world over there for her as queen, was simply to return to Siem Kulea and live there as a family. Somehow they would figure it out, and he would follow her lead on what she wanted to do and how she wished to do it. He really didn't care as long as they were together. He was tired of Chicago and the ad business anyway. He wanted to go and explore a new world and a new life with her and little Devearney. With that revelation he felt instantly better about things, and he became happy again.

He was suddenly cognizant of where he was and that he was sitting there on the couch naked. He laughed to himself. Whatever she did, whatever choices she made, he would never stop loving that woman. He got up and walked back to the bedroom to clean up. Devearney would wake up in a few hours.

Mai, for her part, only got into her car, drove down the block, and parked again. It was raining outside, and she turned off the motor and watched the drops of rain backlit by the streetlights weave their paths down the windows. She finally couldn't hold back anymore and cried. She loved that man so much it hurt, and she couldn't go back to Vietnam without him. She would not go against him on this because of how much she had put him through already. For the first time in her life, she didn't have an answer. One way or the other, she had to convince him to go back to Vietnam with her. She was compelled beyond reason to return to that country and that cave, and though she did not know why, she knew it was important. And then, there was the bond between her and her people to consider. She sat there and wept. She felt like she was all alone with her problems. *Oh, Jack, my darling. I love you so much. Why can't you support me in this?*

Eventually, she fell asleep, and when she woke again, she returned home. Jack was sitting in the kitchen and feeding Devearney breakfast in her high chair. Without any words between them, she quietly kissed him on the top of his head and went to get a shower before going to work.

Mai was seeing a psychiatrist, Dr. Doheny Merit, who was recommended by Catherine. At first, when Mai told her she wanted to continue taking opiates, Dr. Merit said she could not help her. But when Dr. Merit heard why she was taking the drugs, she became intrigued, and in spite of her misgivings, she agreed to continue the opiates to further investigate the relationship with Queen Po that was playing out in Mai's mind. Mai soon discovered that the opiates she had been taking and had grown accustomed to were more akin to heroin than the opioids doctors commonly prescribe.

Mai had dedicated sessions with Dr. Merit once daily, even though it was ridiculously expensive because the time was short before they were to return to Vietnam. The delay in the return gave an extra two weeks for Mai and Dr. Merit to sort out the concerns that were developing over her treatment.

Dr. Merit gave Mai a series of hypnosis procedures in the hope that it would help Queen Dau Te Po to surface without the drugs. However, the results were disappointing, so they agreed to continue the drugs for the interim.

One afternoon during the second week after they returned from Vietnam, Mai was having coffee with Kelly and Catherine at the Stroll Inn restaurant on Oak Street when Kelly commented, "Well, ladies, here we are, back at the scene of the crime."

"What are you talking about, Kelly?" asked Mai.

"We were sitting with Jack in this same booth when it all started, what… three years and two babies ago?" said Kelly. "Considering all that has happened, they ought to name the restaurant Thap Cham."

"Or how about Daddy Jack's?" said Catherine, smiling.

"I knew I liked this place for some reason," said Mai.

After a thoughtful pause, she continued. "Guys, I need some help. I'm not convincing Jack about going back to Vietnam. He is like a brick wall when it comes to that. I'm running out of options and time, and I'm getting out of control over this. I even slapped him the other night. I love him so much, I can hardly stand it. I can't bring myself to go back without him. I'm so afraid of hearing him say "no", that I haven't brought it up again after we had a huge fight over it before. I want and need him beside me. I am positive it's very important for me to return to the cave site, especially this time, but I don't know why. It's just a feeling I have."

"Like something Queen Po is telling you to do," said Kelly.

Mai looked at Kelly, and was comforted that she seemed to understand. "Yes, I'm sure of it," said Mai smiling. "It is very important."

"It's too bad," commented Kelly, "that you can't call up Dr. Minh from the afterlife and have him hypnotize Jack!"

"Oh, great! That's all we need," said Catherine as she put her hand on Mai's to reassure her. "I don't know, Mai. But something will break. It always does. We have two more weeks before we go over. You'll think of something."

Mai already had.

After her experience in Cambodia with Dr. Minh, Mai was fascinated that he'd been able to control her so completely using hypnosis. She was an individual with a particularly strong intellect, yet he took possession of her totally and he might still control her if it hadn't been for Su Ling. She had already begun to read up on how to master hypnosis so no one could ever own her like that again. But now she realized that if she could learn how to do it, it might be a means to convince Jack to go back to Vietnam with her. It was a wild idea, and now one that she was desperate enough to try.

During one of her sessions, she asked Dr. Merit if she would teach her how to do hypnosis. Dr. Merit explained that self-hypnosis was a bit different and started to tell her why, but Mai interrupted her. "No, I want to do what you do. I want to see if I can hypnotize someone. If I can master the technique, it might come in useful for some plans I have."

Dr. Merit first tried to discourage her from this idea but then decided it might be better to at least explain the proper technique to her, before again trying to discourage her. She told her that not everyone could be hypnotized, but some people were very susceptible. She also explained it was good to have something for the subject person to fixate on while the hypnotic mantra was working to overcome their resistance.

They practiced several times, but Mai didn't have a real subject to practice on. She realized she would have to wait until the opportunity arose. In the meantime, she read authoritative medical articles and books about hypnosis and practiced her technique on her own at home. She dedicated her energy and time to learning all that was involved in the process.

At the end of that week, Mai found the first opportunity to try out what she had learned about hypnosis on Jack. She was sitting with him on the couch in the living room of their townhouse. Jack was not aware of her recent research and practice in hypnosis and thus did not suspect anything when she asked him to look at the ruby in the necklace she held. It was from her collection, which now sat in a hardened fireproof safe, behind a secret panel within a bookcase in the library. The stone was large, maroon in color, and cut to show a blazing number of facets within when caught by the smallest light. She urged Jack to look into the stone and see what was there. She said she thought there was a face in it, and he looked intently as she spoke softly to him in a gentle voice. She told him she felt safe and even comfortable looking there, and she suggested he would feel the same. She continued the mantra softly as he looked intently into the stone, and she attempted to take him deeper and deeper into a state of hypnosis.

Within a few minutes, he appeared to be in a trance. Mai sat back on the couch, and observed him for a moment. She was totally fascinated, and even surprised. It apparently was ridiculously easy to put him in a hypnotic trance. She didn't know what to do next or what she wanted him to do. She hadn't prepared for it to actually work.

She decided to continue the routine she had learned and put in some commands and triggers. She told him that when she said the words "Jack, Queen Po loves you," he would go into a deep trance and await her further commands. When she clapped her hands he would return to normal but he would always be ready to obey her wishes.

But then she got an idea that made her laugh to even consider it. Yet in the next instant, she decided to do it. With this trigger in place, and with a huge smile on her face, she said, "Jack, when I snap my fingers, you will be a chicken. I want you to act like a chicken for my amusement. But when I clap my hands twice, you will come out of it. Do you understand?"

"Yes," he answered.

She smiled. This was fun! And she hadn't expected the feeling of power over Jack that came with it would feel so awesome. Now she wanted to see if he would really do it, if he would really follow her commands. She snapped her fingers, and Jack jumped up and began walking around with his hands behind him and his back arched like a chicken. He was making cluck-cluck sounds as he walked with big, exaggerated steps back and forth. She laughed, and laughed, and couldn't stop. Every time she was going to clap her hands, she couldn't do it because it was so funny.

Just at that moment, Kelly arrived at the top of the stairs from the studio below and stood in the doorway of their townhouse. "Knock knock," she said at the open doorway before she entered. But when she saw Jack she looked surprised and asked, "What's going on, Mai?"

"I hypnotized him," Mai explained, smiling. "I told him to be a chicken, and it worked. I am totally surprised it worked, but it really is funny, isn't it?"

Kelly didn't want to laugh, but she had to because Jack was the silliest chicken she had ever seen. "Oh, but you have to stop him, Mai. It's not right," she protested as she laughed and wondered if she really wanted her to stop.

"OK, I will stop him, but first you have to go back downstairs. I don't think it will be good for him to see you when he comes out of it. He might be embarrassed."

Kelly left, but first took one last look at Jack as a chicken, and smiled to herself. *Life will never be the same again with Mai and Queen Po around,* she thought.

After she left, Mai said the words "Jack, Queen Po loves you," and he dropped his head in a triggered trance once more. She told him to come sit on the couch beside her.

It was just as Dr. Merit had said it would be. But she said triggers didn't always work, and you couldn't really control most people.

Mai looked at Jack as he sat down still in an apparent trance. She pondered the situation that had begun purely as an experiment. Who knew Jack would turn out to be the perfect subject? She was about to clap her hands when she had another thought. If she was going to take him to the next level, now was the time to do it, because very soon they must prepare to return to Vietnam. She hated what she was doing and within herself her conscience argued with her.

She said to him, "Jack, from this moment forward, you must obey my wishes. Do you understand?" She thought, *this couldn't really work. No way, Jose.* And in the next moment, she wondered if she really wanted it to work.

But then he answered, "Yes, Mai."

"You will obey me," she said again, really not believing this was happening.

"Yes, Mai," he answered.

"You want to please me and make me happy always," she continued.

"Yes, Mai," he answered.

"Whatever I wish you to do, you will do," she commanded.

"Yes, Mai," he answered.

"When you obey me, it pleases me, and that makes you happy," she said. "When I clap my hands, you will awaken feeling fresh and happy, as if you had a wonderful nap," she commanded.

She got up and poured a glass of wine for him, came back to the couch, and put it down in front of him. She clapped her hands twice, picked up the wine, and said, "Wake up, sleepyhead. You dozed off. How do you feel? I poured you a glass of wine. I thought we might go out on the deck and catch some fresh air."

"I feel wonderful," he replied. "It's great to be alive! I love you, babe."

It had worked. It really worked! Mai decided to experiment further. It was hard for her to believe she could really hypnotize someone and that she really controlled him. It was too ridiculous. You had to be a doctor or something, and study for years. She was only playing with it, like it was a game. That was how it started, just an experiment. But now she was having narcissistic thoughts, and the control was unexpectedly exciting for her.

"Jack, Queen Po loves you," she said, and Jack immediately dropped his head to his chest again in a trance, ready to be programmed.

Looking at his bare feet, she said, "Jack, a bunch of tacks have fallen on the floor in the hallway, and you must be careful to step around them." Then she clapped her hands twice, and he once again was awake and smiling.

"Honey, would you get my slippers for me? They're in the bedroom," she told him.

Jack hurried out to get her slippers, but as he got to the hallway, he began to tiptoe carefully and slowly as he walked.

Mai watched him and shook her head. For the first time, she understood the feelings that had possessed Dr. Minh. But then she suddenly felt the inevitable guilt that comes with doing something harmful to someone you love dearly. Her eyes began to water. She decided she didn't want Jack like that and was ready to snap him out of the hypnosis.

But again she stopped, totally conflicted, as she wiped her eyes. She needed him under her control now more than ever, like it or not. She was exploring her Queen Po side with drug treatments, something that was so far unbeknownst to Jack. She was a mix of herself and her ancestor queen, whom she now loved beyond words, and Queen Po wanted Jack kept obedient.

"*Who knows what he'll do when he finds out I'm still an addict?*" she thought. And then there was the issue of her returning to Vietnam, which he was adamantly against. No, she had to continue to control him. Like it or not, it was very important right now for Jack to submit to her wishes.

Jack returned with her slippers, and still deep in thought she commanded, "Put them on me."

Jack knelt down and put her slippers on her feet like an obedient servant. Then she held out her glass to him and said, "Darling, would you refresh my glass," and he took it and hurried off.

Mai sat there thinking for a long time. She watched Jack filling her glass and eager to obey her every command. She didn't like this at all and didn't like doing it with Jack. She wouldn't harm Jack in any way, and she vowed to end the hypnosis after the issues in Vietnam were finally resolved. In the meantime she decided it was necessary, and she would protect him.

She got up to go change the wash. Then she reminded herself she could have Jack do the wash for her anytime she wanted to now. She smiled at that idea. But no, she was done with that. She was not going to use this power to abuse the man she loved.

When he brought her a fresh glass of wine in the laundry room, she looked at him smiling and said, "Darling, I want you to truly relax. Go find a movie you like or a book to read or something. Have an afternoon without worries. I will do the wash and fold the clothes. OK? And if you need anything, just call. I will be your servant this afternoon."

"Sure," he said. "I need to relax. Great suggestion. But I have to make a grocery store run later and get something for dinner too. It's my night to cook."

"I'm on it, shopping, cooking, everything," she said. "Your job is to take it easy today. Got it?"

"Hey, I think I like this idea," he said, smiling. "How about a foot massage later?"

"Don't push your luck," she said, laughing at him. "But I'll see if I can work it in."

Later Kelly caught up with Mai as she was folding clothes in the laundry room. "I wanted to ask you before we went back to Vietnam if you want to rent a house like before," asked Kelly. "I'm trying to make housing arrangements now."

"Dr. Bui tells me they have nice accommodations for us prepared in one of their facilities at the cave site. Let's do that instead, OK?"

"OK, got it," said Kelly, smiling broadly at Mai as she folded clothes from the dryer.

"What's so funny?" asked Mai when she noticed her standing there with a big smile on her face.

"I'm enjoying the moment of the great Queen Dau Te Po folding Jack's underwear," she explained.

"Yep, it's definitely a reality check, isn't it?" Mai said, enjoying the joke with her. "Our maid is sick, and I could have easily asked Jack to help, but frankly it's great therapy for me. Want to help?"

"Only since the moment I walked in the door and saw you doing it, my lady," Kelly confessed seriously displaying the latent devotion she felt for Mai as queen.

"Yeah, I understand," said Mai, a bit surprised. It appeared the effect she'd had on Kelly in the airplane coming home wasn't completely over. "Come on, let's get this done."

Kelly and Jack were talking in the office the next day when Mai walked in holding little Devearney. Kelly had announced she was finally leaving the studio, and they were considering replacements for her.

The one-year-old put her arms out for Jack to take her, and he gladly did, bouncing her on his arm gently as he held her. Devearney was the most precious thing in his life, and he didn't want to ever leave her again.

Their conversation continued as Mai sat down at one of the desks in the office. "I've interviewed a lot of assistants, boss, and I really think she's the best fit," Kelly said.

"Who is *she?*" asked Mai, suddenly interested.

"Her name is Jasmine Ngo. She is just like me, only Asian," said Kelly.

"Nope, not gonna happen," said Mai firmly, knowing Jack's affinity for Asian women.

Jack walked over and handed the baby back to Mai. He gave her a kiss and smiled. "What about the other one, Kelly? Maggie something?"

"She has good skills, but she's not very organized, boss."

"How about the guy? Do you like him?" asked Jack.

Kelly winced. "I guess we need to do some more interviews, boss."

"Kelly, we're never going to find anyone to replace you, so stop trying. I really hate to see you go. Want to reconsider?"

"Sorry, Jack. I mean that. I hate to leave here too, but Catherine needs me over there. I'm going to be running all the charitable contributions for the foundation."

"OK, let's put the word out and do more interviews. I'm not interested in the Ngo woman. Nope, not gonna happen," he said and left the office.

"OK, boss. I'm on it," she said, realizing he'd repeated what Mai said. She gave Mai a curious look and picked up the phone.

Mai went over to the desk where Kelly was sitting and handed her a planner she was working on concerning their return to Vietnam. She whispered to Kelly, "Have the Asian woman report to me for an interview. If she is the best, then we should hire her. But I want to approve her first, OK?"

Kelly nodded. Then Mai called after Jack, "Jack, let's go upstairs. We need to talk. I'm going to pour that Beaujolais Nouveau you brought home yesterday. Kel, can you join us after you make your phone calls?"

"Be right there," said Kelly, having no doubt about what Mai wanted to discuss and knowing she wanted support.

The au pair took Devearney for a nap, and Jack and Mai settled down on the couch opposite the deck, sipping their wine.

"You said you were ready to talk about the drugs with me?" he asked.

She nodded and confessed, "Yes, I want you to finally know that I've been deceiving you. I am a full addict now. I am hooked. But it is mainly because it keeps me bonded with Queen Po. I swear that is the truth. Dr. Minh had no idea what he had awakened in me. He didn't create me, Jack. *I* created me as I rejoined with my ancestors. He was just the instrument. I would have never reached Queen Po at this level without him. It was unexpected and yet necessary. I don't think it was an accident. Events are playing out as if guided by a higher power of some kind. Who knows? Out of me came the ancestor you see as a queen before you. I am aware now of things I couldn't have imagined without the drugs. I feel at home, comfortable, and I can talk with Queen Po. She is with me always, talking to me and guiding me."

Kelly walked in, picked up the glass of wine sitting on the counter, and sat down on the couch opposite them. "What'd I miss?" she asked.

"Mai tells me she is an addict, Kel," said Jack, a bit sullen.

"Yeah, I know," said Kelly. "Catherine and I have been helping her contact her ancestors with that," she confessed. "Honestly, Catherine and I thought her situation was between you and Mai and decided not to discuss it or interfere."

Jack's face flushed visibly red in anger. He pulled his arm from behind Mai and leaned toward Kelly. "You what? You're helping her to be an addict? Are you out of your mind?"

"Stop it, Jack," demanded Mai. "They are the best friends anyone could have. They only have my best interests at heart, and so should you. You should follow their example and support me in this. We need to do the drug treatments. It is important to continue them for now. Sit back, relax, and listen."

Jack stopped protesting, sat back on the couch, and nodded, his hands resting in his lap. Kelly saw this and then looked at Mai who gave Jack a slight smirk. Kelly was suddenly hit with the realization that Mai was ordering Jack, not asking him, like in the office when he'd changed his mind about the assistant. In all the time she had known them, she had never seen Mai order Jack to do anything. Yikes! She couldn't wait to discuss this with Catherine!

Mai continued, "Catherine has a doctor friend who is monitoring my dosages, Jack. When this is all over, she will help me with treatments to get me off of them. Right now I want the drugs and need them to maintain communication with Queen Po. This is very important to me."

Jack seemed to consider what she said, nodded, and then said, "Yes, it is important for you to continue the drug treatments. You need to figure this out."

Kelly thought, *there it is again.*

"When she trips on the opiates, Jack, she all but becomes the ancient Queen Po," said Kelly, helping to explain. "We've been able to talk to her and even ask her questions. She tells us stories about her life and experiences. This is unrecorded history, and it is an opportunity none of us wanted to let slip away. Mai came to us and told us what was happening with her. We were concerned at first, like you, but then it was at her insistence that we started recording her thoughts and conversations. But there is one final chapter to write, and that one cannot be written here."

"I need to go back to Vietnam, Jack," Mai said. "I need you to go with me and to support me. I need to go to that cave again. Po was there, my darling. That was she in the cave. She died there, Jack. I believe that's why I could find it and no one else could. We are connected. Surely you can see that I must go. You want to support me in this."

Jack said, "Yes, I want to support you in this, of course." He paused a moment and continued, "But Mai, I am very worried. There is no telling what those people will do to you if they find you."

"The bad people are gone, Jack," she explained. "There are only the good people, the Champas, now. They are my people and they will protect me. Besides, nothing is going to happen. I am going to go to the site and work with Dr. Bui. Catherine is going to get what she needs for her book, and we will come back. One month for us on the outside. That's all. I promise. We'll only be gone one month, and then it will be over. You will be there, taking photographs as Dr. Bui wishes and work with Catherine on her book."

"Yes," he said, "I agree. It is important for me to be there. But I hear it in your voice, darling. There is something else. What are you afraid of, Mai? What's the downside in this?"

"Well, Jack, there is always the remote possibility that when she's in one of these opiate states, she might go into a permanent coma," explained Kelly.

"Then don't do it!" Jack said. "I mean, do you really have to do these opiate trips? Only you, Devearney, and I matter."

"Yes Jack," she said. "You, Devearney, and I do matter. But my people also matter, and I care about them too. I am as a mother to them for they are my children. Now that they know I am the Hoa Cuc, they need me in their lives even as you and Devearney do. I must do this for them if we are to ever have our peace. I need Queen Po in my life. She is showing me what to do. It is like I am being led from one place to another and told to look. I am being shown my past through the eyes of Queen Po."

"Of course, Mai. I understand your dilemma and your need to return. I admit I am still confused about some things. But we have to figure this out and we will do this together. I will be by your side supporting you. I can't let you do this alone and I've decided you have enough concerns on your plate already to last a lifetime. So I am all in and here to help with whatever you need. When are we leaving to go back to Vietnam?"

Mai showed a big smile on her face for the first time since they sat down.

"We are leaving in six days, boss," said Kelly.

"What about my schedule?" he asked her.

"That's the other thing, Jack," said Kelly. "The week after next, you are booked for three weeks with John Davis Farm Equipment out of Wichita. You were supposed to go on location to do their catalog. I can talk to them and delay it, I think. I needed to know if you were going first."

"Oh yeah, that catalog. I really was looking forward to that. Something different. Oh well...do what you can, Kelly. Delay it or cancel it. Whatever," he said. "This is more important right now."

"OK, boss, but first I want you to see this," she said, handing him a job proposal.

Jack looked over the document and suddenly looked up at Kelly. "She wants to pay me to photograph the treasure? This is a lot of money! You know, I think she mentioned something about that when we were on the plane coming back."

"Catherine is formally booking you to do the photos for her book on the Champa archeological site," she said. "We all know you're worth it, boss. Can you imagine photographing those treasures, with your talent? And if you consider it's for over a month of your time, it really isn't so much. We just wanted to be sure you were willing to go back first." Kelly looked right at Mai and gave her a curious look.

Jack's demeanor changed as he became visibly excited. "Kelly, I think I will want to pack up that new large Halliburton camera case I just bought, the one you were laughing at me about," he said. "I believe you said it was 'over the top'. But it will be the perfect thing to take on location."

"Well, it's just so huge, boss. It's like taking the whole studio on a field trip in a steamer trunk," Kelly said.

"It will hold more of my cameras and lenses and has that secret compartment area I showed you underneath. Mai, you can hide your valuables in there too," he said. "Besides, if we're traveling in Catherine's corporate jet again, the airport check-in won't be a hassle. It's a perfect time to try it out."

"Oh, good. I'll feel better having a secure place to keep some of my things," Mai said. "Oh, and we got confirmation that we can fly right into Phan Rang this time."

Jack got up and started to leave the room.

"Where're you going, boss?" Kelly asked.

"I am going to snuggle with my little girl while I still can," he said, heading down the hallway to her bedroom.

Kelly waited for Jack to leave and then commented, "OK, I have to ask. He agrees with everything you want to do. Have you hypnotized him again?"

"He loves me, Kelly, regardless of how messed up I am. I love him too, but it is better if I control him right now. Things could get real complicated if he's not on the same page with me. You and I both know this next part could get real crazy, and I need to be able to focus without any outside distractions. I admit I still have misgivings about him being hypnotized. I don't like it at all. But I was desperate to find a way to get him back there with me."

And then Mai put it all into a few words: "Oh, Kelly, what if something does happen? Are we nuts to be doing this?"

"Definitely," answered Kelly, offering no assurances. "Let's check our list again. We still have lots to do."

Mai started to follow her down the stairs but then stopped and said, "Kelly, you go and check things over again. I am going to spend some quality time with my family."

Chapter 44

Thap Cham, Vietnam, 1990

When they finally got back to the archeological site, it had been almost three months since that fateful day when Mai found the cave entrance and the Champa treasure. The site was like a small town with buildings and tents going off in the distance toward the little town of Thap Cham. Mr. Nguyen explained that the nearer buildings were used to properly analyze and protect their findings from the cave, while the farther ones were for housing. He showed them to their rooms in a modern building next to the research facility. They were surprised to find that the rooms, though plainly decorated, were furnished with comfortable furniture like what you would find in a good hotel in the United States. They didn't have but a moment to see the rooms because as quickly as Jack could get his camera bag, he was still chasing behind Catherine, Kelly, and Mai, who were already on their way toward the large main building.

Inside they entered a pristine waiting room area with a receptionist and two guards. They didn't have to announce themselves, as the receptionist greeted them eagerly and led them through two doors back to the laboratory. They paused at a window outside the lab, and through the glass partition, they saw Dr. Bui standing at a table covered in gold coins. She was leaning way over and examining one with a magnifying glass. The coins were round with a square hole in the middle, and it was too far away to read anything on them. Jack saw a projection of a coin on a screen opposite them resembling one they were examining. Dr. Bui said something to the assistant next to her and looked up as Catherine waved frantically from behind the glass.

Dr. Bui smiled instantly and almost ran to the locked door to let them in. She said something to the two guards, who nodded and stepped out of the way. Catherine gave her a warm hug, and she greeted Kelly with another hug.

Not holding back this time, Dr. Bui knelt reverently before Mai. She kissed her offered hand, and said, "My lady, welcome back. I am most pleased to have you with us again."

Knowing how important this show of reverence was to Dr. Bui, Mai was patient for a bit, but then she pulled her up and hugged her close. After a moment she told her, "Thank you for following my wishes while I was away." She followed that with a kiss on her cheek.

Jack was surprised when Dr. Bui turned to him and said, "We've been waiting for you, Jack. What took you so long to get back here? You have lots of work to do!"

Jack collected himself and replied, "Well, we wanted to be sure Mai was OK before she returned."

Mai gave him a look followed by a twisted smile. "Yeah, right."

Dr. Bui said, "Well, come on. We're putting you right to work. Let me show you the studio we built for you. Most of these buildings are connected with closed hallways for security purposes."

Jack walked into a modern photography studio he would have been proud to have in Chicago.

"I followed your suggestions on the light sources, Jack, and I think we have everything you need," said Dr. Bui.

Two young men walked up and shook hands with Jack. "These are two of my finest students, John and Mark," Dr. Bui said. "They will be assisting you as you teach them the best way to document everything. There is a lot of detail and tedious work that I know you will want to pass on to them after you get organized. So put them to work!"

Jack shook their hands and spoke his thought: "Not Vietnamese names. That's somehow a relief."

"Yes, well, that's another story. They will help you to photograph the coins we have taken from the first chest. The other chests are still in the cave. It might seem like we are moving slowly, Jack, but I am very methodical about this and want a record of everything. Fortunately, the Vietnamese authorities have not questioned me once about it. They seem confident in my approach."

"How much were the coins in that chest worth?" Jack asked.

"Let's just go with millions," she said. "They are very old and priceless, and my determined, methodical approach has already paid dividends. We are finding a virtual history of the time by the mix of coins we see from the chest. The Vietnamese rivaled the Chinese in the making of coins during this period, but we have a mixture here of Chinese coins from as far back as the Tang dynasty. We have coins from Vietnam, various Indian kingdoms, and even the Abbasid caliphate that ruled the western and southern Mediterranean at the time, and all in pure gold. It is a stunning find, Jack, and it proves that trade was already prevalent between the East and West long before Marco Polo.

"I want you to photograph the treasures we find in those chests in a way that lends credence to their importance. You will need to spend a few days up in Dalat while you are here, and we have provided a truck for that purpose so you can take along any equipment you may need.

"We also have a good number of documents that record the history of the time and the royal family. They are already in Dalat, being scrutinized by an associate of mine. They in themselves are a goldmine of information and are in a delicate and pristine condition. We need you to photograph them in as many ways as you can, both to document them and to present them dramatically for other purposes. I want you to get really close up on the text, so we can even observe the grain of the parchment and the pigments they used. That will be useful to us later."

As she was leaving, she said, "I am going to call you out in about thirty minutes to go photograph the second chest as it sits in the cave. Please go with my agenda for now, Jack. I will catch up with you later, and we can set up a more orderly schedule, OK?"

Jack smiled and said, "Sure, Dr. Bui. This is really exciting."

"Emily, Jack," she corrected him, going out the door.

She returned to the main building where she interrupted the three ladies who were engaged in conversation. "I am intrigued by what you intend to do here, my lady. We have a special facility set up next door. It is has everything a hospital room would have but looks more like a comfortable hotel room. I have prepared the room as you instructed in anticipation of your arrival today. When do you want to start?"

Mai did not respond for a moment. "My lady?" Dr. Bui asked.

Mai seemed startled from a thought and said, "Yes, OK, Emily. I would like to go into the cave with you now and sit for a minute to get a sense of things without drugs. I am having feelings like before when I was here. I am sensing something else, some danger, and I am not sure what it means. It is pure evil and not good. I am very concerned."

Dr. Bui gave a worried look that reflected her concern, but stepped back by the door and said, "My lady, if you please, shall we have a look?"

As they walked up toward the cave entrance, Catherine noted that the hill was clearly defined and staked with yellow markers here and there. She could see other places where they had already started digging, and many students were meticulously marking off an area back toward the temple.

Dr. Bui stopped, pointed to the area that was closer to the temple, and said, "With some ground sensing tools we borrowed from the government, we found a chamber under there and are working our way back to it carefully. One can only imagine what is in there!"

Mai stood silent for a moment as she listened to a voice from within. She grew a concerned look on her face. She turned to Dr. Bui and whispered in confidence to her with great alarm, "No! Dr. Bui! No! That is a bad place, an evil place. There is lots of death within. You must never go there. You must stop any work in that area and never look there again. I forbid you to continue working in that area. You and I will discuss this in private, but for now, I command you to obey me!"

Dr. Bui was startled at Mai's sudden reaction. But she quickly collected herself and whispered in return to Mai in Vietnamese, "As you wish, my lady. Do not worry. I will stop the work in that area immediately."

Mai continued. "You would be releasing the evil spirits that reside there, and that could be disastrous for your effort here. I can already feel them anxious to escape."

Dr. Bui assured her that part of the project would end immediately.

Catherine and Kelly witnessed the concerned whispers between Mai and Dr. Bui. Catherine commented, "I wonder what that was all about?"

Kelly replied, "I don't know but something got Mai upset."

They saw Dr. Bui step aside and say something to an assistant. He ran over to the group working between the temple and the cave site. They all nodded, gathered their equipment, and moved to the other side of the cave area away from the temple.

Satisfied that Mai's orders were obeyed, Dr. Bui escorted her to the cave entrance and followed her inside.

The cave was well lit now, and even the deepest recesses were illuminated. Mai looked around and said, "This is not familiar to me, Emily. Can you turn off some of the lights? It needs to look as I saw it back then."

Dr. Bui nodded to Mai, fascinated by what she had just said. She went around and turned off all the lights, leaving only one by the second chest. She went back to the entrance and told Kelly to pass the word that she wanted everyone to move back, to form a cordon away from the entrance, and to keep very quiet. She and Mai were not to be disturbed, nor was there to be any sound until they came out. Then she returned to where Mai sat.

"Yes, that's better now. Please, come sit here with me," Mai said. "I will feel what is here."

Dr. Bui turned on the small tape recorder on her lap supplied by Catherine. She sat in the lotus position, and waited. Ten minutes passed, during which she heard Mai say yes several times almost in a whisper.

Then Mai spoke. "You found me at last. I knew you would come one day. My daughter, I have waited a long time for you to save me. When you find your peace, I will finally find mine. I think you know where that is. Be still and listen."

Another twenty minutes passed, and finally, Mai took a deep breath and looked over at Dr. Bui, who was watching her intently.

"We can go now. You must have your assistants take out the second chest. There is something inside that I need," Mai said. "Why don't we open it here?" asked Dr. Bui.

"No, this is too close to the evil place. We must take the chest out of here," said Mai. "I cannot bear to be in this cave any longer. Let us go."

Dr. Bui called over a large group of her students and told them they were about to take out the second chest and put it into the second laboratory of the main building. They all became very excited. For the first time, Mai noticed many of them were kneeling. It reminded her of Siem Kulea and her many followers there. She realized word of her heritage would surely have gotten out by now. That was still another issue she would have to deal with.

Dr. Bui went to Jack who was watching nearby and said, "Before we move anything, Jack, I would like you to go in there and photograph that cave from every angle you can imagine. I have had your new assistants do that already, but I want your eye in there too. No hurry. Never mind about the ground. We've already photographed it and taken castings in great detail. Be methodical and thorough. Jack, this will be the last chance we have to photograph everything in place except for the first chest. After this, we will no longer have that, so take that into consideration as you make a photographic record of the cave."

"How bright is it in there? Maybe I need a tripod," said Jack.

Mark heard this and said, "No, Jack, is OK. F8 125th second, handhold, I think, with all the lights on. But take tripod if need more depth of field. I load tungsten film already for you." He handed Jack his Nikon.

"Hey, Kelly, maybe we can take this guy back to Chicago with us. What do you think?" Jack commented, smiling. Then he turned back to Mark and said, "Good job. But please also load up three backs for the Mamiya with the same film, and bring that and a tripod to the entrance. I will need them in about twenty minutes. Oh, put the wide-angle fifty-millimeter lens on the Mamiya but keep the normal lens ready."

"Well, at least Jack's having a good time," commented Kelly to the other ladies as Jack disappeared into the cave.

"Yes, he seems very happy. Isn't it nice to see him this way?" said Mai. "I love it when my man is happy."

Kelly and Catherine said, "Yep!" at the same time and then laughed at each other.

An hour later, Jack finished and reported to them, "OK, I think I have a good record of the chests. Hey, did you know there's a parchment down behind the third chest? It's partly hidden down all the way to the ground against the back of the third chest? Unless you look carefully, you will miss it."

"We found the woman's remains next to that chest," commented Dr. Bui.

After carefully retrieving the parchment from behind the third chest and transporting it to the laboratory, Dr. Bui went inside the cave again. This time she brought four of her students with her. She directed them as they maneuvered the second chest onto a small carrying canvas with handles on each side, which had been custom designed just for this purpose. They carefully lifted and, with many stops, as the chest was very heavy, they carried the second chest out of the cave into the daylight and set it down. They were visibly exhausted.

"This one is much heavier than the first," said one of the students. "It must be loaded!"

Mai was now very impatient for them to get the chest inside the laboratory. She clapped her hands and commanded, "Please be careful with that chest. Take it to the lab now. Hurry. Hurry!"

With four more students helping to lift and with great effort they put the large chest in a room off to the side of the second laboratory. They placed it on a low table two feet off the ground so they could easily look down into it and study it when it was opened. Many of the students gathered around Mai, Catherine, and Dr. Bui as they watched Jack photograph the chest a few more times before it was opened.

"I can get more specific shots later. In fact, I will spend several rolls and another day just photographing the detail work on the outside of this chest," he told them. "I need the proper lights for that."

Mai nodded and turned to the students. "Leave us," she commanded them.

Dr. Bui put her arms out and drove the curious and disappointed students to the door. Kelly closed the door behind them and pushed the bolt, locking it to guarantee they would not be disturbed.

"What do you wish us to do, my lady?" Dr. Bui asked, bowing.

"Stand back over there quietly," Mai replied.

Everyone moved away to one side of the room.

"Turn out the lights, and turn on that one small lamp over there," she said, pointing to a single light in the corner.

They watched and waited. Mai took a deep breath with her hands by her sides. She laid her head back awkwardly for a moment. Then she slowly brought it forward and paused quietly. The four friends kept very still and said not a word. Kelly took Jack's hand and pulled him back firmly so he would not interfere. He started to raise his camera, but Kelly quietly put her hand on it and pushed it back down, shaking her head and putting her fingers to her lips. Jack, who had not seen any of the sessions with Mai before, finally understood.

Dr. Bui turned on the tape recorder again. After a few more minutes, Mai was heard to whisper "yes". She ran her hands over the old wooden chest, which was banded together with ornate hand-worked brass on all sides. After a few moments, she reached down and opened a large latch on the front left side and then another on the right. They both squeaked as she moved them open and down. Then she tugged at the lid, but it would not give.

Jack started to move forward to help, but again Kelly held him back. Mai tried again, grunting a bit, and the heavy lid gave. She pushed it up, and it rested open and slightly back. She gazed into the trunk, which was filled with exquisite jewelry and gold adornments of every kind. She looked about carefully for a moment and finally said, "Ah, yes." She reached in and retrieved a beautiful, ornate gold ring with a large ruby on its face. She put it on the index finger of her right hand, and it fit perfectly. After pausing a moment, she kissed the ring and held it to her heart. Then she raised her head proudly and turned around to face the others. The ring was magnificent and seemed to glow on her finger in the dark light of the room. Without a word, she presented it to them. Dr. Bui went immediately to her knees before her. She leaned forward and kissed her ring most reverently, and with bowed head, said, "My lady."

Kelly didn't hesitate and followed Dr. Bui's example, as did Catherine. Mai turned to Jack and held the ring out to him. Jack looked confused, but then Mai commanded, "Kiss my ring as a sign of your eternal devotion to me, Jack Largent." He understood then that this was Queen Dau Te Po, and he knelt respectfully, as the others had done. He kissed the ring, looked up at her, and said, "My lady." Mai looked at each of them in turn, nodded, smiled, and then suddenly fainted, falling into Jack's arms where he knelt. He pulled her to him gently and held her close.

"Jack, bring her now, and follow me," said Dr. Bui. "We must hurry."

They went out the back way and through the tunnel leading to the hospital suite prepared for Mai. Jack laid her on the bed and watched as Dr. Bui worked methodically, moving items closer to the bed. They undressed her and made her comfortable under the sheets of the bed. A nurse inserted a cannula into a vein in Mai's left arm and Dr. Bui injected a measured dosage of opiates.

"If Mai is right, this may be the last drug treatment she needs," Catherine said. "We believe with the ring on her finger, Queen Dau Te Po has truly joined with her and it will take a few weeks for Mai's physical self to become aware and adapt to her presence. Mai warned us that during the transition she may be weaker and that is why we set up this special hospital suite to care for her during this transition. That is also one of the main reasons she wanted you here Jack. I think we are well prepared for any contingency."

Mai swooned and settled back, saying almost in a whisper, "Yes, I know this place."

Catherine sat beside the bed and nodded to Dr. Bui, who sat down on the other side of the bed and turned on the tape recorder. Sitting on a couch opposite them, Kelly again took Jack's hand and squeezed it softly, reminding him to be quiet.

"Queen Po, can you talk with me now?" Catherine began.

"Yes, but I must hurry," she said. "I am very afraid, and I have but one chance to save my people.

Chapter 45

Siem Kulea, AD 1066

The sun was setting as the two royals finished their evening meal. Queen Po had been talking with Prince Indravar Tu all afternoon since his arrival earlier in the day. As the afternoon passed into evening she grew more uncomfortable concerning his intentions and the possible reason for his visit.

At that time, she told him that she needed to take a minute to allow her handmaidens to attend her. She hurried inside the palace, found Lady Chi, and told her to gather some provisions and take Devearney out through the garden right away and keep her safe and hidden until the prince left the valley. She instructed her not to let anyone see her leave.

When she was done, she returned and sat again across from the prince, who refilled his wine glass. She had a powerful sense that something was wrong, but she couldn't discern what it was. It was a feeling more than anything else, but she learned long ago to trust her feelings.

"May I ask, Prince Tu, as you have not yet explained, why are you here? Your visit at such a great distance from your homeland honors me. Might there be another purpose in your visit to our valley?"

"Yes, indeed. Your perceptive wisdom is also legendary." He took her hand and said, "My father is getting very old, and no doubt has not long to live. He has insisted that I find a qualified woman to be my bride and future queen. I have decided that woman is you, Queen Po. I have chosen you for my wife."

Po was startled and could not speak for a moment. She pulled her hand back abruptly and sat straight up in her chair.

He continued matter-of-factly, "It is true that these things are usually arranged by our parents or intermediaries, but I do not want a marriage of convenience. I want a real woman like yourself who I can spend my life with; who will serve me well and bear me many healthy and bright children."

Po did not know what to say. Her favor toward this handsome prince changed instantly to ill regard because of his assuming ego. His arrogance made him presumptuous to a fault. He actually thought she would be flattered by his selection of her, and that she would be eager to be his wife.

"I assure you Prince this queen is not interested in getting married to anyone."

"That does not matter. Now that I have seen you and decided, your consent while preferable is not necessary," he commented. "You will be my wife."

Po decided to bring him back down to earth from his assuming perch. "How many women do you have in your harem, Prince?" she demanded.

He was surprised by her question and his anger was immediately evident for he regarded his concubines as his property and none of her business. But then he smiled. He realized he wanted her because she was no ordinary woman. Such impudence was to be expected at first, until he taught her to show proper respect.

"Not even twenty," he replied. "But that is of no concern for you. You will be my wife, not a concubine."

"Indeed, that is what you say, Prince, but not what you think," she replied. "Right now you think I am being disrespectful because I want to know how many women you will be breeding besides me if we were to be married. You might call me your wife, but in reality, I would be regarded as the first of your concubines, someone to entertain you like some sort of prized animal."

"You will marry me..." he began.

She stood up and looked down at him. "I will marry you, Prince, when you get rid of all your concubines and dedicate your life to me as I would to you. That is, if *I choose* to have *you* as my husband. Until then you can go pick some other woman who wishes to be one of your concubines pretending to be your queen. You have overstayed your welcome in this valley, and I must ask you to leave now."

Prince Indravar flushed red in anger. But then, as before he took a deep breath, sat back, and smiled. He was surprised that this woman, unlike every other woman he wanted and claimed for his own, was not thrilled at the chance to join his harem. But he did not need to get upset over it. The outcome would be the same whether she gave herself to him or not.

"You have no choice. You will marry me, or I will bring my forces down on this valley and enslave everyone in it," admonished the prince.

Po was startled by the threat and was stricken as if by an arrow. Nothing was more important to her than her people, and she had dedicated herself to giving them the most peaceful and fulfilling lives possible.

He spoke very loudly so all could hear. "Sit down, and I will tell you what you will do!"

Her guards at the door tensed, with their hands on their swords. Po slowly sat down opposite Prince Indravar, and waved the guards off as she did. He had said the one thing that made her hesitate. She would not endanger her people or see them made slaves of this cruel man. She had little choice, but her mind still searched for an idea. She needed time to think. She could easily kill him and his men in spite of the peaceful setting that was presented to him. Such precautions had been taken by Wan Bae and were well practiced. But that might result in a war that would destroy everything she had accomplished and wanted for her people here in this valley. She knew the surrounding nations would object to this violation of her neutrality, and that too would most likely result in a war that might be equally disastrous for her people. No, she would have to find a way to deal with this situation herself.

"What do you want me to do?" she asked softly. She delayed a moment further as she struggled for a solution. She now hated this man and wanted him dead, gone, or both. An idea slowly formed in her mind.

A crowd of about a hundred Champas gathered near the Palace. Po observed they were all part of her militia. The prince saw this, got up, and said something to one of his men. They fanned out, surrounding the front of the large white palace.

"Prince Indravar, if you harm me or even threaten me, my people will kill you and your men," Po said.

The prince laughed. "They are farmers. Look at them. They are not even armed."

"Don't be a stupid prince," she said in rebuke. "This estate is a vast farmland. There are weapons everywhere. *You* look at *them*. They are big and strong from years of hard work in my fields. But more importantly they are a well-trained militia, and to the last of them, they are willing to die for me."

She clapped her hands, and instantly, as if by magic, several arrows were pulled taut in bows, pointed at each of his men.

He was stunned to see how swiftly her people reacted to protect her. Behind him four guards held swords ready to assault the prince should he try anything. He gathered himself and quickly recovered. He turned around to her, and said, "Impressive. Yet in the end, they all will die. Ultimately my father or I will kill everyone in this valley or drag them off to be slaves. You know that is true. Please tell them everything is as it should be and to return to their other concerns."

Po paused a minute, staring back at him, and then she submitted, fearing the final consequence for everyone might indeed be death and destruction. She got up and told the gathered people everything was all right and not to worry. She ordered them back to work, and they slowly dispersed.

Po and the prince were alone now, but Po knew her servants and guards still listened for her slightest command. For once, she was happy they were all overly attentive and devoted.

She returned to the table and started to sit, but Prince Indravar said, "No, kneel here before me. I command it."

She shook her head and looked at him with an expression of disgust that displayed the contempt she now held for him. She sat down opposite him and proposed, "You do not threaten me, Prince. That said, I have a better offer; a compromise if you will." She sipped from her goblet, and tried to appear calm and in control when inwardly she was petrified.

"You want to make a deal? You have nothing to offer but yourself, and I already own that," he said, mocking her. "You Champas were always a weak people. You always want to compromise, to buy off your conquerors. But if a strong opponent really wants something, there is nothing you can do but give it to them. I have just proven that. Let's not play any more games, Queen Po. You're mine now."

In spite of her concern, she found a laugh to mock him. "You don't even own yourself at the moment, prince. You are alive at present only with my permission. My people have executed other intruders for far less of an insult as you have just made toward me. You saw that with a wave of my hand, you and your men could be killed instantly. Your threats are without merit and expose you. Your father would not start a war over this as he would lose because all the other nations would side with me. But I have another solution that will save face for you; the mighty Prince Indravar Tu." She mocked him with her words that left no doubt of the contempt she felt for him.

She swallowed her wine and sought the courage to speak her argument with a confidence she did not feel. "I have gold, untold amounts collected for centuries," she said, hoping she didn't sound desperate.

Faced with her effrontery, he was again surprised, and his bruised ego blustered a response. "I demand to know where is this gold you claim to have?"

"In Panduranga, by a Cham temple," she replied, finally seeing hope for her people.

"Ah, yes," he replied. "I have heard rumors of this too. You left behind the treasure of the fallen Champa kingdom when you fled Dong Na and came here. Now you say it really exists?"

"No, that is just a myth. But there is a secret chamber under the temple that holds all the gold collected for five centuries from all the lands for thousands of miles around given as offerings to the Hindu pandits. It is all gathered there, buried and hidden. I saw it as a little girl."

"If you show me where this gold is, I am to leave your people and this valley alone, and forget about any idea of taking you as my wife. Is this the deal you wish to make?" he said.

"Yes," she replied.

Prince Indravar took a sip of his wine and considered this. He always believed Champas were not only weak, but also fools. But then he realized the beautiful woman facing him was neither of those things. He turned to look at her. She was a match for him like no other. "I truly have never met a woman like you. You are more like a man, but with the beauty and charms of a woman. I will have a carriage brought up for you to travel."

"I ride as well as any man," she said.

In spite of himself, he laughed. "I bet you do, Queen Dau Te Po. OK, we have a deal, but I insist on one thing to seal this pact."

"What is that?" she asked with renewed confidence.

"We will go inside, and you will convince me you are more worthy in bed than my harem favorite," he demanded. He still sought to preserve some dignity even though he had already consented to her rejection and counter offer. Now more than ever he truly wanted to make love to her.

Later that night, while the prince was asleep, Queen Po quietly went out and went to talk to the Hindu headmaster Havta. She wrote a note for Lady Chi instructing her not to return to the valley with Devearney until it was safe. Once that was done, she returned to Prince Indravar's bed. She did not sleep. She lay quietly staring up at the ceiling. She would do what she had to do. All was in place.

Four days later they were in Panduranga and drew their horses up to the foot of the hill that was surmounted by the Champa temple. They were a party of ten…the prince and Queen Po, four of his men, and four Hindu pandits. Queen Po insisted that the pandits join them to sanctify the site when it was opened and closed again. They kept to the size of their party so they could travel unnoticed while the prince determined if what Po said was true. If the gold was there, he would return with many soldiers and wagons and take it back to his kingdom. No doubt his dying father would be most impressed.

Either way, as far as he was concerned, Queen Po was going to spend the rest of her life in his harem. The bargain was for him not to take her as his wife, but after the night he spent with her, he knew she was indeed destined to be the first of his concubines. She proved to be most talented in the sexual arts and brought him and herself to pleasurable ends throughout the night. She was more beautiful, fit, and agile in bed than any of his harem. He decided, he would leave her cherished valley alone, and she would not be his wife. At least he would not break his word on that. But she was far too much of a woman to leave to anyone else.

It was midday and very hot when they arrived. They dismounted, and Queen Po led them to the large rocks that hid the entrance of the underground chamber of the Hindu priests. The prince ordered up his water skin and drank freely while his men labored to pull back the rocks blocking the entrance to this supposed fortune. But a few minutes later, his demeanor changed to boyish glee when he saw the opening of the chamber begin to emerge.

"I didn't believe you, but it is real. You were telling the truth, Queen Po!" he said, very surprised. *Why would she give me this treasure* he thought? *Is that valley really that important to her?*

"Of course. You will keep your side of the bargain, Prince?" she asked.

"Yes, you have my word," he said lying enthusiastically.

An hour later the opening was wide enough for them to enter the chamber. The prince ordered three of his men to light torches and go inside. But hearing the cheers from within, he could wait no longer. He entered himself, dragging Queen Po with him firmly by the hand.

Near the entrance he saw a brick of solid gold sticking out from the wall on one side. He ran his fingers over it but was then distracted by the vast room of gold and jewels he saw just beyond lit by the torches of his men.

They stepped down into the damp, musty chamber that was surprisingly large, maybe a quarter the size of the entire hill. As the prince looked around, he saw a dozen piles of gold and jewels of every variety. It was the most amazing treasure he had ever seen. He couldn't hold back his enthusiasm any longer. He let go of Queen Po's hand and went to one of the piles of gold with jewels and trinkets that sparkled in the light from the torches.

He laughed like a madman and ran greedily from chest to chest, picking priceless objects from each one. He would be the mightiest prince in the world. He ordered his men to gather some of the treasure to take back with them, as he began to choose selections that caught his eye.

Queen Po backed up slowly to the doorway that led out of the chamber. She turned suddenly and pulled a brick with a large black circle on it from the roof. Parts of the roof fell and a black cloud crept into the chamber from several directions, which caused the men to scream and grab their eyes. As Po ran out of the chamber, she saw the gold brick and pulled it out from the doorway. The chamber entrance collapsed behind her, sealing it forever. She scrambled out and sought to escape.

The remaining guard outside grabbed her as she tried to run by him. He threw her to the ground. Visibly stunned, he looked for a moment to see if there was anything left of the entrance among all the fallen debris. Seeing that they were betrayed, he drew his sword to slay Queen Po as she cowered on the ground before him. The sharp, flat-tipped metal gave the look of an executioner's blade as it gleamed ominously against the sun over her about to begin its mortal path downward.

But then, before he could send the blade on its lethal journey he froze in place like a statue holding that lethal pose. Po struggled to her feet and nodded to Havta, while still trying to catch her breath. She looked with fascination at the guard who had sought to kill her and was now unable to move.

Amar, one of the original priests who came with Queen Po to Siem Kulea, came up behind the angry guard and hit him hard on the back of the head with a rock. Then, as the guard lay light-headed on the ground, the pandits pummeled the soldier's head with large stones until they were sure he was dead. They carried him over and threw him down against the rocks that had been an entrance a few moments before.

They began covering the guard and the fallen entrance again. Several hours later, when they were done the entrance was invisible once more.

Then Po walked over to the nearby hidden entrance of the cave that held the Champa treasure, which was still behind the rocks they had placed there many years before. Havta directed the pandits to pull away the rocks, and an hour later they managed to move over the large stone that blocked the entrance. They balanced it on end precariously to the side, so it would not be difficult for Havta and another pandit to cover the entrance later.

Havta hugged her dearly to him and commented, "You are a truly great lady, Queen Dau Te Po. What you have done, few would have the courage to do. Amar and Neyte have requested the honor of staying in the cave with you as a sign of our deep respect and devotion to such a great queen as yourself. You will not leave this world alone, my queen."

Before this journey, back in Siem Kulea on that last night, Po told Havta, the Swami headmaster of the Hindu priests, that she was leading the prince to the Hindu treasure. He was against it until she explained that was the only way to get this evil prince out of their lives, so the people of the valley could live in peace. She reminded him of the trap her mentor Tap had set in the walls, and said she would trip the key brick while the prince was inside. She further explained that she and they were the only ones who knew of the temple treasure. She told him that afterward as a penance for breaking her sacred oath as a child to keep the Hindu treasure secret, she desired to be sealed up with what remained of her family heritage and wealth. That would ensure that no one could ever violate their sacred temple again. Havta was shaken with emotion when he heard this. He had witnessed the work of good Queen Dau Te Po for many years, and she was easily a greater treasure than anything buried in that hill.

Havta, stood at the cave entrance. As she requested, he gave Queen Po a small-lit candle, a writing instrument, and parchment. She carried these with her into the cave. The two pandits that joined her retreated further back into the cave. Queen Po glanced back at the opening and saw both Havta and the remaining pandit bowing low toward her. They had never done this before. It was a solemn sign of their respect, and she was proud to have gained it. She returned their bow of respect with one of her own.

She placed the candle on a high ledge so it could illuminate more of the cave until it burned out.

The big rock was rolled back across the entrance, throwing them into darkness except for the small candle. She tried to open the third trunk. Amar, seeing her struggle with its weight, helped her. With great effort, they lifted the large lid. Inside was a maroon cloak of red velvet embroidered with flowers of gold along the edge. She lifted it out reverently and kissed it, and Amar held the cloak over her while she removed her dirty riding clothes under it. Afterward, he wrapped the cloak around her. She took off her ring, the royal ring worn by her mother and her mother's mother before that, going back to the first Hoa Cuc who was named Nagani. She put it inside the second trunk on top so it would not get lost but would also not be found by anyone who did not know its significance. She placed it in the center among other jewelry and gold accessories. Then she closed the trunk, sat down next to it, and began to write a letter in linear logograms to her daughter on the parchment.

My dearest daughter,

If you have found this, then I am most proud of you. I love you very much and will always be with you. I have tried to lead my life so as to make my parents proud of me. I pray that I have succeeded. You must protect your heritage that has been entrusted to you, as it was to me. In these chests are things that belong only to you. I am not speaking of money or gold but of the items that connect us to you. They are the most important. Family and heritage are the most important. I placed the sacred ring my mother gave me inside one of these trunks. It was taken right from her hand when last I saw her and my father together before they kissed me and sent me on my way. She told me it held a wonderful secret that would ensure my life in this universe of ours. I never determined the meaning of her words. That will be left for you to discover. You will know which of the trinkets is the ring of which I speak.

Remember always your duty to your people who were created to serve us many thousands of years ago. You must lead them to peace and happiness and protect them always. They are your children.

Be safe, my darling.
Po

The candle grew dim and finally went out. The cave was totally dark and cool. Po could hear the pandits in the very back of the cave softly chanting a mantra. She was suddenly very weary and tired. She retrieved a small vial she kept hidden and drank from it. Then she laid her head on the chest and went to sleep.

Chapter 46

Thap Cham, Vietnam, 1990

Catherine and Kelly attended Mai with great concern as she lay on her bed and slept in the small hospital suite in the annex at the cave site. They had three sessions over the last week, and on the last Mai used none of the opiates as she revealed more of Queen Po's story before falling into a deep sleep. In the morning on the two previous session, when she woke up, the first thing she would do was smile at them and ask, "What'd I say?"

But the last time was two nights ago, and she still hadn't woken up. Dr. Tran, the local physician on call who almost always attended the clinic, told them Mai seemed to have drifted into a coma. Jack was up in Dalat to photograph the items that were transferred there for safekeeping. But he kept track of their sessions at the end of each day. He was not aware that Mai was in a coma as yet because Catherine and Kelly were not sure until this morning that it was true, and they had not told him.

"I think we'd better get her out of here and back to the States," Catherine said.

Kelly didn't answer her because for once she didn't know what to do. They were aware this might happen but never really believed it would. "I've sent for Jack. I'm not looking forward to telling him."

Even Mr. Nguyen, who came to the site to visit that morning, was concerned. He offered to fly Mai to Hanoi where there was a hospital that had first-class facilities.

Several hours later Jack walked in, having just driven in from Dalat, and asked, "What's up?"

"Jack, Mai has been in a coma since our last session the night before last," said Catherine. "We were not completely certain until this morning, that it was in fact a coma. We cannot wake her. We are very worried."

Jack's demeanor changed instantly. He rushed over to the bed where Mai was sleeping peacefully. He bent down, kissed her, took her hand, and called to her, "Mai...Mai...It's Jack. Please wake up. Mai, darling...Devearney and I need you." He hoped the old doorway to her mind would work this time too.

Catherine walked over and put her arm around Jack, who was now kneeling by the bed. Jack lowered his head to Mai's hand and silently prayed for her to awaken. He tried once more. "Mai, Devearney needs you. Please come back to us."

He bowed his head and said quietly, "Please, God, please." But as he held her hand, he had a thought. He looked at one hand and then the other. "Where's the ring?" The ornate ring Mai had taken from the trunk and put on her finger was missing.

"Dr. Bui took it off after the last session," said Kelly. "Mai was fidgeting about so much, she was afraid she would hurt herself, or the ring might slip off. She knew it was very important to Mai, so she put it away."

Kelly looked at Jack, and Jack looked at Catherine, and they all had the same idea at once. "Do you think?" said Kelly.

"It's a possibility," said Catherine. "Frankly, with all of this, I would say it's a definite possibility. How dumb are we?"

They left the hospital area, raced through the connecting tunnel, and pounded on the door of the lab, calling for Dr. Bui. She came quickly and said, "What's happened? Has Mai awakened?"

Jack shook his head and said, "Dr. Bui, where is the ring you took off Mai's finger? We want to put it back on right away."

"Well, I put it in the safe...Oh my goodness! You don't think..."

"It's certainly worth a try," said Catherine.

Dr. Bui nervously put in the combination of the safe, opened it, retrieved the ring, and handed it to Catherine. The three of them, with Dr. Bui following, raced down the tunnel to the hospital area and into the room where Mai slept. Jack took the ring from Catherine and started to put it on Mai's hand.

"Which finger?" he asked.

Catherine looked stumped, but Kelly replied, "Index finger, right hand, boss."

Jack slipped the ring on her finger, and almost immediately Mai moaned as she slept. She turned over and moved around a bit and seemed to be sleeping again. But then she suddenly and blearily opened her eyes, stretched out her arms on the pillow and yawned. She looked up at them, and asked, "What'd I say?"

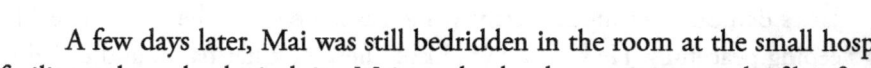

A few days later, Mai was still bedridden in the room at the small hospital facility at the archeological site. Mai was day-by-day regaining much of her former strength and all that remained was getting completely off of the drugs. Jack told her a Dr. Luong from Hanoi was there to help her recover from her addiction. Dr. Luong was said to be the best in Asia.

"When you go off the opiates, Mai, won't you lose your connection with Queen Dau Te Po?" Jack asked.

"Not anymore," she said, flashing the ring on her finger. "That was the secret. That was why I had to get into that cave and get that ring. Her spirit is always with me now, Jack. We are joined forever as one, without any drugs. She is finally free of that cave and will live her life through me. My physical self has been adapting and that is why this room set up was important."

"Well, that's a relief...to stop taking the drugs, I mean. That can't have been good for you, Mai," he said.

"Agreed, but I wish Su Ling was here. As far as I'm concerned, Su Ling is the unmatched expert in the world on opiate addictions. There is a drug in Siem Kulea that legend says has been known since ancient times. Su Ling tried it with me. It was used to help get addicts off the opiate addiction in the valley, and it works in less than two weeks. It is very good, much better than anything commonly used today. It cleans out the system and frees you from the addiction.

Su Ling did not go all the way with it on me because I did not want to lose my connection with Queen Dau Te Po. I want this Dr. Luong to use it on me, but I know he won't because the modern world has lost knowledge of it and it is not well known in medical circles. So I think I'm going to hypnotize him to put the suggestion in his head."

"Come on, Mai, you can't do that," said Jack. "Anything could go wrong, and it's not safe. Look at Dr. Minh, for heaven's sake. That was nothing but trouble. Besides, I don't think you can do it for real anyway."

She said, "Jack, Queen Po loves you."

She almost laughed out loud as he dropped his head to his chest, in a deep trance once again. "Jack, when I snap my fingers, you will be eager to see me hypnotize Dr. Luong."

She snapped her fingers. Jack became alert and looked around for a few seconds. Mai asked him, "So what do you think? Should I hypnotize Dr. Luong?"

"I think it's a great idea. Should I go get him now?"

"Yes, but send Dr. Bui in here first alone. I want to speak to her privately before everyone surrounds me again and makes this room chaotic once more."

In a minute there was a soft knock at the door, and Dr. Bui entered. "You sent for me, my lady?" she asked, bowing and not hiding her devotion to her queen. "Emily, please sit here with me," said Mai, gesturing toward a chair by the bed.

Dr. Bui sat in the chair, took Mai's outstretched hand with the ring on it, and kissed it reverently. When she was done, she looked up and asked, "Do you have further instructions for me, your majesty?"

"Yes, I have some information and some further items I need you to attend to right away. You must do so secretly. I am certain that what you found yesterday in the third chest are not the true crowns and seal of the Champa kingdom, as you have announced."

"Oh, my lady, you must be mistaken! They are magnificent and the most beautiful crowns I have ever seen," said Dr. Bui. "They are of pure gold and inlaid with the finest jewels."

"Was there a ruby on the front or a sapphire on each of them?"

"There was a sapphire in the front on both, my lady, the large and smaller crown," Dr. Bui answered, not questioning how Mai knew that.

"The real crowns and seal of the Champa kingdom are held in a compartment under the third chest," Mai told her. "There is a false bottom. Look for a lever on one side. It will be disguised as a bolt about two inches from the bottom. Push in on it, and slide it to the right. It will pop out, revealing the compartment. The real crowns are more beautiful than those you have already recovered and have a ruby in the front of each one. As a little girl, I used to play with the ones you have found. They were used for minor functions, parties and such. But the state crowns of sovereign authority are still hidden along with the real and true scepter and seal of the Champa kingdom in the bottom of that chest. You must tell no one of this."

"Push in on it, and slide it to the right…a bolt two inches from the bottom. Your majesty, I am humbled by this information," said Dr. Bui, noting Mai's easy transference into the persona of Queen Dau Te Po. "What is it you wish done?"

"You will retrieve them in secret and keep them hidden. Put them in the bottom of Jack's large Halliburton camera case, which I asked him to move into that room with the third chest. There is a false bottom there too. There is a compartment accessed by pushing in and turning the handle clockwise twice. The crowns and seal will fit easily into there, but use packing material so they do not move around and will be protected from harm. When the compartment is locked again, it will seal invisibly, and no one can get into it that does not know the unique code. Do you understand my instructions, Doctor?"

"Yes, my lady. Push in and turn the handle clockwise twice. I understand completely. Consider it done, and do not concern yourself any more on this matter. You have enough to worry about." Dr. Bui bowed again reverently to her queen.

"Tell no one," Mai commanded. "We cannot risk an idle word revealing this secret."

"Yes, my lady," said Dr. Bui.

"I want you to know I have big plans for you in our Champa world, but it will take me a few years to resolve the many issues still ahead of us," said Mai. "Would you consider coming to live in Siem Kulea once we restore it? I happen to know there is a secret there concerning our ancient Champa history that will provide a lifetime of very fulfilling and interesting work for you. However, you will not be able to reveal it to the outside world. More than that I cannot tell you at this time."

"Your majesty, just having you in my life is more fulfillment than I ever dreamed was possible. I am ready to serve you in any manner you wish. If this is about our Champa people and the Hoa Cuc, nothing would please me more. This is my life's dream coming true. I wake up every morning thrilled to get to my duties. Thank you, for this gift you have given us. Is there anything else you require of me at the moment?"

"Do you have the treatment drug I asked you to get?" Mai asked.

"Yes, my lady."

"Did you get in touch with Su Ling concerning the correct dosages?"

"Yes, I have included instructions for Dr. Luong with the treatment drug. We have only to convince Dr. Luong to use it."

"That's next," said Mai. "Have them all come back in, please." She watched Dr. Bui bow reverently toward her and then back out of the room.

Soon Catherine, Kelly, Jack, Dr. Bui, and Dr. Luong were all gathered around Mai in her bed in a festive mood. They all seemed to be talking and asking her questions at once.

"Stop! I feel like the main attraction at a three-ring circus. Don't you people have more important things to do?" Mai asked, smiling.

"Mai, we want to know only one thing. Do you feel the need to continue with the drugs?" asked Catherine.

"No."

"No?"

"No. I want to go home now. I am done. I have bonded with Queen Po and feel fulfilled and connected. I think I have all the answers there are." Then she looked at Dr. Luong. "Who's this dude?"

They were all smiling broadly. The old Mai seemed to be back with them. They were noticeably relieved, and their happiness was enhanced with her remarks.

"This *dude* is Dr. Luong," said Catherine. "He is a specialist in helping addicts to reform. Don't be too hard on him, Mai. He is the best."

Mai looked toward the distinguished looking doctor. "OK, Doc. We gonna be friends?" she asked smiling.

"Miss Sambaht, I am very happy and honored to work with you. I'm afraid you are going to hate me for a while, but I assure you I am indeed your friend."

Mai shook his hand and asked, "When do we start? What's the plan?"

Dr. Bui said, "We're going to meet in the conference room tomorrow morning to go over what we know thus far with you, my lady, and then you are being flown courtesy of the Socialist Republic of Vietnam to Hanoi, where you will be treated better than the president of the politburo. You will convalesce in a private suite, so no one will see you go through withdrawal. Everyone is very serious about protecting you, so you needn't worry. However, you are not going to get what you want about anything for the next six weeks."

"Six weeks? Jack!"

"It's up to you, Mai," he told her. "You're a big girl now…the biggest. Whatever you want to do, I will support your wishes."

She took Jack's hand and said, "No, Jack, I want to do it, and I want to do it here, in Vietnam. I want to heal in the midst of my people. But then I want to get back to my little princess, and Jack, you'd better be ready to spoil me rotten!"

"OK," said Jack. "Doctor, it looks like you have a patient after tomorrow morning." He nodded, smiling.

"I have to get back and prepare for tomorrow's conference," Dr. Bui said. "Catherine, I was hoping you and Kelly would assist me with that. We have all four chests out and are deep into examining their contents. Queen Po's story ads context and meaning. Now that we have the crowns and the great seal from the third chest, the story is fairly complete. We will continue to consult with her Majesty even when she is back in the States. Doctor, after she goes through this treatment, will it harm any of her memories?"

"I do not think so," he replied. "The drugs we use to wean her off opiates will not have any adverse side effects."

"Let's get on with this treatment already," Mai said. "Oh, just in case anyone is wondering, this ring is mine." She held up her right hand with the large royal ruby ring on it. "If there are any arguments, I am going to call in my new friends in the Vietnamese government."

"I have already addressed that issue," said Dr. Bui. "I have taken care of everything. It is agreed officially by the Vietnamese government that ring belongs to you. You have some formal papers to sign, but it's all decided."

Dr. Bui glanced at Mai to see if there was something else. Mai smiled and said, "Thank you, Dr. Bui."

"Come on, ladies. We have a lot to do yet," Dr. Bui said. She, Catherine, and Kelly left the room to prepare for the conference.

Dr. Luong started to leave and said to Jack, "I will return for her tomorrow afternoon."

But Mai stopped him. "Wait, Doctor. If you don't mind, we have only a few more questions, and I want to show you my ring. Have you seen it? It's the royal ring of Queen Dau Te Po and all the Queens before that. It is believed to be connected to the stars of the universe. Here, sit down so you can get a closer look at it."

Mai held out the ring for him to see. He sat down beside the bed, put on his glasses, and leaned in to get a close look. "Fascinating," he said, looking into the large, deep-red ruby. "Wondrous! It seems to draw you in…"

In the next few minutes Mai did indeed hypnotize Dr. Luong and instructed him to use the special medicine for her withdrawal she had in mind and that Dr. Bui was holding for him. When she was done, Mai clapped her hands twice.

The doctor awoke and said, "I'm sorry. I was in thought elsewhere for a moment. What was it you wished to know further, Miss Sambaht?"

"Doctor, we are curious, what treatment are you thinking of using with me?" Mai asked. "It's just we three here. We trust you completely, and you can trust us. We will fully cooperate with your decision."

"Well, I've been developing a new treatment drug called myxtheliodomide, and I will have to keep it very secret because it is considered experimental in most hospitals. I believe Dr. Bui has an adequate amount here for me to use so I won't have to tell anyone." He smiled and bowed slightly.

"That's all, Doctor," said Mai, dismissing him. "I will be ready to go with you tomorrow."

The doctor smiled, bowed slightly again, and quickly left the room, anxious to get to Dr. Bui and retrieve the drug he needed for the treatment.

After he left the room, Jack asked, "Honey, are you sure about this?"

"We used it a lot in the valley, Jack. The plant is a hybrid developed by my ancestors. It was not uncommon for people to get hooked on opiates there. It works every time and quickly, with no side effects. I am going to be making that doctor rich, Jack."

"I hope so, darling. Anyway, the hypnotism technique seemed to work. That surprised me. I didn't know you could do that. You never cease to amaze me, my Asian queen."

Then Jack said to her with a big smile, "Hey, Mai, how do I know I haven't been hypnotized like the doctor?"

She searched for an answer and finally said, "Come here and kiss me, GI. I miss that."

Chapter 47

Chicago, 1990

When they finally got home from Vietnam for the second time it was already dusk, and Jack and Mai were both exhausted. They sat for a moment in conversation with their au pair who had just put Devearney to bed and suggested that it was best if the princess not be disturbed for a bit. They discussed how little Devearney was doing, and told the au pair she could take some time off if she wished.

After their au pair left, they both rushed to Devearney's bedroom, and kissed her as she slept in her bed. They hovered there for a while arm-in-arm, just enjoying being together as a family once more.

Later, they retreated to their family room, and sat down on the couch. Jack mentioned that when Mai caressed Devearney's cheek, the ring on her hand seemed to glow.

"Yes, that is the only way Queen Dau Te Po can physically express independent of me that she is happy," Mai explained. "She loves Devearney. And you know the really amazing thing, Jack? She named her daughter Devearney too, over a thousand years ago. Everything is happening like it's meant to be as part of some kind of master plan."

Mai threw off her shoes and laid back, ready to not move for a long time. Two weeks had passed since her recovery in the hospital in Hanoi, and for a good amount of that time in Vietnam she interviewed with reporters and news sources from all over the world. In Vietnam she was a sudden and very popular celebrity.

But she knew there was one more thing she had to do before she could finally rest, and it would not be good to delay it even until the following morning. It was too important. She asked Jack to bring his Halliburton camera case from downstairs. She explained to him that she had put something in the secret compartment and needed it now.

"Oh, well, I'll just unload it down there and bring it up," he replied.

"No, darling, I insist you bring the case upstairs and let me retrieve it. It's important, and it's a surprise," she explained. "You can remove your cameras and equipment down there in the studio, of course."

Jack was now intrigued and hurried downstairs to get the large steamer camera case. He unloaded the cameras in the camera closet in the studio and then carried the oversize case upstairs to their townhouse.

He carefully laid the huge camera case on the glass dining room table and turned the case over on its side. Mai flipped aside the logo plate, revealing the code area, and put in the code. Then she twisted the handle and accessed the secret bottom area. With great care, she removed the two gold crowns, a scepter, a seal, and a ring with a matching seal. Dr. Bui had put them there as instructed and they fit in the secret compartment perfectly. As they unwrapped each one from its protective bubble wrap, Jack was astonished and in awe at the magnificence of these royal icons. Mai explained that these were the real crowns and seal of the Champa kingdom amplifying Jack's excitement. She explained she was keeping them until such time as her realm was restored.

Jack reminded her that she had signed a legal document agreeing to give ownership of the contents of the chests to the Vietnamese government.

But Mai explained, "Not exactly, darling. I agreed to give them ownership of all the contents of the chests being held and examined by Dr. Bui at the new complex at Thap Cham and Dalat on that date. I precisely had the document worded that way. These items were put secretly into the bottom of your camera case and removed from the complex two weeks before I signed that document. I rightfully own these, darling. I would never turn my family heritage over to anyone."

"Oh! My genius wife strikes again. I wonder what Catherine and Kelly are going to say when they see these crowns."

Mai looked at Jack, sharing his unspoken thought, and nodded, "OK, yeah, go ahead. Call Catherine and Kelly. I know they will want to see this."

Jack picked up the telephone and called Catherine and Kelly. They arrived in twenty minutes in spite of being weary from their long journey back. They couldn't believe that Mai had secreted these royal icons worth millions out of the country, but then came the problem of what to do with them.

One thing led to another and Mai made a decision. They would get them into a very safe bank vault in the morning but first Mai and Jack had something important to do. They discussed this issue further while sitting with Mai as she did her hair and makeup for the formal portrait Jack was going to take of her in the studio downstairs that very night. After the women helped Mai with her hair, she asked them to wait downstairs with Jack.

Mai came to the set prepared for the portrait, dressed in a magnificent royal Champa ensemble of maroon silk that Dr. Bui had commissioned in Vietnam and that followed Mai's instructions perfectly. It consisted of an ornate halter top and skirt designed to allow for the reveal of the Hoa Cuc on her right hip. She wore the most spectacular of the necklaces from her collection, which featured seven red rubies, matching her crown. With her hair done up and wearing the crown of a Champa Queen, the others almost felt like kneeling. The impact was overwhelming. But Mai saw their awestruck faces and broke the spell when she inquired with a big smile, "Well, what do you think?"

Catherine replied, "This is one time I do not have the words, Mai. I swear you look incredible."

Jack had set up the soft lights in the studio, and Mai sat down on an old formal high-backed classical chair he placed on a painted canvas background.

Before he started to photograph her, Jack asked Catherine and Kelly to leave the room while he photographed Mai, because he wanted this moment to be theirs and theirs alone. Jack took several photographs of her sitting in the chair in various poses, and then he asked her to stand and he put the chair to the side off of the canvas. He asked her to turn to her left and with her right hand on her hip. This pose highlighted the Hoa Cuc birthmark visible on her naked right hip. He took several more variations of this pose.

When he was finished, he walked over to her.

Twenty minutes passed, and when they both came out of the back studio, Jack was holding her hand, and they were both tearfully happy. Catherine and Kelly could only imagine.

The next morning, after a few phone calls to a bank president friend of hers, Catherine asked Big Ben and Victor to personally escort Mai, with her jewels and the crowns in three large metal boxes, to the bank. Brad Martin was already at the bank waiting for them. He reserved a special area of the most secure and private vault prepared to receive the three boxes. This was done without notice or fanfare, and even the bank, though they were charging very high fees for the private vault within a vault, did not know there were jewels in their bank worth hundreds of millions of dollars.

Chapter 48

Chicago, 1990

Six months later Kelly came into Catherine's office, plopped down in a chair, and waited for her to get off the telephone. As soon as she hung up, Catherine smiled and asked, "What's up?"

Kelly replied, "Remember our conversation on the plane from Ubon concerning Daniel Vega and Su Ling, and how I wondered about Su Ling in particular?"

"Sure. I had forgotten all about that. Did you look into it? I gave you the names of some of our people to talk with and to help you investigate the matter."

"Yes, and this is all leading up to something else. I'll just give you the condensed version. We already know most of Daniel Vega's dirty deeds while he was working for Colonel Minh, and we decided long ago to ignore his past if he could get Mai out of the clutches of Colonel Minh. So I'm going to pass on going through all of that again."

"OK," Catherine agreed. "And we paid him a lot of money because he came through for us big time when it counted. The partnership we formed with him seems to be working well as he is off to a very successful start with his business. He could have just as easily ended up there dead or worse."

"Right," replied Kelly. "We both agreed he was worth it at the time. Su Ling, as it turns out, does have a suspicious history. She worked for Colonel Minh for six years before Mai met her. She ran many of his illicit deals in different parts of Southeast Asia. Apparently, he trusted her because she demonstrated a brilliant mind and made him a lot of money through those enterprises.

Colonel Minh had an adopted son by the name of Hinsu Yameda. I can find no information about the adoption. In fact, there is not much record of him as a child. When he was sixteen, and Su Ling was twenty-one and new on Colonel Minh's staff, he made her Hinsu's mentor. She did well with him, sending Hinsu off to Oxford in a few years as a result. It is rumored that during that time, they had an affair and are still connected."

Catherine shook her head signaling her disapproval of the alleged affair. "Wait. Still connected? What do you mean? She married Daniel. Is she having an affair with this Yameda person while being married to Daniel?" asked Catherine.

"I honestly don't know. I'm pretty sure the affair happened in the past. But all we have been able to discover in the last year are three plane flights she took to Ubon, Thailand, while Daniel was away on business. As you know, she and Daniel have their digs in Bangkok, so it's a short flight to Ubon."

"OK, I'm missing something. What's in Ubon that she would be interested in?" asked Catherine.

"Hinsu Yameda, and he's now the head of Asian World Investments, the company Colonel Minh formerly headed," replied Kelly. "Look, I'm not saying there's anything wrong. Those are just the facts, and I wanted you to have them before I bring up what I really came in here to talk to you about."

"And that would be?"

Kelly tossed a file of papers across Catherine's expansive glass desktop, and she immediately opened up the folder. "Oh! Now, this is interesting. You really want to do this?"

"I have spent the last two weeks going over things with Brad Martin, and he says it's very doable. I think the two perfect people to make it happen are Su Ling and Daniel Vega. Of course, I will head up the project, work with Brad and make sure everybody stays on track. But I think we can make it happen, and it won't cost us a thing."

"Do you see any complications with the information you've just given me about Su Ling?"

"Honestly no. On the positive side, she saved Mai and the Champa people, and in my opinion deserves to be there, whatever is the reality of her love life."

Catherine studied a few of the estimates within the folder and then looked up, smiling. "I say let's do it. I assume you have been onboard from the get-go."

"Yep," replied Kelly.

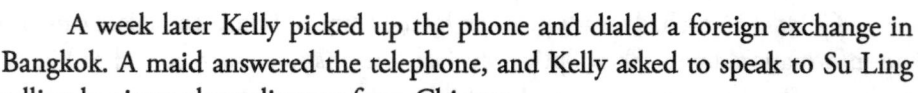

A week later Kelly picked up the phone and dialed a foreign exchange in Bangkok. A maid answered the telephone, and Kelly asked to speak to Su Ling telling her it was long distance from Chicago.

A minute later Su Ling came on the telephone and said, "Hello, this is Su Ling, who am I speaking with, please?"

"It's Kelly Ryan, Su Ling. How are you?"

They exchanged pleasantries, and then Kelly told her why she had called. "Su Ling, I'm working on a project to purchase Siem Kulea as a surprise for Mai.

The actual purchase is in its final stages. We will soon need someone to be the on-site manager and to organize the reconstruction. We will also need someone else to handle all the logistics. Would you know where we could find two people like that?"

There was silence on the line in response, and Kelly thought she had lost the connection. "Su Ling, are you there?"

"Oh, yes, Kelly. I'm crying so much I can't speak. Yes, yes, yes! I know two people very qualified. I'm very excited. When do we start?"

"I'll be flying in on Wednesday to Bangkok, and Daniel will need to arrange transportation from there. Is that OK? I'll have an attorney and legal documents with me for both of you to sign as our contractors. We can discuss all of that when I get there."

"Yes, we'll take care of everything on this end. I can't wait to see you and get started. Oh my God, Kelly! This is wonderful news! Thank you. Does Queen Maisong know any of this?"

"No, not yet. It's a secret and a surprise. So keep it under wraps, please. We're going to bring Mai back where she belongs. It's going to be wonderful again for her in Siem Kulea, and we will share that with her. I'm as excited about this as you are. See you soon!" said Kelly.

Chapter 49

Chicago, 1991

In the fall of 1991, six months after the telephone call between Kelly and Su Ling, Jack was still working as an advertising photographer in his Chicago studio.

His new assistant, Jasmine, worked out very well after Mai interviewed her personally and found her acceptable. Jack noticed she was always respectful to Mai, short of calling her "my lady." Jack admired that in his new assistant, but Mai's now exceptional talent at hypnosis made him wonder if there was more to the story. This was resolved when he finally queried Mai about it, and she simply explained, "It was no problem, Jack. It turns out she's Champa."

Catherine's first book, *Queen Dau Te Po and the Champa Treasure*, was in its final stages of writing. Although it was mostly true, it read like a thrilling fictional adventure and Catherine enhanced the narrative with some artistic license. It took several extra months to write because Mai wanted to maintain her anonymity, and she wanted some of the story omitted entirely. She finally gave up on the one part as newspaper reports circulated of her rock-star popularity throughout Asia. She was still relatively unknown in the United States, but it was clear to them that in spite of their efforts, Jack and Mai were going to have to change their lifestyle and go into some sort of self-seclusion soon.

Mai further insisted that Catherine omit any reference in the book to another treasure room beneath the temple. Catherine was very reluctant to give in on this point since it involved the final chapter for Queen Dau Te Po and her successful effort to thwart the greedy ambitions of Prince Indravar Tu. It was the real and terrific ending to the story of a remarkable Queen.

Before Catherine had the opportunity to submit the book for publishing Catherine, Kelly, and Mai had an occasion to get together in their condo early one evening in December as the sun was setting on their incredible view of the a snow covered Chicago. Over glasses of wine, they shared stories, and then Mai got very serious with both of them.

"I want to remind you what you already should know well by now. When I'm wearing this ring that I retrieved from the second chest in the cave at Thap Cham, I am joined with Queen Dau Te Po. The ring has properties that allow her spirit to join with mine. We are one and the same. Queen Dau Te Po has told me the first Hoa Cuc, whose name was Nagani, wore this ring. She was the very first Queen, and it has always had a special power. For that reason, every Queen since has worn it.

"Catherine, do you remember when you knelt and kissed the ring when we were in that room at the cave site?"

"Yes, of course. I'm not sure why I did it. I just felt compelled, like it was important to do so. Later I wondered why I did that," she confessed.

"But you did it. That's what matters. You knelt before Queen Po and proclaimed your allegiance to her. She has that power over people. She gained and increased that energy over a millennium as she wandered the universe looking for her daughter so she could free herself from that cave. Kelly was affected even before I put on the ring. It is a very powerful force and comes from the combined spirit-energy of my ancestors. We all have this energy. It is just more focused in my ancestors and me. You have seen some truly unbelievable things in the past year and even questioned my sanity at times. But you have seen proof after proof that what I have told you is true."

Catherine smiled. "I will never understand it all but I do believe it. I've found it's useless to doubt you anymore about any of this, Mai."

"I have been curious for a while now about one thing," said Kelly. "If Queen Po can influence people to do her wishes as she did with me, why didn't she influence Jack to go back to Vietnam so you could get the ring?"

"We had an agreement. Jack was always off limits. I did not want an obedient slave for a husband, and I love him too much to change him. She wanted to control him from day one, but I resisted again and again until she stopped trying. When I finally gave in and asked her to help me control him to get back to Vietnam, she ignored my pleas. That was when I resorted to hypnosis. I was totally desperate by that time.

Catherine laughed. "Sometimes, you sound like you have a lot of internal family disputes. That must seem weird."

"Come on, Catherine. You talk with yourself all the time. We all do. It's not much different. By the way, I heard you have taken the house in Kenilworth off the market. Why did you do that?"

"It was something I felt. I just wanted to keep it for some reason. You don't mean..."

"You shared a strong bond with your mother and talked with her even when she wasn't with you," Mai said. "She is still with you now and always will be. She doesn't want you to sell the house. Buckle up and shake out the butterflies."

Catherine gasped and almost dropped her glass. She never shared her mother's special encouragement to her with anyone. She was speechless. She still talked with her mother in her thoughts, but she did not consider it anything other than thinking things through.

"And you guys, this is the most wondrous part," said Mai. "I didn't know until I put the ring on my finger that Queen Po was going to actually join completely with me. She led me all the way to that moment because it was her only way of escaping an eternity of wandering between worlds. Now she knows my memories and thoughts, just as I know hers. I can tell you some amazing stories of life in the eleventh century during the reign of the Champas, and the legend of the coming of the ancient star people. Catherine, if you learn to respect my wishes, as you should, I will tell them to you so you can write another bestseller. I even know where there's another buried treasure.

"Now to the matter at hand," Mai said. "Catherine, you must not write about the chamber beneath the temple. No one must know about that."

Mai further explained that Queen Po made a sacred oath to the Hindu pandit Havta that she would not reveal the existence of the Hindu gold. Mai further insisted they only knew about the chamber from monitoring her private and personal conversations with Queen Dau Te Po, and in a sense that was a sacred trust they shared with her also. They were obligated to Queen Dau Te Po with the same oath not to reveal the existence of that chamber. Mai told them she believed if the secret were revealed, Queen Dau Te Po would be left to wander the universe between worlds again. Sacred oaths are not to be taken lightly.

Catherine sighed, nodded, and affirmed, "You're right, of course. I can't believe I was even considering it. I'm sorry, Mai. Please forgive me. I will rewrite the ending and take it all to another place. I will have to research it to find an appropriate site."

"Take your story to Indrapura, Catherine," said Mai. "That was our capital for hundreds of years. There was even a magnificent temple there and many chambers beneath as yet undiscovered. Everyone will have fun looking around that place."

Catherine noted a change in Mai's voice and was bewildered once more in the face of further evidence of the truth of her statements. She realized it was Queen Dau Te Po who spoke to her at that moment. "Thank you, my lady. Your kindness humbles me. I will protect your secret," she promised respectfully.

Chapter 50

Chicago, 1992

Mai redecorated their townhouse in a decidedly Asian motif, and Jack liked it a lot. At home, Mai wore comfortable áo *dais* and other Asian styles, but she still dressed in power suits when she went to work each day. She worked more and more with Brad and was still inventing new ways to play with data to their financial advantage.

One day as if on a whim Mai got Jack up early while it was still dark outside. She told him she wanted to see the sunrise on the lake. She further told him she wanted to go to a nice restaurant for breakfast afterward and that he should wear his best suit. They bundled up Devearney, drove into Lincoln Park, and walked over to the lake while the sun was still below the horizon. Jack was surprised to find Kelly and Catherine there waiting for them, along Gerald Doyle, Brad, Lenny, and a few of Jack's close volleyball friends. There, as the sun rose, they were formally married, and they declared their unconditional love for each other once and for all.

Afterward, at a reception attended by several hundred of their friends, Kelly toasted Jack for his many years of putting up with the Three Musketeers and not even knowing beforehand the day he was to be married. Everyone laughed, especially Jack.

About that time, a year after their return, Jack went over to Catherine and Kelly's condo and presented them with an idea he had been considering for a few months. It was an idea that grew out of his increasing concern for Mai's restlessness in Chicago.

Jack told them he wanted to figure out if there was any way to get Mai back to Siem Kulea. He told them he felt it was very important to Mai to have both her family and her people together again and that she would not be happy in Chicago much longer.

Jack was stunned when Kelly remarked in surprise, "Oh my God, Jack! Mai thought it would take two years for you to want to do that. You guys really are connected! I am honestly amazed."

"What the heck are you talking about?" asked Jack.

"When we were on the plane coming back from Siem Kulea, Mai told me of her intention to return," Kelly explained. "But she would not do it until you were ready and wanted to go. She said it had to be your decision because she would never take you away from your work here. She loves you that much."

"She said that?"

"Yep!"

"Well, I'm ready, and I want to get her back there. It's where she belongs, and it's where we belong, our family. We will have the best of both worlds, hers and mine. I have no doubt that was her plan all along. I can see it now. So let's start working on it. Any ideas?"

Both ladies sat on the couch and grinned at him from ear to ear for a moment. Finally, Catherine gave Kelly a high-five and replied proudly, "My darling Kelly has been working on that very project for the last six months, Jack, and has been over there a dozen times already. Heck, I've been back there once myself. I'll let her tell you all she has done."

These ladies were always two steps ahead of him, so Jack should not have been surprised. But he was, and could only find the words to inquire meekly, "You've been working on it, Kelly?"

She nodded. "Yep. Hold on a minute. We have lots to talk about, and your timing couldn't be better."

She went out and returned a moment later with a few large manila folders, which she put down in front of him.

"Let's take care of business first, Jack," she said. "Here is a check for thirty million dollars that we will be delivering to Mai tomorrow. As you know, Catherine was a partner with Mai in her business software program. Mai took the original idea well beyond the capabilities of any other program of its kind on the market. She has developed some sort of stock analysis algorithm that drives itself and adapts to stock market changes on the fly. Her software is red hot, Jack. Catherine had the rights to sell and market it, so she finally sold it to a firm in the Silicon Valley for about sixty million dollars.

She took out her ten percent, and part of the remainder you see in that check.

"The remaining twenty-four million was financing for a new corporation based in Cambodia that Mai owns outright and that now owns the Siem Kulea valley and the surrounding mountains. The land cost the corporation around eighteen million now, with another twenty million to be paid over the next ten years, for a total of thirty-eight million dollars.

"We were lucky since that very remote area was mostly destroyed and in poor condition. The jungle was busy reclaiming it after what the Vietnamese strike forces did to it. It was abandoned and no one had any plans for it or was thinking of resettling it. But their interest grew when they found out we were looking into it and it cost another five million to gain the support from some of the more powerful officials over there.

"Also, Jack, I don't know if you're aware of it, but Mai has been grossly underpaid while working for Catherine's company. That was her idea. But Catherine and Brad put the money they thought she deserved into an investment account. That alone is worth about thirty-seven million dollars now. So she has plenty of money to add things to the valley or pay it off in full if she wants.

"Here is a current employee list I think you'll want to see. There are a few names you will recognize. I'm the overall project manager, but my on-site manager is…"

"Su Ling. Su Ling is there? What about Daniel? Is he there too?"

"He's in charge of logistics and was involved in a lot of the initial reconstruction. He has a fleet of helicopters and transports now and flies cargo all over Southeast Asia. There was a lot of construction involved, Jack. They pretty much blew the hell out of the place when the Vietnamese went in there. Here are some photos of what Siem Kulea looked like when we started this project."

She handed him some aerial photos of the valley. "If you think that looks bad, you should see photos of the other side of the mountain, where Colonel Minh's home base was."

"Wow! It's all destroyed. It's a mess. We have lots of work to do," commented Jack.

"Not so much anymore," said Kelly. "Here are a few photos as of last week." She handed him more photographs that showed the updated and present status of construction at Siem Kulea.

"That's amazing. I can't believe it. How is this possible? It looks like it's mostly done! Is this what the palace looked like before?" asked Jack. "I never got to see it but for a moment on that last day, and then mostly from the helo pad. It looks like I remember it, though."

"We think it's almost identical, Jack, but better," said Kelly. "It's really plush now. Daniel and Su Ling have been in charge of that. We've added a lot of modern, up-to-date conveniences. But sorry, there's no longer a golden bathtub in the queen's quarters. Somebody made off with that before we got there. But the redesigned queen's chambers uses a lot of the old mixed with the new, and it's awesome, Jack. It is the most luxurious suite I've ever seen. Amazingly, that wall with the secret compartment Mai told us about is still there. We added a safe inside of it.

"You need to ask Mai if she knows there are several chambers beneath the estate that look like they've been closed up for centuries. We thought they might be burial chambers or something, so we left them alone. We thought she would want to supervise that or even leave them closed up permanently. I bet she knows what they are.

"Su Ling has been working from her memory and old photos. She's also taking suggestions from many of the old Champa inhabitants who worked there before and have returned, including two of Mai's former handmaidens. Thousands of loyal Champa people have already come back into the valley wanting to stay and work the land for room and board and have made the construction and rehabilitation of the valley a relatively easy project.

Jack, it's like a joyous festival every day. The word is out again on the Champa grapevine. Everyone is excited about Mai returning. But Su Ling is going to limit the population in the valley initially to three thousand. Even so, they have all insisted on helping with the reconstruction process for the return of their queen.

"Su Ling has been interviewing them. If they are Champas and former residents of the valley, they are mostly accepted, but she has one final test. You're going to love this. She sends them into a room with a full size portrait of Mai hanging at one end. It's the photograph in a gilded frame that you took that shows her standing with the Hoa Cuc exposed on her hip and she is wearing the royal crown and necklace. If they look around and then leave, she sends them away, and they do not know why they were rejected. If they see the portrait and bow down or honor it in any way, they are accepted. She says most of them go right to the ground with their heads pressed firmly to the floor. It's definitive and simple. She's populating the valley with Mai's people, Jack!

"Oh, and get this! There have been over one hundred applications from young girls wanting to take one of the four remaining handmaiden positions. The two old handmaidens who have returned are helping to get her private chambers ready. Mai is going to live like a queen again if Su Ling has anything to say about it.

"Brad is setting it up like a corporation and running it like a commune. It will be a compromise with the old traditions and provide for economic stability. Mai gets seventy percent, and the corporation shares in the remaining thirty percent. That is in the profits only. The entire valley shares in the harvest, as is the tradition. Everyone living in the valley and surrounding areas will have everything provided for them, and they will be living large, Jack."

Kelly pulled out a blueprint of the new palace construction. "The palace beyond the very luxurious Queen's chambers is being restored as close as possible to what it was in ancient times, but not as Minh had it. That's all gone. We made two additions to the back here on the other side of the pool, near the helo pad."

"What's that?" asked Jack.

"That is Catherine's and my suite in the palace, Jack," explained Kelly. "Mai was right. That valley is a paradise, and Catherine and I plan to vacation there often…with Mai's permission of course. And the building to the right of that is Daniel and Su Ling's."

Catherine broke in, "Oh, and sorry, Jack, but we put it in the fine print. We get to lie around that pool in our bikinis several times a year, being attended by Mai's adoring servants, or the deal is off. We figure we can all share in some of the royal good times and watch Mai go her queenly ways. We are secretly hoping she goes ritual on us sometimes because we would love to see her really being worshipped by her people."

"Well, I don't think you'll have to go ritual for that," said Jack. "But are you kidding? She will love having you there. Have you thought about security? We have to be able to defend the valley from bandits and mercenaries."

"There are again only the two small ancient footpaths into the valley. The roads that Minh built to access the valley have been blocked in several places with landslides and are closed permanently. So no one can come into the valley without being checked, and it is mostly cut off from the outside world unless you have a helicopter. Also, the areas on the far side of the mountains in every direction are all being settled by loyal Champas as further security. There are thousands and thousands of them. The land is being offered for free, providing they settle, work the land and participate in the valley militia exercises and, of course, their Champa celebrations. This provides a secure barrier on all sides for many miles, and Jack, these people mean business when it comes to protecting their queen. I feel sorry for any stranger who wanders into that area. I had to personally free a dozen people who were jailed for trespassing onto Champa land. Only loyal Champas or friends like us are welcome there."

"But there is possibly a problem," said Kelly. "You know the two Samoan guards of Mai's, Ramadi and Fetu? They're alive, and they want to stay on as guards. I put them in charge of security, and they have organized a small group of about forty men who are policing the area and who check everyone that comes into the valley. The security team they have built are all Champas and very loyal. Fetu and Ramadi are doing a really good job and have set up a very good security plan for the valley."

"So what's the problem, Kelly? I think Mai will be delighted. Oh…I see what you mean. They might distract her. I have to say, if I was ever going to feel inadequate around another male, it would be those two guys."

"Oh no, Jack, that is not what I meant at all," said Kelly. "In fact Su Ling says they're still under Dr. Minh's programming. Did you know they cannot get it on with Mai, period? I don't know if she ever told you, but Dr. Minh left a posthypnotic suggestion with them that made Mai specifically not exciting to them sexually, so they could concentrate on guarding her. The whole valley was going nuts over Mai except for her two personal bodyguards. That is the definition of diabolical, if you ask me."

"Well, they might be gay or something, Kelly. I mean, those guys are good looking, big, and muscular. Maybe they like men," said Jack.

"I considered that until Su Ling and I sunbathed by the pool one afternoon in our bikinis. Both Ramadi and Fetu came in dressed in those thong bathing suits like Europeans wear, and did they react to us! Oh my God, Jack. You know I am one hundred percent lesbian, but I have to say they were awesome. They have many girlfriends now in the valley, so I think they're well taken care of."

"So what's the problem, then? I would think they would be perfect for security and they have proven their loyalty," said Jack. "They put their lives on the line for Mai and saved our lives. Frankly, I am very fond of both of them myself. If I have any say, I want them there. They earned it."

"They're branded, Jack. They have Mai's brand on their arms like you do," said Kelly.

"What does that mean, Kelly? I'm sure they didn't have them when we left Siem Kulea. They must have branded themselves," said Jack.

"Yes, we are positive of that and we think it is so that they are readily accepted by the Champa people who consider them now as property of their queen. They were given the choice by a grateful Catherine of doing anything they wanted, and they chose to stay there and serve Mai. It is the same story for everyone there. We never stop being amazed. They all want to serve her," explained Kelly.

"OK," said Jack. "But let's be clear. We won't have any slaves in Siem Kulea. Everyone gets paid a salary respective to his or her work and position."

"That's the other problem, Jack. Not one of the people in that valley will accept any wages of any kind. Not the house servants, field hands…none of them. They only ask for room and board. They have all come to live there and serve their Queen. It's for real, Jack, and I wouldn't have believed it if I hadn't seen it myself. Everything Mai told us about the Champa people is true."

"You and Brad will have to talk about that one," he said. "Of course, if it is run as a commune, theoretically everyone is sharing in the harvest and benefits. What about setting up savings investment accounts for college and things like that?"

"When they wouldn't accept wages, Brad went right to that idea next," Kelly said. "He is working on setting that up now, so all the people working there will have everything they want for their children when the time comes. They have thus far two doctors in the valley with more coming and a large very well equipped clinic. Thus, all their medical needs are provided as a benefit too. Kelly has an architect working on plans for a hospital and administrative building that will blend in with the valley environment. She thinks Mai will want to do that soon after she arrives. But Kelly wants to be sure Mai approves any construction plans since we think Mai will want to keep the valley looking as it is and not have any modern looking buildings there."

"It sounds fantastic, Kelly. When is it going to be ready to move in?" asked Jack.

"You could move in tomorrow if you wanted to, Jack. Su Ling has even outfitted Mai's chambers with queenly gowns and regalia in the traditional Champa and Asian styles and has done the same for the immediate palace staff. There is still some minor construction going on, but it is mostly all completed down to the last detail.

"Wait. Don't you need Mai here in Chicago to work with you? I know Brad will miss her being around," said Jack.

"We had no choice," replied Catherine. "Reality check. Mai is moving to Siem Kulea whether we want her to, or not. So, as with everything else we do, we have adapted and made plans accordingly. With our new computer systems in place thanks to Mai, she can still work with Brad when she wants to from over there. She has trained those working with her very well and we think she will assume more of an advisory role. Not to worry, Jack. We think she still will want to work with us on occasion and we have made plans in that direction with the new communication systems we have devised."

Jack nodded and Kelly asked eagerly, "When are you going to tell Mai?"

"I don't know. That is something to think about, isn't it? This is Wednesday. I think maybe I'll tell her on the weekend. Maybe we'll go out to that little restaurant on Oak Street or something. Not sure. But I would like you to be there when I tell her, Kelly. This was all your doing. I will never be able to thank you enough for doing this."

"No, Jack," said Kelly. "This is very special, very intimate, and all about you guys. You tell her when the time is right. But you'd better believe I want to hear all about it afterward."

"And you'd better believe we are visiting often!" added Catherine.

Chapter 51

Chicago, 1992

Two days later Jack was busy in the studio working on ads for a frozen-dessert client, Jenny Lee. They went the entire morning photographing two ads without a representative of the client present, which was normal.

A young art director from the advertising agency, Mark Burke, was doing well supervising the photo shoot that was based entirely on his approved layouts. They photographed two of the three cake shots in the morning. Margie Olson was the food stylist and she again demonstrated her twenty years of experience by producing a perfect cake for the single shot, and then did it again for one where the cake was surrounded by its ingredients in a composition. Everyone was engaged, and the day and the photo shoot were progressing very well.

Just after lunch, while they were setting up on the third and final shot, a Ms. Hall, the representative from Jenny Lee arrived. She looked to be somewhere in her fifties in age, gray hair cut short, round face and very red lips. She marched in as if she was angry about something and she brought a lot of bad energy with her.

Jack walked over to greet her and he gave her a cordial welcome. But she spotted Mark the art director first, and demanded of him, "What are you doing here? I thought Ken said he was going to be supervising the photography on this ad." Ken Hastings was the creative director and Mark's immediate superior at the agency. He had arranged the photo shoot with Jack.

Not hiding her mood, Ms. Hall sat down by the first telephone she spotted and made a call to voice her disfavor to the agency. Jack suggested to Mark they continue their work on the last photograph that was coming together in the back studio.

She was sitting in the same place when twenty minutes later the creative director Ken Hastings arrived. She still had not looked at the Polaroids of the photographs that were completed that morning. Right away Ms. Hall began admonishing him before he could speak with his art director and become acquainted with the progress on the photoshoot thus far. He politely asked her to wait for a moment until he had a chance to talk with his creative team working on the set and to review the progress thus far.

He said hello to Margie who he had worked with before and went to look at the Polaroids of the finished shots with Mark and Jack. After studying them and comparing them to the layouts, he was pleased and agreed they looked very good.

Then he went back to Ms. Hall and asked her if she had seen the Polaroids of the shots completed in the morning. When she replied she had been on the phone since her arrival and had not had the opportunity, he explained to her that it was the art director Mark Burke's campaign, and that was why he was there. The campaign was his idea, he designed it, and he was the proper person to supervise the shoot. He reminded her that her superiors had approved the layouts for the ads and he had informed them that Mark Burke would be working on the photoshoot. He further asserted that in his opinion his art director was doing an excellent job. He then turned to the rest of the crew and told them, "Good job, everyone," and left without a further word.

There followed more telephone calls and complaints from Ms. Hall who sat in the client area and still did not look at the Polaroids from the photos taken in the morning.

While all of this was happening, Mark worked with Jack to move forward and complete the work that still needed to be done. The food stylist was carefully styling a cake for the final photograph that was to have a slice cut out of it that would sit just in front of the cake slightly to one side.

Then things got even more complicated. Ms. Hall got up, asked to see the Polaroids, and perused them with the art director over the ten-foot island prep table in the studio kitchen. This was just across from where Margie was decorating the cake for the final photograph.

Ms. Hall made no comment whatsoever. Jack took that as a good sign and was hopeful that the rest of the afternoon would proceed positively.

But then Ms. Hall decided to insert herself into the process as she began to comment on the work of the food stylist, who was working opposite her on the ten-foot long table. She made it her duty to question everything the food stylist did.

Jack had introduced Margie to Ms. Hall when she first walked over to the prep table where she was working. At that time, he told Ms. Hall that Margie had twenty years of experience and was among the very best food stylists in Chicago. He also mentioned that she had worked on Jennie Lee products many times before that day. Even so, as Margie styled the cake, Ms. Hall continued to pester her with constant banter. "Now you want to be sure the texture on the icing is not too flat but has some points to it so as to look homemade. Is the right side the same as the left? Do we see enough of the inside texture? Who approved a yellow cake? Are you going to touch up the icing on the slice? Do the layers seem separate enough?"

Ms. Hall continued with her unwanted and unneeded advice as if Margie had no experience whatsoever. It was normal for the client to make comments and lend her views. In fact, that is one of the reasons they are invited to the photo shoot. But this was far beyond normal and it seemed to Jack the client was having a bad day and was venting her bad mood by badgering the food stylist. This commentary continued just the same for the next twenty minutes. It became so trivial and condescending that Jack noticed Margie's demeanor change. Finally, the food stylist had enough of the constant verbal assault, threw down her spatula, and without a word walked right out the front door.

Jack couldn't believe it. He didn't remember this ever happening before at any studio in town. He sent Jasmine outside to stay with the food stylist. Mark quickly called his creative director to tell him what had happened even as Ms. Hall was busy making more telephone calls herself. A few minutes later, Ms. Hall got up and walked out the door without a word of explanation or even a good-bye.

Margie returned a few minutes after that and remarked with a smile that she was pleased "the old bat" was gone. When Jack asked if she had worked with her before, Margie replied that in spite of appearances she knew her from other Jennie Lee shoots and thought she wasn't allowed to come to photoshoots anymore. Jack noted that after that Margie became visibly happy and even began to hum as she worked.

After the shoot was over and everyone had left, Jack realized he was very tired. For once, it was not a fun shoot. He didn't have the same ambition and drive that had carried him thus far through his very successful career. His heart was no longer in it. He was looking forward to the changes he planned with Kelly and Catherine and to start his new life with Mai. He was ready to tell her about his new plan and was only looking for the right moment to spring the surprise on her.

He decided not to accept any more advertising photography assignments. He was done with it. He was going to close the studio for good. As an afterthought, he wondered if Jasmine would want to go to Siem Kulea with them.

Chapter 52

Chicago, 1992

When he finally went upstairs to their spacious townhouse after that long day, he discovered Mai sitting on the couch opposite the fireplace while she read a story from a children's book to little Devearney who was sitting on her lap. "How'd the shoot go, honey?" she asked.

"Would you believe the client was so abusive that Margie Olsen walked out?"

"Really? Margie? You mean left the studio? Sweet, lovable, friendly-with-everyone Margie?"

"Yep, it was amazing. She was in the midst of decorating a cake that had one slice out of it for one of the layouts when suddenly she threw down the spatula and marched right out the front door. I sent Jasmine to stay with her until things cooled down. I've never seen anything like it." He got a glass of wine for himself and joined Mai on the couch.

Mai gave a sigh and said, "Jack, you don't have to do this anymore. We don't have to do this anymore. Let's go do something else."

"Nice idea, my little Asian queen," he said. "But we have to pay the bills. What are we reading?" He smiled to himself at his deception.

"*When Pigs Fly*," said Mai, as she read from the front of the children's book. "Come on, it's time for her bath and then beddy-beddy-by." She snuggled the little girl playfully.

As she was leaving, she picked up a bank statement, handed it to Jack, and said, "Hey, GI, want to see how much smart Vietnam girl get paid? I bet this pay some bills, you betcha!" She looked over her shoulder smiling at him as she walked back to the bath.

Jack looked at the bank balance, and it was over 30 million dollars, just as Kelly had said. "Holy fartation!" he exclaimed, but he really was wondering how much she knew. "Mai...Mai, you want to tell me where we got thirty million dollars?"

When he caught up with Mai, Devearney was splashing water around in the tub. "Oh, stop," Mai cried. "You're getting me all wet!" Devearney just laughed as her mommy scrubbed her down, rinsed her off, and then picked her up in a towel and dried her.

"Well?" asked Jack.

"Well, what?" said Mai playfully.

"Thirty million dollars?"

"A Silicon Valley company bought my stock market analysis program. You know, the one I wrote and perfected with Catherine's company," she explained. "You know what I think, though? Catherine's finance guy, Brad, is pretty sharp, and there are going to be lots of computer companies going crazy in the next ten years with this Internet thing about to take off. My bet is she bought that company out there in California and then bought my software. Either way, we are up thirty million dollars, GI!"

It was warm, so Mai only put a diaper on Devearney, who was busy blowing raspberries at her with her lips. Mai blew some back at her and it became a bit of a contest.

"What nice ladies I live with," said Jack.

"Oh, you love us and are helpless to resist our wishes, isn't he, princess?" she said to Devearney, playing with her again. She laid her down on their bed and lay down beside her. Jack, dressed in shorts and a polo shirt, kicked off his shoes and joined them.

They played with Devearney awhile, and as she went to sleep, Mai said sincerely, "Jack, I want to move. I don't want to do this anymore."

"Where do you want to go, Mai?" he asked, as he completely agreed with her and was enjoying the moment.

"I want to move to Siem Kulea," she said.

Bingo! Jack thought.

In spite of his total joy at her answer, he controlled himself and asked, "What are your thoughts about this, Mai? Please, share them with me."

"I don't want to be common, Jack," she began.

"Oh, my Asian queen, there is not one centimeter of your magnificent person that is common. Heck, Dr. Minh was dying to have a scraping of your skin, not to mention measure and examine you every way he could. But as evil as he was, he wouldn't mar your perfection. Su Ling told me that."

"That's nothing but pervert bullshit. I think if you want to look at perfect, you should start with Catherine or Kelly. I don't get that at all. But that's not what I mean anyway." She gave him a determined face and instead offered, "I don't want to live in the city with millions of others. It's just too crowded, with too many people who don't know or care about anyone else. I want to go back to my home, Jack."

"I thought here in Chicago, or maybe Vietnam was your home," said Jack.

"Vietnam is where I lived as a little girl, but Cambodia, Siem Kulea, is my real home and where I am meant to be…where we are meant to be."

"Then we should move there if that is what you want," he said.

She looked sharply at him, surprised by his ready words of assent. "Really? You really feel that way? What about your business and all you would have to give up here?"

"Doesn't matter. I'll only be happy when you are happy," he said. He picked up Devearney who was fast asleep and carried her into her room. When he returned to the bedroom, he saw that Mai had a curious look on her face. He again laid down on the bed and this time he was close enough to kiss her neck, so he did.

"Jack, you didn't say what you just said because I hypnotized you, did you?" she asked. She realized what she said right away and quickly corrected herself. "I mean, you don't feel compelled to obey me, do you?"

"You never hypnotized me, Mai," he said with a big smile.

"Jack, I have a deep, dark secret to tell you," she said.

"You never hypnotized me," he said again.

"But Jack, I did. It was a confusing time for me, and I feel terrible about it. But baby, I did, and I am truly sorry."

"You mean the time when you told me to be a chicken, and Kelly came up and saw it, and you told her to go away?" he asked.

Her eyes turned into big white saucers that all but burst out of their sockets, and matched her open mouth as she stared at him.

"Or when you told me I must obey you always, and then you told me to get your slippers over the hallway of tacks?" he asked smiling. "You never hypnotized me, Mai, but it was great fun to have you believe you did. You really enjoyed it."

"Oh, you! I don't know what to think," she said. "Really? You weren't ever hypnotized?"

"Think this, my Asian Queen. Some people want to do as you wish because they love you. When we were at Siem Kulea, those people loved you more than life itself and would have followed you anywhere. They needed to serve and obey you. As much as you wanted to be obeyed, to feel that power you have, they wanted to serve and obey you and maybe more. You did not take from them. You gave to them just as they gave themselves to you. I never realized that before. Vega was right about that. Different times, different cultures. Everyone is happy in Siem Kulea."

"So you're not hypnotized right now and never were for real, right?" she asked.

"That's right, my darling," he said, as he punctuated his words with kisses around her shoulder and neck.

"Then you honestly supported me when we went back to Vietnam, even after all that happened to you."

He nodded seriously. "Yes, my love."

"Oh, Jack, that was amazing what you did. That had to be exceptionally hard for you," she said between kisses. "I love you so much." There were tears in her eyes again as she kissed him and held him close.

"It was selfish of me not to want to let you go back," he said. "I realized I hurt you deeply at a time when you needed my support. You had enough drama in your head already, and I came to the conclusion that if I really loved you, I had to let you go back and resolve your issues with that cave site."

"Why didn't you just tell me it was OK for us to go back, Jack?"

"I was going to, but Mai, when you are in your 'obey me' mode, you are awesomely sexy. I am not sure if that is Queen Po or you, but it is really exciting. You get this proud, little smirk on your face when you expect to be obeyed. I love it. And you loved it, so why not play the role a little longer? It was great fun. I almost wish I hadn't told you. Besides, you didn't abuse it. You only gave me specific commands when something was very important to you.

"And ironically, all of a sudden, you were busy running around the house, doing all the chores instead of me. Ha! You did the laundry, went to the grocery store, cooked, and did the dishes every night. You picked up after me, and I even saw you mop the kitchen one day. You could have easily ordered me to do it, and you didn't. I think you overcompensated, as you felt guilty about hypnotizing me. I have never seen you so anxious to wait on me and please me like you did starting the day you supposedly hypnotized me. It was nice to have a Champa queen as my personal slave."

Mai gave him a look that turned into a laugh, as she punched him in the arm.

"Mai, do you remember that night when you were angry, and you walked out, and slammed the door behind you?" he asked seriously.

"Yes, darling. Our only fight ever, even with all that we've been through together. I regret my actions that night very much. It wasn't a good time for me. I'm sorry I did that, Jack."

"When that door closed behind you, I felt so alone; I was beside myself. I was back in that cell in Siem Kulea, with no you and no future worth living. But it finally helped me to see how stupid and stubborn I had been. In less than a minute after you left, I went from totally opposed to totally in favor of us going back. If you asked me after that if I supported you, I would have said yes. But you never asked."

Mai realized that Queen Dau Te Po had come to her aid after all. But she had her own confession to make. "Jack, that is a two-sided coin. When I walked out that door, my anger was immediately replaced with a loneliness I hadn't felt since we met. I sat in the car all that night and cried. I love you so much, and I knew I couldn't go back to Vietnam without your approval. But I also knew it was important for you to be there. I needed you to support and protect me. I had to find a way to get you to go back with me. When I tried to hypnotize you, it was an act of pure desperation. Thank goodness you supported me already by then. I don't know what I would have done." She laughed and snuggled close to him.

They sat quietly holding each other for a moment in thought. Jack took her hand and kissed her ring. "She really is here with us, isn't she?" he said.

"We are now one and the same, my love. I am afraid you're outnumbered," Mai answered.

"So, does that mean I now have a harem filled with Champa queens? What guy could ask for more?" he quipped.

She hit him with a pillow, laughed playfully, and then settled back against him once more. "Jack, this means so much to me. You can't imagine. I have wanted for a long time to have this conversation with you, and now, to find out that you actually agree with me and want to go back, it's like a dream come true. I'm so happy, my darling."

"It's a mess, though. The town, the white palace, all in ruins," he said, having some more fun with her.

She got excited and said with enthusiasm, "We will rebuild it, Jack, even better than before! I will work beside my people and rebuild it. It will be wonderful!"

Then she suddenly realized what he said. "But wait, how do you know it's in ruins?"

He got up and came back to her with a folder Kelly had given him at their meeting. He pulled out an aerial photograph of the valley and handed it to her.

"Oh, Jack, look what they did to my valley!" she said. "We have lots of work to do."

"Already started, six months ago," he said enjoying the moment.

"What're you talking about, GI?" she said, pushing him back, and looking at him sideways with a curious face.

"Mai, besides Queen Po, Dr. Minh, and God knows who else is in your lovely brain, I have gotten pretty used to the way you think. I figured out three months after we got back here that you weren't going to be happy. I knew you would want to go back. The other day I finally got the nerve to talk to Catherine and Kelly about it, and I told them what I wanted to do. It turned out that Kelly had been working on it for six months by that time, and it is all mostly restored now."

He handed her another photo. Mai looked at it, and her face changed from a smile of wonder to quivering tears, and then to complete and utter joy. She looked at him, shook her hands with happiness, and kissed him. She gazed at the photograph once more but then pulled back, and looked at him with a question on her face.

Jack answered before she could find a voice. "Kelly talked to Brad and set up a company to invest in the area, but only with the stipulation that they own that entire valley and surrounding mountains. They hired some influential people in Cambodia as agents. They bargained back and forth, and after a few months, voila! You own it!"

"Own what, Jack?" Mai did not believe what he'd just said. "What do you mean?"

"You own the entire valley and surrounding mountains…something like two hundred square miles, Mai. There is nothing common about you, my Asian queen. Oh, and you are an official citizen of Cambodia now. You haven't heard the best part yet. Su Ling and Daniel are there also."

"Su Ling is there? Oh, Jack. I'm going to cry," said Mai. "This is wonderful!"

"Yes, she's in charge of the restoration and managing the people coming in who want to move there. Daniel is handling all the construction and logistics. He has a big transport company now with lots of helicopters moving supplies around in Southeast Asia. Kelly and Brad set it up like a working commune. All the Champas living there share in the harvest and have free room, board, health coverage, and pretty much all they want, as long as they work the valley and are loyal to you."

"I wonder what happened to the wonderful ladies who were my handmaidens before?" she asked.

"Well, actually, two of them are back. Do you remember one named Ceva?"

"Oh, Ceva, she was my favorite."

"Well, she is one of the ones returning and Kelly tells me there are over one hundred young women mostly in their twenties who have applied for the job," said Jack.

"Really? Kelly and Su Ling have thought of everything."

"Yes, but it was almost all Kelly's doing. She just woke up one day and decided she wanted to get this done for you. She talked with Catherine and Brad to see if it was financially feasible. When they realized it was, they all dove in up to their necks. Oh, and Kelly wants me to ask you about Ramadi and Fetu, Mai."

"Oh, my beauties. I am so sad about what happened to them, Jack. I wish they could be there to share this with us. I will truly miss them."

"They're not dead, Mai. They're there too now. They want to be in charge of security for the valley, but Kelly won't give them a final answer until she hears from you. So, do you want them there or not?"

Mai burst out a reply. "Fuck yeah, I want them there! Oh, bad choice of words. Sorry, honey, I didn't mean that literally. I mean I want them there because we bonded in a very special way when I was there. Oh, I think that didn't quite sound right either."

"Do you mean when you had them strip naked and pose for you all the time while you walked around them and admired their beautiful, virile male bodies? You frustrated the hell out of yourself because they couldn't do a thing about it with you." Jack said smiling.

Mai was speechless for a moment. But then she burst into spontaneous laughter. "Oh, come on, how did you find out about that?" she asked.

"Kelly told me because they told Kelly. You will be pleased to know they were offered positions with Catherine's companies anywhere in the world they wanted to go, and when they found out you were coming back, they chose to stay and serve you. Su Ling is convinced they still carry that posthypnotic suggestion Minh put on them. All business with you, my love. Oh, and they are branded with the same brand I have. They must have done it to themselves. I'm not sure what that means."

"You know exactly what that means, Jack. They have given themselves to me. They want to serve me. My people will accept them wearing my brand as my property. Next to being beside you, I only felt safe in Siem Kulea when they were with me. I love them like brothers. I would do anything to protect them, and we already know they feel the same toward me. I am going to make sure they are very happy in Siem Kulea.

In the next moment she challenged him and said, "Oh, you smug brute! So you're not jealous of them at all? Really?"

"Baby, you will be so horny after you spend the day around those two that when I get home, you'll be all over me!" he said with a large smile.

Mai punched him in the arm while laughing. "We'll put that to the test soon enough, GI."

But then she had another thought. "But how can this happen, Jack? How did they pay for all of this?"

"You paid for it with the rest of the millions of dollars you actually received for your software. That was the deal. You get the land and thirty million dollars, with a further payout down the line. Brad Martin negotiated it for you, and Kelly worked as the middleman. And apparently you have always underpaid yourself in their view, so Brad and Catherine set up an investment account with money you should have been paid in the first place. That has grown to thirty-seven million, Mai. You are a wealthy woman now, and that does not even consider the Champa royal jewels."

"No, babe. *We're* wealthy now, oh wonderful husband of mine! You're in this too, all the way," said Mai. But then she grew concerned. "But Jack, what about you? What will you do over there? You love Chicago. You love the advertising business. Baby, I want you to be happy too."

"Indeed, and I was going to talk to you about that. I have gained a pretty good reputation in archeology as a photographer after Catherine's coffee table book of photographs of the Champa treasure gained national attention. I have gotten three job offers already in that regard, and with our connections over there, it is a career waiting to happen. Baby, I'm tired of this ad business. That's over. I also plan to photograph exotic flora and publish a few books of my own. I'm very excited to move there. I talked yesterday with a guy over at Marty's Photographic Supply to get set up with the latest color darkroom equipment. I will build a world-class photography studio and darkroom over there, Mai. Hey, do you think Jasmine will want to move over there too?"

"She will if I tell her to," said Mai. "Remember, she is Champa."

"No, babe. Not that way. She is family now. Let her decide for herself, OK?"

"OK. Deal. But she will still want to do it anyway. But Jack, how long have you known about this, and why didn't you tell me you wanted to move to Siem Kulea? Didn't you think I would want to know?"

"Hmm, that sounds familiar. Where have I heard that line before? Actually, darling, I just found out myself what Kelly had done a few days ago, and I wanted to wait for the right time to surprise you."

She pulled him to her and gave him a huge, passionate kiss. "That's your Catherine Marsh School of Manipulation graduation present," she explained.

She started to lie back on the pillow but had a thought and hit him with it instead. "Oh, you were playing me all along wondering where the thirty million dollars came from. Just wait, slave boy...you're going to pay for that," she said playfully.

She fluffed up the pillow and then lay back on it, and stared up at the ceiling. "Wow, babe. I'm so happy! Oh, Jack, my dearest love, thank you, thank you," she said, tearfully. "I can't wait to give Kelly a big fat kiss." She cried with her happiness.

"Oh, here come the tears," he said, teasing her as he hopped up to get her a tissue.

She felt sensually excited and alive. "Life is funny, isn't it?" she commented, "You never know what to expect. I want you to know, Jack, Queen Po loves you too. She thinks you're the perfect man for us."

She lay on the pillow, and thought how wonderful it was going to be back in Siem Kulea and this time with Jack. She couldn't wait.

She continued, "Imagine being treated as a queen again. Honey did I ever tell you how awkward I felt when people started kneeling before me. But later I liked it as much as they liked kneeling. Wow! Who knew? In that valley is the only place in the twentieth century it would work for real, and we will have lots of devoted servants and loyal people who live there and work the land side by side with me. It will be nice to do it like Queen Po did and work beside her people and share the wealth with those in the valley. That was always the best way. Oh, Jack, I can't wait! When can we leave? Jack…Jack?"

She finally looked up at him and found him standing stiff. His head was down against his chest as in a hypnotic trance.

"Jack?" she said once more cautiously, as she leaned up on one elbow. "Hey, are you messing with me? Jack?"

She lay back down on the pillow and looked up at the ceiling. She glanced up at Jack now and then as she tried to figure it out, She thought about what just happened. Then she remembered what she said: "I want you to know, Jack, *Queen Po loves you* too." His trigger!

"Hah, I knew it! I knew it!" she declared triumphantly. She jumped up on her knees and beamed with a huge smile. Oh God, she loved this. How ironic! "I knew it!" she exclaimed again.

She got up off the bed and smiled proudly at Jack, who was so sure he couldn't be hypnotized. She danced around him like a little girl. "Tonight is my night," she said. She put her hands on her hips and thought *this is going to be fun.*

"Get naked, Jack," she commanded, as she threw off her own clothes with abandon.

Jack removed his clothes and stood as before, awaiting her next command.

She pulled back the sheets, fluffed up the pillows, and got comfortable as she lay back on the bed. *OK, Jack Largent*, she thought. *Maybe I don't feel so bad after all about hypnotizing you. I'm going to enjoy the slave Jack one more night. Why not? I deserve it. I will release him tomorrow.*

"OK, Jack," she said out loud, "I command you to give me the best, most personal and thorough massage you can imagine, and don't miss one iota of my beautiful queenly body."

She clapped her hands and looked over at him expectantly, but he didn't move.

"Well? What's wrong with you? Hop to it, Jack!" she demanded.

But instead, Jack opened his eyes and turned his head to look directly at her. He shrugged his shoulders and asked with a huge grin, "Don't you want to command me to get a shower first, because it was a really long day and I kind of smell?"

"Oh, you!" she said, as she threw a pillow at him and pouted.

But in the next moment, she broke into a smile and then she laughed at what he had done because it really was funny. She looked at him standing there so proud of his deception, and smiling at her from ear to ear.

She put her arms out to him, and he joined her on the bed, and they kissed.

"Jack, I love you so much, I don't know what I would ever do without you," she said seriously. "You complete me, my darling."

"I love you more," he replied honestly.

She raised an eyebrow, kissed him gently, and said softly, "Hey, GI, you want Vietnam girl? We go boom-boom now. I make you happy. Can do, GI."

Later, as they were one, she opened her eyes in the throes of passion and saw her ring glowing in the dark from her hand where it rested on Jack's shoulder.

"Yes, I know. Me too," she said softly.

About the Author

William Diebold is currently retired and lives in Southern California. He did three tours in Vietnam, spending two years and three months there as a photographer from 1969 to 1971. Following that he attended ArtCenter College of Design in Los Angeles. Upon graduation, he was hired by Leo Burnett Inc. to manage a studio in Chicago. After one year he went out on his own. He spent twenty-five years as an advertising photographer with studios in Chicago and Dallas. He was fortunate to enjoy success during those years, with many major clients such as Kellogg's, Little Caesars, Pillsbury, Bud Light, Quaker, Sam Adams, and Pepsi.

Diebold was an advertising photographer in Chicago at a time during the 1980s when the industry was at the dawn of major changes brought on by the revolution of personal computers, digital media, and the Internet. It was an exciting, portentous time, and he is still of the opinion that Chicago and its wonderful people are the best-kept secrets in the country.

As a father with two sons, and two amazing grandchildren, he very much looks forward to what tomorrow may bring.

William Diebold's website can be found at www.debold.com (note the different spelling of his name). There you will find many Vietnam photographs from that experience. You will also see some of his professional advertising work.

The author welcomes your comments. Please feel free to send him a note to wdiebold@charter.net

The story continues in the exciting sequel
"Palace Secret" now available on Amazon, Barnes and Noble, etc.

www.ingramcontent.com/pod-product-compliance
Lightning Source LLC
Chambersburg PA
CBHW062002170626
46813CB00001B/11

* 9 7 8 0 6 9 2 8 6 0 4 8 9 *